I0760513

# KRISTOPHER JEROME

THE GODS AND MEN CYCLE

# WRATH OF THE FALLEN

THE BROKEN PACT
BOOK 1

*Wrath of the Fallen* is a work of fiction. Names, characters, places, and incidents are the products of the author's imagination or are used fictitiously. Any resemblance to actual events, locales, or persons, living or dead, is entirely coincidental.

Cover art by Sanjin Halimic

Cover design by Miblart

Maps by Ralarismaps

Illustration by Patrick Buermeyer

Hardcover ISBN: 978-1-951138-12-7

Paperback ISBN: 978-1-951138-13-4

eBook ISBN: 978-0-9970542-1-7

First Edition, March 2016

Dark Tidings Press LLC

PO Box 593

Albany, OR 97321

darktidingspress.com

# ALSO FROM DARK TIDINGS PRESS

## THE GODS AND MEN CYCLE

By Kristopher Jerome

The Broken Pact Trilogy:

- Wrath of the Fallen
- Cries of the Forsaken
- Tears of the Godless

The Nightbreaker

White Wings from Grey Ash

Before the Breaking:

- A Bandit's Balance
- A Voice from the Darkness
- In the Shadow of Light
- The Sons of Lighthammer
- The Bard's Demons
- Disciples of the First Cycle
- Ten of Seatown
- The Last Gift of Kane Darksend
- The Grey God's Edict
- The Blood-Soaked Sacrament

*Forthcoming

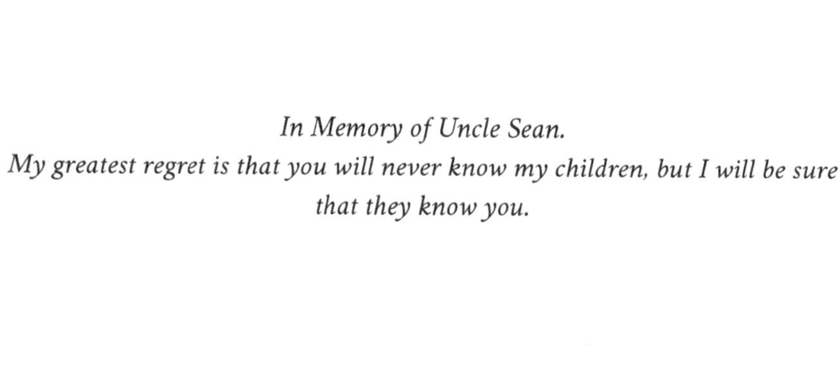

*In Memory of Uncle Sean.*

*My greatest regret is that you will never know my children, but I will be sure that they know you.*

Artorus
The Rim of Paradise
Lioss
The Grey Temple
Rimwaithe
Eligan
Dyeth
Seatown
Kliwen
Aniel
Serega
Illux
The Great Chasm
Ostarth
Ryun
Firan
Marna
The Nameless Sea
The High God's Tears
Godsend

The Grey God's Shrine
Ayyslid
The High God's Throne
The Basin
Infernaak

“Sacrifice is the greatest gift a man can give. For what is sacrifice but a choice? And choice is the greatest gift given to man by the High God. Any who is willing to sacrifice themselves in the service of others is truly Divine.”

— SERMON BY SERAPH ARENDT, AGE OF THE PACT 487

# WRATH OF THE FALLEN

# PROLOGUE

## 1034 AP

The bits of ash mixed with falling snow, making it look as if pieces of the drab and sunless sky itself were drifting onto the thatched rooftops. Terric watched as the black rent in the heavens made the white world around him turn a shade of grey. The horizon of buildings, some made of loosely assembled wood and others of rigid stone, slowly faded into a colorless void where earth and sky were one.

For the last several days Illux, the City of Light, had been a shapeless white mass; now it was becoming even bleaker than it had been before. Overhead the sun could not be seen, but Aenna, the opening to the Divine Plane, was still ever present, just as it was on even the darkest of nights. Terric turned to look at his little brother, Trent, who had also never averted his eyes from the strange sight.

"What do you think it is?" Trent asked, shaking the snow from his red hair.

"I don't know," Terric responded distantly. "It looks like smoke."

"That's a bigger fire than I've ever seen."

"So it is."

Terric turned and walked across the cobbled street toward the small crowd of people who had left their homes to watch the smoke. Before reaching them he rubbed his frozen hands together in a vain attempt to gain some measure of warmth. He found limited success.

*We can't sit out here all day; Trent is likely to freeze to death.*

"What do you think is burning?" Terric asked no one in particular as he squeezed into the throng of onlookers.

"Can't say for certain," an older man replied through chipped teeth. "Borden walked a few streets over. He says that the city watch is in a tizzy running back and forth to the fire. They say it's near the Grand Cathedral. Maybe it *is* the Grand Cathedral. Who knows? I don't want to get close enough to find out."

The old man went back to watching the smoke, leaving Terric to muse over this nugget of information.

*What could have caused the Grand Cathedral to catch fire? What does this mean for the faith?*

Terric remembered the few times that he had seen the great stone building in the heart of the city up close. Elise had taken the boys to see it last year before the snows came. Usually she was content with praying at home, but Terric and Trent had insisted. It was an immense structure: it was made of the purest white stone; its blocks were cut to a size larger than any house on their street. The cathedral had five tall spires: one for the High God and one for each of the Gods of Light.

*Not anymore. There are only three Gods of Light now.*

Terric began walking back toward Trent; his younger brother didn't seem to have moved an inch. He studied the other boy for a few moments as he crossed the frozen stones. His brother looked just like him, from his worn shoes to his torn brown shirt. Trent had a mane of bright red hair and a freckled face while his older brother kept his brown hair cropped close to his scalp. The younger boy was enraptured by things that he had never seen before. When they had first visited the Cathedral, he couldn't keep his eyes off of it—until he saw his first Paladin, of course. Even Terric had found it hard not to stare at the hulking men and women in white and golden armor. He couldn't remember exactly when he had seen his first Paladin. Had it been when his mother had taken him to the Cathedral to give thanks when Trent was born? Or before?

But that seemed like it was a lifetime ago now. Terric wiped a lone tear from his cheek before it had a chance to freeze there. He couldn't allow his brother to see him crying; as the oldest, it fell to him to be strong.

"Borden says that it might be the Grand Cathedral," he announced when he finally stood beside Trent again.

"How could the Grand Cathedral catch on fire, Terric?" Trent's shiver crept into his voice. "Why don't the gods stop it?"

"You know the stories just as well as I do. The Gods can no longer directly interfere with us down here. That's the Seraph's job."

"And Paladins, too."

"Paladins, too. I wouldn't worry. It was probably just the big candles Elise complained about when she took us there."

*The Seraph won't allow the fire to spread. He can't. They will save the Cathedral. They have to.*

Terric had never seen the Seraph, not even during his two or three trips to the heart of Illux. The Seraph's duties were too many and Illux was too large of a city for him to be seen by every boy in the slums who wished for it. Still, the winged emissary of the gods must surely have been a sight to behold. After all, it was said the Seraph was endowed with as much power as all the gods could muster below the Divine Plane. Not only had they gifted him with wings, but their blood too, if Elise was to be believed.

*I will see him one day. I have to if I am to become a Paladin.*

"Come on, little brother. It's time we head back to Elise," Terric told him, grimly.

"I want to watch the smoke. Couldn't we get closer? Please, Terric?" Trent begged.

"No. You don't want to get a lashing again, do you?"

Trent said nothing and merely hung his head in dejected silence. Elise was a good woman, and it was only by her charity that the boys had lived this long. Without her they would have died in the cold last year, alone on the streets. Still, she was stern and didn't tolerate the adventures of young boys. The old woman supported the three of them by washing all of the neighborhood's clothes, a process that she often required help with. But that didn't stop Trent and Terric from sneaking away to walk the streets near the outer walls of the city from time to time.

*If only mother were still alive. If only father weren't such a bastard.*

Terric could never forgive that man for what he had done. His new wife and daughter would bring him more joy than his two sons ever had. Once the woman was with child, Terric and Trent had found themselves out on the street begging for food. Of course the faith would never have allowed such an injustice to occur had they known about it, but the sprawling slums of Illux were just too far from the Cathedral to make any bit of difference. And, as often happens to people who are down on their luck, the two boys' prayers went unanswered. Elise had found them only a few nights after their ejection from their father's house and had taken them in at once. She was a righteous woman who couldn't bear to see two boys starve in the cold.

It didn't matter. Once Trent was old enough to watch out for himself, Terric was going to begin training to become a Paladin. In time his brother would follow. He had wanted to join the ranks of the holy warriors of the faith for as long as he could remember. They were respected above all but the Seraph by those who followed the Light. Images of himself and Trent armored in white while charging hordes of shadowy Demons flashed through Terric's mind. He could feel the grim line that his mouth had formed turn up into a slight smile.

The two boys slowly began their walk back to the hovel that they shared with the elderly woman. Her home was typical of those in this part of the city: small and falling apart. The white stones that made up the taller buildings and homes near the center of the city marked the original border of Illux, before it grew out to the walls. The ground that Terric walked on now had probably been a rudimentary farm back then, but today it was a muddy thoroughfare bustling with activity. By now Elise would probably be furious that they were late in helping her wash the neighborhood clothes. The process took on more urgency during the winter, when the multitude of drying lines were taken down in favor of laying the clothes in front of the hearth. When they walked back in she would already be through the first batch, most likely. Unless she had gone further into the city today on some errand. The thought made Terric's stomach twist up in knots. Thankfully, the temperature around him numbed the sensation.

*It will be good to get out of this biting cold.*

"I had the dream again," Trent mumbled, not looking up at his older brother.

"The dream about the birds?"

"Yes. It was the same as it always is. The black bird is eating the white one, and I have to stop it, but I don't have any wings yet." It was more than the cold that made the smaller boy shiver.

"Elise says that it is just a bad dream and you should ignore it. You talking about it so damned much is probably why you keep having it."

*Don't lose your temper. Not like him. Never like him.*

"Why can't we live with father again?"

"Because father is a bastard, that's why."

"When I become a Paladin, I want to kill him."

"It's the duty of the Paladin to protect men, not to kill them, Trent."

"It's the duty of the Paladin to kill evil. Father is an evil man."

Terric had begun to mull this over when a commotion began in the crowd of onlookers, now several houses behind them. Before Terric could stop him, Trent was running back toward the mass of people, bounding through the snowdrifts like he didn't even notice them. The residents of the slums had begun pointing and yelling at the sky, matching their crazed shouts with exaggerated gestures. A second charcoal smear was quickly rising up to join the first. Then, without warning, black smoke began to billow upward from several places all around the center of the city.

"Gods! The city is burning!" a small woman cried out beside them as Terric rejoined his brother.

Behind them, the sound of rapid footsteps crunching through the snow and rapping on the stone beneath assaulted their ears. In unison, the onlookers turned to see armed men and women running down the street toward them. Without a word, a dozen members of the City Watch barreled past with their weapons drawn, cloaks fluttering wildly behind them. Their chain mail bore the insignia of the city: a five pointed spire on a gold circle.

*Why do they need swords to battle a fire?*

The intervening moments of silence seemed to go on forever, broken only by whispers and sharp gasps from within the crowd. No one was brave enough to voice the concern they all felt. Finally, a solitary figure, far larger than those who had just run by, sprinted past them. He was easily a head taller than any of the previous men they had seen in the watch, and he was far better armed. His heavy plate was a brilliant white, trimmed with gold. He wore no helm, allowing instead for his raven-colored hair to flow freely behind him as he ran. As he got closer, Terric got a good look at his sword, which the man easily carried in one hand even though any normal man would require two. It was forged from the sharpest steel, its pristine surface reflecting the snow and making it appear to be as white as his armor.

*A Paladin.*

The copper-skinned giant continued on without a second glance toward the crowd, who were now staring in open shock. It wasn't every day that Paladins were seen in the slums, and certainly not armed and on the run. Something was terribly wrong in the center of the city. Soon another group of armed watchmen ran past, but this time the older man with whom Trent had spoken earlier flagged one of them down.

"What's going on? Is the Cathedral burning?" His voice shook with his frail body.

The watchman looked around nervously before he responded. The way in which he held himself almost made him look too small for the armor that he wore. His sword was clutched so tightly in his left hand that it rattled against the metal on his legs. Terric could clearly see the fear in his eyes.

"The center of the city is burning. The fires cannot destroy the stones of the Cathedral, but I cannot say the same for the insides. It isn't just the Cathedral that is burning. The flames are spreading, quickly."

"How could this have happened?" asked another, younger man. "Is the Seraph calling in the guard to fight the blaze?"

The soldier seemed to choke on the words coming out of his throat. Terric thought the he looked like he might run rather than speak. "There was an attack on the Forth Spire," he said at last. "The reports say that it was Demons."

The immediate uproar in the small crowd was deafening. Cries and gasps were drowned out by curses and prayers, all mixing together into a cacophony.

"That is not all. They say that the Seraph lies dead."

With that the man quickly turned and continued down the street, chasing after his comrades, leaving behind the screams and wails of the gathered crowd. Tears filled the eyes of many of the onlookers; others stood quietly in shock. The older man who had been speaking with the guard looked more confused than afraid, and he clutched weakly at his chest while dumbly working his jaw. Terric was in disbelief. Demons had never entered the city in his lifetime. Although he knew that they were real, at times they seemed like nothing more than a bedtime story that kept children from misbehaving. Looking down, he realized that Trent was clutching tightly at his side and he hadn't even noticed.

"How can they have breached the city?" one man shouted out over the din.

"The Seraph cannot be dead; who then will speak for the gods?"

"Arra, Lady of Light, watch over your people." Terric wasn't sure if the prayer had come from him or another. The numbness in his face and ears had begun to recede, flushed out by the adrenaline that had begun pumping through his body.

*We need to go home, now.*

"Come on Trent, we have to go."

Terric grabbed his brother by the collar and pulled the sobbing boy off of him. Frantically, Trent's little fingers clutched at the shabby fabric of his older brother's breeches in a hopeless attempt at finding safety. But Terric knew that there would be no safety on the street now. Grabbing his hand, Terric led Trent down the street as quickly as the boys could manage. He made them cut between ramshackle hovels and down twisting alleyways in an attempt to stay off of as many of the main streets as possible. Sometimes the snow made passage difficult, but Terric would not allow his brother to slow for any reason. The numbness of their legs slowly subsided from the pumping blood answering every harried footfall. Their feet made wet crunching sounds that were quickly drowned out by shouts from around the corner. Terric continued to pull his brother along, rounding the large house in front of them. Then they stumbled into a main road.

*Did we go the wrong way?*

The street before them seemed to stretch on into the distance, a snake winding away as far as the gloom allowed for him to see. In the grey blanket of snow and ash, all of the wooden buildings looked alike, piled atop one another like discarded toys. Terric began to worry that his nerves had clouded his mind, causing him to lose his sense of direction. He couldn't tell why, but he knew that they were somehow heading the wrong way.

It wasn't the biting cold that brought him back to the world, but the sobs of his brother beside him. Again they were running, now back the way they came, heading toward sanctuary at last. From one street over, Terric could hear shouts again, and sounds that he couldn't quite place.

When they rounded the next corner Trent pulled on Terric's arm wrong, sending both boys sprawling. Chills wracked Terric's small frame as he pulled himself out of the snow bank that they had stumbled into. When he looked around to orient himself, he shivered from far more than the cold. Just down the street, coming from the heart of the city, was a dark shape lithely bounding across the rooftops. Dozens of armed men and women were running along the ground behind the shadow but failing to keep pace with it. City watchmen came from behind Terric, quickly brushing past him and knocking him back into the snow bank. He barely noticed when Trent weakly grabbed onto his frozen hand and began tugging on it.

The dark shape came into focus as it drew near, still maintaining a steady speed from grey rooftop to grey rooftop, sending showers of snow and ash to the street below. Somehow the roofs of the houses held, even though the thing was clearly of a monstrous weight. It stood out from the muted background like a black stain on a white shirt. A battered smear of red, dark as blood, fluttered behind it in the wind. The figure was as large as any Paladin, but armored head to toe in jet-black plate covered in small, wicked spines, with a horned helm that had no opening for eyes. Its armor was oddly reflective, like the carapace of a beetle.

*A Demon.*

"Terric."

Suddenly the Demon, for that is the only thing it could have been, jumped down onto the street, crushing one of its followers in the process. The other men cried out in fear, raising their swords and spears before them to prevent the armored monster from advancing. The air in the street seemed to go still; even the snow and ash flakes hesitated to continue falling for a few brief moments. Although surrounded, the Demon showed no signs of hesitation. It reached down and grabbed the head of the gurgling remnant of a man beneath itself, tearing it from his shoulders. The way in which the head was thrown into the face of one of the other men was almost casual.

Then the creature struck.

The Demon swung its black-bladed sword through a man and a woman at once, severing arms and legs in a bloody arc. Those behind it tried to press the attack, thinking that they had some kind of advantage by flanking the beast. They were wrong. In a swirl of its red cloak, it was completely turned about and ready for their advance. Steel clashed with steel for only the briefest moment before the next two men fell and the third found his head in the grip of a giant mailed hand.

Terric never felt the small hand tugging on his own; he never heard the frenzied pleas for him to run, nor the sobs and curses that only a small boy could make. What Terric did hear was a wet popping sound. More men were running to fight the creature, but Terric knew that they would face a similar fate. Behind him, Trent released his hand and had fallen to his knees, beginning a frantic prayer.

"Arra, Goddess of Light, protect us. Samson, God of Light, protect us. Luna, Goddess of Light, protect us."

*The gods aren't thinking about us. Not now.*

Suddenly a cheer rose up from the men, returning Terric's mind to the battle. From behind them the raven-haired Paladin from earlier bounded into view, greatsword at the ready. The surviving men of the watch quickly parted for him and began backing away, maintaining a loose circle around the pair from a safer distance. The snowfall had stopped altogether, the High God even holding his breath, it appeared.

The Demon raised its left hand.

A red glow began to encircle its gauntlet before launching a beam of fire into the Paladin. A wall of blue energy flashed up, deflecting the attack at the last moment. A hoarse noise was emitted from inside the helm of the creature, almost as if it were laughing. It attacked with magic again, but this time in a sweeping motion that ignited the ground at the Paladin's feet. Smoke and snow flew into the air, obstructing the visibility of the entire road.

It was then that they charged.

Once the Demon disappeared into the smoke, Terric could no

longer see what was happening with the combatants, but he could hear it. The sounds of clashing swords echoed off the sides of the buildings, ringing down the street behind them like a hammer on an anvil. Terric could feel the heat from the haze; the smoke was the only smell that his nose could recognize. Then a snapping noise followed by a high-pitched scream emanated from within the swirling mass. A flash of bright light split the murk and illuminated the two fighters; the Paladin was now cradling his left arm, which had been crushed above the elbow. A soldier standing outside the battle bravely charged in from behind the Demon and stabbed her spear through its cloak toward its lower back. In the blink of an eye the monster had spun around, removing the spear from her grasp with a twirl of the ragged cloth, and caved in her chest with one solid punch.

The Paladin saw this opportunity and leapt into the air, using his one good arm to bring the sword crashing down into the exposed back of his enemy. Blood followed his leap in a steady stream, welling out of the crumpled plate around his arm. Terric heard himself shouting "No!" just as the Demon rolled out of the way of the incoming blow and swung its sword upward into the chest of the injured Paladin. Before the blood could finish escaping his open mouth, the man's head was split in two. The awestruck men watching the engagement began to back away in the hopes that the invader would continue on its path out of the city and leave them be. It let out a wretched howl before sending more of the red flame into the men and the buildings around them. Houses quickly caught fire and the street again descended into a hazy darkness.

Fear finally broke Terric from his trance and the boy grabbed his brother and began running down the street and away from the smoke. The cold had been replaced by the heat of the flames jumping up around them and licking hungrily at the grey sky. Trent screamed loudly as he ran, tears streaming down his small face. In moments they were clear of the smoke and again running through the icy cold when the hairs on the back of Terric's neck stood on end and he felt eyes upon his back. Quickly the boy turned. Emerging from the red and black miasma was the shadowy figure of the Demon. He still felt its eyes upon him even though he could see that it had none.

Without warning the Demon began running toward the boys, throwing up a flurry of snow in its wake. Terric grabbed Trent by the hand so hard that the smaller boy began to scream in pain, but he refused to let his brother go and continued to pull him along as fast as he could. The loud crunching of snow behind them came closer and closer until Terric was sure that the Demon was directly behind them. He could still feel the eyes upon him, and he was sure that its hot breath was on his neck.

Without a second thought, Terric let go of Trent's hand and pushed his little brother hard into the snow beside them. He turned around just as the Demon was upon him. Lightning fast it swung its sword. He never felt it touch him. Shouts from within the smoke drifted to his ears: by the sound of it, dozens of men and women were heading this way. The Demon bounded off, brushing past Terric, spinning him around so that he was facing his little brother.

*He's safe.*

The sounds of their rescuers pounded in his ears, forming a rhythm that he latched onto in his mind. For some reason he was finding it hard to focus on anything other than the thumping. Suddenly Terric felt warmth across his stomach and hands. Numbly, he looked down and saw that he had been split open from side to side. Blood was covering his shirt and skin. He could see parts of himself squeezing out into the cold. Terric tried to push them back into the warmth of his body but it was no use. Suddenly his vision was filled with white, and he couldn't tell if it was from the snow rushing to meet him as he fell forward or something else.

TRENT SCREAMED as his brother fell into the reddening snow beside him, and he didn't stop screaming until the pain in his throat became too much for him to bear. The snow had begun to fall again, large flakes of the sky lazily descending onto his head and face. He didn't notice. Before him the grey and white ground turned scarlet.

Trent never even noticed the giant armored figures that bolted past him, hot on the heels of the Demon. His senses were full of the smell of his brother's blood.

# CHAPTER 1

## 1054 AP

*The harsh squawking of the large, black bird chilled him to the bone. That sound flayed him bare every time he heard it; never once had he found himself used to it. The beady red eyes bore a hole into his unprotected face, challenging him. Strands of moist sinew hung loosely from its beak, dripping blood onto the pure white plumage beneath its talons. Sickeningly, the black bird swallowed the meat and returned to squawking.*

*The Vulture.*

*He hated the Vulture with every fiber of his being. The way it looked into him. The way it accused him with its squawking. As always, the carrion creature was covered in blood, both red and black, and yet it seemed that it hadn't lost any strength. Not all of the blood belonged to the Vulture, though. Most of it belonged to the white Dove that struggled beneath its talons.*

*Red rivers flowed from the sides of the smaller bird where the talons of the Vulture squeezed and clawed. From time to time the Dove struggled weakly, but this only caused the Vulture to tighten its grip. Her throat was torn open at the base of the neck. The eyes of the light colored bird pleaded with him.*

*-Help me.-*

*But he couldn't. He never could help her. He had no wings. He was too weak. He was nothing without his wings. His own form was that of a pigeon, the likes of which he had often thrown stones at as a boy in Illux. Yet he was a pigeon with no wings, a useless and misshapen piece of creation. Without wings he could never hope to traverse the great chasm that lay between them. And even if he could, he knew that he wouldn't be able to chase off the large bird.*

*-Help me.-*

*The ground around the Dove began to turn red as it was stained with her blood. The earth was blanketed by something that had once been the same color as her plumage. What was it? It was snow. Just like before. But when?*

*Squawking again.*

*-Help me.-*

*He must act. He had to do something. Perhaps if he tried to jump the chasm, his wings would return and he would be able to fly to her. Dumbly, he stumbled to the edge of the rocky cliff and launched himself into the air. His eyes locked with those of the Vulture. All of his strength failed.*

*Now he fell. On his way down his eyes again locked with hers.*

*-Trent.-*

*All he could see was the blood red of the snow. But this snow hadn't been white to begin with. It was grey. Now he was somewhere else. Somewhere new.*

*No, not new.*

*He was standing in the middle of a cobbled street. In front of him a Paladin in brilliant white was lying face down in the red slush. He knew this Paladin from somewhere. But where?*

*-Trent.-*

*Standing over the Paladin was a great shadow, darker than anything he had ever seen. It had been the one who hurt the Paladin, of this he was certain. If he didn't act, the Paladin would surely die. Slowly, he looked down at his own hands; they wore white gauntlets just the same as the Paladin before him. He was a Paladin too.*

*But where was his sword? Why did he not have a sword? How could he ever hope to help without a weapon of some kind?*

*The shadow began to laugh at him, a deep rumbling sound that was alto-*

*gether inhuman. He had heard this laugh somewhere, when he was a boy. He must do something, anything. But what? Then he heard the squawking again. Vainly, he searched for the accursed Vulture, but it was to no avail.*

*Had the shadow made the sound?*

*At once the Vulture materialized from within the shadow and fluttered down to land on the Paladin. It hunkered over him, somehow seeming far larger than was naturally possible. Its gimlet eye flitted up at him before looking back down at its perch. Without warning it bent down to pick at exposed flesh from beneath the armor. He was filled with revulsion. He knew that he must act.*

*-Trent.-*

*Another Vulture exited the shadow and landed on the Paladin. Then another. And another. Soon the body was covered in feasting scavengers drawn to fresh carrion.*

*-No.-*

*He must stop them. He tried to step forward, but his legs refused to respond. His armor was too heavy. He still carried no sword.*

*All he could do was watch and listen to the squawking of the vultures.*

TRENT SLOWLY OPENED his eyes to see the light filtering in through the cloth that hung over the window in his small room. He sat upright and swung his legs over the sides of the miniature bed. His sheets were drenched in sweat again, like they had been almost every night of his life. The dreams had begun when he was only a boy, yet he had never truly grown accustomed to facing their horrors every time he slept.

Judging by the amount of light in his quarters, he guessed that it must be just after sunrise. It would soon be time to join his comrades in the mess hall for breakfast before beginning his daily practice and patrol duties. Devin would surely be up and waiting for him already, just as he was every morning. There was never a time when Trent could expect to be separated from his friend and brother-in-arms for more than the length of a single night's sleep.

He stood and walked the few paces to the opposite wall where the small bucket of water that he had filled the night before sat. The stones of the floor chilled his bare feet, still slick with sweat from the terrors of the night. The cloth that he used to clean himself every morning was hanging from its usual place on the side of a small wooden bucket, ragged and dirty as it always was near the end of the week. He took the washrag and dipped it in the cool water before wringing it out and wiping his already naked form down. He preferred the water cold rather than warm as it helped to counteract the heat of his body after a restless sleep. As he cleaned himself he examined his unnatural form with the same sense of awe that he had every morning since his transformation.

First he ran the damp cloth over his arms, then his abdominal muscles. Trent stood, stretching his powerful legs and rotating his broad shoulders as he began to clean the rest of himself. He knew that he was surely a sight to behold, being nearly twice as broad as any mortal man living. And yet Trent was not unique. His same physical traits could be said about any Paladin, man or woman. This was just one of the many gifts bestowed upon him by the Gods of Light when he had undergone the ceremony. His pale skin was not without its imperfections, however. He traced his fingers over the scars, small and large, that marred his near-perfect form, remnants of past victories and near escapes. Most of them caused him no discomfort, but some could still be felt when the muscles they marked were tightened.

*I have been watched over many times, haven't I?*

Trent put the cloth back into its familiar position before walking over to the wooden rack that held what few pieces of clothing he owned. He picked up a pair of linen undergarments and quickly dressed himself as he eyed his armor on the adjoining rack. When it came time, he put that on as well, a small ritual that he performed every morning. Like all members of the order he wore plate enameled in the purest white, each piece crafted from the strongest steel. His was trimmed in an icy blue that matched the flowing cloak that was clasped upon his back. It was a hardy garment, meant for warmth as much as decoration, that he would not go without. When he had finished, he strapped his sword upon the outside of the cloak, and above that his circular shield, emblazoned with images of the three Gods of Light.

On his way out of the solid wooden door, Trent stopped for a brief moment as he always did, speaking a prayer to the goddess whom he favored most.

"Arra, Lady of Light, watch over your servant today. Keep him safe from danger, but should he champion your cause in battle lend him your strength."

Trent briskly walked through the halls of the barracks, occasionally stopping to nod a greeting to those he passed. The walls and floors were made of white stone, lit by torch in the interior passages and small square windows for those near the outer walls. Tapestries hung between these light sources showcasing glorious scenes of battle and heroism. Trent never gave them more than a passing glance, his familiarity with the tales upon them being unmatched. Terric had told them all to him as a boy, he himself having learned them from their mother. Besides, Trent needed no glory but his own.

None walked these halls other than the hulking, armored forms of the Paladins. They had no servants or retainers, each being responsible for his or her own washings and chamber pot emptying. The only normal men who ever stepped foot over the threshold were the kitchen staff, and even they were only allowed in shortly before and after mealtimes. The Paladins were the guardians of mankind, not its rulers. Allowing them to have servants would have damaged this distinction.

Every hallway that Trent walked through was lined with wooden doors, each leading to a small room not unlike his own. No names were carved upon the doors, in case a Paladin were to fall in battle and his or her room filled by another. They were expected to remember where they slept all on their own, which had proven to be difficult for some.

Within minutes, the quietness of the sleeping quarters was

replaced by the low din of the mess hall. Trent entered the cavernous room at the rear, making his way through the wooden tables to the back of line that had formed to get food. The daily rations were bread, meat and cheese of no singular variety. Sometimes the meat would change from beef or pork to fish when a good catch from Seatown was brought in, but this made little difference to the overall flavor. Life was not meant to be pleasant for a Paladin, only tolerable.

Not two minutes spent standing in line had passed before a strong hand slapped him across the shoulder and pulled him in close. A voice boomed beside him.

"Trent! Glad to see you awake early for once on this blessed day!"

"I always wake shortly after sunrise, you thunderous dolt," Trent shot back with a smile. "Not all of us can be well-rested before the moon even decides to hide herself behind the horizon."

Trent turned to see Devin beside him, already filling his mouth with old bread. The brown-skinned warrior smiled through his short black beard, crumbs falling onto the floor. Devin was rarely still in bed after sunrise, for he seemed to require less sleep than any of his companions. He attributed it to the good breeding of his forebears, many of whom had been Paladins themselves. Trent, on the other hand, simply knew him to be stubborn.

Sticking up above the other Paladin's short-cropped hair was the white shaft of his double-edged battle axe. Whenever Trent saw it, he was instantly reminded of the savage ways it had been used to hack the rotting flesh of their foes. Trent pushed the face of their fallen commander, who had wielded it before Devin, from his mind. The two laughed and joked as the line slowly moved forward at a sluggish pace. Finally, Trent was able to grab a bowl of food before they moved back into the endless sea of wooden tables and benches. The two Paladins found one off to the side where they could talk without needing to shout over the clamor of the mess hall.

"I suppose you want to witness the initiation this evening?" Devin asked as he sat, clearly knowing the answer already.

"Of course. I can never miss the chance to relive the glory of that day," Trent responded, smiling.

"I figured that you just didn't want to miss the sight of the Lady Ren using her full power."

*He can't leave that be, can he?*

Trent said nothing as he toyed with his food.

"You not talking about her is how I always know I am right."

"Do you deny that she is a beautiful and intelligent woman? That it is an honor to serve under her?" Trent queried through a full mouth.

"Of course not! No man on or above the Mortal Plane denies it. Even the Fallen One, in his miserable musings, cannot deny her brilliance or wisdom," the other Paladin intoned, tearing gristle from bone. "Yet she is our Seraph, the mouthpiece of the gods, and no man can have her. That doesn't mean that they don't think about her at night while they are alone in their beds. It's the same with every Seraph, I imagine. They are the most desired because they are the most out of our grasp. But you don't want her like that, do you?"

"No, I respect her. That's all."

"You can lie to yourself but you can't lie to me. You love her. I know this even if you do not. I expect that she knows it too."

"I don't have to listen to you, you know."

"Ah, but you do. Ever since I saved you from that Demon, you've followed me around like a lost dog. If you aren't smitten with her then surely you are with me."

"What Demon would that be?" He tried to hold back a laugh.

"Don't play coy. You know the one. All of them, really."

"Don't flatter yourself," Trent said, smiling. "I believe it was *I* who saved *you*, once or twice. And have you forgotten when I proved myself so much better than you in training that you asked to be my friend just so that I would go easier on you?"

"All lies!" Devin boomed out another laugh and then drained his cup. "Let us be off, the day is ending already!"

Both men laughed as they pushed out their chairs and walked from the mess hall, depositing their bowls and cups into a large basin for the kitchen staff to gather after the meal. From there they traveled through the winding halls and down a great staircase onto the ground floor of the facility. Here the crowds of Paladins coming and going were the largest, choking the great metal gate of the building with their travels. The floors above held rooms for the hundreds of holy warriors stationed in the city. The floors below were used as storage for weapons and supplies, with this center location serving as the hub between all of them. Trent figured that it could always have been worse. The leadership of the order could have been stationed here as well.

*Then we would never be able to make it through this flood.*

After finally wading through the throngs of fellow Paladins, Trent and Devin made their way through the opened gate and out into the bright summer day that awaited them. The barracks were located on the outer edge the giant plaza of smooth stone at the heart of Illux. Just opposite where they now stood was the Grand Cathedral itself, center of the worship of the Gods of Light. The crisp white stone of the building caught the light of the sun and reflected it as if it were polished glass. The cathedral towered hundreds of feet into the air, a marvel of construction that could only have been completed with the aid of the gods. To see the tip of the center spire, one had to crane his neck even from across the plaza. High above, wisps of cloud floated past, reaching out every so often to brush the stone. The four lesser spires only reached to half its height. It was toward the northernmost of these that the two Paladins made their way: The Fourth Spire, the base of military operations and home of the Seraph.

The Paladins may have all been housed in the barracks on the eastern edge of the circular plaza, but each day they were expected to report to the Fourth Spire of the Cathedral for orders, training, and, in special cases, initiation ceremonies. A practice yard had been erected around the outside of the spire to facilitate the rigorous physical training that all Paladins engaged in before and after initiation into the order.

As they made their way directly toward the practice yard, Trent thought about how serene the entire center of Illux was. It was a far cry from the outer slums where he grew up. Something of an unofficial class system had sprung up based upon where one lived in relation to the Cathedral. Those who lived in the heart of city got to enjoy better food and solid stone houses, sometimes multiple stories high. Crime near the cathedral was almost nonexistent, which many thought was due in no small part to the piety of those who spent their time near the great structure. Trent knew it was simply because those in the inner city had no need. They did not starve as the people near the walls did. As he had. Those in the outer city worshipped the gods just as those in its heart. But the gods didn't feed them more than just enough to survive. The gods didn't give them the space to build solid homes like the center of the city had been given hundreds of years past. It was for these reasons that they stole and killed. It was for these reasons that Trent and Terric had found themselves on the street. Not for lack of piety.

Many of the people living near the center of Illux knew nothing of the troubles right on their doorstep; knew nothing of the evils that plagued the wilderness and villages beyond their walls. Paladins, on the other hand, had no choice but to know all of the troubles that plagued the land, as Trent's scarred body could attest to. And yet not a single incursion of enemy forces into the holy city had occurred in some twenty years due to their vigilance.

*Not since the day Terric died...*

And the last Seraph. Trent had never seen the Lady Ren's predecessor, but by all accounts he had been a valiant leader and a great loss to the city and its inhabitants. Perhaps he had even been too valiant. He had preferred open incursions into the wilderness to hunt down raiding parties of Accursed and their Demon masters. This focus on attacking over defending had made him very popular with the Paladin leadership, and even the people. Victories were an easy way to get one admired. But it had been reckless, and some said it may have been what got him killed. The attack on the city was likely a response to the campaigns that he had led, bringing the wrath of the Gods of Darkness upon himself.

The Lady Ren was different. She valued the lives of every last person under her command, from Paladins to mortals. Her goal was not the complete eradication of evil, but the protection of the Light. Under her leadership even the slums near the outer walls were beginning to flourish again. Food flowed freely, and crime had lowered dramatically in the intervening years since Trent had been a boy. Perhaps if she had been Seraph when Terric was alive, things might have turned out differently for the both of them.

*But she is my commander. I cannot think of her any other way.*

Trent knew that what Devin had said earlier about the Seraph was true. He loved her, as he had for quite some time. In fact, he knew deep down that it was his love for her that had kept him from spiraling into depression and melancholy over the death of his brother. Sometimes destroying evil was not enough, and he needed her to bring his mind back from the brink. She had taken a liking to him as well, recognizing his intelligence and battle prowess early on during his training. Because of this he was moved up very quickly after his initiation. In some ways he was one of her most trusted confidantes, much to the chagrin of her other, more experienced commanders.

Soon they passed the large, golden statues of the three Gods of Light, rising from the plaza like giants watching over those who passed the polished stone and small gardens on their way to the cathedral. The sculptures were a relic of another age, made when the gods still walked the earth before the Grey God's Pact forbade them to do so. Each looked majestic, even in this still form. The three stood as equals, none being given prominence over the other. Samson and Luna bore looks of courage, each shouting a silent battle cry. Arra looked far more contemplative than the others, but no less powerful. Trent's eyes always fell to the place of the fourth statue, however, of which all that remained were the broken golden feet.

*Lio. The Fallen One.*

Not long after the war between Light and Darkness began, the greatest of the four Gods of Light had taken for himself a lover from among the ranks of the Paladins. He raised this man to become one of the many Seraphs that served the gods in that age. Their love for one another continued on for some time before it was spoiled by the chief God of Darkness, Xyxax. In retribution for what Xyxax had done to his lover, Lio challenged him to a duel on the Mortal Plane that raged for three long days, leaving much of the wilderness in ruin. The battle was finally ended when Lio struck Xyxax deep into the bowels of the earth, leaving a giant scar upon its surface. For his crime of deicide, Lio was cast down from the ranks of the Gods of Light by the High God himself.

*Not even the gods are invincible.*

After a few more moments of walking, as the corner of the northern spire grew closer, the ringing of blunted blades against sturdy shields greeted their ears. Devin, smiling as always, picked up his pace and rounded the corner of the great white building. Spread out before them was a large swath of land upon which no stone rested. The practice yard cut into the white of the plaza like a great brown stain on fresh linen. At its farthest edge it was hemmed in by the first buildings that circled the plaza, mostly home to the families sired by Paladins in the days of old. Paladins and recruits alike sparred and practiced archery all across the field. Here and there, flashes of blue light could be seen where magic, the greatest gift from the gods, was honed and tested.

Trent scanned the area and saw the winged form of the Lady Ren herself standing on the large steps leading into the spire, surrounded by her commanders. No doubt they were evaluating the recruits who would enter the cathedral that day as men and women before walking out as Paladins. Trent still vividly remembered his own initiation with Devin and Gil standing by his side. Many of the others that they had trained and fought beside were no longer living.

*Her beauty will never fade. She will never age a day from this moment.*

The two men made their way toward the steps to greet their

Seraph as custom dictated. After exchanging pleasantries, she would then give them assignments, if there were any; otherwise, they would spar alongside their brothers and sisters in arms. It was possible that they would be sent on patrol along the city wall, a most basic function of the order, or perhaps sent beyond the walls on a ranging mission. As they approached, Ren's eyes moved to them, and her previously taciturn face revealed a small smile. The smile quickly vanished as the man closest to her leaned in and whispered something in her ear, pointing at one of the recruits in the yard.

*Castille.*

"It always brightens my day to see that old bastard make others just as miserable as he made us," Devin said with a smirk.

"Made? He will continue to be an irritation right up until his death."

"And even after, I expect. The High God will grow tired of his spark and send him back down to the Mortal Plane to inflict more irritation upon his fellow mortals."

The thought made Trent chuckle. Castille was the oldest living Paladin, and by far the most hated. He was a tough, cruel man who didn't accept failure in any setting. Castille had been a close confidante of the last Seraph, as even then he was a veteran commander of the order. As such, he had thought for sure that when the next Seraph was chosen, it would have been him. When it was decided to be the Lady Ren, a woman his junior by some fifty years, he couldn't even pretend to hide his resentment of her. Trent wished that he could have seen the old man's face when the word was passed down from the gods that it was some girl who would gain the Divine Blood.

His experience was all that allowed him to keep his position as senior Paladin, commander of all but Ren herself. But ever since the Seraph had begun taking a liking to Trent and Devin, the old man feared that he was being pushed out, or worse, that somehow the gods would pass him over again in the unfortunate case that a new Seraph was needed.

Trent and Devin approached the base of the stairs and knelt before the Lady Ren and their commanding officers.

"My lady," they said together. "Our blades are yours, for the glory of the Light."

"Stand, my champions," she replied in her strong yet lyrical voice.

They both stood and awaited further instruction. Trent knew better than to speak first in front of the other Paladins, who would have seen it as overstepping a clear boundary. The light of the early morning sun crept around the corner of the cathedral and illuminated Ren's features with a dazzling brilliance. Trent drank her in as he always did in such moments, locking the images away in his mind to remember her by on his long treks into the wilderness.

She wore armor just as any Paladin would, and yet on her it seemed all the more magnificent. At her side, the ancient sword Nightbreaker hung, the black blade carried into battle by champions of the Light since the beginning of creation. It had first been carried by the warrior Daniel as he led the armies of Seraphs against the Divine Beasts. It was with this very blade that the creature Rexin the Blasted was felled. Yet what made her stand out among all other servants of the Light were her large white wings upon which she could soar through the air like she had been born to it. Even so, it was her mortal beauty that Trent remembered most. Her strong eyes, that gazed at him even now, were of a deep green that almost seemed black from a distance. Flowing between her shoulders was her brilliantly white hair, the final physical mark of her status, a result of the Divine Blood that flowed through her veins. In stark contrast to her otherworldly hair, her skin was of the darkest ebony, and to Trent it seemed flawless in every way.

"Perhaps you two wish for special privilege," Castille quipped, looking as irritable as ever. Surely he had noticed how Trent had looked upon the Seraph. "Or so it seems since you decided to approach your Seraph rather than join your comrades in the yard."

Trent tensed as always when his special relationship with Ren was brought up in front of her. He clenched a gauntleted fist and prepared to say something when Devin cut him off.

"You know us so well, Commander. Your two best warriors and scouts who still always look for the easy way out."

"Your arrogance-" the grizzled Paladin began.

"Was meant in jest, Castille. You forget yourself," Ren interjected sternly. "Now go see to the arrangements inside."

The old Paladin glowered at the pair for another few moments before turning to leave. Trent locked eyes with the man as he did so, never looking away. Devin simply smiled at him, but it was not his normal smile that he flashed at the old warrior, but one laced with malice. As Castille turned to leave, Trent thought that he saw the man's hateful gaze fall upon the Seraph for a moment. But, just as quickly as he noticed it, the man was gone. Most of the other Paladins surrounding Ren followed their commander back inside, leaving only a few as a token guard. They too were waved away, leaving Ren alone. She walked down the large flat steps to greet her champions.

"He grows bold, my lady," Devin said to her when she reached the bottom of the steps.

"His distaste for me has never been a secret, but in the last few weeks he has grown more difficult. Paladins are unnaturally long lived, but only those with Divine Blood are truly immortal. Castille must know that he has only another decade or so before his own time comes and he must rejoin the High God. I think he wants to achieve some greater glory before then."

"Or greater rank," Trent said in a low tone. "He covets your power."

"He would not be the only one," she replied, looking over the practice yard. "But his desires mean nothing to me, nor should they to either of you. He follows my commands, if begrudgingly, and the gods would never choose to bestow my rank upon one who raised his hand against me. What you should worry about is your duties to the Light. And on this day that means the induction of several more into our ranks. The few volunteers seem worthy of the challenge to me, but

Castille has given his recommendation that several of them be dismissed and not partake in the ceremony tonight. I would like you two to train with them this morning and give me a second opinion. When you are through, report directly to me."

"My lady," they said, bowing.

With that Ren opened her wings and launched into the air, soaring up and around the cathedral. The sunlight glinted off of her armor until she was just a speck in the upper reaches of the clouds, disappearing behind the great spire. Trent thought that the feeling must have been exhilarating.

*All men wish to fly, my lady.*

# CHAPTER 2

Clang!

The practice sword glanced off the side of the recruit's armor. Even with blunted edges on the sword, Trent could see the man grimace in pain. With a Paladin's strength Trent could easily kill the man, even with a blade such as this. It had seemed like a lifetime ago that he had been in the same position as the warrior before him, learning under the tutelage of those more powerful than he. His adversary still came on, even with what now seemed to be a damaged arm. This was good to see. Pain could not be allowed to interfere when Demons were involved; they were the masters of pain.

*Don't keep letting your guard down.*

The recruit continuously repeated the same mistake, and Trent had yet to take full advantage of him. Whenever the smaller man moved in to strike he lowered the shield in his left hand so that he could bring his sword to bear with more leverage. His blows against Trent's shield were ferocious, as if he were desperately fighting for his actual life. Trent imagined that in many ways he probably felt that he was. If he failed here he would not join the ranks of the holy warriors that he wished to become a part of. Who knew what reasons drew the man to covet this position? His faith? His family? Trying to escape a life in the slums? Still, his mistake would cost him his life in a real battle, and as such Trent could give him no special privilege here.

*This will hurt.*

The man lunged again, this time the pure desperation on his face turning to outright fear as he saw what was about to happen. Trent pivoted to his left, easily ducking the swing of the practice sword and bringing his own to bear just over the top of the lowered shield. He pulled back slightly at the last moment so as not to cave in the other man's chest. The recruits wore only the light armor favored by the City Watch during training, and it wouldn't do much to protect him from the blow.

As the sword struck, Trent felt a change in the air around him. He turned just in time to see three other recruits descending upon him from the rear. The Paladin attempted to raise his sword to block their advance, but he reacted too slowly. Two of the three landed hits along his sides, blows that could have caused serious damage coming from a real opponent. Behind him he could hear the fallen recruit moaning in pain. The man would need healing in a moment, as soon as he had finished with these others.

*Working together to fight a larger foe. They are learning.*

Trent lowered himself into a crouch and prepared to return the favor, taking the moment to study his new attackers. Two of the three were women he had seen in training before; each was armed and armored in the same fashion as the other recruits. The third was a man who had disposed of his shield in favor of a second sword. They stood together in a half circle, wisely choosing not to separate themselves, although surrounding him might have been the safer choice. It was decisions on matters such as this that would make or break them when they faced actual Demons.

They moved in as one, not rushing to him but keeping a forward momentum that hid any sense of trepidation. Trent cast aside his own shield and took his sword in both hands. If they would approach as if he were a Demon, he would fight like one. They struck at him simultaneously, each blow being narrowly blocked by the faster Paladin. The man with two swords broke off from the others, distracting Trent with a flurry of strikes from both of his weapons. While dealing with this new threat Trent was exposed from the side, a fact that both of the women took full advantage of. The Paladin almost let out a laugh when he admitted to himself that the three recruits had begun to best him.

Then he made them regret the attempt.

Trent turned aside one of the man's swords with his own before knocking the other away with his forearm. The blunted blades skittered across the dirt just out of reach. The recruit quickly found himself upon his back with what would be several bruises forming across his ribs. Turning next to the women, Trent dispatched the first with a well-placed kick that sent her careening backward. When he turned his attention to the second, she lunged at him in one final, desperate attempt to land a blow before her inevitable defeat. He easily sidestepped her attack and placed the point of his sword into the small of her back.

Their battle was interrupted by booming laughter.

"Enough already," Devin called out as he moved into view. "Haven't we beaten up enough of these children today?"

The other Paladin was standing at the front of a rather battered group of recruits whom he had surely bested time and time again. The rest of the recruits who had not been battling one or the other of the two Paladins had gathered around to watch the three on one fight. Upon hearing themselves being called children, many of them lowered their weapons as they glowered at Devin. Clearly insulting them had not helped their moods. Trent attempted to heal the wound.

"Although some would say that three on one isn't a fair match, I would say that it was an intelligent choice." He raised his voice so that the others who had begun to gather around could hear. "When facing a larger or stronger foe it is sometimes necessary to have help bringing the beast down. There is no shame in that. Never allow foolish pride or arrogance be your downfall, or the downfall of a comrade. In this war each Paladin could be the last hope for keeping the Light alive. Each of you that falls could doom us all. Remember that. I say that you all have done well."

Trent turned and reached down to help the fallen man whom he had bested earlier rise. He was clearly still injured from the final blow Trent had given him to his chest. When he was on his feet again he avoided looking him in the eyes. The man's face was aged beyond its years, but it still held a softness that Trent could recognize.

"You have nothing to be ashamed of," he said. "You held out against a stronger foe for longer than many others would have. But you cannot allow yourself to lower your defenses even for a moment, it will be your life."

"Thank you sir," he replied weakly. "I am honored to have fought you."

"What's your name, recruit?"

"Edmund, sir, of the City Watch."

Suddenly Trent recognized the man from his dealings with the Watch. He was more than a simple grunt. If Trent remembered correctly, this man was next in line to be the captain of the entire force. A man in his position should have no reason to want to leave.

"And what makes you wish to leave the Watch for the Paladins?" Trent asked, now intrigued.

"I..." Edmund began to trail off. "I don't feel that I can do enough. I wish to be able to save more people. I see the suffering of those in the slums and I cannot do anything to ease their pain, even from within the Watch. I was born and raised near the outer wall, sir. I know what it's like."

Trent felt his pain, but he also knew that becoming a Paladin wouldn't necessarily give him the purpose in his life that he sought. Joining the Paladins would give him the power to fight the evils of the gods, but he would face the same struggles against the evils of man.

"I lived in slums as well, Edmund. I have seen more than my share of suffering there. But I will warn you that by becoming a Paladin you give your life to a greater cause. You will fight and die for the safety of the people of this city, yes, but not for their comfort. I think it would do you well to consider this choice before you. The Watch needs men like you who care."

The man gingerly bowed and then began to make his way to the small healers' tent in the middle of the yard. Trent watched him go for a few brief moments, clutching his broken arm tightly against his chest. The tent in center of the plaza would have healers of the mortal sort, who would bandage some of his wounds and relieve his pain with balms they had concocted. If his injuries were serious they would contact a Paladin to use some healing magic on the man. Trent felt that he owed him that much.

"Wait."

He approached Edmund and placed his hands upon him before he even had the chance to turn around. Trent closed his eyes and offered a silent prayer of supplication to the gods. Slowly he could feel the energy welling up inside of himself as a blue glow began to emanate from his hands. The glow enveloped Trent's arms before finally moving into the body of the recruit. Within a few moments the glow faded and Edmund was standing a little straighter. He looked visibly stronger from the attempt; moving his arm in wide circles to make sure that everything worked properly.

All Paladins were gifted with healing powers from the gods, although they were mild compared to those which the Seraph employed. The healing magic took its toll as all magic did, and Trent could feel himself slightly weaker for his effort. Edmund's injuries were relatively minor, and so too was the expense of energy and the fatigue that it generated, but he noticed it all the same. For a brief moment Trent stared off into the distance, noticing that his fellow Paladins trained around the field taking little notice of himself and the recruits. All except one...

"Why don't we teach them one final lesson?" Devin asked as he unclasped his axe from his back. "I'll give them a battle they can learn from."

Without waiting for a response the large warrior was jumping through the air, bringing his axe down at Trent. The other Paladin had only moments to react, bringing his own sword to bear, blocking the strike. All thoughts of the future of the idealistic recruit from the City Watch faded as Trent's feet were visibly pushed deeper into the dirt below them from the force of the blow. The practice sword broke in two, allowing Devin's axe to come uncomfortably close to Trent's face.

*He certainly isn't holding back.*

Trent spun to the side, pulling his real sword loose from its fastenings. He rolled under another broad swing from his companion's axe before launching himself behind him. Trent cut upward, slicing Devin's golden cloak in half. He stepped back and picked up his shield from where he had dropped it before, raising it to protect his open side. As he did so, Trent shot a smile at Edmund, who smiled back. Their struggle had cast more of the heavy dirt into the air than usual, filling his nostrils with a pungent earthy scent. Devin turned to face him. When he noticed the damage to his cloak he began to laugh, unclasping it so that it fell to the ground.

"You owe me a new garment."

"You owe me a new practice blade."

The two warriors sprinted at each other, kicking up more dirt as they did so, each clashing his weapon upon the defenses of the other. This fight would only end when one side gave in, something that rarely happened when they decided to duel. Devin brought his axe mere inches from Trent's face with a mighty swing that was only just stopped by the other's sword, which this time refused to break. Blocking the blow shook Trent's entire body, the slight fatigue of healing Edmund beginning to draw his attention. With Devin so close, Trent could make out the sweat forming upon the other's brow. He was expending more of his own stamina that Trent would have expected. He used this to his advantage by striking the larger warrior in the side of the face with his shield.

Devin stumbled back, hooking Trent's sword as he did so. The dazed Paladin used all of his strength to pull the sword from Trent's grasp. Once the blade landed in the dirt he let out another thunderous laugh.

"Tell me you are ready to admit defeat."

"I was about to ask you the same."

Trent bounded forward with great strides, his shield held before him to deflect the blow of the axe sideways, leaving Devin open to assault. Savagely, a gauntleted fist glanced across Devin's face, sending him careening backward. Casually, Trent bent down to pick up his blade again and settled into an offensive crouch. Devin still rocked back onto his heels, fresh blood welling out of the wound to his face.

"See how he lets his guard down when he prepares to strike?" Trent addressed the recruits. "His weapon may be large, but this also makes it unwieldy, leaving him open after every attack."

"The best defense is a strong attack," Devin growled as he spat blood onto the ground.

"No. The best defense is caution." The voice that answered the Paladin came from above. In unison, the recruits looked up to see the Lady Ren making her slow descent from the sky. "Watch your opponent, study their movements and kill them. Do all of this without exposing your own weaknesses."

She landed between the two Paladins, smiling.

"Devin, I am glad that you have grown out your beard as of late, otherwise you would ruin my ceremony with your broken face."

The bruised Paladin laughed again and lowered his weapon, spitting out blood once more.

"My lady, I would never pollute your presence with such ugliness. For that reason, I recommend that Trent be barred from the proceedings. His face is beyond repair."

"Surely you are the expert on ugly men. I hear that is all that fancies you."

"We do tend to stick together, my lady, this is true."

Ren turned and addressed the recruits. "Go now, prepare yourselves, for in a few hours you will no longer be simply human, but something much more."

As the men and women began to disperse, Trent and Devin returned their weapons to their backs and approached their Seraph. Ren put her hands upon Devin before he could protest; a familiar blue glow enveloping them. Within seconds the wounds to his face were healed. When the recruits were all out of earshot Devin finally spoke.

"All of them, my lady?"

"Yes. Do you disapprove of my decision?"

"Some of them could use some work, of this I am sure."

"Trent?"

*Some could use more time. And I fear that Edmund truly belongs in the Watch. The people of the city need men like him...*

"I stand by you, my lady," Trent responded, ignoring the look Devin shot him. "Some are more ready than others, but they all have the drive to serve the Light to the best of their abilities."

"Could they not do that from within the City Watch or the army?" Ren asked.

Trent hesitated. "Not for these. If any of them are like I was, they will accept no substitute for being a Paladin."

"If even one of them is like you then we truly are lost," Devin laughed.

"Castille will not be pleased with my decision, but we need more Paladins," Ren said.

"Has there been recent enemy activity that we are unaware of?" Trent asked, concern seeping into his voice.

"No, and that is what worries me. The gods do not share my fears, nor do my advisors. As always I find more receptive ears from you two than anyone else. Castille wishes for us to march out into the wilderness like we once did and destroy the forces of Darkness root and stem, but I refuse to put so many lives at risk. When the ceremony is over I am going to send you two ranging to see why our enemies have been so quiet of late. Hopefully I am wrong, but gods help us if I am right and did nothing."

Trent and Devin were often her first choice for men to send on ranging missions into the wilderness. Lately there had been very few forays into enemy territory that they were not involved in or leading themselves. It was up to Paladins to scout the uninhabited regions of creation in order to track enemy movements to prevent attacks on the villages. It also fell to them to hunt down and destroy the few roving bands of bandits that had formed from various exiles from Illux over the years. Most Paladins serving under Ren found themselves either stationed in Illux full-time or defending the small farming villages. The only other sizable assignment was for those who stayed at Seatown, many of whom had begun to think of themselves as not being under the direct control of their parent city. Very few found themselves getting any duties between those three. These two were her champions, though. They were the ones she could count on the most to journey into the lands of the enemy, kill what they could and make it back every time. It seemed their skills would be called upon once again.

*Another ranging mission could take weeks. Weeks without her.*

The two men dropped to their knees before her.

"My lady," they said together.

THE TWO PALADINS spent the next few hours gathering the supplies that they would need for the journey. These trips were usually arduous, filled with danger from Demons, Accursed, and even starvation. It was much easier to hide from the enemy without horses to care for or a large assortment of supplies to carry. This meant that what little they brought needed to fit upon their backs. That didn't leave much besides weapons and hunting gear. For this reason, these trips were not often envied by their fellow Paladins. Some did fight for the honor, but enough had never returned that the very notion seemed foolish to many who were given the choice.

This was nothing new to Trent, and yet his mind raced as he went through the usual preparations. Was Ren's uneasiness unfounded? Or would they find something worth reporting while they were out there? They could rest assured that they would come across Demons and Accursed; it had never before been otherwise. But what if this time they found something somehow worse? The dangers of these missions had never bothered him before, but now some deep fear picked at his mind like a scavenger at a carcass.

*The Vulture. Ren's uneasiness must be infectious.*

Devin, on the other hand, seemed completely unfazed by the situation, as if this mission were no different than any other. The smile never seemed to leave his face, even while his friend looked as if he were marching to his death. It hadn't always been that way, but it seemed that his old friend had done away with those ghosts. Trent thought at first that Devin didn't notice his own discomfort, but he quickly realized that it was far more likely that he was simply choosing to ignore it. His lack of fear had served him well as a Paladin until now, but Trent was sure that it would get both of them into trouble before long.

He pushed the issue out of mind while finishing the preparations. Horses were gathered and saddled from the stables near the outer wall; they would serve as mounts to the last village before they were left behind so that the rest of the journey could unfold on foot. Bedrolls and foodstuffs were gathered, as well as Devin's favored hunting bow that he brought along each time they went ranging. Much more than that would prove to be too much for them to carry. They gathered these supplies with the horses and left them hitched near the barracks until it was time for them to be off. When they felt that they were finished, they began to walk back toward the cathedral in order to help prepare things for the proceedings that evening. It was on the walk back that Trent felt he could leave his concerns unspoken no longer.

"Doesn't something about this assignment feel wrong to you?" he asked.

"Your lack of enthusiasm for the chance to kill Demons is certainly disconcerting."

"I'm being serious, Devin. I have a bad feeling that I don't usually get before we go ranging."

"And this should affect me why?"

"Because you are my friend and partner. My brother-in-arms."

"This is exactly why I am ignoring your fear: tough love. I imagine that you are simply afraid that you won't get to see the Lady Ren any more if you die out there. Don't worry, I won't let that happen."

His words were more patronizing than the tone of his voice, but Trent still felt stung by them.

"Don't you ever take anything seriously?"

"No, and neither should you. Enjoyment cannot be gleaned from serious matters. I remember when you used to take great pleasure in the chance to rend the skull of some Accursed or split the helm of a Demon. Each time your sword bit into an enemy you felt a little better about your brother's death."

*Don't mention Terric. Don't you dare.*

Trent could see his brother falling again. Dying there in the snow. He could smell his blood on the air.

"Leave my brother out of this."

"I would if you would, but you won't. I know you better than any other man alive. I know the dream that keeps jolting you awake every night just as I know what it is that brought you to join the ranks of the Paladins in the first place. It wasn't faith in the gods, or some sense of civic duty. Your search for vengeance is not a weakness, Trent, but a strength."

"How could it possibly be a strength?"

"You have never seen yourself fight. It is truly a sight to behold. Not as magnificent as myself, I would imagine, but terrifying all the same. But you have to admit it, embrace it, or else it will weigh you down like a stone."

"You may think you know my pain but you don't!" Trent spat, rage giving life to his words. "Your early life was spent growing up in the inner city, listening to the glorious tales of your ancestors, not scrounging for food. The first time you saw a Demon was in the field, with other Paladins at your back. When I first saw a Demon it had split my brother in two. I will never forget what I saw that day, even when my spark returns to the High God! Don't ever act as if you can understand that!"

With that final pronouncement Trent turned and stormed away from his friend, each angered footfall sounding like thunder in his ears as they reverberated off of the plaza stone. Dimly he could hear Devin calling after him, but the sounds faded as he made his way into the city and away from his pain.

# CHAPTER 3

Trent hoped that, if he had any luck at all, a walk through the winding streets of Illux would clear his head and help him shake the anger that he still felt toward his friend. Devin was never one to worry about the opinions of others, and as such, his words often cut deep. Trent had thought himself used to this behavior by now, but being reminded of Terric and his death those years before never ended well. Trent knew that this was simply because he blamed himself, a fact that Devin was never slow to point out. Terric died pushing him out of the Demon's path. He died so that Trent could live.

*I should have been the one to die that day. Terric should be the Paladin. If only I had moved out of the way on my own...*

His thoughts trailed off as he allowed them to get lost in the cobblestones beneath his feet. The smooth construction of the roadways and thoroughfares of Illux didn't provide much in the form of a pattern to focus on, so his mind quickly returned to its grief. There would never be a way for him to rationalize what had happened that day, and in some ways he felt that he didn't really wish to. Deep inside, Trent knew that there was a comfort in his guilt. That gnawing emotion was the only way that he could cope with the random and senseless evil of the world.

Guilt and anger.

Anger was the emotion that he relished most, although he kept it hidden where few could see. It was for this reason that Devin found it so easy to bother him, for who knew him better? It was the anger that made him excel in his Paladin training, just as the other had said. It was the anger that made him seek out the enemy with such fury and satisfaction. It wasn't just hatred of the Demon who took Terric from him, but hatred for himself.

There was one aspect of his darker emotions that didn't rely upon self-loathing, however: his feelings toward his father. Trent hated the man even more than the Demon who cut Terric down, even more than he hated himself. After all, if his father hadn't cast his two boys into the streets, they very well might have never found themselves in the path of the Demon as it cut a bloody swath out of Illux and into the darkness beyond. To children with nothing, the streets were a paradise where the imagination was the only plaything. Trent knew that he and his brother would have watched the blaze outside no matter where they had lived that day, but if things had been different, it would have been from a different vantage point. As it was, the two boys would have most likely starved or frozen to death that winter, long before the attack took place, if not for the goodwill of a kindly old woman. Injustices seemed to breed in the slums of the outer city, just out of the watchful spires of the Cathedral. Yet some kept the Light alive in their hearts.

*Elise. She deserves a visit. Perhaps that will quiet my mind?*

Trent often found himself returning to the aging woman in-between his treks beyond the walls of the city. He didn't visit her as often as he should have, always finding more reasons to stay away than to make the trip to the outer wall. He knew that this was most likely because each conversation that he had with her brought too much pain welling to the surface. And yet he could never stay away for long. He loved that woman as he had loved his own mother, herself now nothing more than a face in his memory. Elise still lived in the same ramshackle hut near the wall that she had raised Trent in, refusing any offer that the Paladin made to get her closer to the inner city.

"The slums are dangerous," he would tell her. "Wouldn't you like to be closer to the cathedral, in any case?"

"This is my home," she would stubbornly reply. "And I don't need stone walls to pray to the Light."

He supposed that she was right, so he never found himself forcing the issue. As it was, the slums had begun to gradually repair themselves after hundreds of years of neglect once the Lady Ren had taken control of the city. Paladins now actively patrolled the streets rather than hunting the Accursed in the wilderness. As a result, crime had begun to lessen. The main duties of keeping the city safe from the dangers within still fell to the Watch, and men like Edmund were still the first lifeline that the citizens of Illux looked to. The number of people living in impoverished conditions had barely abated, however, even with the Seraph's increased attention and aid. There were just too many people living off of too few resources.

The inner city had sprung up around the Grand Cathedral in the beginning, long before the walls of Illux were constructed. As time went on, the people of Illux began to multiply and spread farther and farther outward until they were pressing against the walls that they had built for protection. Some left for the villages to farm, as the lands once tilled within the walls made way for more and more homes. Others founded Seatown on the coast, fishing what they could from the salty ocean waters. Most just continued to cram into the space between the walls and the inner city, building their houses in the small spaces between those already constructed, pressing up against one another like bodies in a grave. From there it was only a matter of time before they found themselves struggling against one another for comfort.

Once Trent had decided to go and see Elise, his path changed from a steady meandering through the heart of the city to a direct walk toward the outer wall. The tall buildings of white stone around him matched the architecture and the beauty of the cathedral at his back, stretching away almost beyond his vision. Many of the homes here were tall and broad, some reaching up to hide the streets from the sun above. Even so, the walkways were wide enough that the inner city never felt as closed in as the slums near the wall. The stones beneath his feet somehow remained mostly polished and intact as judicious cleaning in this part of the city helped to keep it so.

Large trees and elaborate hanging gardens decorated street corners and walkways, adding needed color to the shining thoroughfares. Some of these elaborate buildings belonged to the older families of the city who claimed direct, unbroken descent from the first men made by the High God. The very notion was ridiculous, as all who now lived had to have been descended from the first in some fashion or another. Yet these special few had kept records and chosen to live where their ancestors did, many of whom stemmed from the oldest children of these early lines. Devin came from a family such as this, his own forebears belonging to some of the first Paladins in the war against the Gods of Darkness. Trent had no such esteem for his ancestors, knowing little and caring less about those who had predated his father and mother.

*My family is the order now. Devin, Gil, Ren...My blood no longer matters.*

His boot plunging into a water-filled hole signaled that the inner city was slowly being left behind for the gradual descent into the slums. As if on cue the buildings began to cluster tighter together and take on an altogether muddier texture. The smells that wafted to Trent's nose changed from aromatic and floral to pungent and all too human in origin. Gone were the brilliant whites of the inner city, replaced instead with a far less vibrant grey stone. Trees and gardens were nowhere to be seen, replaced instead with visible wash lines and merchant stalls selling poorly made wares or foodstuffs imported into the city beyond what was rationed by the faith. Often people traded these rations for extra blankets or handmade clothes. In theory,

Seatown and the farming villages produced enough food to feed the entire city, but in practice, mankind could never share limited resources that well.

And these weren't even the worst areas of Illux. Trent had only just left the border of the inner city behind. Here the houses were still made of stone, and every road paved, not just the main ones. The closer one got to the outer walls the more cramped the conditions became. Stone houses were replaced altogether with poorly built wooden shacks with thatched roofs. Beggars sat upon every corner, and thieves still prowled the streets here and there when Paladins and the City Watch were occupied elsewhere. Ren tried to visit these areas often, bringing with her extra food and clothing, even offering shelter to those in need. Many, however, refused her gestures, too proud to take even the charity of the faith.

Elise was one such woman.

Ever since he had been a boy she had refused the charity of others, instead relying only on her own determination to provide for herself and the two young boys she had taken in. Her trade was the washing of clothes for her neighbors or even others who lived farther from the wall than she. The work took up most of her time, and rarely did it pay her more than enough to gain food and pay for her housing, yet she was content. When she had been a younger woman, Elise had been a maid to one of the older families in the center of Illux. She'd quickly tired of their ways and put her skills to use closer to home.

*Not even the Fallen One could bring down this woman's spirits.*

It was the war against the Darkness that had allowed for the slums of the city to fall into disrepair. Trent's walk had now fully changed from pleasant to depressing, the reminders of how little the people of the outer city were cared for finally becoming all too apparent. Martial action had taken precedence over the care of the people of Illux, from its founding until now. The High God had created a paradise for his creations to enjoy, and had gifted them with the Gods of Light to govern it, while the Gods of Darkness threatened. The safety of mankind was of paramount importance to the gods, but not, it seemed, its wellbeing. Trent often wondered what it was that he was really defending every time he killed a Demon in the wilderness. Was life, no matter how wretched, really worth preserving? The open vices of the Gods of Darkness were punished by the faith and the City Watch: theft, rape, murder. But it was the hidden ones that went unchecked and remained all too insidious: hunger, poverty, hopelessness…

*Abandoning one's own sons.*

As the great wall continued to rise above him and the air continued to grow more rank, Trent knew that he was now only a few minutes' walk from his childhood home. The streets here were mostly dirt, with stones only loosely covering the main roads that led from the wall to the heart of the city. Few homes here stood over two stories high, and even those housed more than one family. From within one such house Trent could hear the sad wailing of a child, most likely crying out in hunger. He had wanted to change this place once, even thought that he could. Now he knew different. Now he knew better.

As Trent had walked through the inner city, most of the people out on the streets had paid him no heed. The closer one was to the Cathedral and the barracks, the more regular it was to encounter a Paladin out on a walk of one kind or another. Out here, on the other hand, they were far less common. Most still ignored Trent as if he were any other man, though some nodded in recognition or reverence. There were a few who watched him with suspicion from their windows, thinking that he had come to stop some illicit activity at the behest of the Watch. That often ended with a door being kicked open and criminals dragged into the street.

The thought made him smile. Trent hadn't been given such duties for years, not since he and Devin had proven themselves in the field and earned the respect of the Lady Ren. The few times that he brought his sword to bear against men nowadays, occurred only when the small groups of bandits that plagued the countryside became too much for village Paladins to handle alone. They were made up of runaways and cowards, men who had been banished or had chosen to seek a life of freedom, unconfined by the rules of society. They made their living by raiding the villages and the shipments of goods sent to Illux from afar. When they did so it always resulted in death, eventually their own. Turning against your fellow man was as good as forsaking the Light.

Children ran across Trent's path, playing a game not unlike what he had played all those years ago. One of them, a lanky girl who couldn't have been older than ten, chased the others about with a stick. Trent gathered that she was playing the Paladin, and the others running from her were Demons or Accursed. If only the reality of things were like these children's games. In his experience it was the forces of Light who fled for safety before the forces of Darkness would. Humanity was too fragile for it to be otherwise.

Finally, Trent saw the familiar house as it leaned ever so slightly against its northern neighbor. Clothes lines stretched from within the open windows to the nearest buildings on either side, each holding enough sopping linen that they had begun to sag earthwards. The four walls of the little building each stood at a slightly different angle, leading to gaps in several places where he remembered that the light from the street was able to penetrate in. The roof was thatched with old brown straw that barely supported itself anymore, and had never kept out all of the rain. Even from his vantage point on the street, Trent could see Elise working inside, scrubbing and hanging clothes all by herself. He couldn't help but smile. She certainly didn't plan on changing anytime soon.

Trent stopped short of her home, listening to the din of the slums around him. In the distance he could hear the children still playing, beyond that the shouts of a market corner or the familiar slosh of a chamber pot being dumped from a window. The sound brought back more memories than he cared to face. Slowly he ran his hands through his long red hair. Surely she would comment on his appearance as she always did. He was never quite kept up enough for her conservative tastes. His smile returned as he walked forward, knocking on her loose wooden door.

When the door opened, Trent was greeted by a wrinkled face, split across the middle by a wide smile.

"Trent! I thought you had forgotten me," she wheezed, her breathing more labored than he had remembered.

"Forgotten you? I'd die before I'd forget you." He could tell that he looked as hollow as he felt.

"Die? Why are you always so dramatic? And don't you ever cut that hair? They let you marry in that order, don't they? How will you ever attract a woman with that mane?"

"I wear it how I like." Trent thought he sounded like a boy again. "Yes we may marry, but few do—I..."

"Well, come in! I'm only washing clothes."

Trent tried not to chuckle as Elise abruptly turned and hobbled back inside, ushering her ward back into the house he was raised in. She hadn't ever mentioned marriage before, not once he had talked of joining the order, and he knew that she herself had never married either. The very notion was almost humorous. As she walked, he could see that her posture had gotten worse, old age hunching her over like she carried a great weight upon her back. She shuffled as if her joints had begun to fail her as well. He knew that it wouldn't be long before she finally rejoined the High God.

*Don't think like that. Elise isn't one to go quietly.*

"Don't let me put you out," he said when she began to quickly move things aside so that he had a place to sit.

"I thought that I taught you better than to stand when you are told to sit!" the old woman snapped, pulling out a chair and shoving it in front of him.

Trent cracked a toothy grin before he replied. "You haven't told me to sit yet."

"Then sit!"

The great Paladin slowly lowered himself into the wobbly chair, its wood audibly groaning beneath his immense weight. Elise spent the next few minutes finishing her work with the wet clothes she had been hanging, leaving Trent to survey the room in awkward silence. The multitude of laundered garments made the entire house smell of damp fabric, something he hadn't smelled in some time. For as small and shabby as her abode was, the old woman took pride in keeping it clean: not a speck of dust was evident within the entire breadth of her home. All of her belongings were kept in an orderly fashion, and even the laundry that she hung inside and out to dry was kept so organized that it prevented any semblance of clutter.

The house was divided into just two rooms. The front room in which they sat included a three-legged table and some chairs, a washbasin, and a small hearth with a great black kettle sitting over the fire for when Elise made her daily broth. The second room at the rear of the house was home to a single, large bed, and a chamber pot, both of which Trent had made use of while living here. Almost nothing about the house had changed since he had last called this place home, shortly before joining the order. The only differences that he could see were on account of the age of the house and its sole resident. Elise wasn't able to keep up with the building as she once had, and it showed. Small spots of sunlight streamed through fresh holes in the roof, and the front door didn't seem to hang right.

*When we get back from this mission I will come and fix this place up.*

He had tried convincing her to move several times in the past, but by now he knew better than to press his luck by trying again, so he had kept his mouth shut as he watched the little shack get worse and worse over the last few years. When Elise finally passed on, Trent figured that he would knock the old building down and let something new sprout up in its place. He couldn't tell her that, of course, or else he would risk getting boxed on the ear.

"How have you been?" he finally asked, as she moved from the laundry to the hearth, checking her broth.

"The same as the last time I saw you. My bones hurt more now, but I don't expect that to change anytime soon."

"I see that the neighbors keep you busy with the clothes washing."

"There will always be clothes to wash. Even when my old bones don't hurt anymore. Do you want some broth?"

"I can always eat a bowl." He couldn't. They both knew he hated it, but she always offered and he always accepted.

Elise poured two bowls of the milky-brown liquid and brought them over, seating herself across from him. Trent made an honest effort before giving up and setting the bowl down on the table beside him. She continued to slurp hers loudly, seemingly paying Trent little attention. Seeing her eating with such vigor made him feel somewhat guilty, so he lifted the bowl and made a second attempt. The smell was only vaguely reminiscent of meat, and it left a sour film in one's mouth. Still, he finished this time, using as few spoonfuls as possible. When Elise finished hers, she eyed Trent suspiciously upon seeing his own bowl empty.

"Where is that big friend of yours? Darren?"

"Devin. He is preparing supplies. There is to be an initiation tonight, and then we are being sent on another ranging mission."

"Aren't there enough of you big brutes already? You would think that we worship the gods through fighting rather than prayer at the rate that they make new Paladins."

"Somehow there always seems to be more of them than us, I'm afraid."

*Until now, that is.*

The ranks of the enemy always seemed to grow at a near exponential rate. The legions of Accursed were fed from those evil men who gave themselves to the Darkness and found their souls consumed. It was said that a Divine Spark could not return to the High God while it was shackled inside the rotting body of an Accursed. And yet the living death that they faced was not just forced onto those with evil in their hearts. The manner through which the enemy made their armies was not entirely known, but forced transformations were not unheard of, nor was reanimation. Those who fell in battle or found themselves on the edge of death could sometimes expect the gift of immortality, bestowed at the most heinous of costs. Some believed that it was possible that there were still Accursed in existence that were made in the beginning when the gods still walked the Mortal Plane.

"We wouldn't need to worry about them if more people would just stay here where they belong. I never understood why so many would choose to live beyond the walls of Illux. Demons and bandits alike prowl the wilderness. Fools both! Even those monks in the hills are dangerous. That is why I have always been content to live here where it is safe."

*In squalor. Living yes, but even Illux isn't safe.*

"The villages aren't all bad. My friend Gil is stationed at one of the villages to the north, and he doesn't mind it. And there is Seatown, of course." Trent's response sounded weaker than he had anticipated.

"Seatown! Bah!" The old woman spat. "That glorified chamber pot thinks that it can be independent from Illux. Well, I think it needs to be dumped into the ocean. They are nothing but trouble out there."

Trent shook his head laughing. "I won't argue with you."

"No, you won't, or I'll clout your ear." Elise was smiling again.

The old woman reached her gnarled hands out across the table and grabbed hold of Trent. Her old shawl that kept her thin white hair hidden slipped farther down the back of her neck while she looked at him. He could feel that there was some vitality there, deep inside her old body.

"This old crone missed you, Trent."

"I know. I have no excuse for not visiting more often, when duty allows."

"You and your duty. I still don't understand why you chose to join the order. It won't bring Terric back."

Trent tried not to clench his hands with hers inside. He knew that her callous demeanor hid a sadness as deep as his own. On the day Terric died, Elise had cried in front of Trent for the first and last time. When he had finally left to begin training as a Paladin he thought that she would cry again, but if she ever did she waited until he was gone.

"I know I can't bring him back. But I can't let anyone else die on my account. Inaction is just as bad as causing their deaths myself."

"If I could spare you the pain of that day I would. You shouldn't blame yourself as you do. Just know that I am proud of you. Proud of my boy."

Quickly, Elise stood up and gathered the bowls and spoons, taking them over to her small wash basin so she could begin cleaning them. Trent rose to help her but she shooed him away, making him return to his seat. She ignored him again while she cleaned their bowls and didn't speak a word until they were done.

"Why are you still sitting around?"

"I didn't think that we were done talking?"

"An important Paladin like yourself doesn't have time to waste doting on an old woman. Don't you have responsibilities, or is that shiny armor just for show?"

Trent laughed and stood, walking over and gently hugging her. In his arms she felt even more frail than he had remembered. What little strength she had left was due more to her iron will than any physical source. As they parted their embrace she leaned in close and whispered in his ear.

"Forget what I said earlier about your brother. Kill them all for me."

Trent silently nodded and turned away, attempting to hide the tears that had begun to gather in the corners of his eyes. He thought for a moment that hers had some as well. He slowly opened the crooked door and stepped out onto the street without another word. As he turned to wave goodbye she was already back to work cleaning clothes.

*I won't wait so long to see you again. I promise.*

With that final thought Trent began his long walk back to the heart of the city. Within a few minutes he would be leaving the slums and his past behind again, just as he had all of those years before. As he kept walking, Trent tried to push how frail Elise was becoming from his thoughts. The woman had been old even when she had taken him and Terric in, and yet she had always seemed so strong to him. At times he couldn't help but wonder what she would have been like had she decided to push herself to become a Paladin in her youth.

*If that had happened the war would already be over.*

The thought made Trent smile to himself as he walked along, no longer in any rush to get back to the heart of the city. Devin would surely be missing him by now, but the other could wait; the initiation ceremony was still several hours off, and even then it would be a while yet before they left the city. He was going to enjoy this moment alone for once. His thoughts of Elise soon turned to Lady Ren in her brilliance, another strong woman whom he had the good fortune to have the respect of. In some ways they reminded Trent of each other, and he often wished that the Seraph would visit his surrogate mother before she passed from this world.

The pungent odor of the slums began to recede as the buildings around him were no longer built on top of one another. Trent decided that he would take the long way back and walk the streets of the middle ring of the city, just between his past in the slums and his present in the inner city. There was almost something poetic in the notion.

As he rounded a corner Trent stopped short at the sight of a squat man with thinning red hair. He was carrying himself with a sour disposition, and those who passed him on the street quickly moved out of his path. His gait was slowed from a slight limp that he exhibited, but he still trudged onwards as if he had somewhere that he needed to be.

Sweat began to form on the Paladin as he watched the man walk past, the faint aroma of alcohol wafting off of him. The older man didn't even give Trent a second glance as he shuffled close to him on his walk down the street. Trent didn't even stop to think as he turned around and followed the heavy man at a distance, making sure that he hung back far enough to avoid attention. He had recognized the man from the moment that he had seen his face, and hatred had boiled up deep within him in an instant.

It was his father.

# CHAPTER 4

The heavyset man that Trent had recognized as his father continued ahead, oblivious to the seething Paladin who stalked him from behind. His brisk walk continued unabated as he plunged through the throngs of midday traffic in the middle ring of the city. Something about the way that he carried himself told Trent that he still had the same vile personality that had plagued him before. Even from behind, Trent could tell that the hateful man had a grimace plastered across his face.

Trent continued his advance at the same slow pace as his quarry, not wanting to draw attention to himself or his motives for following the man. He could feel the cramping in his fingers as his fist tightened like steel, the hatred rolling through him like molten rock beneath the earth. It was this cruel man who had thrown him onto the street. It was this man who had left his sons to starve during the winter. It was this man whose actions allowed for Terric to be killed.

*You might as well have killed him yourself, you bastard.*

His father suddenly turned right, making his way around the corner faster than Trent had anticipated. Trent's pace had slowed while he was lost in his thoughts, and now he risked losing his target.

He sped up and took the corner just as quickly as the older man, knocking a woman over in the process. She tumbled to the ground, spilling her armful of bread and vegetables into the muck of the street. Around him the world reeled for a moment, the sounds of the city drowning out his thoughts of pursuit, his face becoming flushed from his embarrassment at knocking over a stranger. When Trent locked eyes with her she became visibly afraid, crawling backward upon the ground, soiling her patched dress with dirt and mud.

The look that she gave him caused Trent to pause, stopping him from plowing forward as he had been planning to just moments before. She looked so young and small where she lay upon the ground, cowering in fear just within the shadow that he cast over her. The Paladin quickly gathered her food and handed it to her after she finally began to pull herself upright, now no longer cowering. He barely heard his own apology as he took off running to find where his father had disappeared to. Running headlong through the crowds of people had finally drawn some attention to Trent from those about the area on their afternoon errands. Ignoring them he pushed on, shoving his way through those who didn't heed his passing on their own, still keeping a watchful eye ahead for the sight of the thinning red hair. It wasn't long before he caught sight of the other man rounding another corner and he sprinted after him.

By now they were completely in the middle of the city, no longer near the real slums, but not yet in the nicer districts near the cathedral. Gaining the sight of his prize again, Trent slowed his run to a walk, hoping to lose the slight attention that he had generated. Now with his father just out of reach he needed to fade back into the crowds so as to not be noticed. As he followed closer again, his mind wandered to what exactly he planned to do once they had reached the other man's destination. Would he confront him? Bare his soul as he had always dreamed of? Or was there a darker motive crawling deep in his breast that he dared not admit?

*It is the duty of the Paladin to kill evil. Father is an evil man.*

His own words from childhood cut through him like a knife,

bringing bile to his tongue. He knew what he wanted to do. What he had secretly wanted since even before Terric had died. When others around him dreamed of slaying Demons or crushing the Accursed under heel Trent's mind always wandered back to his father, replacing the shadowy forms in his mind with a familiar one. There was no reason to deny it now, not to himself.

Ahead, the older man slowed his walk in front of a small two-story house nestled between two larger stone buildings. Without stopping he opened the little wooden door that led inside, pulling it shut behind himself. Trent stopped just short of the door, left alone to stand without. The city almost seemed quieter here, as if he stood not in the middle of Illux but in another world. His breathing intensified as he stared at the wooden door, almost certain that he was boring holes through it.

*Arra, Goddess of Light, bring me strength.*

He continued to stand outside the moderately sized home, a monolith of hatred, smoldering within the shell of his armor. Those on the street who took notice of him moved away in fear, some even pointing and whispering before rounding a corner and disappearing into the city. Trent paid them no heed. Paladins only took this much interest in people that they intended to kill or arrest. Surely they thought that this champion of Light had tracked a thief or murderer to his lair. In some ways they were correct.

*What are you going to do now, you fool? Talk to him? Threaten him? Killing him would be an unforgivable sin.*

The sights and smells of the city faded as Trent's mind returned to the day he and his brother were cast out into the street. Their father had stumbled home from his work in a foul mood, already halfway drunk before he even stepped through the door. Terric had tried to approach him, even welcome him home, but had instead found himself rebuffed. His new wife came down the upper stairs with a smile, informing her husband that she was with child. Trent only barely remembered her face, and each time he thought of the woman her hair color was a different shade of brown. Even her name was no longer present in his thoughts. The details of this portion of his life were fuzzy at best, but the emotions that he had felt had crystallized in his mind where they would stay unchanged until his death.

He wasn't sure who his father had struck first, his wife or his youngest son, but once the old drunk had started swinging so did Terric. The older boy couldn't have been much past the age of ten, and yet he stood between his father and little brother without a single flicker of fear in his eyes. He had fought this battle before, and he would fight it again and again to keep Trent safe. Each blow that connected with his face crumpled him to the floor, and yet he stood again each time. Trent recalled the sound of his father's new wife screaming at first, but she silenced herself when she realized there was no other way to protect her unborn child. The next thing Trent remembered was being thrown into the street beside his bleeding brother, left to freeze to death in the snow.

"I can't afford to feed you with another little bastard on the way," were the last words that the hateful man slurred as he shut the door. Once he was gone, the reek of wine still lingered over the street where they lay.

In his mind, Trent vaguely recalled that the child had turned out to be a girl when it was born some months later. How he and Terric had come by this knowledge he wasn't entirely sure, but having heard it from his older brother he had taken it as fact. He had never seen his father again before today, Elise living some distance away from their old home in the slums. Two whole weeks they had lived in the streets, stealing and begging for food. At night they found warmth under old blankets while curled against the outside of a hearth, the flames within just heating the stones enough to prevent the boys from dying. When Elise had found them, shivering and near death, she took them in at once, never asking a second question about what brought them to her door. The Seraph at that time cared more what transpired without his walls than within, allowing for the city to decay from the inside out. When they finally related their story to the kindly old woman she considered bringing the matter before the faith, but then decided that the gods would surely punish the man for his sins in their own time.

*I'm just going to confront him. If I harm him, I am no better than a Demon...*

The sword swung at Trent, but he tumbled onto the ground just out of its reach, Terric standing there in his place, keeping his younger brother from harm just as he had when their father had struck him. Terric had looked so confused as his insides sloshed onto the ground, staining the snow red. The Paladins had rushed past, but he never saw them. He didn't see anything again until he was in the arms of Elise, both of them crying in heavy sobs. All he could remember was the smell of his brother's blood as it mixed with the smoke of the street as it burned.

Before he realized what was happening, the wooden door was burst off of its hinges and Trent was storming into the house, every muscle in his body tense and ready for a fight. Outside on the street people began to scream and run to alert the City Watch. They knew that something bad was happening in this little house in the middle of the city. Trent quickly searched his surroundings, seeing that the slightly furnished home was hardly different from the one in which his father had lived before, if not smaller. There were dishes of half eaten food scattered about, mostly covered in moldy bread or the partially gnawed bones of a bird. Unwashed clothes were draped across the small wooden chairs and table in the center of the main room. The blackened hearth in the corner looked as if it hadn't been lit in ages. A steady sheen of dust covered most surfaces in the house, clearly showing that the place had never seen the touch of a woman. It was obvious that his father's existence had been a lonely one.

Trent saw the man on the landing above, coming out of a room half-dressed to see what the crashing sound made by the shattered door had been. His screams and protests fell upon deaf ears. Almost blindly Trent stalked up the stairs, gripping the wooden railing until it splintered, sending shards of it in every direction. His father returned to his room for a moment before reappearing with a large knife in his hand. By then Trent was already at the top of the stairs and well within range of an attack with the small blade. Before the man had a chance to bring the weapon down upon his attacker Trent had already grabbed his wrist, the bones shattering inside with no effort. His screams were cut off as Trent's iron grip closed around his throat, hauling him into the air and tossing him down the stairs like a rag doll. At the bottom he crumpled into a bloody heap, weakly moaning from the pain.

"Why are you doing this to me?" the older man choked, tears filling his eyes.

Trent bounded down the creaking steps and landed beside him, rolling the broken mess over to confront him face to face. He looked weak now, far weaker than Trent had anticipated. His body had broken quicker than the Paladin would have assumed; the strength that he once held over his sons in had evaporated to age. He was pitiful now, no longer the vile creature that he had been in his youth. Now he was just a wretched, lonely man who was being beaten by his only son. Sympathy for his hated father welled up inside him and quenched the fire in his breast. The Paladin pulled his father upright and dragged him over to the center of the room, pushing him up against the small table. He was vaguely aware that he had moved his victim out of sight of the street upon which a small crowd had gathered to peer in through the open doorway.

"I don't understand."

The warm magic had already begun to flow from Trent's body, the blue glow moving from his arms and hands into his father. What wounds the fall had caused began to knit, stopping what bleeding had surely begun inside. Within moments the older man no longer relied upon the other to hold him up, now fully healed from the beating he had taken. He reeked of wine again, like he had all those years before.

"Who are you? Why have you invaded my home?"

The sound of Terric's belly tearing open rang out in Trent's ears. He struck his father across the face, sending bits of tooth and blood onto the floor.

"Have you forgotten what your own kin looks like, you old bastard?" Trent struck him again, pulling his punch at the last possible second before the full force of it connected with the man's stomach.

Cold realization filled his father's blue eyes. What had moments ago been fear was now replaced with defiant anger, if only for a fleeting moment. His breathing had become short gasps, each exhalation sending small droplets of blood onto his chin. Using the support of the table behind him the older man pushed himself upright in a weak attempt to stand more level with his long lost son.

"Trent."

"Father."

"You and your brother never had much love for me, but why this? Why now? By what right does a Paladin break into the home of a pious man?"

"We never loved you because you never loved us!" Trent was only inches from the other's face. "I didn't ask to live my life without a father. You ask what right I have? I have the right of an abandoned son to seek justice from the man who robbed him. Don't hide behind the faith, you share no more love for the gods than you do for your own flesh and blood."

"I never asked to lose my job! I couldn't afford to keep all of you fed! Not once that bitch bore me another. The whelp wasn't even mine. I found out when the little whore began to come of age. By then we had moved here and I threw her and her mother out as well. I never asked for the gods to curse me with such shame." His bitterness was palpable. Trent felt disgust welling up inside. He clenched his fist to prevent himself from landing another blow.

"You have only ever brought the shame upon yourself. When mother was alive you never acted like such a fool! Did the gods steal your wits?"

"No, but they stole my wife from me. All of the light in my world was taken away when she died. No amount of whores or sons could fill that void. I hated you because you reminded me of her."

Trent saw fleeting glimpses of his mother again; her laugh, her warm smile. For a brief moment he considered if what his father claimed was true. Was his pain really as great as Trent's? He hadn't been like this before he lost his first wife. New guilt began to spring up from the wound he had inside.

"You aren't even worth my rage. I've wasted my time."

Feeling empty, Trent turned to leave, abandoning all thoughts of conversing with the other. Calm did not return to him, but his mind had begun to clear from the fog that had overtaken it. Behind him his father stumbled forward, still clutching at his arm as if the wounds had never been healed. In between curses he spat onto Trent's back.

"Do you really think that your white armor protects you from me, boy? You had no right to harm me like this! I know the rules that you bastards are sworn to live by. You've broken your code."

*He's right. I am a fool.*

Trent continued to make for the door, a cold sweat forming on his brow. His lapse in judgment might have just cost him his place among the ranks of the Paladins. When others of the order abused their power as he had, they were often banished or killed. The order was meant to protect the people of Illux, not rule over them with an iron fist. What would Ren say when she received word of his crimes? He would have to plead for reassignment to Seatown. It was his only chance of remaining in service to the Light.

"I knew you were a coward! Just as you hid behind Terric then you hide behind your rank now! Where is that mouthy little shit? I want him to face me as well."

*Oh gods, he doesn't even know.*

Trent stopped in place, considering whether or not it would be worth even telling his father the truth of what his misdeeds had wrought. Even though common sense screamed in his ear to keep his mouth shut he couldn't. He slowly turned and faced his father again.

"He is dead. Killed by one of the Demons that took the last Seraph from us."

His father stared blankly ahead for a moment, clearly taken aback by what he had heard. Trent thought briefly that what he had said had finally broken through the wall the man had placed up all of those years past. But then he seemed to regain his senses and return to his tirade.

"He was a fool. I knew that attitude of his would get him killed."

Trent tried to stand firm against the torrent of anger that again flooded his body, overwhelming his senses. He failed.

*Arra forgive me.*

He charged his father, slamming him into the table so hard that it shattered. Blow after blow landed on the man's face; blood vessels burst and bones cracked beneath the onslaught.

"Don't ever say his name again! You killed him, bastard! He is dead because of you!"

Trent could feel the tears welling up in his eyes as he spat out the words. On the ground underneath him his father cried and gurgled as well. But Trent knew that he would not kill him. No, he could not give this man the freedom that death would bring. He had raised another mailed hand into the air with the intent of breaking one of his father's arms when he found himself spinning through the air and crashing into the floor. His head cracked into the wall so hard that it left a small hole in the wood. Trent lay there for several minutes, the world spinning around him. Somewhere in the distance he could hear the sound of boots upon the hard floor. Trent's eyes weakly fluttered open, revealing Devin standing over his father. His friend quickly approached him, grabbing him by the neck and hoisting him up to eye level, locking his gaze with Trent's own.

"What in the High God's name have you done?" Devin asked, his normally jovial face a mask of distaste.

"My fath-" Trent began.

"I know who he is. How did you think you could get away with beating a man to death in his own home? What gave you the right? Ren would have had to execute you if you had killed him!"

"I had every right!" Trent's mind had finally begun to clear from his fall.

"This man deserves death or worse for what he did to you and your brother, on that we agree. But can't you see what this is? This isn't righteous, Trent. This is evil."

"How can you judge me? You have always told me to embrace my anger. To use it in battle against our enemies."

"Against Demons! Not against men! This isn't justice, this is madness!"

Trent tried to struggle against the other's grip like a caged animal, his emotions raging inside just as madly as his body. He knew that his friend was right, and yet every second his father drew a blood-choked breath upon the floor he could do nothing else but wish to silence him. He knew that what he had done was wrong, but he had been so fully consumed by his rage that nothing else mattered. Finally, Devin struck him across the face with an open palm. His struggling ceased and he looked his friend in the eye again.

"I will not lose you to this. He did not take your brother from you, a Demon did."

"He needs to suffer-"

"Listen to me!" Devin interrupted, covering Trent's mouth. "He has suffered. I am your brother now. I love you more than any man living. You have made him suffer enough. Now it's my turn."

Devin released his grip on Trent and stepped back, leaving the other Paladin to stare at him in confusion. The dark skinned warrior walked over to the bloody wreck on the floor and placed his hands upon him. Within moments a blue glow had transferred from Devin to Trent's father, healing his wounds and bringing him back from the brink of death. Devin pulled away as the man let out a loud exhalation and slowly tried to lift himself up. He never had the chance as the large Paladin pulled him to his feet and pushed him toward the door.

"What are you doing to me?" the older man rasped, trying to cover himself meekly as he realized that he wasn't fully clothed.

"Open your mouth again and I will cut out your tongue," Devin barked. "Trent, get your ass out here with me."

Still confused, Trent pulled himself together and followed his father and friend out of the shattered door and into the street beyond.

Outside, a crowd of onlookers and City Watch alike had gathered to see just what had brought two Paladins crashing into the home of a bitter old man. The looks of fear and shock that some had worn slowly faded when they saw that the man was himself not much more than bruised as he stumbled ahead of the two Paladins. Devin nodded to two members of the City Watch who were standing nearby. The man and woman approached and quickly tied Trent's father's hands behind his back with a length of cord, the remainder of which they passed to Devin.

"Everyone return to your homes!" Devin called out, parting the crowd as he walked forward. "This man is a criminal against the people of Illux, and he is being treated accordingly."

Some murmurs of dissent moved through the crowd, but it began to disperse as Devin prodded the old man on, with Trent following meekly behind, now feeling the full shame of his actions.

*I don't deserve this power that I wield.*

The old man tried to protest, but a few sharp shoves from his captor made him keep his thoughts to himself. Devin led them straight to a main road, avoiding as many clusters of people as he could. To Trent, the city almost seemed to be in a trance; everyone around him speaking in hushed whispers, watching to see what would happen next. They kept a steady pace, never once slowing so that the heavier man could stop to rest. Trent followed along wordlessly, barely hearing the shallow breaths of his father, himself in the same trance that the city seemed to share. They were heading for the outer wall just a few short miles away. Overhead the sun began to make its descent from its apex where it rested each day next to Aenna, the night now just some hours off.

*And the initiation. I have been such a fool.*

Finally, the dream ended. The great wall loomed above them, an immense structure made of the same polished stone as the cathedral. The ramshackle houses in this district pressed up against it hungrily, but never fully encroached on the wide walkway that circled the city just within the wall. Hundreds of feet it rose, its shadow engulfing the three men before they were within a stone's throw of its base. Cut into the middle where the cobblestone road met the wall was a set of gigantic golden doors, wide enough for ten men to come and go on horseback at the same time. Rarely were the gates left open, and since the assassination of the last Seraph they had remained closed at all times, only opening to permit Paladins to leave or to allow crops from the villages to enter. As they approached, Devin called out to the men in the gatehouse to open them and allow the three of them to exit. From here Trent could see the swirling patterns that covered the golden surface of the gates behind the iron portcullis as it was raised.

After a few moments the portcullis lifted and the great grinding gears began to turn, allowing the golden doors to swing inward. Trent looked at Devin questioningly, but the other did nothing but flash a knowing smile and continue to prod his charge until they were standing outside upon the road leading from Illux to Seatown. There he pulled a knife from his belt and cut the bonds holding the other man to him. In the distance the wind began to blow over the lush grasses in their direction. When he was done, Devin kicked Trent's father in his back, sending him sprawling to the ground where he lay whimpering, his lower body still naked. The great Paladin unclasped his axe from his back and pointed it him.

"Your crimes against the Light are numerous, but it is for the sin of abandoning your own sons to die on the streets that you are to be punished. Under my powers as a Paladin of the order, by the right bestowed upon me by the Gods of Light through the Lady Ren, I hereby banish you, Brandon of Illux, from the city of your forebears for all time. If you attempt re-entry, you will be killed on sight. Should you wish to repent you may find solace in one of the villages or in Seatown, but know this: if Trent or I see your face again, you will die."

In one final act of defiance the old man pulled himself to his knees and tried to spit at his captors, but the attempt simply ended with him face down in the dirt once again.

"Gods curse you!" He cried out, never lifting his head. "Curse the man who would do this to his father. I am a pious man! I deserve justice."

"Justice is what you have been given. The nights are cold and the food is scarce, just as it is on the streets to which you condemned your sons. This is what you shall reap."

After speaking again Devin motioned for Trent to follow and the two Paladins turned to reenter the city, the golden gates closing behind them. Once inside, Trent looked to his friend for some commentary on what had just transpired, but the other Paladin had already returned to his jovial self, a great grin upon his lips. They walked for a time down the main road leading back to the center of the city in silence with only the sounds of the slums to comfort them. The shadow of the wall continued to lengthen as their journey progressed, the spires of the cathedral looming in the far distance. Finally, Trent could take it no longer and broke the silence himself.

"Why did you do that?"

"Because he is a bastard who deserves death. If he can make it to one of the villages at his age without being killed, then the High God must have some greater plan for him; otherwise he is as good as dead. I could not allow for his blood to be upon your hands. That would have been the end of you."

"I wasn't going to kill him. I am better than that."

"You are, but who is to say what you would have done had I not arrived? Even so, we couldn't have let him stay in Illux and tell his side of things. Who knows what would have happened then?"

Although Devin laughed, Trent didn't find any humor in the situation. He allowed for the silence to return for some time before asking his next question.

"How did you find me in the first place? I don't understand how I could have been so fortunate." Trent muttered this last part, more to himself than to his companion.

"You got lucky on that one. Or I suspect that one of the gods was keeping close watch." Devin seemed to be surveying the houses that they walked past before he continued. "When you had been gone for so long I figured that you had gone to see Elise, so I decided to track you down and apologize. When I was halfway there I saw a commotion beginning as people began to gather the City Watch claiming that a Paladin had busted in a door for no good reason. I never suspected that it was you, but I felt that I needed to see just what was going on myself."

Devin was smiling in his self-assured way, clearly pleased with the act of heroics that he felt he had just performed. They continued to walk for a few more minutes; then Trent felt Devin's arm around his shoulders. The other Paladin didn't say anything, and he didn't have to. As hard as it was for him to admit to himself, Trent knew that he was now forever indebted to his old friend. Without Devin he would have lost himself to his past and committed a crime that he would never be able to live with. As it was, the guilt of how far he had gone would surely haunt him for the rest of his days.

Soon the silence was broken by the bells of the cathedral, signaling that the initiation was to begin shortly. The two Paladins quickened their pace and made for the white spires ahead.

# CHAPTER 5

The ringing of the bells continued as the white spires drew closer overhead, the setting sun bathing them in a luminescent glow. Direct entry to the Fourth Spire would most likely be blocked for the ceremony, so the Paladins headed for the great oak doors that were between the spires. These great openings led to the central chapel, which was dedicated wholly to the worship of the High God. Throngs of people began to congregate in that direction, mostly members of the elite from the inner city. Few from the slums ever found themselves at an initiation due to matters of distance. Trent had never seen one himself until he had experienced it firsthand.

Some of his uneasiness had abated, but deep down the wound was still there. He would not soon find comfort from the realization of what he had done some hours before. Would he have truly killed his father had Devin not intervened? As much as he wished that he could deny it, Trent knew that it was possible. This hadn't been the first time that his emotions had gotten the better of him, nor would it be the last. More than once he had questioned whether or not the

Balance Monks of the Grey Temple would have been a better fit for him.

*I wouldn't get my revenge there. But I would be at peace.*

His mind wandered again to his father, now alone in the wilderness beyond the walls of the city. What would become of him now? Most likely he would make for one of the villages, possibly to live out the end of his bitter life there. Trent felt more guilt rise inside of himself. He knew that to be little more than a fantasy. His father was a doomed man now, more likely to die of starvation or exposure to the elements than to ever speak with another living soul again. There was a time when this would have brought him the greatest joy; now it just left him hollowed out and empty. The man deserved justice, but did he deserve the death sentence that the two Paladins had been so quick to thrust upon him? That his own son was so quick to thrust upon him? And what if he faced a fate worse than death? Chills raced down Trent's spine as he thought of Demons conscripting his father into the living death of an Accursed.

Perhaps they had made a mistake?

Now Trent would look at the face of each Accursed and wonder. It would be the same now as it had been with every Demon Trent had come across, always wondering if they were the one who had killed Terric and ruined his life. Each bore a helm that was slightly different; Terric's killer's helm was forever burned into his memory. He had yet to see its like again, but deep down he always wondered if he was misremembering, if he had truly faced that monster again already. And if he had, was it now dead? This thought brought him no comfort, but instead the same hollowness he felt over the fate of his father. His entire adult life had been spent chasing ghosts through his memories, shadows and vultures in his dreams. Even when he finally did bring justice to those who had wronged him, it brought him no peace, only more pain.

*Where is the gods' work in that?*

The crowds began to gather close, funneling toward the open doors that led into the stone edifice before them. General excitement rumbled through the Paladins and normal men and women alike as they made their way to the giant steps of the Cathedral. Children upon shoulders pointed and called out, men laughed and women sang. All across the crowds, prayers to the gods were upon every tongue, thanking them for the safety that their blessings brought. Trent looked above at the now darkening sky to see Aenna above, looking down on him with its watchful gaze. He wondered if the gods looked through the opening onto the Mortal Plane still as they once did, or if they had finally forsaken their subjects as the High God had. It would be their power that fueled the initiation, but was it truly their will?

Finally, the two Paladins bounded up the steps into the entrance of the Cathedral amidst the crowds of people wishing to see the power of the gods on display. The stone steps were wide and flat; a gradual ascent to the landing above where the people made their way inside. Standing at the top, beside the great oak doors, were two Paladins, ever on watch for any intrusion of the enemy. The last time the Grand Cathedral had been stormed its guards had been killed to the last man, each dying in turn to protect the most holy site in all of creation. Trent prayed that he would never live to see that happen again. If one looked hard enough and in the right spots, the white stone of the building still held some scars from the fires that followed the fighting.

Once inside the great archway, the cathedral opened up around them into a giant singular chamber that rose higher than the eye could see. In the upper reaches the lights of the candles on the lower levels didn't quite illuminate the darkness, instead being replaced by hundreds of small windows that let in the daylight. The ringing of the great bells was magnified here, they themselves being located just out of sight in the upper shadows of the center spire. Pews of lacquered wood filled the massive chamber, circling about the central altar. Beautifully woven rugs lined the pathways between the wooden benches, each leading from the giant slab of white stone to the outer doors. It was from here that priests of the faith spoke in great sermons every day, decrying the evils of mankind and begging for the High

God to return to his creation. As they walked past, Trent could see the forms of men and women, clothed in white, coming and going from the small side rooms that encircled the Cathedral. The clergy were always on duty, answering only to the Seraph herself on matters of faith.

Above where they walked were windows of stained glass, each depicting a scene of creation. The glowing figure of the High God brought order to the chaos of existence, and created a paradise. One showed him raising the mountains to the north known as the Rim. Another showed the great sea being filled with the tears of the High God when his creations began to struggle against one another violently. The largest and most favored of the images depicted the High God creating the lesser Gods of Light to serve his will. At the four corners of the room were the entrances to the lesser spires, each of these having its own stained glass image depicting the patron god whose primary worship occurred within.

It was toward the northernmost of these entrances that the crowd made its way: the Fourth Spire. The image above this entrance still bore the likeness of Lio, the Fallen One. The fallen god stood in polished white armor that complimented his golden skin. In his hand was clasped a large sword with the point facing downward at the entrance to the Fourth Spire. Before he was cast down, this spire was home to the worship of the fourth God of Light. Once his crimes were punished, however, all worship of him ceased, and the Paladin order took up command within his temple. As he passed under the image, Trent couldn't help but realize just how similar the fallen god looked to a Paladin. His stomach churned as the images of his father's shattered face flashed before his mind. Just as Lio had lashed out in anger and struck down Xyxax in a blind fury, damning himself for all time, so too had Trent nearly done to his own father. The difference, he supposed, was that Trent had the love of a friend who would never abandon him, something even the gods did not have. Still, the thoughts brought him little comfort, and only served to remind him of how far someone with his power could fall.

The dimly lit passage that they were ushered through was choked with wisps of smoke from the multitude of candles burning in the rooms beyond. The murmur of excitement began to rise to a fever pitch as the crowds pressed their way into the central chamber of the Fourth Spire, a much smaller chapel facing the northern wall of the city. Unlike the main Cathedral chamber, this room was not altogether circular, with the altar standing on the wall between the door from which they entered and the greater set of doors leading to the practice fields beyond. The rows of pews were packed tighter here, with a large opening in the front where orderly rows of recruits kneeled with bowed heads. Trent and Devin split off from the people filing into the pews to join the rest of the Paladins lining the back wall behind the small altar. When the pews were filled, the rest who had gained entry stood at the back in front of the great wooden doors leading outside.

The walls of the chapel were lined with openings leading to passages and stairwells that continued to the upper levels where the Paladin leadership conferred about how to govern the city and win the war. Above these floors, nearer to the pinnacle of the spire, were the chambers of the Seraph, accessible both by air and staircases from the floors below. To accommodate these extra rooms and floors the ceiling of this chapel was only slightly higher than a normal room, eschewing the vaulted ceilings of the other three for added space above.

Standing behind the altar was the Lady Ren in all of her glory; silently looking over the men and women who would soon be joining the ranks of her command. Just behind her was Castille and his retinue of cronies, the governing elite of the Paladin Order. Castille's grim countenance was relatively unchanged from how he had seemed earlier in the day, although he might have been a shade redder. No doubt he found the Seraph's choice to induct all of the recruits enraging.

Trent looked over the faces of those gathered on their knees upon the stone floor. All of the recruits that he had fought and trained with over the previous months were in attendance. He recognized several from that morning, seeing the three who had attacked him together kneeling side by side, still united in purpose. The first smile Trent had made since seeing his father earlier that day passed his lips. They were not unlike how he had been when he was still just a recruit, inseparable from his friends. As he continued to scan the faces below he realized that there was one missing.

*No Edmund.*

The veteran watchman was nowhere to be seen. Perhaps Trent's advice on where the man was truly needed had struck a chord with him. After the events of today he was even more sure that the city needed more men like Edmund, and fewer men like himself. Hopefully, some good would come out of the recruit staying in the Watch and not joining the ranks of the Paladins. The people of Illux needed small heroes just the same as they needed large ones.

The dull murmur of the crowd quickly died off when the chamber was finally filled to bursting and the door shut to prevent anyone else from entering. Just as the silence was absolute, Devin leaned in to whisper in Trent's ear.

"I bet some of them are pissing their pants right about now. What a glorious moment this was."

"Yes it was."

Trent remembered his own initiation perfectly, as if it had happened to him just days before. The floor upon which they had knelt, the same as the recruits knelt upon now, was made of the hardest stone. By the end of the proceedings his legs had been numb from the discomfort. The air had smelled of more than just smoke, the tightly packed bodies giving off their own pungent odor. The fear and excitement about what was to come had sent shivers down his back, his ceremonial white silk feeling inadequate to cover him. Devin and Gil had been kneeling beside him then, the only time in their lives that Devin had seemed at all afraid. The Seraph had stood in front of them and spoken the words, every one of which Trent could recite by memory even though he had been lost in her brilliance at the time.

Ren had barely known he had existed then; he'd been just another recruit who had shown more potential than others.

Then had come the pain.

And then the power.

Ren finally broke the silence, her voice filling the chamber with an otherworldly magnitude. It was at times like these that none could doubt that she spoke for the gods, or that they spoke through her.

"Gathered faithful, I thank you all for coming to witness the strength and power of your gods. As you know, today we welcome more men and women into the ranks of their most trusted and holy soldiers. Today the Light gains more champions!" With each exclamation a renewed cheer rose from the crowd. "Today we take one more step against the encroaching darkness! Today the gods give us their strength! Today we are reminded of those we have lost and the sacrifices that we have made. Today we gain more Paladins!

"But first, let us give our thanks to the High God for the blessing of life with which he has gifted us. Let us give thanks to the Gods of Light for leading us against the Darkness at our door."

The cheering subsided and heads began to bow in reverence.

"As with each initiation from the first until the last we begin by remembering why we are here. In the beginning the High God created all things out of chaos."

"He created our world and bathed it in warm light, making it a paradise," Trent murmured, his voice joining that of the multitude.

"Connected to this realm was the Divine Plane, the home that he made for himself to watch his creation from. It was then that he filled our world with life." Ren paused here, looking at those gathered in the room. "I see this same life gathered here now. But this paradise was unlike our own. This world existed with no pain or suffering, but also without courage or justice."

"A perfect world cannot truly be perfect if there is no choice to be righteous," they answered.

"Seeing that this was so, the High God created choice for the world, choice for mankind to do good or ill and thereby earn his place in paradise," Ren continued. "To allow for this to come to pass he created the other gods."

"To appeal to our lesser nature, our greed, lust, and violence he created the Gods of Darkness, because we are not worthy."

"And yet to enable us to be just, courageous, moral and righteous, to give us an ideal to strive for, he created the Gods of Light. As you know, it was not long before war broke out between those who served the Light and those who served the Darkness, war which has lasted until this day.

"In the beginning of the war, the Gods of Light created the Seraphs to serve as their voice and stewards on the Mortal Plane. And they also created the Paladins to serve as the vanguard against the forces of evil. So it is today that we add to that vanguard and strengthen our position against our enemies."

Ren paused and motioned for those kneeling to stand. Slowly they did so, attempting to refrain from showing signs of the fatigue that their legs undoubtedly felt. The hushed silence still hung over the room in anticipation of what would come next. Those in the crowd held their breaths for fear of disturbing the ceremony. Without warning, Ren spread her wings wide and continued speaking, her voice taking on a fuller and more commanding tone than it had before with the crowd echoing her words.

"Arra, Goddess of Light, give us your blessing. Samson, God of Light, give us your blessing. Luna, Goddess of Light, give us your blessing. Arra, give these recruits the wisdom to heal. Samson, give these recruits the strength to fight. Luna, give these recruits the honor to serve. Gods, bathe these recruits in your light!"

With those final words, Ren drew forth Nightbreaker and aimed the blade squarely at the recruits. The room was suddenly filled with blinding white light that had no discernible source. Crackling blue energy lanced down the blade of Nightbreaker before surging into the bodies of all of the recruits. The men and women began screaming in agony as their bodies smoked. The crunching of bone was the only sound that could be heard over their screams as their bodies twisted and contorted, becoming visibly larger in the process. Clothing tore and fell to ground as new muscles rippled forth from their previously weak flesh. Trent noticed that some in the pews hid their faces in fear of the grotesque sight. Trent never once looked away, the sight reminding him of the experience of his own initiation those years before. At his side Devin laughed as always, exhilarated by the energy in the room.

Then it was over.

Just as suddenly as it began the light faded and the recruits fell naked to floor as Ren closed her wings. They lay there shivering and smoking for several long moments, no sounds escaping any of them. The new silence that filled the room was deafening compared to the sounds that had been present moments before. Trent felt that his own breathing was the loudest sound in the room, everyone else silent in awe at what they had just witnessed.

"Rise Paladins," Ren said, sheathing Nightbreaker.

Cautiously each newly made Paladin stood; all of them were now naked giants that looked as if they were carved from stone. Trent noticed that many looked at themselves in the same dumbstruck confusion that he had, unbelieving that they were still within their own bodies. The gods had granted them a great gift. Each now had a strength and endurance that surpassed any mortal man, and with it too, elongated life. They would not age in the fashion that normal men did, retaining their strength far into their years. They also would now possess some powers of magic: power to heal, to protect, and even to kill. The magic of the Paladins drew upon their own energy to sustain it, but the source came from the gods above. Only Divine Blood could actually create magic on its own, which meant that Ren was the only servant of the Light on the Mortal Plane with access to this force without the aid of the gods. When the reserves of energy failed them the Paladins would die from magic use, their bodies unable to stand the strain of channeling such immense power. Trent supposed that the same was true of Seraphs, themselves immortal but only half-god.

"Do you all swear to obey the Light, to champion its cause, and to serve its gods?"

"We do," they intoned in unison.

"Will you defend the righteous, and strike down the wicked wherever they are found?"

*Father.*

"We will."

"May your service be rewarded, and your sacrifice mourned. May the High God return to his creation and bring glory upon you. You are now Paladins all. Rejoice!"

Cheering went up from the veteran Paladins along the wall as well as the audience seated in the pews. The doors were thrown open and members of the clergy entered the room carrying armfuls of new armor. While the new Paladins stood at attention they were clothed in silk and covered in white armor, some trimmed in gold, others in blue. Ren and her most trusted Paladins stepped forth and clasped colorful cloaks around their necks. Trent and Devin were each entrusted with this duty, along with Castille and some others. Trent smiled at the woman whose cloak he bore; she returned his smile with a curt nod and took the honor with dignity. By then the ceremony was ended and the Gods of Light had gained many new champions.

The new Paladins were warmly greeted by their veteran fellows with handshakes and hugs while the audience in the pews and at the back of the chapel filed out into the night. Trent and Devin shouldered their way through the rejoicing recruits to find Ren warmly welcoming her new charges into the order. When she saw them the Seraph broke away and took her favored champions aside to speak.

"They will do well. This ceremony should occur more often, not less."

"Yes," Trent replied, his mind briefly fluttering back to his father. "We have prepared our supplies. On your command we leave for the wilderness."

Ren looked sideways at Trent for a moment, casting him a questioning glance. He was sure that she knew something tore at his heart, but she decided against questioning him here. Instead, she simply nodded.

"Go forth, my champions, and return to me safely. If you find anything of note, make haste back to the city. I hope that I am wrong, but I fear that there is something happening out there that we are unaware of. May the gods watch over you."

"My lady." Both men bowed low and turned from Ren, making their way through the outer doors into the night.

They headed back toward the barracks in silence. Overhead, the moon now sat next to Aenna, both glowing softly up in the silky blackness. The stars tonight shone fainter than usual, a slight sheen of cloud obscuring their light. The city had begun its nightly ritual, the sounds of activity emanating only from the celebrations in the Cathedral. As they walked along, Devin finally turned to his friend and spoke.

"I cannot promise you that we will return as we always do so that you can look on that pretty face again. But should something befall us, know that you will never die alone."

"Nor will you. We are brothers now, until the end."

"Now let's go hunt some Demons."

Once the two Paladins reached the barracks they gathered their supplies and horses and made for the outer wall of the city. Within the hour they were on the southern road, beginning their long trek into the wilderness.

# CHAPTER 6

"Life is balance."

*The struggle between creation and destruction. Life and Death. The war between the Gods of Light and the Gods of Darkness is a necessary part of this balance.*

So mused the solitary Balance Monk who sat cross-legged on the cold stone floor. Teo often sat like this, deep in meditation long after his peers had journeyed outside to greet the day. He couldn't allow himself to break concentration before he was ready, and the peace that he felt while alone in the empty room was far greater than any he would experience outside. The monk was clothed in simple grey robes that only just hid the swirling tattoos of similarly hued ink that covered his body from neck to ankle. With his eyes closed and his mind detached from his surroundings it seemed as if he were floating, with reality nothing more than a distant memory.

The order of the Balance Monks lived a simple existence in their temple high in the mountains. The beginning of each day was spent in group meditation, the monks collectively drawing on the power of their god to keep them at peace. When the others had all gathered themselves and left to begin the day, training and reading and praying,

Teo had chosen instead to remain and continue to focus his mind. On some days he was joined by others who needed more time to meditate, but often he sat alone for another few hours, kept company only by the reassuring presence of his god, who was always just a thought away.

Those who sought more to life than the endless struggle between Light and Darkness found their way to the temple and dedicated their lives to the service of the Grey God. It was Ravim, the Grey One, who maintained the balance between the warring pantheons of Light and Darkness, and it was the Balance Monks who enforced his will upon the Mortal Plane. Those who served him came from all backgrounds and experiences, some good and some evil. Teo had been such a man once, a lost soul who had no purpose or reason to live beyond habit.

*A murderer.*

He reflected on his previous life, as he often did when meditating, playing out the choices he had made again and again, in the hopes that some further insight would bring him greater peace. Teo's past life had been built on pain and suffering, both committed by him and against him. Growing up in one of the outer villages around Illux had spared him from the rough life of the city slums, but not by much. Life was spent tilling the fields and making just enough to survive off of before seeing all of it shipped off to feed those who still lived in the city. Living in the villages also meant constant fear from attack by Demons and Accursed. Everything about his wretched existence had felt constricting, which was why he had left home when he was barely old enough to be called a man and became an outlaw.

He'd joined a group of bandits that pillaged the countryside, always evading the pursuing Paladins sent out by the city or the villages. Mostly they had lived in the wilderness, sleeping under the stars or under the watchful gaze of some tree. His life then had felt so liberating, so free that he no longer cared about what harm he caused to others. He had stolen. He had raped. He had killed. The Gods of Darkness had grasped firmly onto his heart, leading him down a path to ruin.

Finally, he and his companions sought the forces of evil out directly, hoping to gain even more freedom and power than they already possessed. They had hoped that they might be turned into Demons. The reality was something far less appealing. Teo fled from these horrors until he could run no further, his bloodied feet finally giving out as he reached the base of the mountains. It wasn't long after this that he stumbled across the Grey Temple.

*All men may change. Even our Grey God was a servant of darkness once. You too may find peace in the balance of things. The same peace that he himself has found.*

This is what he had been told at the temple gates that day, and the words had never once left his mind. It had been another life that he had lived, a life that had ended when a weary bandit collapsed before a stone building hiding deep in the forests of the Rim of Paradise. Teo was a new man now, a man who had been born the next day when he began his induction into the Balance Monks. After he was taken in, his black curls were shaved to the skin, his head never bearing hair again. Over the following few months his body had slowly become covered in the swirling grey tattoos that marked him as a servant of balance. He had been taught not just how to find peace, but how to live. The transition from a life of violence to a life of tranquility and meditation had come far easier than Teo would have believed possible. It was as if something had been missing from his life, and the Grey God had given him the means of finding it.

"Light cannot exist without darkness, nor darkness without light," he said aloud.

*The scales must never be tipped in one direction or the other, or both will be destroyed.*

Learning to meditate had not been the only skill that his time with the monks had taught him. All of the monks were also expected to read and write, for they were charged by the Grey God with the preservation of a detailed history of the Mortal Plane. They also grew their own food on the mountainside below the temple, an activity that took much of their time. Tilling the fields was in its own way a form of meditation that the monks did not take for granted. Although the men and women of the Grey Temple lived a life of peace, they were sometimes called upon by Ravim to restore balance to the world.

This required the skills of battle.

Combat training was seen as one of the most important ways for a monk to spend his time, honing his mind and body to be the perfect weapon to carry out the will of the Grey God. Whenever the forces of Light or the forces of Darkness gained the upper hand in their struggle for dominance, the Balance Monks would enter the war and turn the tide. So they had done, time and time again, for the last thousand years.

Teo knew that it was time for him to join his brothers and sisters in combat training this day, finally relinquishing that extra moment of peace that he had allowed himself. The solitary monk always spent extra time in meditation to cleanse himself of his dark past before beginning a day of work. Today he felt more at peace than he had in quite some time.

*Surely the Grey God takes notice of me this day.*

Teo's eyes snapped open and he surveyed the empty room around himself. The room was sparse, empty of all but the torches used to light it. The same grey stone that made up the entirety of the temple was here as well, a solid material that brought no comfort after hours of sitting upon it. This room was one of many such areas where the monks could focus their minds without the distractions of the rest of the temple. Teo slowly stood and walked out of the single doorway, an arch with no physical door present. His near-silent footfalls were the only sounds that echoed from the bare walls as he made his way from the chamber.

The hallways of the temple were completely silent; not a single monk seemed to remain inside. Teo continued along, noting that the sun shone brightly through the small windows cut into the walls of the structure. His path outside was a short one, the branching halls leading to the library or the cells in which the monks slept all connecting to the front entrance in a direct fashion. Soon he found himself in the central chamber of the Temple, a large room with a vaulted ceiling in which the giant iron doors to the mountainside were located. It was within this room that the main shrine to the Grey God stood. Teo made sure to show the holy site the proper reverence as he passed by into the daylight.

He walked along the outside of the temple for a time, enjoying the gardened paths that led around the building. From the outside the Grey Temple was an imposing structure, a monolithic creation of godly proportions. It was wide and flat, disdaining the height favored by the buildings of Illux for a wider spread upon the mountainside. The forest had been cleared for half a mile in every direction, allowing for the flat temple to dominate the landscape. The walls of the Grey Temple were covered in small windows to allow for the natural light to flood each of the rooms within. Connecting from the walls to the earth were hundreds of arches that made the structure look more akin to a giant insect than a place of worship.

The Balance Monk made his way toward the meadow on the side of the clearing where his brothers and sisters would surely be practicing by now. Those who were not would be writing in the library or just down the mountainside working in the small fields that they shared. Teo's lot for this week had been the afternoon shift in the field, after he had trained and read for the day. Their duties in the field wouldn't become more involved until it was time to harvest this batch of crops.

As he got closer to the meadow he could hear the muffled grunts of exertion and the quiet pops of human hands and solid wood landing blows upon exposed flesh. They were heavily trained in the use of both hand-to-hand combat and staves, with those who had mastered both styles able to choose a preference. Teo had chosen the staff because he favored the added reach that it gave him, not quite admitting to himself that he still felt uncomfortable without a weapon in his hand. It had been over thirteen years since he had last held a blade, but the wood of the staff felt natural in his grip.

The temple was now some distance behind him by the time Teo

reached the meadow, the wild grasses and flowers giving way to a neatly trimmed arena where the monks were gracefully practicing combat. To the uninitiated it would have appeared more as a dance than a battle, but Teo knew that each fought with a controlled power that could bring an army to its knees. The unnatural calm and focus that the Balance Monks exerted during combat came not only from years of training and discipline, but from a spiritual connection to the Grey God himself. The ascetic deity sat on the Divine Plane in constant meditation about the balance of the world. While doing so, he connected with his disciples in order to communicate his wishes and to share a portion of his power. While the servants of the other lesser gods were gifted with strength and magic, the Balance Monks were given speed and clarity.

Teo entered the field and took up his place alongside his fellows, preparing his mind and body for the rigors that would follow. A slight breeze wafted up to his nose, bringing with it the scent of the forest below. Once they noticed his presence, two younger monks turned to allow him to engage them in combat. Teo studied them both for a moment as they presented him with a staff. They were a man and woman, both of whom had been shaved in the manner of their faith. The woman bore the tattoos of a full-fledged monk while the man still had the clean skin of an initiate. Teo recognized the female from around the temple, but the other was clearly new. Her face had soft features but a fierce determination lurked behind her hazel eyes.

After taking his staff, he placed himself into a defensive stance and waited. He traced the swirling grey lines upon the woman's body, a pattern unique to her alone, applied over months of training by the other members of the temple. Both she and her companion remained weaponless, each taking a similar stance as the other.

*She must be training this one. Now it is my turn to contribute.*

The young man struck first.

His eyes flitted to the right momentarily before he lunged that direction. Teo snapped his staff into the air, halting his attacker's advance and sending him spiraling to the ground in a heap. The woman was far more cautious. She lunged to the left in a feint, sending her body right at the last moment to avoid the swing of Teo's staff. Catching the wooden pole between her arms she deftly twisted it, almost removing it from Teo's hands. Once she saw that he wouldn't let go that easily she spun away from the staff, landing two powerful blows on Teo's midsection before spinning back out of his reach. By this point the man had pulled himself back up to his feet and returned to the woman's side. He would not make the same mistake again.

Teo took a deep breath, quieting his body for a brief second before taking the attack to them. He sprinted forward, planting the end of his staff into the ground in such a way that he was able to vault past them in one smooth motion. The other two monks turned to face him as he was landing, but not before he struck them both with his staff, now removed from the earth. The man was again knocked off his feet, but the woman was able to roll with the strike, preventing herself from receiving the brunt of the attack. She turned toward Teo and outstretched her hands. Instinctively, the older monk tossed her his staff and put himself in the proper stance for hand-to-hand.

To prepare herself for the use of the new weapon the female monk twirled it around her body, feeding it over one shoulder and under another. Her eyes stayed locked with his, almost as if she were studying his mind more than his body. They stayed like this for several long moments before she charged forward, clearly ready to begin.

*She is a master with her body, but what about the staff?*

Teo found his question quickly answered when the younger monk met him head-on with a flurry of strikes, each only meant to probe his defenses. He lithely deflected each blow with the sides of his hands, the effort causing him minimal discomfort. Finally, she relented in her assault and took a step backward. Then Teo pushed forward, punching and kicking at her from all directions, spinning and dodging each thrust from her weapon intending to knock him backward. She still continued to evade his attacks just as well as he had evaded her own.

*So we are evenly matched. Life is balance.*

The female monk found a hole in Teo's defense and lunged forward, sending the wooden staff directly into his chest. Teo was able to catch the weapon with both of his hands at the last possible moment, small slivers of wood working their way into his palms. Gripping tightly, he exerted all of the strength that he could call upon from the Grey God and lifted the staff high above his head. Sensing his plan, the other monk gripped on just as tightly and jumped while Teo lifted, sending her over his body as well. When she reached the apex of his swing Teo could feel her shift her weight downward and bring the staff to the ground behind him, still firmly within her own grasp, but no longer in his. He spun around to defend himself, but was a moment too slow. The wooden staff struck him directly in the temple, knocking the light from his vision.

Dazed, Teo remained on the soft ground for several minutes, not opening his eyes. A small trickle of warm blood ran down his face from the site of the blow. It had been a long time since he had been bested by one of his companions. The pain reminded him that he was not immortal, and that even the experienced would find themselves defeated in time. It was the nature of things for the young to defeat the old, for even experience had its limits. He listened to the sounds of the others fighting around him, muffled by the sounds of the breeze drifting over the grass of the field. When Teo opened his eyes he stared at the bright sky, allowing them to adjust before he would look around again. Overhead, Aenna glowed softly beside the sun, the great white disc unmoved as always. The sight brought him comfort, for it was through this hole in the heavens that his great god looked down upon him.

Finally, Teo sat upright and surveyed the meadow around him as he wiped the blood from his face. The two monks whom he had fought just minutes ago had already resumed their training as if he had never interfered. The young man would be expected to continue to train for some time to make up for the lack of skill that had caused his defeat. Teo's defeat, on the other hand, was not at all due to his lack of training but to the superior skills of his opponent. The answer to this was to return to meditation.

Teo allowed the sounds of the world around him to fade away as he again closed his eyes, this time focusing on the sounds of the two combatants closest to him. Even with his eyes closed he could visualize each blow that was landed on one or the other. Within a few moments he could even tell who was who, just by the sounds that they made: their breaths, their footfalls, each parry and strike. These were sounds that would have been imperceptible if he had been watching with his eyes. Just as it had been before the woman maintained the upper hand, her flurry of strikes disarming and then disabling her opponent every few cycles of the mock battle. Teo began to picture himself fighting her now, in place of the other monk. His mind slowly quieted again, removing now even the sounds of the surrounding practice and replacing them with a concentrated silence.

In his mind the female monk swirled and flourished around him, her speed and lithe movements almost too fast to follow with the waking eye, but not too fast for the well trained-mind. He replayed her movements again and again, slowing them down and then ramping them up, looking for any sign of weakness. He lost track of time, studying the female warrior in his mind for what could have been hours. Each spin and lunge that she had used repeated itself over and over until it became so well known to him that he could have predicted every movement.

His eyes snapped open.

The female monk still battled the other, his own defeat beginning to manifest as slight bruising around his body, taking the place of the tattoos he had not yet earned. Slowly, Teo rose from the grassy earth and approached the two younger monks, staff again in hand. As he neared they each acknowledged him with a curt bow. It was the male who spoke first.

"Even after defeat you return, Master Teo?"

"Have you not continued fighting yourself?" Teo replied in his baritone voice, the first time anyone else had heard it that day.

"I am training to get better, I must continue to learn more. Mistress Rella is teaching me how to fight more effectively. But you lost a contest of equals."

"Life is balance," Rella interjected. "Even victory is balanced by defeat. Master Teo lost to his opponent and now he has come to right the scales."

Teo dropped his robe from his upper body, revealing more of the tapestry of tattoos beneath. The swirling lines spoke to him when he traced their mark, reminding him of the path that his life had taken, from darkness to peace. Even though he was middle-aged, his ascetic lifestyle and rigorous training had made his body a lean mass of hardened muscles, pulled tight like the string on a bow. He lowered himself into an attack stance, his staff held before him, not like a weapon but like an extension of his arm. The other monk, whom he now knew as Rella, stepped away from her pupil and began to circle Teo, her own arms outstretched and ready for attack. She continued to circle him for minutes, never changing her expression from the mask of calm that it had worn all morning. Teo studied her still, never letting his guard down even though he knew her movements now as well as he knew his own.

Finally, she advanced.

Rella charged forward, striking away with her fists at Teo's body, each blow being parried by his staff, each of her movements known to him before she even made it. The Grey God had taught them focus just as he had taught them to study their enemies before bringing an attack to fruition. Now that he had studied her, Teo knew that he could not lose. Rella moved in close now, within the extended reach of his staff where it could do him no good. He relied upon his own body now to duck and dodge her attack, blocking her strikes with his upper arms. He jumped backward, swiping the ground beneath her feet with his weapon. Rella leapt over the staff and returned to her assault, bringing herself closer and closer to him again, trying to keep the older monk from bringing his weapon to bear.

Teo remained calm, following her motions more with his mind than his eyes. When she had again brought herself inside the reach of his staff he threw the wooden object high into the air, matching all of her blows with his own fists; each monk moved in a flurry of motion that no normal human could ever hope to match. Overhead, the staff reached the height of Teo's throw and began to return earthward, the female monk barely taking notice. Finally, Teo saw what he had been waiting for: a small lapse in her defenses that she had repeated from the previous battle. He quickly took advantage of the momentary gap and slammed the palm of his hand into her chest. Rella stumbled backward just as Teo's staff returned to his hands.

Two quick jabs knocked the female monk to the ground in a heap. Teo found himself standing over her with his staff pointed downward at her face; still a mask of serenity. Rella nodded in acceptance of her defeat and the older monk extended a hand to pull her up. The other young monk stared at the pair in dumbstruck silence, finally sitting cross-legged on the ground and closing his eyes to meditate on what he had witnessed.

"What is your secret, Master Teo?" she asked as they began to walk back toward the temple, leaving the practice meadow and the other young monk behind.

"The Grey God gave my life purpose when he took me in to study his ways, Mistress Rella. There is nothing a man with a purpose cannot do."

"Wise words. How long have you been in the god's service?"

"It has been at least thirteen years now." His reply became more thoughtful as his mind slowly drifted back to his earlier life. "I was once a lost soul, not unlike our god before his ascension. Our ways have saved me. How about yourself, when did you join the temple? I have seen you many times although we have never spoken."

They walked through the serene gardens that covered much of the landscape behind the grey structure. Small rock-covered pathways wound this way and that, surrounded by well-maintained trees and wild flowers. It was a place of beauty, maintained to keep the monks connected to the natural world whose balance they sought to preserve. The clearing that the Grey Temple was built upon looked as if a side of the mountain had been scooped out by the Grey God himself. The meadow where the practice yards were located sat off to one side near the border of the forest, where the wildness of the mountain still held sway.

"It has been seven summers now. My husband and I were farmers. He was killed by bandits one day while working in the fields. At first, all I wanted was revenge, so I considered joining with the Paladins in Illux, thinking that somehow that would give me the strength I needed to bring his killers to justice. Soon the very thought consumed me. Once I recognized that I came here instead, to find peace."

There was a time when her story would have filled Teo with an all too familiar guilt over his own actions during his previous life. Although he had not brought any harm to this woman himself he had done the same to many others like her. But that was long ago, and now he had the strength of his god to fall back upon.

"Have you found it?" he asked, his voice neutral.

"I have found a balance between my emotions. Now I rule my passions instead of letting them rule me. I find this to be more important than simply finding peace."

*It is.*

Teo smiled at Rella before finding a suitable place to sit upon the ground and meditate before taking his turn in the fields below. Before traveling down the mountain path he would again quiet his thoughts and reach out to touch the mind of his god. He could sense that Rella had sat beside him, most likely closing her eyes as well. When Teo finally felt the gardens fall away he reached out and touched the familiar presence of his god in the Divine Plane above. Slowly the magnificent being reached out and touched his consciousness back.

# CHAPTER 7

They had been riding for hours now, without stopping to rest once, sunrise having come and gone some hours before. The two hardy Paladins could easily handle this pace, but the same could not be said for their mounts, who struggled under their immense weight over such a long distance. The two large animals were a mottled brown color with hair growing near their hooves. They didn't move with the speed of a smaller horse, but they could shoulder the weight of a Paladin over a longer distance. They were nearing the outermost of the farming villages now, and their ride would soon be over. Trent spent the quiet moments of the ride contemplating the nature of the landscape around them to better keep his mind from straying back to the events of the preceding few days.

The lands around the City of Light had once been a paradise, but ever since the beginning of the war they had slowly become more untamed and dangerous for mankind. Now the paradise had collectively become known simply as the Wilderness. Pockets of this wilderness still called back to that earlier age when creation was new, teeming with life of all kinds. Most of it, however, had become fouled by the presence of evil, and the land wept for what it had once been.

Much of the wild was unexplored by the forces of Light due to the roving bands of Accursed and Demons that prowled the countryside.

The north was of no concern to the Paladins because it was hemmed in by the mountains known as the Rim of Paradise, an older name from an older time. It was here that the servants of Ravim made their home in the Grey Temple, spending their days meditating rather than intervening below. Even so, the Rim was considered dangerous, for here the corruption of the south had not yet crept into the world, and old things still crawled along the ground or clawed their way below the mountains. It was said that the Balance Monks would keep the forces of Darkness from crossing their borders and the Rim would keep out the forces of Light.

Similarly, to the east was a vast body of water that had no known end. Any ships that had sailed across its often tumultuous surface had never returned to tell of what lay beyond the horizon. The great sea was teeming with fish, however, and for this reason the city of Seatown had sprung up on its shores to better feed the people of Illux. Other villages populated the distance between Seatown and Illux just as they had between Illux and the Rim. These villages to the east and north fared far better than those to the south or west when it came to Demon activity, although for this same reason they were more often the targets of bandits.

The west had an unofficial border in the Great Chasm, the giant crater that marked the site of where Xyxax was crushed into the earth by the Fallen One. It was a wicked place that gave off a foul aura that even Demons shunned. It was whispered that even the High God himself dared not walk there, for Xyxax still clung to life, deep in the bowels of the earth. Trent figured that if that were true then Ravim would have never been made the Grey God to maintain the balance of the world, nor Lio cast down in penance. Still, the rumors persisted and the place was avoided by all but the foolish.

That left the south as the direction with the most enemy activity, which is why Trent and Devin had chosen it as the way that they must head to begin their search. Several villages populated the southern expanse; each tilling the land in order to bring crops to Illux before the winter set in and food became short. Trent knew that without the sacrifice of the farmers and the other people in the villages, Illux would never be able to stand on its own. It would be the last of these where the two Paladins would hitch their horses and begin the remainder of their journey on foot.

Even this far south the landscape was still just as lush and vibrant as it was closer to Illux. They were riding along a large dirt road that cut a swath across miles and miles of grassy fields. Small rabbits and other furry creatures darted about at the edges of road, keeping well away from the clomping hooves of the horses. They would be able to survive out here for weeks if they had to, living off of the animal life that still called the wilderness home. From time to time they could hear the trickling of small streams that crisscrossed the plain; clean water from which they would be able to fill their skins, if need be. Trees popped up here and there as they went along, but never in any large quantity. The heavier forestlands were generally farther south or along the Rim.

On hot summer days the lack of shade between Illux and the outer villages made a trek such as this far more of an ordeal. This day the sky was thankfully blanketed by an impenetrable wall of ominous clouds. The sun weakly tried to break through the barrier, but to no avail. Beside it, Aenna glowed as always, its faint light cutting through even the darkest of cloud cover on the blackest of nights. Even so, it never added any illumination to the ground below. A light breeze blew across the grasses and tickled Trent's face, stirring his red hair as he rode. It wasn't a cold wind, but for some reason he felt that it carried a wicked chill.

*Finally, we are here.*

The first signs of human habitation for the last several miles sprang up to greet them from among the grasslands. The breezy meadows had finally given way to freshly tilled fields that stretched on before them for some distance. Trent knew from experience that it would be an hour or more before they reached the village proper, but this was progress at least. Each village was surrounded by miles of farmland in order to grow the food needed to cart off to Illux. Those in the north even supported livestock on the foothills of the Rim where the proper grazing grounds were more abundant and the threat of attack was less.

After a few more minutes of plodding forward, Trent and Devin saw villagers working the fields. There were several of them, men and women of all ages bending low to pull up weeds or to inspect the crops. Most of them had sun-browned faces hiding under long straw hats. The loose clothing that they wore was not unlike what one would expect to find among the poorer districts of Illux. Those who noticed them waved in greeting or simply nodded in recognition. The smaller children who accompanied their families stopped whatever they were doing and ran up to the edge of the road to get a better look at the large warriors.

"You would think that they had never seen a Paladin before," Devin said, laughing.

Trent simply smiled and waved at them all as they passed. A small girl pointed at him and giggled before being dragged back to work by her mother. They both knew that all villagers had seen their fair shares of Paladins in their lives, especially in the villages this far from Illux. Every village had at least one Paladin assigned to it, and some, such as this one, had three or four. Raids from bandits were not uncommon, and the looming threat of Demons and Accursed never allowed for any real sense of security.

The rest of their journey to the small village passed without any more activity of note. Trent and Devin remained mostly silent, each mentally preparing for the weeks ahead. They knew that this would be the last time either of them would gaze upon another human face or sleep under a solid roof for quite some time. Trent still felt the uneasiness that had permeated his thoughts since Ren had given them this assignment, sure that something was lurking just out of reach, watching him. Devin seemed to feel the same brash courage that he always felt, even when looking death in the face. Soon the small ramshackle houses sprang up around them with no clear rhyme or reason to their existence. Each was a simple wooden structure with a thatched roof, not unlike the one Trent had grown up in back in the slums of Illux. The only major difference between the two was that the homes here had more space between them, although this usually just allowed them to sag more to one side.

*People sacrifice safety to come out here for better living, but is it really any better?*

"I could never live in a place like this," Devin murmured, his smile finally leaving for a brief moment.

"You could never live anywhere that wasn't the barracks. If you aren't fighting you aren't living. At any rate, the location has nothing to do with it," Trent replied, himself breaking into a small smile.

By now the faint smell of livestock had replaced that of raw dirt and grass. The air here was cleaner than it was in the slums at least.

"I could so! I rather like to think that if I weren't the most important Paladin in the order, I would make a fine bandit. Imagine living out in the open, always on the run, never tied down to one place."

"I don't care to imagine, because I know how it always ends, with my sword or your axe buried in their gut."

"Better to die from a man than to be turned into a monster."

The sight of Terric numbly trying to hold his innards as they squeezed out of his open abdomen flashed through Trent's mind.

*And what if you are killed by a monster?*

A new thought crept in, just under the last, that chilled Trent to the bone. Something about what Devin had said brought images flashing through his mind that overrode any thoughts of his dead brother. He was reminded of his father, left alone on the road outside of Illux, weakly crawling through the dirt.

Trent pushed the thoughts from his mind as they found themselves again greeted by village children who had come out of their homes to see the newcomers in person. The two Paladins dismounted and led their horses through the mud-covered village street. Their destination was the Paladin's retreat, a building located in the center of the village that was slightly larger than the rest. This building was of a sturdier construction than its neighbors as it was the home of the local Paladins as well as any who needed a place to stay while ranging. Every village had a similar building at its heart, as well as a small stable around the back where they would be leaving their horses until they made the return journey in a few weeks or more. The faithful animals would be cared for by the local Paladins, and most likely the village children as well, until they returned.

When they finally reached the central building, Trent took a moment to take in the surroundings while they walked the horses around back. The village was cleared away from the Paladin house for several yards in each direction, flowing outward like the spokes on a wheel. Everything in the small community led to this one central point, a feature that provided the Paladins with easy access to the rest of the village in case something was to go wrong. This clearing was also home to a rather large well that provided the drinking water for the residents. After hitching their horses inside the stable alongside several others, the two warriors made their way back around the front of the building, stopping to fetch some water from the well. Trent filled his skin from the bucket and drank heavily from it while Devin simply drenched himself directly from the source. When they were done they bounded up the steps onto the small porch.

"Who is it that is stationed here at the moment?" Devin asked, taking Trent's skin away from him to drink more.

"Jakob?" Trent replied, shrugging.

"As if I would know who that refers to. There must be half a dozen Jakobs in the order. And of those, I've met three."

After a brief moment of waiting Devin knocked loudly on the door, calling inside to any who might have been home. Several minutes passed with no answer, so the two weary Paladins made their way inside. The room that was before them was a large common area with a small hearth for a fire and several stools on which to sit. The sturdy wooden floor made barely a creak as they walked inside, letting the door lazily swing shut behind them. The room was lit from the sun streaming through the windows, but even so Trent found himself lighting several candles above the hearth for added light. To their left was a large staircase that led up to the second floor where there would be rooms and beds for them to sleep for the night. On the far side of the room was an open doorway that must have led to the kitchen. They had stayed in many such rest stops before, and this one more than once if he could remember right; after years of ranging, all of the villages began to blend together.

Trent removed his weapons, his shield, and what other provisions he carried and set them down on the floor beside one of the stools. He then casually sat down himself, causing the wooden object to groan in protest. Devin walked through the doorway to forage for food, returning with a cup overflowing with ale in one hand and a piece of old bread in the other. His mouth was already full by the time he sat down next to Trent; the sounds he made caused the other to salivate. It had been half a day or more since they had stopped to eat, and Trent had begun to feel the pangs of hunger. Even so, he struggled against his slight fatigue as well, causing him to lean back against the wall and close his eyes.

They would wait like this until news of their presence had trickled through the villagers to the ears of one of the local Paladins who would then rush to greet them. Usually the reunion was pleasant, and war stories were swapped until nightfall, but there had been times in the past when meetings had been tense. Some saw a divide between city and village Paladins, a divide that Trent could never understand. All were tasked with the preservation of the Light, but some saw the village assignments to be less desirable positions. Others craved the freedom that it gave them, which often led to other concerns. The Paladins who protected Seatown had become more unruly as of late, so much so that there were rumors that the city planned to declare itself independent from Illux in the near future. Trent knew that if that happened it would come to blood one way or another.

It wasn't long before the front door was thrown open and a blonde-headed Paladin entered with a wide grin upon his face. The man wore his hair in a braid down his back with a small beard upon his chin. Trent and Devin instantly recognized him, jumping from their stools so quickly that they clattered to the floor.

"Gil!" They shouted together, rushing to meet him.

The man let out a hearty laugh as he wrapped his arms around his old friends.

"We thought you were stationed up north," Trent said as he righted his stool and sat back down.

Gil pulled up his own seat next to Devin and took the mug of ale from the other, draining it.

"I was, but I moved down here where I was needed more. One Paladin is all a northern village needs, so they gave it to some green boy from the city. But a southern one, especially this southern one, needs a good three or four at least. It used to be that we had armed patrols down here even, but lately that hasn't been needed."

Gil slapped a hand down on Devin's armored leg and let it rest there. The other man looked at him and let out a laugh. Although the three of them were equally good friends, those two had been lovers once, before duty took them separate places. For a while Devin had seemed lost without the third member of their group, but over the years he had moved on, or simply found better ways to hide his sadness.

"And what brings you two rugged bastards outside of those pretty walls?"

Trent's smile left as he began to answer. "The Lady Ren is nervous that the enemy is planning something. Attacks have begun to lessen as of late and she wants us to find out why."

"You remember that poor Trent here is smitten with the Lady Ren, don't you?"

"Can you blame him?"

"Of course not, but I think that it clouds his judgment. He worries about what we will find out here."

Gil visibly tensed and removed his hand from his friend's leg.

"I wouldn't be so quick to mock, brother. Things look awfully different from outside those walls. It's easy to get lost in the glory and the grandeur of being a Paladin from inside Illux, but out here, out in the muck of it, there is nothing glorious about it."

"You act as if we never leave the city. You know Trent and I range more often than not. You did too, once."

"And when is the last time that you went much farther south than this? When is the last time that you hunted anything more than a bandit? Things have changed out here, Devin. Ever since they moved me south, sightings of Demons and the Accursed have lessened. It's as if the enemy is withdrawing."

"Then why all of the apprehension? This is good news. They have finally given up!"

Both Trent and Gil stared at the other Paladin, causing his smile to quickly recede.

"You don't believe that, surely?" Gil asked solemnly.

"Of course not. But I refuse to soil my pants like some frightened child. This doesn't mean that some new threat is looming on the horizon. You both know that all battles between us and them are mere skirmishes compared to what they once were. The Grey God would never allow for one side to outmaneuver the other. Do neither of you remember what happened when the Light thought that it could overtake the Darkness?"

They both knew of the event of which he spoke. Some five hundred years before, the armies of Light had marched into the wilderness and so thoroughly cut out the forces of Darkness root and stem that the Balance Monks where forced to stir themselves from high in the mountains. The loss of life in Illux had been catastrophic. It had been said that Arra wept for a hundred years after the purging of Illux. None had dared to violate the pact of the Grey God and shift the balance that drastically again. Even the previous Seraph had checked his ambitions of conquest in the wilderness due to this event.

"The Grey God and his disciples may step in to right the scales, but the last time that they made that much of an impact the other side was already decimated. They may preach that they preserve the balance of the world, but the truth is they only correct it." Trent spat his words as he added, "How many have to die before Ravim sends his monks to save Illux?"

The other two remained silent. Devin had become visibly flustered since his enjoyment of their reunion with Gil had been squelched by his morose companion. Finally, he stood and entered the far room again, this time returning with enough bread and ale for all three to share. Gil accepted his happily, while Trent shot Devin a venomous glance but remained silent.

"Who else is stationed with you?" Devin asked through a full mouth.

"An Albert, a Clarissa, and a Jakob."

The look that Devin shot Trent caused his smile to quickly return.

"Were any of them initiated with us?"

"No."

"Good. Then I doubt I know them."

They laughed at this, the tension finally broken. From here the conversation varied from what activities Gil engaged in every day to what life had been like living outside of the city for the past several years. It wasn't until the conversation returned to what things were like in the city that the mood began to sour again.

"And what of you two? Has anything exciting happened in the last few weeks?" Gil inquired.

Trent looked at his hands silently, knowing that there was no way to hide what he had done from one of his closest friends.

"Don't make Devin tell me."

"I won't. Trent needs to tell this one," Devin said.

It took him a few moments to muster up the courage, but he finally choked out the words. "I saw my father."

"Ah. And that didn't go well I presume?"

"Not in the slightest. He damned near killed him," Devin interjected.

"So much for letting Trent tell me himself, you dumb bastard."

"No. He is right," Trent replied. "I lost myself to my rage and it nearly cost me my rank. If the gods hadn't sent Devin at that moment, who knows what I would have done."

"Where is he now?"

"We banished him from the city. If he headed south, we didn't come across him."

"I will keep my eyes open. Now enough of this. Let's make the rounds!"

With that Gil pulled himself to his feet and made for the door, motioning the other two to follow him. Slowly the three old friends made their rounds about the village, learning the names of the villagers they passed or the children who followed at their heels.

Gil told his visitors that he walked the pathways of the village and the fields beyond every day, keeping close watch for any sign of bandits or Demons. From time to time he would place himself in the middle of a disagreement between villagers, but he told them that this was a very rare occurrence.

Finally, they were introduced to the other three village Paladins who greeted them warmly if not a little distantly. It was when the grey clouds above began to turn black, signaling the beginning of night, that they made their way back to the center of the village to finally rest.

"They didn't seem too fond of us," Devin observed as they walked back up the wooden steps. "Jealous, perhaps."

"I told you that we see things differently out here. Some say that the walls of Illux should come down, so that all of us can live as equals."

"But the walls keep our people safe."

"Not all of our people. I know that those who live in the villages made that choice, but we need them to grow food as well. All I am saying is that their sacrifices cannot be forgotten. The inner city knows little of what happens beyond Illux."

"They know little of what happens in Illux. Although I don't disagree with you Gil, you are starting to sound like a Seatown Paladin."

Gil turned to Trent and laughed.

"Am I? Gods have mercy."

After another round of ale and food the Paladins retired to their rooms above, the other village Paladins joining them soon after. Trent found himself alone in a small room with only a chamber pot and sleeping pad, while Devin slept with Gil down the hall. It was another hour after he laid down that he was finally able to find sleep, his friend's words clawing at his thoughts right up until the world faded from view.

*Squawk.*

*The Vulture screeched at him mockingly between beakfuls of sinew from the white bird ensnared in its talons. The smaller bird twitched violently with every string of meat that was ripped from its throat. By now most of its breast was stained red with blood.*

*Trent struggled in vain to reach them, but he still had no wings. Just as he did every night, he fell into the abyss that separated him from the other bird and spiraled down into blackness. It engulfed him utterly, leaving not a sight or sound for him to see or hear.*

*Squawk.*

*Now he was a Paladin again, armed in the whitest armor that he had ever beheld. Upon his head rested a helmet with a great blue plume sprouting from it. Beside him was another Paladin armored the same. They were running together, side by side, but from what he could not remember. A great black shape blocked out the sky above them.*

*The Vulture.*

*The sound of beating wings drowned out everything else. Trent couldn't make himself move fast enough; the winged beast seemed as if it were breathing down his neck. He turned and saw that the other Paladin was falling behind.*

*-Trent.-*

*He couldn't remember who the other Paladin was.*

*Terric?*

*It must be. It must be his brother. Trent tried to yell to him, but his screams were drowned out by the flapping of the great beast's wings. He was now engulfed in its shadow, preventing him from seeing anything beyond himself.*

*Suddenly the shadow was gone, and with it the other Paladin. Trent fell to his knees and tried to cry out in anguish, but no noise escaped his lips.*

THE NEXT MORNING the two Paladins gathered their supplies and prepared to continue out into the wilderness bereft of mounts. Each carried a rolled blanket, a hunting knife, weapons, and a skin for water. Devin also brought his bow and quiver for any game that they might come across. By the time they were ready to depart, the other Paladins had already left to begin their own duties. Only Gil stayed behind to see his old friends off.

"Trent," he said, patting Devin on the back. "I expect you to keep this fool safe."

"I can't protect him from himself," Trent responded, laughing.

"Nor should you try, for that is a battle you will always lose."

The blond Paladin tightly hugged each of his old friends one last time. When Devin and Gil broke their embrace, the dark-haired Paladin patted his old friend on the shoulder.

"Do try to make it up to Illux sometime. Or better yet ask to go ranging with us, we could use that sword of yours."

"Admitting you need something? You better go before you show other signs of madness. We both know Castille would never allow it after I told him how ugly he was. Besides, I do like it out here."

Gil waved them off and the two Paladins left the last village behind. Trent was sad to say goodbye to Gil, but he knew that he would see him again in a few short weeks at the latest. Turning his mind from the sadness he felt, Trent looked forward to what they must now do. Ahead of them lay untold miles of wilderness upon which only the forces of Darkness tread.

# CHAPTER 8

The motes of light parted as the solitary figure passed between them. She slowly made her way through the trees that stretched taller than any others in all of creation. The great sentinels had stood this tall for nearly as long as time itself had existed, unchanged as the world around them. At their base, large ferns sprouted upward, providing cover for the dark shapes that flitted to and fro in the shafts of gold at the edges of her vision. Beside her a babbling stream wound between the trunks of the trees and flowed farther into the heart of the wood. The only sounds besides the meandering of the water were the chirps of the birds as they hunted higher in the foliage above.

*Truly this is a paradise.*

Arra, Goddess of Light, walked amidst the forests of the Divine Plane, as she had since the gods had been confined to it. She often walked alone like this, sometimes for days, never growing tired or lonely. Her only companion, the creature she had named Divinity, often hunted in other parts of the forest, checking in on the goddess every few days. Arra enjoyed these forays because they gave her a respite from the other gods. Samson and Luna wished to endlessly debate the war and discuss tactics that they should employ in order to gain the ultimate victory that they wished to achieve. Or they did once, before it became all too obvious that Ravim would never allow for such a victory.

Thousands had died in Illux to prove that point.

Arra had grown tired of such discussions long before that. After all, it had been Lio's thirst for victory and poor judgment that had resulted in his condemnation. Perhaps the High God had reacted too harshly when he punished his most loyal servant, or perhaps Lio had reached too far.

Or loved too much.

What had been done to him was monstrous, just like his rage afterward. Her memories of that day a thousand years before still cut her deeply. She had lost two of her greatest friends to madness. Arra never did learn what had become of Daniel after Xyxax had cursed him.

The prayers from the devout on the Mortal Plane below filtered up to her ears dimly, like whispers at the back of her mind. There were too many to hear them all clearly, and most of them came to her as emotions rather than thoughts or words. She would expend what powers she could to answer some of these in time, many of them being from Paladins seeking a replenishing of their strength. Her apathy for the war did not extend to those mortals in her charge. The High God had entrusted her with the well-being of the human race and the Divine Spark within each of them. Her fellow gods had begun to lose sight of their true purpose in the hopes of becoming victorious over the Gods of Darkness. It was as if they had learned nothing from Lio's fall, and yet they scorned him still like some mad beast.

*I don't scorn him. I pity him.*

The Grey God was the only thing that stopped Samson and Luna from reigniting the war to its full ferocity as it had been in the days of old. The onetime God of Darkness had constantly checked the advances of either pantheon since his ascension. The High God had decreed that Ravim would speak with his voice and carry out his will in order to maintain balance between the two factions. Never again would Light overpower Darkness, or Darkness, Light. Never again would one god kill another. There had been flare-ups since the Pact was formed, but the Grey God had always stepped in to set things right.

Arra was not the first to lose taste for the conflict. She had watched as apathy and inaction had slowly overtaken the gods on both sides of the struggle. Recent exchanges with Vardic and Rhenaris had shown them to take little care over the actions of their servants on the Mortal Plane either. Of the Fallen One she was unsure. He rarely made himself known since his condemnation, and was viewed even by his new companions with disdain for his role in the destruction of their greatest member.

*Xyxax. Even among the damned he was abhorrent.*

She followed a small stream for some ways before coming to a halt and kneeling close to the ground where she saw a shadow in the brush. A rabbit came to her from underneath a nearby fern; hopping directly toward her outstretched hand. The goddess gently stroked the furry creature, feeling its soft coat brush against her fingers. Like much of the life on the Divine Plane, this rabbit had a docile quality that was unlike its brethren on the Mortal Plane below. There was a marked difference between the creatures here and those the High God had populated the rest of his creation with. After several minutes she sent the animal on its way and returned to her trek, reflecting on recent events.

The ceremony to initiate new Paladins had occurred over two weeks ago, so Arra had been forced to commune with her fellow gods to lend as much power to Ren as they were able. The experience had left her embittered toward Samson and Luna as usual, and she hoped that she would not need to see them again for some time. To give herself the respite that she craved, Arra had begun one of her many forest strolls. Her walks never took her far from the others, even as much as she wished for it. The Divine Plane and the forest that she walked through extended on indefinitely; a never-ending paradise filled with tranquil life. Yet something kept her from fully giving in to her desire to leave her duties behind forever, so she always kept Ayyslid close.

It was the thoughts of two of her Paladins ranging in the wilderness that gave her pause now. Ren had sent two of her favored rangers out past the last villages in order to discern why the forces of Darkness had been so quiet recently. The Seraph had informed the gods of her apprehensions and desire to send Trent and Devin out the same day as the ceremony. They knew that Ren feared the inactivity of the enemy was simply the calm before the storm, a hidden sign that something was looming on the horizon. Arra wasn't completely sure that she agreed, but she wasn't one to second guess the choices of her champions. As she walked through the forest, the goddess had come to share her Seraph's uneasiness, and began to question the activities of her enemies on the far side of the Divine Plane. She knew from her discussions with the others, however, that they not only didn't see any merit in Ren's fears, but felt that she was showing weakness and should be doing even more to combat the forces of their enemies.

*They want to finish what we started so long ago. Can't they see it was for this reason that the High God left us?*

As her thoughts became more troubling, Arra decided that the only way to put her mind at ease would be to visit the Basin and gaze through Aenna onto the Mortal Plane. Perhaps seeing what Trent and Devin were experiencing would calm the feelings that had begun to stir in her breast. Still, doubts dug into her mind, telling her that something was wrong. It didn't seem likely that Vardic and Rhenaris would be planning anything. The two embittered gods entertained themselves by using what limited influence they had to corrupt the hearts of men, rather than trying to physically enslave them as they once did. If only she knew more about what Lio was doing, alone in his tower.

*Vardic and Rhenaris don't have the drive to crush the Light as they once did. Not since the Purge. But what of Lio? I can't see him wishing violence against his own people? Those who he loved so...*

The enigma of her fallen friend plagued her even as she changed her course and made for her companions, seeking their council before she made her way toward the Basin. She knew before even fully making up her mind that she wouldn't be able to adequately explain her concerns to them, nor would they be likely to heed them even if she could. And yet Arra felt compelled by duty to head back to the keep and broach the issue with them.

The forest sprawled for endless miles in either direction, seemingly unending no matter which way she turned. The goddess had walked these woods for a millennium, however, and she knew each path that led to and from Ayyslid without a second thought. The journey back would not take long, for though she usually traveled away from the fortress in a meandering fashion, now she returned to it by the quickest route she knew. Time passed differently to the gods, the cycles of day and night not applying to the Divine Plane. Her walk might have taken her hours on the Mortal Plane below, or it might have even been days. The shadows of the trees passed her by and she walked in an endless pattern of lights and darks.

Finally she saw it.

Ahead of her, rising out of the trees, was a great fortress made of living wood. It was in the center of a clearing, in which rested a small grove within the larger forest. All of the trees in the grove had weaved together to shape the giant edifice, which had taken the vaguest outline of the mortal strongholds below. Stray branches and leaves poked up from the upper reaches of the living structure, giving it the most uneven of outlines. It swayed back and forth gently even without the presence of any wind, and a faint glow emanated from within.

*Ayyslid, fortress of Light.*

So it had been named when the High God had called it forth from the wood, bringing to life a place for the Gods of Light to call home.

The gods needed no sleep or shelter, and yet their time on the Mortal Plane had made them crave their own fortification to gather within. Arra found Ayyslid to be beautiful, but she still craved the openness of the woods that stretched infinitely beyond it. The goddess walked into the clearing toward the living building, drinking in her surroundings just as she did every time she approached. The air here was almost thicker than elsewhere in the wood, bringing her mind from its usually frantic activity to a drowsy comfort that she both loathed and loved.

As she approached, the curved boughs that made up the walls of the fortress spread before her, admitting Arra into the inner sanctum of the Gods of Light. After she had made it past the outer layer of trunks and branches, the opening closed behind her just as quickly as it had spread. The entrance to Ayyslid was just a small hallway that led into a larger central chamber. No windows or candles were needed inside, for it glowed with its own luminance. Without a doubt her companions would have sensed her presence by now, and she could expect them to be out to greet her shortly. It was after she heard the sounds of carnal pleasure from the rooms above that she realized they were indifferent to her arrival. Luna called out passionate cries of lust that were clearly meant to be heard by Arra below.

*As if there are no better ways for gods to spend their time. Not that I am any better.*

She had partaken of Samson herself many times over the centuries, when her boredom or loneliness became too much to bear, and yet she still looked at the activity with disdain. Pleasures of the flesh were one of the favored ways that the other two passed their time. It was those same kinds of feelings that had led Lio to his doom. All love came from the Light, but it was the emotion most easily exploited by the Darkness. Even so, what Samson and Luna did could hardly be called love.

Irritated, Arra sat down on a limb that rose up from the floor to meet her. She would wait. It wasn't long before the sounds from above stopped. The silence that followed was almost as uncomfortable as the sounds of the two lovers that had assaulted her ears before. After a few moments the limbs from the ceiling in the corner of the room began to part and lower themselves, carrying the two lovers to ground level.

Like Arra, the two gods were clothed in armor that shimmered a thousand different colors as the light of the room bounced off of it. Each carried a different weapon strapped upon their back, crafted for them by the High God himself. Samson carried a bow made from the very trees they lived in, the living wood willingly giving itself to their cause. Luna's weapon was a large warhammer tied to her back. The weapons had seen almost no use since their banishment from the Mortal Plane. Arra kept her large great sword on her back as well, although as of late she had begun to wonder why.

Samson left his companion and walked across the room to the wall closest to Arra. A small alcove opened from the branches there revealing several goblets and a pitcher, all made of wood. He took the pitcher and poured himself a full goblet of clear wine before walking back to the center of the room where he began to drink, his eyes never leaving Arra. She studied him as well, noticing that his posture conveyed his usual arrogance. His features were chiseled stone, hard and beautiful at the same time beneath his tightly cropped white hair. Luna walked up beside him and leaned against his rough body, never truly allowing his form to dominate her own. Luna's soft-featured face always carried a mischievous look about it, even when she seemed irritated, just as she did now. Clearly, Arra's presence was unwanted.

All three of the gods were white of hair and gold of skin, not unlike the statues of their likeness on the Mortal Plane below. They resembled the mortals under their care in general outline only, the rest being purely divine. Within their veins flowed the same silver blood as the High God himself, drawn from within his breast at the beginning of all things. Only a few drops of this precious substance flowed within the Seraph Ren.

Luna began to speak first, using the overly musical tones that she often employed when she was unhappy. "Arra, dear. Why do you still refuse to join us in our fun? You did once in the past, I am sure."

*Why do I?*

"Because I do not wish to shirk my duties as a god for the pleasures of the flesh." Her voice was cool, but beneath her temper had already begun to flare.

Samson snorted derisively. "And it is for this reason that you walked amongst the trees for years on end without a care for the dealings of the world below. You engage with the mortals far less than we do. Do you even hear their prayers anymore?"

"I still hear their prayers, and unlike you I try to answer them! I still care for our people, just not this war!"

"Why have you come here, dear Arra?" Luna asked, drinking from her own cup now. "We have no need of you. And we certainly have no want for you."

"I worry about our Paladins, who currently traverse the wilderness alone. Trent and Devin, they are called."

"That wild goose chase that Ren has sent her favorites upon?" Samson replied, draining his goblet. "There are no merits to her fears. None."

"That may be, but I cannot sit idly by while they risk themselves."

"You have never taken this much care before. Why now?"

Why *did* she care so much? Endeavors such as this were undertaken by Paladins every day. What made this time any different?

"It is because she has feelings for all three of them." Luna was almost singing now.

*She certainly grates upon the ears. How does he stand her?*

"Ah yes, how could I forget," Samson said. "It is because of Arra that we have been left with this lackluster Seraph in the first place. She is unwilling to follow orders, and even worse, she is unwilling to crush our enemies as we once did."

"Crush our enemies?" Arra was clenching her fists now, tightening them with each syllable. "And thereby incur the wrath of the Grey

God? You know as well as I do that any sweeping victory would quickly be turned to defeat."

"We were charged with defeating the Darkness, no matter what Ravim has to say on the matter. If we must, the armies of Light will engage the Balance Monks as well. Ravim will not stand in our way forever. That fool is still no better than when he was Xyxax's sniveling lickspittle."

"This is the same folly that caused the Pact in the first place! It was by this madness that Lio fell!" She felt the branches beneath her retract as she bolted to her feet. "We were not tasked with the destruction of the other, we were meant to provide mankind with a choice."

"Your weakness will not stop us from our course, dear," Luna said. "Lio had the right idea, even if his madness caused him to falter at the last moment. If this Seraph of yours will not obey our commands then we will find a replacement."

"Castille would do nicely, I think," Samson added.

Arra walked over to the alcove and filled herself a goblet, draining it in a matter of moments. The cool liquid warmed and tingled as it went down, quenching the fire in her belly that had begun to rise. Samson and Luna each sat on branches that rose to meet them. Arra returned to her previous location and did the same.

"That pompous excuse for a servant? I know that you poison his mind while he sleeps, filling his dreams with treacherous delusions of power."

"We only remind him of what he already knows," Samson replied.

"It matters not. You both know as well as I do that it was my turn to choose the Seraph, and I chose. Now we must abide by that choice until she is killed in battle."

"Which is why she refuses to engage in battle then? To keep her goddess in control of the workings of man a little while longer? Your petty attempt at dominance is of no consequence. We have eternity to wage this war. Victory is inevitable."

"If you really thought this was possible then you would have broken the Pact by now. You both fear him. You are not as confident as you claim."

"Leave, Arra," Luna commanded, her lyrical tones replaced by a sternness unbecoming of her. "We have no need of you here."

"As you wish." She sounded more defeated than she felt.

Arra stood and walked to the nearest wall of the room. The trees split before her, allowing her to quickly exit and leave Ayyslid behind. It was painful to walk away from her home, even though she had rarely thought of it as such for quite some time. She had not seethed with this kind of anger in just as long. Had the desire to win this unwinnable war really turned them to madness? What had once been duty had become apathy, and now treachery? How could they hope to defy the Grey God?

She continued from the clearing, leaving her former companions behind to work their plots and delusions at their leisure. Her destination lay ahead, in the center of the Divine Plane: the Basin. It was through this mystical window that she could look through Aenna and directly observe the Mortal Plane below. Without the use of Aenna and the Basin, the gods only had limited knowledge of the actual workings of the Mortal Plane. Those servants who carried in them Divine Blood could communicate events to them, but the gods could never truly witness anything without looking into the Basin. While she was there she would also be just paces away from the clearing where the Grey God meditated.

*Should I tell him that my companions wish to defy him? Would they really even dare?*

After several minutes of considering the idea she decided that she must wait to approach him, whilst her fears were still mostly unfounded. Samson and Luna would be fools to actually attempt any disturbance of the Pact. Ravim was not a being to be trifled with, nor was his anger something to be called down lightly. If she brought these accusations before the Grey God, there was no telling what he might do.

The great trees around her began to thin as she got nearer to her destination, a sign that she was soon to be leaving her beloved forest behind. The Basin lay at the exact center of the Divine Plane, under the watchful gaze of the High God's Throne. This neutral location allowed for it to be used by any god, Light or Dark. Using it had dangers of course, as enemy eyes could look into its surface just as easily as Arra could. Still, she doubted that it got much use in recent times, for the Gods of Darkness seemed to care little for the Mortal Plane as of late.

*Unless what Ren fears is true.*

Eventually, even the grass beneath her feet disappeared, replaced instead by flat white stone. This new surface covered all of the area between the two halves of the Divine Plane, serving as a sign that Arra now walked in neutral territory that was protected by Ravim. The ground was smooth and polished, showing no visible cracks or seams, as if it were one solid piece from end to end. She traversed this new material for quite some time before anything else appeared on the horizon. Then, all at once, it loomed before her. In the center of the stone sat the giant throne, which towered over twice her height. The throne sat empty, just as it always had since the day Xyxax was killed.

*Come back to us. I have need of you now, as I always have.*

The disappointment of the High God in his children was rarely spoken of by the lesser gods. They would rather ignore the issue that he had taken with them than address it. Arra's conversation with Samson and Luna showed her that they were even keen to repeat the mistakes of the past that had led to the throne sitting empty. Once the High God had sat here and watched his creation with great joy. Now doing so would only bring him sadness, so he abandoned it for some other realm. It was rumored that he created other worlds besides this one. Perhaps he traveled there now, the pain of his creation a distant memory.

Several yards from the base of the throne sat the Basin of Aenna. It was a giant bowl, some several hundred paces in circumference that was made of the same stone as the ground beneath it and the throne behind it. The Basin was filled to the brim with a highly reflective silver liquid.

*Divine Blood.*

When he created the Divine Plane, the High God had filled the Basin with his own blood, creating a window down onto the mortal world for the lesser gods to peer through. This Basin was his gift to his most powerful children, granting them a small portion of the omniscience that he himself had. Then he sat upon his throne and watched as the other gods looked down in wonder on the world that their father had created. On the Mortal Plane the window was known as Aenna, the Opening; a great glowing circle that hung in the sky day and night, unmoving and unchanged.

*Unchanged since Xyxax died.*

With the death of the dark god, Aenna had become slightly dimmer; as had the Divine Plane itself. The very existence of this realm relied upon the continued survival of the gods. If all of them were to fall then there would be no reason for its existence, and all of what she saw around her would vanish as if it had never been. What would happen to Divinity and the other creatures that called this place home she could not say.

Arra looked behind the High God's Throne toward a circle of pillars in the distance. Sitting within that shrine deep in meditation would be Ravim, the Grey God. It wouldn't be hard for her to walk over and speak with him now if she so chose, but her misgivings won out again and instead she merely walked up to the Basin and looked into the surface of the Divine Blood.

The silver liquid never rippled, nor showed any signs of change. She considered looking for the servants of Darkness to see just what they were doing at this moment, but something told her it would be fruitless. There were too many for her to focus on specifically besides the Herald, and even then she would learn little. The most trusted servants of the gods had learned ways to shield themselves from the prying eyes above.

Once her thoughts turned to Trent and Devin she could suddenly see them in the Basin as if they were standing just below its surface.

Arra gasped as she saw the scene that was unfolding on the Mortal Plane below her. Her servants were outnumbered and in grave peril. Both were suffering from grievous injuries, and seemed to have little time left. Almost as soon as she gazed upon them a prayer filtered to her ears, distinct from all of the others.

*Arra, Goddess of Light, protect your champions.*

# CHAPTER 9

It took only a few hours for the previously tamed landscape to become wild and unhindered by the pursuits of man. The land this far south was not withered and dead like it was to the west near the Great Chasm, yet it still gave off the air that humans didn't belong. Where there were once fields of short grasses there now stood chest-high clusters of brush. Trees rose in more frequent numbers now, with large copses appearing every so often, which the Paladins chose to move around. Trent knew from previous ranging missions that this would soon change as the presence of evil began to taint the landscape further away from Illux.

They moved at a brisk pace, not quite a run, and yet quicker than any normal man would be able to keep up over any length of time. Although the area showed few signs of any activity beyond that of animals, they still kept a watchful eye out for Accursed or Demons. There were no roads this far south, the last having ended in the village where they said goodbye to Gil and their horses. Humanity had never tried to colonize much further from Illux than the current villages, and Trent supposed that no one other than Paladins had ever even traveled out this far. Bandits usually stayed hidden in safe pockets between Illux and the coast or in the foothills of the mountains. Even the armies of Light feared to march into the wilderness.

As the first day came to a close, the two Paladins unrolled their blankets in a small cluster of trees that stood alone for miles in all directions. After relieving themselves, they ate a sparse meal of dried goods that they had been given by Gil earlier that morning. They made no fire, and slept in shifts so that one could keep watch while the other regained his strength. Both men knew firsthand the dangers of being caught unawares in the open by Demons. Even Accursed, who usually posed little threat to Paladins, could be dangerous in the dark.

The next day brought more of the same. They continued on for most of the morning and into the afternoon without encountering a single trace of Demons. When the sun had begun to lower itself toward the horizon, Devin spotted several deer grazing in a meadow near a small wood to the east of where they walked. He removed much of his armor and crept along the ground, getting as close as he dared. Trent sat back on his heels, himself unmoving as he watched his friend on the hunt. When Devin was halfway between Trent and the deer he stood upright with an arrow nocked in his bowstring. His aim was true, bringing one of the smaller animals collapsing onto the earth. Both men rushed to the injured animal to end its suffering and stop its bleating from alerting anything to their presence. Trent held his hand on the animal's breast, feeling its weak breathing give out as its life flowed into the dirt.

That night they made only a large enough fire to cook their kill, dowsing the flames as soon as the meat was thoroughly browned. Once they had eaten their fill they butchered what remained of the animal and wrapped the meat in their blankets to provide them with food for the next few days. Trent filled their skins with clean water from a nearby stream before they left the site of the fire to make their camp for the night elsewhere. They finally rested a mile to the north, having slightly backtracked to prevent any chance of discovery.

Neither spoke a word to the other, each choosing instead to listen to the silence of the night around them. When it was finally Trent's turn to sleep he dreamed of the Vulture picking at the fallen dove as he did every time he slept. Devin finally woke him, more to prevent the sounds of his nightly struggle from alerting nearby Demons than because it was his watch.

This continued on for days on end, with no discernible change in their situation. The landscape around them was different even if the signs of those they searched for were not. Scrub brush and trees were replaced with dry and rocky earth, as most living things withered and died in the prolonged presence of the evil squatting in these lands. Now they were forced to eat less and less of their food in an attempt to keep their limited supplies for as long as possible. When the meat from the deer began to sour they were forced to track and kill smaller game, such as the rabbits that darted from stone to stone around them. When they found fresh water, which was rarely, they filled their skins to the brim and drank them empty again before moving on. Throughout all of this there was never a sign of the servants of Darkness.

*We never have to go this far south. We should have at least found some tracks by now.*

Finally, on the seventh day after they had left Gil and his village behind, Trent decided to break his silence and make his fears known. His voice cracked from disuse and the dryness in his throat.

"Something has changed out here," he said. "We have never been out this far without so much as a boot print to show us that the enemy has been here before us."

Devin scratched his beard ponderously before answering. "I agree. It seems what Gil said was true, enemy activity has lessened dramatically. They have withdrawn for some reason. I wonder if they are clustering somewhere other than south? Could that even be possible?"

*West is most likely, any significant numbers in the north or east would have been seen.*

"You know as well as I do that they rarely act in tandem anymore.

We are looking for separate roving bands, not a singular force. Why would they move together? The Gods of Darkness have not directly commanded their servants in over a generation."

"Then the answer is obvious. They are being commanded again."

"So you finally agree with the Lady Ren's fears?" Trent asked, feeling somewhat vindicated.

"I never said that. This doesn't mean that some large strike is in store for us. It simply means that they are no longer running wild, even this far south. Perhaps the Herald has finally pulled his horned head from his ass?"

"We can't go back until we find out what is really happening. We have to press on."

"Which way do you suggest?" Devin asked. "Continue south or make our way west?"

"I say that we continue south as we have been for at least another day before we change direction. They cannot have completely abandoned the south without leaving a sign."

They continued south as Trent had suggested, moving quicker than they had before. Uneasiness permeated their every action, and both men were in agreement that something had changed in the wilderness. It was halfway through the next day that they found out what.

The terrain here was rocky and uneven, inhabited only by carrion birds and large lizards. The grass and trees had fled from them some time ago, and now they truly found themselves in the heart of enemy territory. Every small sound sent the hairs on the backs of their necks on end, and even Devin seemed to be jumping at his shadow. Overhead, the twin lights in the sky beat down upon them, ever watchful. The two Paladins were crossing the rim of a shallow valley of slate when Trent caught sight of several rotting bodies stumbling behind a giant in black armor. He quickly signaled to his companion and they dropped flat against the stones.

The Demon-led band of Accursed was at least thirty strong; most likely too many for even these seasoned warriors to handle alone. They were far enough away that Trent was sure that they would remain unnoticed and the band would pass them by. The creatures were coming up from the southern direction at the edge of the valley opposite the Paladins. Then the Demon called them to an abrupt halt with a simple motion of its hand.

*There is no way that he can sense us up here. Have we been seen?*

Beside Trent, Devin quietly set his rucksack on the ground and then unclasped his axe from the strap that held it in place. Every muscle in the big warrior's body visibly tensed as he prepared for what was coming. Trent unloaded his own gear before closing his eyes and beginning to say a prayer to the gods. He was interrupted mid-thought by a sharp tap on the shoulder from Devin. Trent opened his eyes to see that his companion was pointing at the eastern side of the valley where another troop of Accursed led by several Demons was marching toward the first.

"Damn," Trent whispered under his breath.

"High God help us."

Now they were sure that there was no surviving this encounter if they truly had been noticed. Silently they watched as the two groups greeted each other in their own fashion before continuing on through the valley toward the northwest. Most of the Demons moved at the head of the column, but some stayed at the rear to keep the Accursed moving forward at good speed. They continued on this way without slowing, now numbering well over a hundred. When they were far enough away that it was safe for the Paladins to speak, Trent did so.

"We have to see where they are headed. A troop of this size could pose a considerable threat to the villages."

"It is as I said, they clearly have renewed leadership. We must take caution," Devin replied as he returned his gear and weapon to his back.

The two men cautiously entered the valley, slipping down the rugged slope while trying to avoid leaving any signs of their passage.

When they reached the bottom they followed their quarry far enough back that they could not be seen, always keeping an eye in each direction to make sure that another party did not stumble across them. The tracks left upon the ground were not hard to follow; it was clear that the Demons did not fear being discovered this far south.

They trudged on this way for hours, never once stopping to rest. After a time, the sun set behind the horizon and it became more difficult to discern whether or not they still headed in the right direction.

By this point they had found themselves struck by hunger and out of any suitable food. They stopped just long enough to catch two of the larger lizards that inhabited this area, using the creatures' night lethargy to their advantage. Once the animals were in hand they continued on their way, skinning and eating the reptiles raw while still on the move. The sour meat almost caused Trent to retch more than once, but he knew that stopping to cook would only cause them to lose their quarry or draw attention to them from other monsters in the area.

When the sun rose the next day they were able to see the tracks clearly again. It was obvious that at least two more bands of Accursed had joined the party they were tracking.

*What is going on here? Why do they keep heading in this direction? Surely we are west of Illux by now?*

That day continued much like the first, but this time water ran short before food did. Rationing their last drops from within their skins kept the Paladins from being able to continue on at full speed. Most of the water that they came across was fetid and stank. Just as the sun was finally setting they came across a small spring that was safe to drink. After dipping their heads and filling their skins they decided to rest for a few hours and make up for the delay in the morning. Trent took the first watch, allowing Devin to sleep for three hours before waking the other for his turn. He wasn't rested when Devin shook him awake just before dawn; the dream of the Vulture had seen to that.

They continued their hunt at nearly twice their previous day's speed to make up for the six hours that they had lost over the night. The blood pumping through Trent brought with it heightened senses; each footfall from their running seemed to echo off the stones around them. It appeared that any who would have wished to look for them would surely notice their passing. Finally, after a few hours, they could see from the tracks they followed that the number of Accursed had stopped growing. Trent estimated that the party they followed had grown to some eight hundred Accursed and Demons. A single force of this size had not been seen in over a hundred years or more. This paled in comparison to the number of Paladins in Illux, and yet Trent knew that if they attacked the city or the villages they would still cause considerable damage.

The enemy troops continued northwest with no signs of changing course for the next few days. Trent guessed that they must be only a day or two from being within sight of the Great Chasm. The giant rent in the earth was almost directly west of Illux, several days by horse. In recent years, farming settlements had cropped up just out of sight of the place, but none dared to get any closer than that. Not that it mattered, for the land for miles around was even more withered and dead than the wilderness to the south. Even lizards and carrion birds stayed away from the place.

*What could they possibly want out here? We will have bypassed the city and villages both at this rate.*

Devin kept any theories of what the enemy forces were after to himself, seemingly preferring to keep all of his energy focused on moving forward rather than speaking. It had been at least a week that they had been tracking these Accursed, and fatigue had fully set in. They both knew that if they kept up this pace for much longer, they would be of no use in a battle of any kind.

Finally, their journey came to an end when the enemy tracks descended down a steep precipice onto the plain below. The ground here was littered with loose stones, and here and there a sun-bleached bone jutted from the earth. Trent couldn't remember how many days it had been since they had set out from Illux, nor the exact amount of time that they had been on the heels of these monsters, but it seemed that they had finally reached some sort of destination. An air of expectancy hung before them when they finally came to a stop.

The two Paladins knew that they would be able to overlook the entire plain for miles from the edge to which they tracked the troop. Before climbing over, they collapsed onto the ground to finally allow themselves a moment of rest, no matter how brief. Trent's legs cried out in pain, and his armor chafed him. He could feel a rash forming from the sweat that had beaded on his body but had not been removed. Both men were at the brink of exhaustion; their skins were again dry, and there were no lizards to be had for some distance. Trent was sure that he could feel blood in his boots from blisters that had formed and burst over the course of their journey. Any normal men would have dropped dead days before, but these were Paladins of the Light. Still, even their superhuman endurance had its limits, and they had surely found theirs. Normally they would have employed healing magic to aid their recovery, but such a drainage of energy would have rendered them completely useless in battle.

After several minutes Trent and Devin crept along the ground to the rim of the stony ridge and peered at the plain outspread below them. The land stretched beyond in a muted grey, flat from where they lay to the horizon. What they saw gathered below caused both men to pull back from the rim in shock. The troop of Accursed that they had been following must have been just one of many, for below them gathered thousands upon thousands of the Demon-led filth. It was a veritable army that would be able to sweep the defenses of Illux away without a second thought. There had to have been Accursed here that had walked the Mortal Plane for hundreds of years, for there was no way that recent generations of fallen or evil men had been enough to produce such a force. Even as they sat watching the gathered forces below them, more trickled in from nearly every direction.

Trent looked above at Aenna, hoping beyond hope that some god looked back and saw the horrors that he did.

"This can't be," Devin stammered.

This was the first time Trent had seen true fear in his friend's eyes in many years.

"We must warn Illux. The Lady Ren was right."

"You both were. But I'll waste no more time apologizing. We have to get back to the city."

The Paladins quickly moved back from their vantage point along the rim of the incline and only stood up when they could no longer be seen by those below. Without a second look back Trent and Devin turned and began their forced march east, where Illux surely lay. Their path led through rocky hills that prevented them from being seen from a distance, a blessing that neither man overlooked. With any luck they would come across a village within a day or two and be able to get new horses to speed their progress homeward. Gil would miss their return, but there was no time to travel that far southeast again before heading back to the City of Light.

For the next few hours they headed back toward Illux, again refusing to rest or eat, but forging onward as if the army were on their very heels. They knew that if this large a force marched upon the city and caught its defenders unawares, the war would end quickly and cruelly. Illux had a standing army, but it was mostly made of green boys who didn't want to volunteer for the actual duties held by the City Watch. Fighting a force such as this would require more courage than Trent was sure that they could muster. Even now he felt a pang of fear strike at his heart as he recalled the images of the rolling sea of bodies milling on the plain below.

Soon they came upon a shallow ravine that once held water. Even though the ravine wasn't deep, its edges were very precipitous and covered in loose rock. As they descended in their haste, the loose stones gave way under Trent's advance, causing him to lose his footing and tumble to the bottom.

He lay there for a moment in a daze, listening to the sounds of his companion stumbling down the rocks to his aid. The dust from Trent's fall stirred through the air, making a thin haze at the bottom of the ravine. Trent continued to lie there for a moment, probing his body for any signs of injury. Suddenly the sounds of Devin's descent became much louder, as if many more feet were headed toward Trent than the lone Paladin. Then Trent heard the sound of Devin's axe scraping his armor as he unhooked it from his back.

They were no longer alone.

"Trent!"

He rolled to his stomach and pushed himself upright, scanning the immediate area for the new threat that approached. Descending the ravine on the end opposite of where he had fallen down were several desiccated bodies of the Accursed, with a large armored Demon urging them onwards. The sounds of tumbling stone filled his ears while the haze thickened. Quickly, Trent threw his supplies to the side and unsheathed his sword and strapped on his shield. The first of the Accursed stumbled to the bottom of the ravine just as he was pulling himself to his feet.

The sight of the decaying monstrosities always filled Trent with the most primal of revulsion. He resisted the urge to retch as he set himself into a battle stance. They bore the shapes of men, for at one point all of them had been such, and yet their countenances were more closely related to a corpse than a living creature. Their bodies were completely naked, down to their rotted genitals; festering boils covered their decaying flesh, oozing black putrescence from each orifice. Numbly, they stumbled forward on unshod feet, blood and blisters having deserted those appendages long ago, replaced instead with a leathery covering. No eyes gazed upon him as they approached, the two holes set back into each skull having been gouged out at some prior time. Below that their mouths were sewn shut, keeping what sickening sounds these things were capable of from being uttered.

Trent supposed that there was a mercy in that.

He lifted his shield and set his sword before him, ready for the clashing of steel and iron that would ensue. Worst of all the deformities visited upon the servitors of darkness was the cruel surgery that replaced the hands of every Accursed with rusted iron swords, attached to bone at the wrist. These blades had no pommels that could be seen as the rotted flesh grew haphazardly up the first inch of the blade. These horrors were mindless servants who knew only pain and death.

The usual laugh with which Devin threw himself into combat had been replaced by an inhuman snarl as he met the first creatures on the floor of the ravine. This battle would be nothing to take any enjoyment from; their chances of survival were significantly lessened due to the fatigue of their long trek, but the cost of failure if they didn't warn Illux of the impending doom was too high. The first enemy to face Devin's attack fell with a single swing of his axe, the corpse-like flesh splitting in two and dropping the creature's bowels onto the floor of the ravine with a sickening plop. Trent could see that the second met Devin's attack in a more prepared fashion, blocking his initial blows and nearly landing some of its own.

Trent returned his focus to his own struggle, sprinting ahead to use his shield to unbalance his closest adversary so that he could attack its fellow standing close behind. As he got close, the stink of the things filled his nostrils, a sickeningly sweet smell that reminded him of the slums in more ways than he cared to admit. His sword easily split the creature's skull as its companion stumbled to the ground from his shield's strike. Trent spun to the side and thrust his blade into the falling Accursed as the creature swung its swords wildly at his arm. He tried to bring his shield to bear against the flailing thing's attack but he was a moment too slow. One of the blades found its mark, denting his armor and slicing the flesh beneath. Crying out in pain, the injured Paladin pulled his sword free and finished the Accursed with a kick to the back of its skull, bursting it open. A crossbow bolt buried itself into Trent's shield, just missing his arm beneath. He had forgotten to look for the ranged variety of the creatures during his initial assault.

Then Trent was knocked to his knees by a concussive force.

A ball of blood red fire had rocketed between where Trent and Devin stood, sending stones and flames flying in all directions. Both Paladins had been thrown by the blast, which had also singed their cloaks and hair. Dazed, Trent could vaguely see that Devin had regained his footing, smoke rolling off the large warrior like steam from fresh food. The Demon coalesced out of the newly blackened haze and began hacking at the Paladin with its wicked black blade. More Accursed began to converge on where Trent had fallen, while the rest moved to catch Devin from behind.

Trent ignored the blood in his mouth and reacted without thinking; throwing his sword into the nearest of his attackers. The next Accursed nearly stumbled onto him as it swung both of its sword arms down at where he lay. At the last possible moment Trent blocked the attack with his shield that he now grasped with both hands. Using the brief moment after blade and bulwark connected he planted his feet firmly beneath himself and launched upward, using his shield to push the Accursed backward into one of its comrades. He sprinted past the body of the first attacker, pulling his sword free as he did so, making straight for the Accursed that were gathering behind Devin.

The Demon was furiously swinging its sword with both hands into the blade of Devin's axe, forcing the large Paladin to remain on the defensive. Trent could see that each swing drained more and more of Devin's resistance, slowly forcing him to lower his weapon and step backward. The Accursed behind the great Paladin staggered forward with blades raised, ready to overwhelm him from the rear. On the hillside behind them, two Accursed stood loading their crude crossbows. One hand on these creatures was a wood and steel crossbow, while the other was the hook with which they loaded and set the weapon. Trent knew that he would need to deal with them quickly lest their bolts punch through his friend's lowered defenses.

He was seconds from reaching the Accursed that had gathered behind Devin when the Demon took one final, massive swing; this time gripping its weapon with only one hand. Devin was forced backward into the reach of the accursed while the Demon quickly raised its free hand, which had begun to glow with red energy. White hot flames lanced down the creature's arm and directly into Trent. He had only just enough time to throw up his own magical defense before he would have been incinerated. The blue barrier would only be able to hold for a few moments as Trent felt his energy drain, the crackling of the two conflicting magics deafening in his ears.

*I can't keep this up. We are done for.*

Trent's fear turned to anguish when he saw Devin fall to his knees after several blows and bolts found their way past his armor. Blood spurted from his mouth as he gurgled in pain, his eyes already glazing over. The Demon continued its barrage toward Trent while the Accursed raised their blades to strike again, or loaded their crossbows for another barrage. Trent's anguish became a rage, burning hotter than any fire the Demon could throw at him. The smells of rotting flesh were replaced with the smell of warm blood on a cold winter day.

*Not again. Never will I lose a brother again.*

"Arra, Goddess of Light, protect your champions," Trent gasped under the strain of maintaining his magical barrier.

Then suddenly he let loose a roar more bestial than any animal could ever hope to produce. Even the Demon was taken aback by the sound of his fury. A flood of new energy had begun to fill his body, a direct response to his prayer to the goddess. Surely Arra had watched over him, for now her strength was his own. Trent's barrier surged in response, sending out a concussive wave of force that knocked all of his enemies to the ground. Accursed and Demon alike went flying, the rotted bodies of the former breaking on the stray stones upon which they landed. The Demon's blade flew from its hands and clattered away, just out of its grasp.

The newly empowered Paladin charged forward at the fallen Demon, crying out as he did so. He threw his shield to the side as he bounded into the air, red hair flying behind him and blood running down his gauntleted arm. The Demon weakly tried to push itself upward before Trent could reach it, but the monster was too slow.

Realizing its failure to escape, it let out an inhuman hiss just as Trent's sword found its mark in a gap of armor between helm and breastplate. The Demon writhed furiously as Trent shoved the blade deeper into its throat. In one last vain attempt at survival the creature grabbed the Paladin by the neck and tried to choke the life from him. Trent struggled to free himself from the iron grip that stole the air from his lungs and made the bones in his neck strain. Just as quickly as it had arrived, he realized in panic that his newfound strength was failing. Even the gods had their limits with what aid they could give to mortals. Black spots appeared at the edges of Trent's vision.

Then the Demon's attack was halted by a great axe that separated its head from its body. Devin and Trent collapsed at nearly the same moment, lying on the cold earth beside one another.

Trent lay there for a moment, gasping and wheezing as he desperately tried to draw air into his lungs. The black spots dissipated, but a hollow ringing in his ears persisted. When he regained his senses he pushed himself to his hands and knees before rolling his friend onto his stomach so that he could look over the wounds that had been visited upon his back. Most were of no immediate threat to his life, but at least one bolt had gone deep enough to puncture internal organs. Without healing, Devin, already severely weakened from their journey, would surely die. Crying out to Arra to give him one last bit of strength, Trent attempted to heal Devin with what little bit of magic he had left. When no response came from above, Trent knew that what energy he would need to expend would push him to very limits of his own life force.

He had no choice.

The magic poured out of him and into the body of the other Paladin, a cool warmth that left Trent and entered Devin. He could feel through their connection that the wounds within Devin's body were healing to the point where his life was no longer in danger, but no further. Trent pulled the bolts from his friend's back and watched as the wounded flesh glowed a faint blue before knitting itself closed. Pain began to flare up in his own body, the wound on his arm getting worse from the expenditure of energy. Finally, Trent knew that he could do no more, collapsing back onto the ground beside his companion. He had used too much energy during the battle, and now his mind desperately clung to his surroundings as he tried to stay awake. His struggle was soon lost and he closed his eyes. Any further protection that either of them received that day would have to come from the gods.

# CHAPTER 10

As the sun slowly set behind the horizon, a small shadow dropped out of the darkening clouds and descended earthward, staying well out of the last remnants of sunlight. As it swooped in low, a light fog had begun to rise out of the hills and encroach upon the small village nestled between freshly tilled fields. From the air the patchwork landscape was a tapestry of color—lights and darks spotting the valley from the sunset and the upturned earth. The shadowy figure landed in one such field, just out of sight of the torchlights that had begun to flicker into existence as the sun had begun receding from view. The dusk was eerily silent. There were no sounds but that of a cool breeze that carried forth the smell of fresh earth.

The creature folded his black leathery wings against his body and wrapped himself in a worn shawl that had been clutched in his hands. He pulled up the hood to prevent any passerby from seeing his inhuman countenance and alerting the other villagers. He couldn't risk being discovered this early in the night. Once he had found what he was looking for it would make no difference if they knew him or not; by then it would be too late for all of them. The thought brought him great pleasure, and his wicked tongue flashed out of his mouth to lick at where his lips should have been. Death was a clean end compared to the horrors that he visited upon mankind. Human and Paladin alike would fall before his unbridled power. A village this far south would surely have at least three of the big brutes, if not more. That would be just enough to give him the challenge that he had been craving.

*I must enjoy this while it lasts. His plan will not fail. Not tonight.*

The creature became his disguise: his once tall stride was replaced with a lurching hobble, his body bent as if he had been humped by old age. In the darkness he would be mistaken for an old man, barely given a second thought until the chaos had begun. In reality, he was far older than any of them could have imagined, and far more powerful. The Paladins and villagers would be on the lookout for Demons, but he was something else entirely. Long fingers ending in cruel claws clutched tightly at the grey shawl, keeping the small breeze that brought the fog from exposing what lay beneath as he approached the village. The mist signaled his arrival as if it were called upon, a portent for the wicked things to come. If his master had made this occur by some show of divine power, he had said no word. Sometimes everything fell into place on its own accord.

Beneath his feet the upturned earth was soft and inviting, a far cry from the hard stone upon which he regularly walked. Trailing behind him were clawed footprints that belonged to no mortal creature. The neat rows of turnips and other green things were crushed beneath his talons, his focus upon the flickering lights ahead. From this vantage point the buildings of the village jutted up like broken bones before the blood red sky behind them. He pondered this comparison for a brief moment, thinking that it was an image that would be recreated before the night was ended.

The cloaked figure entered the perimeter of the ramshackle houses without being noticed, slipping from shadow to shadow as a snake slithers from stone to stone. Some figures walked about here and there, laughing and talking, unaware of what walked among them.

None that passed the shape of the older man took particular notice of him, most not even bothering to cast a second glance in his direction. He studied each figure intently, looking for the one that would serve his purpose the best.

As the minutes passed on he continued to navigate the streets, slowly working his way from the edges of the village to its center, hoping that some villager would catch his eye before the descending mist forced all of them indoors. At his sides the lights in the houses began to flicker on as candles were lit and the farmers prepared to end the night.

It was then that he saw her.

A young woman crossed the street before him, leisurely making her way home from some errand through the village. He could tell that by human standards she would have been considered beautiful; her red hair was almost the color of flame.

Suddenly she turned and looked back at where he crouched in the shadows of a house, clearly having felt his eyes upon her. Looking chilled, the young woman bundled herself up tighter and began walking faster toward her destination. When she was out of sight the creature looked about to be sure that he couldn't be seen and made his way to where she had been standing, crouching low to gain her scent. Once he had the smell of her in his nostrils he continued to make his way to the center of the village, ignoring the path on which she had gone. Now that he knew her she wouldn't be hard to find; other matters needed seeing to first.

A large building in the center of the village was known to the creature, for within it would surely be the Paladins who guarded the settlement. Once it became visible above the surrounding houses he slowly wheeled his way toward it, taking to the open streets when it was less suspicious to do so. The scent of the woman was lessening, replaced now with the smells of human waste and cooking food. Soon he was in a clearing in the heart of the village, the great Paladin retreat looming before him. There were no lights on inside, but he decided to move in closer to see if he could sense any of his quarry. The side from which he approached gave him access to the adjoining stable in which he smelled several horses.

They could smell him as well.

The sounds of the now restless beasts drifted to his ears, breaking the silence of the street around the building. Without being dealt with, the animals would surely alert someone to his presence. Quickly he moved into the opening of the stable, bringing the nervous whinnies of the horses to a crescendo. In a flash his claws lashed out, tearing throats and splattering gore upon the wooden walls. He moved between each animal in a rush, not giving any of the pitiable beasts the time to react.

In the ensuing silence he stood motionless, listening for sounds of his discovery. The blood that dripped from his fingers joined the pools forming in the muck of the stable floor, disturbed only by the shudders of the dying horses. After several interminable minutes he crawled from the stable closer to the ground, keeping away from the windows of the adjoining house. He couldn't be certain, but the lights from within told him that none of the Paladins were yet inside, and his senses told him the same.

While readjusting his shawl he pulled away from the house and began to move about the streets again, casting about blindly for any sign of his enemies. The fog had by now begun to fully blanket the village, keeping him even more protected than he had been before. The new miasma served to force the villagers back into their homes for an early night, leaving the streets to the hidden intruder. He continued walking about, the scent of the woman returning to him. He decided to deal with her first, rather than wasting his time ferreting out the Paladins in this haze.

Shortly after he made this decision, one of the armored warriors rounded the corner, almost stumbling upon the cloaked figure. The creature was able to pull himself off of the street and into a doorway just in time to avoid detection, choosing instead to study his opponent before striking. He watched the broad figure with a cold indifference; he wore his blonde hair in a braid down his back, a matching beard upon his chin. At his side was a short sword, and upon his back a shield. The creature detached from shadows behind the warrior and paused, the warmth of the horses still upon his fingers.

*I could kill you in a single blow. Rip your head from its shoulders.*

They would all die tonight, in time. The direction of the breeze changed and he picked up her scent again, stronger this time. Allowing the Paladin to continue on unscathed, he made an about-face and followed the smell, weaving between homes while he looked for the one that would stand out to him. His orders had been simple, and he could have carried them out without ever alerting the Paladins to his presence, but even his master knew that he could not be expected to operate in such a fashion. Mindless obedience was for Demons and Accursed, not a creature such as himself. Finally, her scent led him to a small home set slightly apart from the others. He approached the house just as the lights within were blown out, the last candles extinguished until morning.

It was perfect.

Slipping up against the door, he clenched his claws around the edges where there were gaps and forced it open. The splinters rained down on the floor, but no one within stirred. The house reeked of the woman that he hunted, preventing him from following to the exact room in which she slept. Even so, his large eyes were perfectly suited for darkness, and as such he had no trouble finding his way about the small cottage. He saw that there were three rooms attached to the one in which he stood, with minimal furniture blocking his path. Keeping the shawl wrapped tightly around himself, the intruder climbed up the wall onto the ceiling like an insect, finding footholds above with ease. His passage made small scraping sounds that disturbed the silence of the home, but none awoke from their night's rest. He entered the first room still upon the ceiling, finding an older man and woman asleep upon a straw bed.

This was not what he was looking for.

Dropping without a sound he landed upon the unsuspecting couple and in one instant had removed both of their heads from their bodies. Disinterested, he tossed both heads aside and leapt back to the ceiling above, exiting the room and returning to the emptiness beyond. He turned right and entered the next door, quietly pushing it open and making his way within. It was inside this room that he found what he had been searching for. Lying asleep in her bed, undisturbed by the deaths of her parents in the next room, was the young woman, not yet old enough to live on her own.

Once again he released his grip on the ceiling and dropped onto the bed, quickly covering the woman's mouth as he brought his face close to hers. Her eyes flickered open, instantly filling with fear as she tried to recoil from the sight. By now his fangs were fully exposed, a grim smile forming as he noticed that the blood from her parents was smudging across her face. Even muffled, her scream was loud enough to be heard throughout the small house.

He could hear the sounds of footfalls outside the door, and then a boy burst into the room. The lad was some years her junior, and yet he held a large knife aloft, more stupidity than bravery clouding his soft features. The shawled creature lifted his arm in one careless motion, sending a torrent of red flame into the boy, turning most of him to ash in an instant. His cries of pain were quickly drowned out by the crackling sounds of fire as the flames licked hungrily at the surrounding walls.

It was at this moment that the bells in the center of town began to ring, and the sounds of shouts could be heard out on the streets. No doubt someone had discovered the horses and the townsfolk knew that they were not alone. This outcome was inevitable, and, in fact, it was the portion of his plan that the creature looked forward to the most. Once he had secured the woman he would be able to engage in an entirely different kind of hunt. The fire had begun to spread to the other rooms now, the one in which they still sat being nearly engulfed itself. The air was being choked with acrid smoke that obscured even his powerful vision. She was no longer screaming, but the woman still shuddered with silent sobs beneath the iron grip of the creature, her tears mingling with the blood smeared upon her face. The shouts outside moved closer as the townsfolk had begun to notice smoke was now dancing with the fog.

*Now the fun can begin.*

He clutched her tightly against his breast, allowing for the shawl to fall away as he spread his wings and launched into the air, tearing a hole through the thatched roof. They lifted into the sky just above the village, the sounds of screaming beginning to intensify on the ground beneath them as the villagers noticed the unnatural creature above. The robes that he had been wearing underneath the shawl fluttered madly as he flitted about, scanning the ground below. The fog made his attempt at scouting out the Paladins before they found him difficult, an unfortunate effect of the fortuitous weather that he had not foreseen.

He was a moment too slow.

An arrow launched from below punched through his left wing, throwing him off balance and sending him careening toward the earth. He corrected at the last moment, flying through another thatched roof and collapsing onto a table. The woman cried out in pain upon impact, but a quick glance after he regained his footing told him that she was largely unhurt. The air in the house was clear, allowing him a moment of respite from the lack of visibility outside. He scanned his surroundings, seeing that no one was about, the inhabitants most likely having joined with their fellows already. The winged creature pulled the woman close again from where she lay on the floor, bringing her near his face. Outside, the sounds of pursuit had begun to get closer.

"Stay here, or I will find you again," he hissed. "And when I do, you will not die, but you will... suffer."

It wasn't often that he heard his own voice. When he did, it sounded foreign to him, as if he were listening to a long-dead corpse suddenly rasp out a few words. The woman seemed to understand his meaning, or perhaps she was in such shock that she didn't have the strength to try and flee. Instead she simply crawled away from him to the corner, where she shuddered and wept. He was filled with satisfaction again for a brief moment before he quickly exited the house onto the street beyond, still confined to the ground due to his injured wing. It didn't take him more than a moment to heal the small hole, but he decided to stay out of the air where he would be blinded by the smoke and fog again. In the distance he could hear the sounds of men approaching, the deep voices of Paladins ushering them on to find the creature and quickly put an end to him. By now they suspected what he really was, and as such would use the utmost caution, but even that would not be enough.

*What fools.*

In the distance the fog glowed a dull orange; the light from the flames still not enough to break through the barrier that he had brought with him into the village. The air was damp, but now the breeze blew a heat from the flames that lightly clawed at his face. Struck with an idea, he moved several houses away from where he had left the woman and lifted his arms into the air. New fire launched forth, shattering the door off of the nearest house and engulfing the interior of the building in a matter of seconds. The blast had been deafening, drawing the sound of pursuit again in his direction. He faded into the fog and shadows of the houses across the street, watching to his delight as the flames spread to the surrounding homes.

It was then that he finally saw the Paladin who had brought him down with the arrow. A copper-skinned man with a large bow ran into the street in front of him, his white armor blackened by soot. His smoke colored hair was cropped short against his head, revealing a large white scar that ran down the back of his neck. The Paladin had several men at his back, each armed with crude weapons as only farmers could craft them. Field tools had become staves, and wood-cutting axes were in abundance. He barked orders in a gravelly voice as his retinue began to fan out, searching the area for any signs of the creature. Some were sent to the well at the center of town for water. If the fires that the creature had set were ignored, the whole village would burn. One of the men came close to the shadows in which the creature crouched, holding a hoe in front of him in a warding gesture.

His head hit the ground before his body.

The creature raised his arms again and lanced red flame at the Paladin, the warrior only just throwing up his own defenses in time. Those around him were not so fortunate; several of the farmers ran from the attack wreathed in flames while others left no trace but a pile of ash. When the attack ceased, the Paladin loosed several arrows in his direction, each one knocked from the air by another barrage of fire. Once the warrior of Light saw his attack had failed he immediately followed it up with a blast of his own blue energy, searing the air around the beast.

It was then that he laughed.

It was a terrible and inhuman cackle that caused even the Paladin to take a step backward. By then none of the farmers remained on the street, for if any did they surely would have fled in terror at the sound.

In the blink of an eye the creature had traveled the short distance between himself and the Paladin, bringing both of his razor-sharp claws to bear. Both of the warrior's legs were torn clear off, sending his torso falling to the ground in a clatter of armor and blood. His face contorted into a grimace as the red from within his body sprayed out for a few moments before sputtering to a slow trickle, ebbing away with what little was left of his life. Before his eyes had completely glazed over, the creature made sure that he could see his own blood as it was licked free from its claws.

*I hope the others put up more of a fight than this one.*

He was soon in the air again, circling over the rooftops through the thick haze that he had created. From this vantage point those who ran through the streets below him seemed as ants, and he was the bird ready to devour them. Trying to flee would save none of them. Those who were smart would hide in their homes and wait for the madness of this night to end. But it wouldn't.

The center of the village drew his attention and he quickly landed there, chasing or killing off all of those who had come to the well for water. Many of these were women and children, but they all died the same.

Just as the last villager's entrails landed in the reservoir below with a satisfying splash, he turned his attention to the house in which the Paladins resided. Even as he felt his own energy waning he again released a torrent of flame into the building, causing the timber to light and the supports to buckle. In moments the building was collapsing under the weight of the flames, engulfed by a hunger for destruction that matched his own. By now the rest of the village had been thrown into pure chaos, the fog illuminated from multiple sides by a sickly orange light as it swirled and intermixed with the black smoke. Screams of fear and cries of pain split the night, all undercut with prayers to the gods.

*Cry to them. They can do nothing here.*

Two more Paladins suddenly appeared before him, a man and a woman this time. He noted with cold indifference that neither was the blonde man that he had spared earlier.

*So there are four.*

The woman was a head taller than the man, her black hair just a shade darker than her skin. The squat man beside her retained the bulk of most Paladins, but did not have the height. He was bald with features that seemed too large for his face. She lifted her large hammer over her head and charged with the man following close behind, his sword and shield at the ready. He could hear their heartbeats echoing in their breastplates as they stumbled across the open plain between them.

The creature met their assault head on, matching each of their blows with his claws; turning every attack away with shocking ease. These two would be even less of a challenge than the previous Paladin had been, leaving his only hope for a real contest on the fourth. He could feel his energy waning from his constant use of magic, so he decided to deal with these two with his body alone.

That included his fangs.

The male Paladin roared in pain and stumbled backward,

clutching at the side of his head where his ear had been, his blood freely flowing over his gauntlets. The creature thought that he tasted more sweat than was normal as he swallowed the ear and other bits of flesh.

The woman brought her hammer crashing into the back of his leg while these thoughts distracted him, shattering bone and sending him to his knees. Somehow she had caught him unawares and done more harm to him than he had felt in over a hundred years. He caught the hammer by the haft before the next blow could land, yanking the weapon from her grasp and throwing it into the darkness beyond even his vision.

"Luna, give me strength!" she yelled as she slammed a gauntleted fist into his face, shattering one of his fangs and sending him careening back into the dirt. The world spun for a moment, and his thoughts with it. It seemed that he had underestimated them.

By then the male Paladin had returned, the bleeding having stopped due to his healing powers. His face still bore the grimace of a man in extreme pain, but he came on nonetheless. The stench of fear was heavier on him now than it had been, even with the creature wounded and on the ground. Pain often had that effect on mortals.

"Jakob, are you all right?" the woman asked.

"I'm fine," he replied through gritted teeth. "Let's get on with it."

The creature pulled himself up to its knees once again before spreading his wings wide enough to force the two Paladins back. The woman stumbled just out of reach, but the man came on, madly swinging his sword at the outstretched wings. He knew that he had allowed them to gain too much of an advantage, so he would need to end this quickly. The injured monster threw himself onto the man, pinning him to the earth by his shoulders in one fluid motion. He smiled wickedly before sinking his teeth into the throat of the Paladin, just as blue energy knocked him several yards away. The cries of the woman faded as he spun into the darkness before landing on the ground in a broken heap. Small trails of steam rose off his body to join their grander brothers in the sky above the village.

In a few moments he had healed himself, although this left him feeling weaker than he had while the wounds were fresh. His own lust for destruction might have robbed him of the strength that he would need to finish this battle head on. He took to the air again, circling the woman just out of her field of vision, his wingbeats taunting her. Her jet-black hair was plastered to her skin from the sweat of fear; the flames from the nearby buildings seemed closer than they had been before. Tears streamed down her face as she tried to follow his movements, the sword of her fallen comrade clutched before her like a ward. But it was in vain. Even in his weakened state he was too fast, staying ever ahead of any direction that she turned. Finally, she stopped turning and cried out.

"Why?"

"Because I was human once." He whispered it in her ear, just as the blood escaped from her mouth, a single claw protruding from her chest.

He let her fall to the ground, landing close to the body of her friend, their blood mingling in the dirt that thirstily soaked it up. The creature returned to the air, winging his way about the village, scattering denizens on the ground as he flew past. By now the majority of the settlement was in flames, with many of its inhabitants dead or fleeing. Accursed and Demons in the hills were prepared to make sure that the ranks of Darkness swelled and word of what happened here didn't go far. They couldn't have the forces of Illux learning of their plans yet.

He adjusted his course and headed back toward the house where he had left the woman a while before, this time staying higher to avoid being seen by the last Paladin, who was, he knew, still out there somewhere. It was possible that he would have to leave that one to the Demons as well. It was an unfortunate truth, but even his pride couldn't be allowed to get in the way of his master's plan. His energy reserves did have their limits.

He landed in front of the house, which had only just caught fire. The crackling of the wood drowned out any potential screams from within. Quickly entering, he fully expected to see the woman cowering in the same corner where he had left her nearly an hour before. To his shock and dismay, she was nowhere to be found in the house at all. Her scent was apparent all over the room, but the stench of the smoke made it hard to trace her beyond the threshold. Another scent was here as well, but they had both been gone for some time now, most likely soon after he had left her.

*She couldn't possibly be that brave?*

Returning to the air he continued to fly around the village, this time actively looking for any signs of the woman. Now that he was trying to find her the fog and smoke had finally become an irritation, and he had begun to wish that he hadn't played so many games with the Paladins earlier. Without his strength and his quarry, it seemed as if his entire attack had been a failure. Any villager would do for his purpose, but he wanted her.

Realizing that few now remained in the village, he expanded his search to the fields and hills surrounding it, hoping to catch a glimpse of the fleeing woman as she attempted to evade him. Out here the air was cold again, and the smells fresh. Within minutes he had her scent again, and made his way toward the trail she had left behind.

It wasn't long before he found her.

And the last Paladin.

"Gil!" she screamed, noticing the creature as he made his descent toward them.

The blonde Paladin had been carrying her over his shoulder, where she had been resting in a near catatonic state until she had seen their pursuer in the air. The Paladin quickly set the woman down and turned to face the creature, placing himself squarely between them. He landed just opposite the man, eyeing him just as coolly as he had the others. There was no stench of fear on this man, and he held himself like one ready to face death.

"I'll die before you touch her."

The creature simply smiled.

# CHAPTER 11

The yellowed pages of the great tome crackled as Teo carefully turned them. The once crisp paper now felt brittle beneath his fingers. The book that he pored over was at least four generations old, itself being a copy of the original as it had been taken down during the time of the Purge. The thick leather cover was loosely held together with hinges that had nearly rusted apart. The Grey God had entrusted the Balance Monks with the preservation of the history of the Mortal Plane, from chronicling the reigns of the Seraphs to cataloguing each of the Divine Beasts from before they were sealed away. This particular tome was one that Teo disliked reading in such detail, for its content saddened him. It was a historical account of the events leading up to and culminating in the purging of Illux by the Balance Monks some five hundred years before. The relatively clean pages might as well have been drenched in blood for the events of which they spoke.

*The cost of keeping the world in balance is often high. But it must be paid. The alternative is chaos.*

Teo took no joy in the slaughtering of innocents, not even to maintain the delicate balance that his order strove to keep. Even so, neither side of the unending conflict could be allowed to gain dominance over the other, which is exactly what had happened when this account was taken down. Never before nor since had such an unbalance occurred, other than the great sin committed by Lio in the age before the Pact. The Seraph at the time of the Purge, a man named Arendt, had marched into the wilderness farther than any force before him had gone. First his army had swept the width and breadth of the Mortal Plane, from the shores of the sea to the borders of the Great Chasm. When they had rooted out all of their enemies their eyes fell south and their march began. It was at the behest of the Gods of Light that Arendt went forth to end the war once and for all. Before these events, the full ramifications of the Grey God's Pact were not as apparent, and the forces of Light and Darkness knew not the full extent to which the Balance Monks would stir themselves. Prior to this, only small engagements had occurred between the servants of balance and the other two factions.

It was said that Arendt journeyed farther south than any man living, cutting down the forces of Darkness root and stem. None were spared in his wrath, including the Herald of that time. The two had battled in single combat over the remains of the evil one's shattered host before the lesser fighter was cast down. This warpath had continued for several months until Arendt and his most trusted Paladins went ranging alone and found something that troubled him so much that the entire army was marched back to Illux.

Over the following days rumors spread of what he had seen out there, but none could guess at the truth. Those Paladins who went with him were sworn to silence, and took the secrets with them to their graves.

It wasn't long after the army's return that the Balance Monks arrived at the golden gates of the city. The rest of the tale was well known to Teo, and he closed the grim work without seeing it to its end.

The monk had not been reading for pleasure; rather, he found himself carrying out the duty of copying each word from the ancient tome to a newer text so that it might be preserved for the next generation. It was a tedious process, watching one's hand trace the lines that the eye read, but the act of writing the ancient words over again allowed him to focus on a menial task while closing his mind to other thoughts. It was at times like this, however, that he wandered down paths which caused him to question the actions of his forebears and the edicts of his god. He would stop for now, finding that the history he was copying brought him more discomfort than it should have, and as such he needed time to recover himself.

The large candles upon the stone slab over which he labored had begun to finally flicker as he stood up. The air around him had started to get choked with the stench of smoke as they sputtered out. The room in which all of the copying took place was set back in the rear of the great library, well away from any windows that could cause distraction from the outside world. Even though it was midday without, within it was black as any night. The small room was only just large enough for two tables, one of which rarely saw use. Teo carefully gathered up all of the parchment and quills, returning them to the large wooden chest on the back wall before neatly arranging the piles of books that were being copied back upon the tables. He blew out the last of the candles and returned to the light of the library beyond, bringing with him the original work so that it might be returned to its place on the shelf until its copy was finished. He closed the wooden door behind him as he left, its subtle creaking disturbing the silence that had cloaked the room.

This tradition of maintaining the history had begun during the very creation of the Balance Monks, with some even going so far as to claim that the first histories and bestiaries were set down by the Grey God himself before he returned for the last time to the Divine Plane.

Teo's padded feet made no sound as he quietly approached the place from which he had taken the great book. He returned the history to its shelf, nestling it between two other tomes with which he was intimately familiar. The first was relatively newer than the others, having been copied from the original within Teo's lifetime. It chronicled the creation of the world and the wars that followed, ending shortly before the creation of the Pact. The second book, however, was misplaced, being a series of lectures on where the High God had gone once he had left his creation in the care of Ravim. None really knew why the great throne above had been empty for so long, but this book attempted to answer that question.

*I doubt any of us will ever know the truth. He has no need to return to us now.*

Teo took the misplaced work and walked to another shelf, where he put it with similar texts. Scholarly writings such as this did not belong beside the histories.

As he walked about the library he saw the usual assortment of his fellow monks studying within, especially newcomers who still needed to commit the histories with which they were unfamiliar to memory. Hanging from the walls above the small tables where the initiates clustered were beautiful tapestries illustrating the creation of the world and the ascension of Ravim, God of Darkness, to his current position as the Grey God. Another of the woven images depicted a faceless man in robes made of stars. Among his outstretched arms were a variety of worlds, each orbiting their powerful creator. Teo knew this to be an interpretation of creation, based upon the belief that the High God had made other realms beyond the Divine and Mortal Planes. He wondered for a moment, as he looked at the image, just what those worlds could be. At the right hand of the High God were two orbs that glowed brighter than the rest, spinning about one another as if they shared some connection. It was within these spheres that he now walked.

*How important we think ourselves, and yet how small we stand.*

Above the tapestries the ceiling was painted a fading fresco that was made to look as if it were the sky above, with Aenna glowing at its center. Off to the side, the sun was hidden behind wisps of cloud so as to not distract from the window to the Divine. Even in the library the Grey God watched from overhead. Teo supposed that the fresco would need to be repainted sometime soon, a project that he would suggest the next time the monks discussed the state of the Temple. It was through their diligence that they kept this place preserved exactly as the Grey God had created it for them, a task with which he had charged them a thousand years before.

Teo left the library, walking through the halls of the Temple at a leisurely pace, the thoughts of the Purge already dismissed from his mind. He had learned early on not to linger on the unpleasant parts of life, but instead to focus on those that brought calm and peace.

At his first opportunity Teo exited the Temple through a small archway into the warm sun of the outside. The arch was protected by two steel doors that could be secured shut in case of a siege, but at the moment were propped open to allow quick access to the garden pathways beyond. He planned to meditate behind the Temple for a time before it was his turn to go down the mountainside to till the fields. His afternoon shift was still several hours off, and he couldn't make himself labor over the histories any more this day. The smells of wildflowers filled his nostrils as he followed the meandering path to the rear of the Temple where the crook of the mountain pressed against it. The sun was less present here, shadowed by the walls of rock and stone on either side.

His favorite spot was here, a secluded willow tree in the midst of silver and purple flowers. Underneath the tree Rella sat waiting, already deep in meditation. This place had become their common ground as of late, the two monks finding relative peace in each other's presence. Teo liked the way he felt around her, liked the very smell of her body upon the air. He knew that his connection to her somehow involved the violence in both of their previous lives. His life as a bandit had led him to commit evil acts, while she had been the victim of the same kind of evil. Even though it hadn't come from his hand, he had at first felt guilt over what had been done to her, but then he realized that the Grey God had united them for a purpose. Bandit and villager, killer and victim, they both now served a higher cause.

*There is a symmetry in that. Balance.*

The monk quietly approached his companion and sat beside her, trying his best not to disturb her meditation. A cool breeze stirred the limbs of the willow as if to signal his arrival as he lowered himself to the earth beside her. Her eyes never opened, but her breathing changed, a slight recognition of his presence. Teo crossed his legs and closed his eyes as he did multiple times every day, slowly closing his mind off from his environment and bringing himself to a true inner quiet. His breathing slowed, forming a gentle rhythm that he focused on to push all of the other thoughts out. But this time there was something that prevented him from reaching his center in a way that he had not felt for some time. A stray thought had burrowed itself so deeply into his subconscious that he struggled to remove it.

Teo's mind returned again to what he had read earlier about the Purge of Illux.

He had thought that he had moved on from the uneasiness that he had felt previously in the library, but, in reality, all he had succeeded in doing was burying it deeper beneath his thoughts. Now with those cleared away it was brought to the forefront of his perception, a great beast that stood between him and his desire to meditate in peace. His own past life had been spent following the ways of evil; he had killed and robbed and raped all across the wilderness. And yet, now that he had found this place and started his new life, the thought of visiting violence upon the innocent, even to maintain the balance of the world, sickened him. Could he ever truly bring himself to harm another human again, even if his god told him that he must?

Teo grappled with this conflict for some time, never fully gaining the peace that he had sought. Then, after an interminable amount of time seated under the tree, he heard the murmur of alarm coming from the front of the Temple.

Both monks' eyes snapped open as one, not just in response to the noises but also to an innate sense that something was wrong. Rella looked quizzically at Teo, who nodded in response to her silent query. They both stood quickly and made their way toward the front of the Temple. They wasted no time following the garden pathway down each of its lazy detours, instead choosing to cut directly through the flowers in a concerned rush. In the short time that it took them to round the great grey building they were joined by dozens of others who had also dropped what they were doing in response to whatever was happening in the front of the Temple. By now the murmurs of alarm had grown to a tumult, disrupting the usually tranquil ambience of the clearing.

When they made it to the front yard where the combat practice occurred, they found all of their fellow members of the Temple standing together in a cluster looking down the mountainside. Smoke was rising a short distance away, in the area where the monks' fields were located. Already the horizon had begun to get blanketed in a thin haze.

*The crops. What could have sparked a fire?*

All of the monks quickly gathered together to come to a consensus on how to appropriately respond. This was not the time for unplanned reaction, not now that it was possible that lives were at risk. They had no singular leader among them, relying instead on the collective to make any decisions that were not directly made by the Grey God.

"We must gather water to fight the blaze!" one monk called out from within the center of the gathering. "That should be our first priority."

There were murmurs of agreement from all quarters, with some even calling out that they should be moving now. There were several natural springs flowing from the mountain behind the Temple. Water could be gathered from them and put to good use fighting the flames.

"We must wait for word from the Grey God. He will command us as he always has!" another man nearer to Teo and Rella interjected.

"No!" It was Rella who spoke now. "We must act quickly if we are to prevent the fire from spreading. We are servants of Ravim, not his slaves. Our god gave us the capacity to act in his name, not just to wait for his commands."

More dissent filled the ranks as the discussion began to turn into a debate. Some already had begun to sit upon the ground and attempt to meditate in order to contact the Grey God. After a few minutes the discussion died down as a consensus was reached that action needed to be taken immediately.

"We must send some ahead to check on the others down near the fire. We cannot leave our brothers and sisters alone and in danger. Who will volunteer to take up this task while the rest of us gather water?"

Many voices shouted out pledges to volunteer for this assignment, ranging from the experienced to the initiate. Teo saw that the discussion was once again beginning to waste too much time. Time that they didn't have. The monks were beginning to show a lack of discipline that he hadn't realized they had developed. There were too many young faces in the crowd, too many initiates and not enough masters. Changes would need to be made when this fire was dealt with, of that he was sure.

"Rella and I will go!" he shouted, silencing all other voices. Out of the corner of his eye he could see Rella's usually veiled expression change to a slight grin.

The murmuring had stopped at his suggestion, the combat prowess of both being highly respected. There were none who could be said to be better suited to undertake this task. If there was danger to be found, there would be no greater agents of the Grey God to face it. The other monks nodded toward Rella and Teo and moved as one back toward the streams behind the temple. Now that there was no decision to argue over, the discipline that they had lacked moments before had returned. Some vices could never be broken, it seemed.

Rella and Teo both bowed to each other, keeping with the formalities of their order, even in a time of danger such as this. Without another word they turned and began running into the woods that led down the mountain. The path that descended down the slope wound around the contours of the rock, keeping well away from any obstacles. They had no time for this path, choosing instead to take the shortest route possible. Both monks agilely leaped over fallen trunks and ducked under low hanging branches without ever slowing their descent. Grey cloaks flowed behind them like smears of ash in between the green foliage as they ran. The walk from the Temple to the fields would usually take two hours, but at the pace that they traveled it would only take a few minutes.

Teo noticed the dark shapes of fleeing animals at the corners of his vision, most likely running before the blaze that threatened to engulf their homes. It wasn't long before the smoke, the plume of which had grown larger as they descended, began to filter in through the forest and obstruct their vision. The haze and the shade of the trees cast the forest floor into night, blocking out all but the faintest of light. The monks were forced to slow as their lungs were choked with the acrid stench of burning fields. Teo's face curled in disgust as the smell sent a memory of his past life flashing through his mind before he had a chance to turn it away.

*The smell of burning flesh. What has happened here?*

Teo turned and looked at Rella, and saw that her face had also become one of apprehension. He realized that it was possible that she recognized that sickly sweet odor just as he had, or that her body had rejected it all the same. The size of the fire, judging by the amount of smoke, made the chance of it being an accidental brush fire seem small. Fires were not uncommon during the summer months, but they were never this close to the fields, which were usually protected by the water that fed them from farther up the mountain.

Suddenly a host of dark figures were before them, moving through the smoke and trees. Teo quickly grabbed Rella and pulled her to the side, crouching low to avoid being seen. It didn't seem that they had been noticed yet, so the two monks quietly moved perpendicular to the oncoming advance in the hopes that they could get around and behind them. Something told Teo that these were not friends that marched out of the swirling darkness, and he did not want to risk finding out for sure.

The size of the unknown force was greater than they had anticipated, causing them to almost stumble upon its outer flanks. Teo and Rella were forced to find refuge within the confines of a large shrub and sit perfectly still or risk alerting the enemy. Teo was sure that those who passed were in fact enemies once he discerned their identity.

*Accursed. Demons.*

It took several minutes for the seemingly endless marching of Accursed and Demons to pass them by. Teo tried to take a count but failed in the attempt, his eyes watering from being held unblinking so long in the smoke.

Once the forces of Darkness had made their way farther up the incline, the two monks quickly returned to their run down the mountain to see what had become of their fellows. They emerged into a smoky clearing, still ablaze in several places. The main thrust of the flames had begun to move into the trees to the northeast, just opposite of where they had been running. The neatly trimmed rows of once-edible plants had been charred beyond repair. The small breeze that swirled the ashes brought the same sickly sweet smell of burnt flesh to Teo's nostrils. He resisted the urge to retch as he looked over the blackened and defiled bodies that were scattered around the field. Not a single soul had survived the surprise strike.

"We must head them off and warn the others," Rella said quietly. "If they attack without warning, all will be lost."

Teo surveyed the terrible slaughter one last time before lowering himself to the ground and crossing his legs. He looked back up at Rella and spoke to her in almost a whisper, his voice sounding weak even to himself.

"You return to the others. I will follow as quickly as I can," Teo said. "First I must pray to the Grey God; this time we do need his counsel."

She nodded in understanding and darted back into the trees, keeping well away from the direction of the spreading flames.

Teo tried his best to let go of the world around him so that he could better commune with his god. There were now more worldly distractions about him than ever, but his determination would win out this time. Again he controlled his breathing, focusing on the rhythm of his chest rising and falling above all other sensations. Somewhere in the back of his mind he was aware that the trees at the edges of the clearing had begun to catch fire; it wouldn't be long now before more of the forest was alight and the fire completely beyond their control. He must hurry if he didn't want to be cut off from the higher slopes of the mountain.

Teo quieted his mind and reached out to his god just as he had many times in the past. There was no response.

# CHAPTER 12

The loud bubbling of the molten rock outside his window never seemed normal to him. The rivers of fire cut between the small keeps of Infernaak like blood running from an open wound. He would often catch himself staring off, as if in a trance, just listening to the liquid death belch and hiss as it floated past the small opening to the outside world. It was a horrid and evil sound, unlike the whispers of the forest around Ayyslid in every way imaginable. Lio had never truly felt that he was a God of Darkness, only a downcast God of Light. The Fallen One, they called him now, a name that he didn't disdain as much as he should have. He was shunned by his old companions due to his new position, and by his new companions because of the crimes that he had committed against them so long ago. He found some irony in the fact that he had been a God of Darkness far longer than he had ever been a God of Light. Now it was as if he were some kind of abhorrent beast that needed to be shut away so that none could gaze upon him.

*Just like what that bastard did to my Daniel.*

Any thoughts of dead Xyxax brought a fiery anger welling up to the surface, which often resulted in the pulverization of the stones in his walls. There were none living that he hated more than the deceased God of Darkness. If it were possible for Lio to kill him again he would have, a hundred times over, each time savoring the moment more than he had the last. He could no longer stand the emotions and memories that clouded his mind—the hate that he could taste in his mouth. He vented his frustrations on his usual place, an indentation in the wall that had faced his wrath more than once. The stones that he pummeled crumbled and turned to dust that slowly drifted to the floor. Once his rage had abated he examined his now ruined hands as the rivulets of silver blood trickled down his wrists. Within a few minutes the flesh would begin to mend itself as it always did when he was injured. That didn't prevent the scarring, though. His body was covered in such marks, some from himself and some from his enemy.

*It's not the scars that came from him that bring the most pain.*

Lio turned and walked to his small washbasin, which was set into the wall on the far side of his chamber. The basin was the only piece of furniture in the room, besides a lone chair that he rarely rested upon. The water inside the stone bowl was cloudy and had a fetid stink that nearly brought him to retch whenever he smelled it. Still, he washed the blood from his knuckles and cupped the steaming sulfuric liquid in his battered hands in order to wash the soot from his grey face. As he did so his fingers traced the ruinous scar that nearly split his head in two, leaving his left eye a solid white orb. That had been the wound that had nearly cost his life during the battle with his accursed foe. The damage done to his once handsome face reflected the damage that he felt inside. If he had been allowed to remain a God of Light he would have kept the damaged eye hidden by strands of his white hair, but since his condemnation he revealed it proudly, a symbol of the crimes done to him. As it was, he didn't allow any of his sickly yellow mane to obstruct the lifeless orb, nor would he ever. Not even if he were returned to his rightful place.

Once he had finished cleaning his face he pulled on his black armor, removing it from the pile in which it had been discarded. The plate was a dark reflection of what it had once been, now looking closer to the arms worn by Demons than Paladins or Gods. He rarely wore it anymore, choosing instead to wander about the halls of his tower naked, not wishing to defile his skin with any signs of his new position. Today was a special occasion, however, and even in his madness he knew that he would need protection where he was going.

When he was finally finished pulling on the various bits of armor, he strapped his curved blade to his side and exited the small room. He walked through the empty halls and spiraling stairs of his keep, feeling more alone than he ever had since taking residence. The small tower had once belonged to Ravim before he had become the Grey God. He supposed that he was grateful that it wasn't the tower that had belonged to Xyxax. He wouldn't have been able to bear the pain of such an insult. The black and grey stones that made up the tower were all unadorned; small torches provided bastions of light separated by vast gulfs of shadow. As Lio continued down the staircase that led to the ground floor, he began to mutter aloud to himself as he often did.

"They sit in their chambers and mock me. I can feel it. Just as their brother mocked me before he fell. He no longer mocks me, not since I crushed his corpse into the earth."

His bitter laugh rang out through the empty halls.

"Once I am done with this, once the forces of Darkness reign victorious over heaven and earth, then they will no longer mock me. The Divine and Mortal Planes alike will shudder in my presence, as they always should have. But even then I will be just, and they will die just as they should have when I held my rightful place."

He approached the great black door that kept him locked in his self-imposed prison, shut away from the grounds of Infernaak beyond. The ominous barrier was nearly twice his height, a warden made of iron and spikes that guarded the threshold to his fate. He looked it over, taking the moment to give himself the chance to turn around and return up the steps to his chamber. It would be easy. He could continue his life just as it had been, drowning in sorrow and self-pity instead of attempting to retake his rightful place. He squelched the modicum of fear that had sprung into his mind.

This was not his choice; it was his right. There was no other course for him to take.

*This will work. My plan cannot fail.*

"And then I will return to my proper place as a God of Light. The *only* God of Light."

With this final pronouncement he pushed open the monolithic door and stepped out into the dim glow of the molten rock. A wave of heat washed over him, bathing him in smoke and fire. It had been some time since he had felt the heat of Infernaak rather than simply listening to the sounds of the flowing lava. It had been even longer since he had gazed out of Aenna onto the Mortal Plane below. All of his knowledge of events on the Mortal Plane had been through his Herald, the winged messenger who commanded the forces of Darkness. His twisted servitor had followed him loyally and without question, for he too had a thirst for conquest that was no longer shared by his other two masters.

*Vardic and Rhenaris.*

His fellow Gods of Darkness had grown distant to the conflict below as of late. They no longer had the will to see the war to its brutal end. Instead, they preferred to hide away in their towers and completely ignore the movements of their enemies. It was the hearts and minds of bandits and cutthroats that occupied them now, not the blades of Demons. This was the effect that the Grey God had upon them, his reign of fear stemming from the powers that had been bestowed upon him. It was said that he spoke at the High God's command and fought with his arm. And yet he had never truly shown these powers to be anything more than a tale.

*Are his powers truly something to behold? Or is he not still just one of us?*

He had asked himself this question many times since he had become a prisoner in his own walls. At first he had believed that the Grey God held power over all of them, but his opinion had changed. If it hadn't, he would not be attempting this long trek.

The isle that his tower rested upon looked as if it were a small stone when compared to the flowing rivers of liquid flame that surrounded it. The air was dark and choked with smoke and ash, the only illumination coming from the fires below. The harsh rock was barren all the way around the tower except for a single stone bridge that connected it to a larger, central island. Lio crossed this small bridge, feeling slightly uneasy as he looked across the lava to one of the other stone bridges that had crumbled into the fire. Once he was again upon solid ground he walked up to the great onyx bell that was the solitary feature of the central island of Infernaak. The large bell hung from a blackened frame in the center of the island, visible from the windows of each of the three small towers. It was only rung when the usually solitary Gods of Darkness wished to commune and discuss their plans for the world below.

It hadn't been rung in hundreds of years.

The Fallen One reached his hands out and gripped the thick black cord that would call his companions to him. All it would take was a single pull and they would answer his summons, angry and confused as to why they were disturbed. He gripped the rope so hard that it felt as if it burned his hands, the flesh of his palms becoming raw. After several long moments of waiting in anticipation, his better judgment overcame his impulse to slay the remaining two dark gods and he released the cord.

*Not now, not yet.*

He surveyed the five bridges that crossed the molten stone that separated all of the islands from one another. The largest of the bridges connected to the solid land that made up the rest of the Divine Plane away from the heat and the death of Infernaak. The four lesser bridges each connected to an island that housed one of the identical towers in which the Gods of Darkness resided. It was the fourth of these that had partially fallen into the lava some thousand years before. The bridge and the island it had connected to had broken and sank into the fire when Xyxax had been killed. It would not be long before all of the islands were submerged into the lava with their brother.

Without another look back he crossed over the largest bridge to the lands beyond. Once the heat and light of the magma had subsided, Lio found himself treading across the darkest of lands. Perpetual night hung over the plain, the only light coming from the fires behind him and the sun on the distant horizon. It took a few minutes for his eyes to adjust to the darkness, but when they did he could easily make out the various slabs of stone that jutted from the earth like so many knives. The path to the High God's Throne wound through these spires for miles, causing the journey to take him an inordinate amount of time. The forests around Ayyslid teemed with life of all kinds, Divine imitations of what lived on the Mortal Plane below. It was not so with the rocky defiles that led out of Infernaak. Nothing crept through the blackness here except a fallen god.

*The darkness can bring only death. I wish to bring life.*

As he walked he remembered the events that had brought him to this point in his existence, memories that had been so painful and became so twisted in time that he sometimes questioned how real they were. He remembered the rage he had felt when he had seen Daniel transformed into that monstrous shape; mindless, with body beyond repair. His cries of anguish that had echoed across both the Divine and Mortal Planes. The challenge to Xyxax to meet him in battle. The pain as his face was split open and his eye ruined forever. The satisfaction when he smote his enemy deep into the earth, never again to rise.

And the shame as his victory was turned to defeat as he was cast down to the ranks of the Gods of Darkness, becoming that which he had hated above all other things. It was then that he had truly known rage and despair. What he had felt at the loss of Daniel was nothing to what he was forced to endure after.

The High God had pronounced judgment upon him for killing Xyxax, but Lio had only seen it as the fulfillment of the original charge that he had been given. Goodness and light could only triumph if darkness were obliterated completely, something that could never be achieved under the watchful gaze of the Grey God. He had decided upon his plan to right these wrongs years before, allowing all of the necessary pieces to fall into place. Once Vardic and Rhenaris had begun to show less of an interest in the workings of the Mortal Plane, Lio had seen his chance. Taking it upon himself to bring the Herald completely under his sway, he began to act. It hadn't taken much for the winged messenger of the gods to agree fully to his plans, and the two of them had put them into motion some twenty years before.

Together they had decided that in order to most effectively destabilize the Light they must remove the current Seraph, allowing for a less experienced commander to take his place. Lio had allowed for the Herald to come up with the specifics of the plan, relying on the natural wickedness of the lesser being's mind to form the strategy. The most powerful Demons were assembled and tasked with infiltrating Illux and killing the man at all costs. They knew that if they failed, the likelihood of getting another chance was very slim.

Their attack succeeded, leaving the forces of Light in disarray and forcing an inexperienced woman to take the fallen warrior's place. She was even less qualified than Lio could have hoped, and as such she did not send her armies into the wilderness as her predecessor had. She merely focused on building up the defense of her city after the attack showed how vulnerable they really were. This allowed for the Herald to begin to play the slow game of building up their forces, just out of range of the small missions that the Seraph sent her Paladins on. Now they prepared the next phase of their plan, which would quickly reignite the war and ensure his own victory.

He came finally to the smooth white stone that marked the center of the Divine Plane. He paused again for a moment, staring down at the unblemished surface that had not seen the footfalls of evil for longer than he could remember. The center of the Divine Plane was supposed to be a neutral place, but Lio still felt that if any Gods of Darkness walked upon it they would surely defile it. It was then that he remembered that one such god still resided here, polluting the sacred stones with his presence. This thought was the final urging that he needed to continue forward.

As soon as he stepped foot upon the polished surface, the night receded and he was bathed in a brilliant light that he had not felt for many years. He resisted the urge to stop and drink it in, choosing instead to push forward now that he was so close. A small silver tear of blood ran from his dead eye as he took in the beauty of it all. In the distance he could see his destination: the High God's Throne. The empty seat would not sit vacant for much longer, of that he was certain.

Once he arrived at the giant stone chair, Lio stopped short and looked over the silver surface of the liquid in the nearby Basin. He gently brushed his fingers over the Divine Blood, shattering the serene calm that it bore. The power that he felt as he did so was exhilarating. Here was the life force that had created all things, the same blood that flowed in his veins. And it was his to control. He gripped the edges of the Basin and gazed out through Aenna at the different events that were unfolding due to his machinations. His army gathered below the surface of the blood in a large valley near the Great Chasm. The site of his fall would also be the site of his rise. The size and ferocity of his followers brought a smile to his wicked lips. This army did not compare to the ones he commanded as a God of Light, but it would surely serve its purpose. The image shimmered and changed with his thoughts, now showing him the force that his Herald had sent to attack the Grey Temple. Within minutes they would begin their slaughter of the unsuspecting monks, removing the last obstruction in his path. Finally he turned his gaze to the Herald himself, waiting patiently for the signal to begin his task. Once he did, there would be no further resistance to their plans.

*All of my pieces are in place. Now I simply have to make my first move. Then I can play this game the way it was meant to be played.*

His own thoughts brought him momentary pause. His wicked side had taken over for a few moments, and now he had to control himself again. This was no game that he played, but an attempt to correct the mistakes of the past and restore order to the gods. If he forgot that, then he would surely die in the attempt. There was still no guarantee that his plan would work, and he must take the utmost caution. He would soon have everything as it once was when he was given his initial charge by the High God.

Lio turned from the Basin and walked toward the cluster of pillars behind the High God's Throne. They were located some distance off, far enough that it was likely that Ravim did not yet notice Lio's presence while he sat in meditation. As he approached, he looked upon the great white stones that rose upward to meet the sky in a perfect circle, evenly spaced with only enough room for a single being to walk through. The columns had been formed of the very stone on which he stood, perfectly smooth all the way around with no marks of craftsmanship upon them. The only seam that was visible was located where they sat upon the earth. At their top the pillars were completely flat, decorated with no ornamentation of any kind. The clean construction of this shrine seemed foreign to him, and made his stomach churn with uneasiness. Taking a deep breath, the Fallen One stepped between the pillars, surely alerting the other to his presence.

The Grey God sat in silent meditation, cross-legged upon the ground with his back to the direction that Lio had entered from. His skin was the same white color as the stone on which he sat, a silent statue carved from rock and adorned in cloth robes as grey as any thunder cloud. Lying across his lap was a wooden staff that looked to have been taken from one of the branches of Ayyslid, no doubt a gift from the sycophantic Gods of Light. He wore no hair upon his head, and Lio knew from memory that his face was hard and cruel. The Fallen One stepped across the polished stone with the reverence that was demanded of such a setting, each footfall feeling to him like a violation of the sacred space. Even the Fallen One could not deny that this place and its resident demanded his respect once he crossed the threshold. When he was halfway between the outer ring and the god at its center he dropped to one knee and waited for the other to acknowledge him.

"Why have you come to disturb my meditation?" the Grey God thundered, his voice echoing off every pillar.

The Fallen One faltered, his words tumbling out. "I have come to talk with you. I have no one else with whom to share my thoughts."

"And why do you think I would wish to converse?"

"Because you are like me."

This gave the Grey God pause. The pronouncement sounded ludicrous, even to Lio's ears. Just when it seemed that Ravim was at a total loss for words he finally spoke again.

"How is it that we could possibly be seen as alike?"

"Neither of us is what he once was, each of us having been charged with a different task than the one originally bestowed upon us by the High God when he created all things. We have no one else."

"I need no one else. You were cast down for disrupting the balance of creation, I was raised up to correct it," Ravim responded in a biting tone.

Lio clenched his fist for a moment, his nails biting into his palm. He seethed at the disdain he was being shown. This was not the response that he had anticipated.

"You are just like all of the others. I am damned for my actions, which only fulfilled the charge I was given by the High God!"

The Fallen One found himself standing now, his rage boiling over to his physical actions. He was losing what little control that he had left. He knew that he must keep himself in check lest the other fear what was coming next.

"You allowed your anger to take control of you, just as you are allowing it to do now. Killing Xyxax was not a part of your charge, giving mankind the choice between good and evil was. And to think that you lost sight of this over love for a mortal."

"You have no right to judge me!" His screams began to make his voice hoarse. "None of you do. You have no right to bring up my Daniel! Why is it wrong for a god to love a mortal? Where is the sin in that?"

"It clouded your judgment and made you weak. We were never supposed to love them, only to guide them."

"You speak as though you have always served balance. You act as though you never tortured and killed mortal and god alike!"

"Calm yourself or I will remove you." The Grey God sounded even more commanding than he had before.

"You cannot command me. I do not fear you like the others do." The rage in Lio's voice had begun to subside as he regained control again.

"Why have you come here, Lio? Truly?"

"I simply came to discuss the irony of the High God's absence. I assumed that you were the only god wise enough to understand."

"Irony?" Confusion now crept into his voice.

The sound of unsheathed steel shattered the silence that followed.

"We all saw it as the reason that we should be kept in line, chained to this Pact of yours," the Fallen One answered coolly. "We were afraid to ever make any moves against each other, afraid to disappoint the High God again. But what we never realized is that his absence is actually our greatest freedom. He has no power here now."

The Fallen One lunged at the Grey God, swinging his sword in a cruel arc meant to sever the head from the shoulders. The kneeling deity spun away from the attack, swinging his staff behind him to deflect the blade downward from his head. Lio could hear the sound of the air moving out of the way of their two strikes, twin blows that would shake the very foundations of the Divine Plane. The Grey God had been a moment too slow in his response; a small stream of silver blood trickled down his lower side where the point of Lio's blade had bit him. The wounded god turned himself sideways and leveled his staff directly with the Fallen One's face. His calm features had become distorted with rage, making him look as he had when he was a God of Darkness.

"You fool! I am the High God's chosen! You know that you cannot walk away from this!" His eyes never left the Fallen One.

"I win no matter the outcome, Ravim. If I die, then not only do I get the satisfaction of knowing that I made you upset your precious balance, but then I also know that you will be forced to kill one of my old companions to regain it."

*Arra, the one who cared for me most. Let it be her that he kills, for she betrayed me first.*

"But if I kill you, then nothing will stand in my way of destroying the pantheon of Light."

The look of anger on the Grey God's face was briefly replaced by fear. The ramifications of Lio's words finally made him realize the trap that he had fallen into. After a moment, the fear was replaced by the calm that he regularly bore.

Then he struck.

Ravim lunged forward, attacking Lio with a flurry of strikes, each deftly blocked by Lio's blade. The Fallen One rested the back of the steel against his free hand as he tried to shield himself from the onslaught. Each time sword and staff connected it shook him to his bones, and made him lose some of his concentration. For a moment he feared that he had been wrong, that Ravim was more powerful than he and this entire plan was for naught. This thought enraged him, giving him the strength to stop defending and take the attack to his foe, forcing Ravim to block and parry each new strike. It was just when he thought that his ferocity would finally win out that his enemy tried something new.

The Grey God sprung into the air, flying toward the outer ring of pillars well away from his enemy. Lio watched in amazement as Ravim began to run sideways along the stone that encircled his shrine. His movements became faster and faster, making it almost impossible for the Fallen One to follow him. The air began to spin in response to this action, forming a small whirlwind that whined in his ears. The grey blur working its way around the pillars finally became clear again as Ravim came flying toward Lio, landing a solid strike against his head and sending him stumbling dumbly to the ground. Silver blood trickled out of the small gash in his temple, leaving him slightly dazed as it pooled on the stone.

"You forget yourself, *Fallen One*," the triumphant god spat, standing over his adversary. "I was gifted more power than the rest of you in order to maintain balance. I enact the High God's will and fight with his strength."

"It is you who forgets," Lio muttered, just above a whisper. "I am the only one who has killed another god."

The Fallen One swung his sword at the legs of his attacker, causing Ravim to jump into the air, again bringing his staff downward in a counterattack. This was just as Lio had hoped. Before the other was even fully off the ground, he was rolling out of the way and to his feet. The wooden staff struck empty stone where he had been lying only moments before, sending a flurry of rocks into the sky. Lio's sword flashed through the air, spraying silver blood along the pillars. The Grey God stumbled backward, clutching at the stump of what had once been his outstretched arm. Shock played across his face as he backed into one of his columns and slid downward.

"I was never as weak as I made myself seem, nor were you as strong," Lio cooed, almost sounding caring as he stepped closer to the dying god. "Xyxax and I fought for three days on the Mortal Plane. And yet you only last for three minutes."

The Grey God simply looked at him, confused. His mouth moved without forming any words before he was able to mumble, almost to himself. "My monks, they cry out to me. I can hear their pleas."

"They are all dying," Lio said as he crouched down to eye level. "I commanded the attack to begin just minutes ago."

"Why? Why have you done this to me?"

"Because," the Fallen One leaned in close so that Ravim was forced to look directly into his dead and good eye alike. "No matter what title you decided to call yourself, you have always been a God of Darkness, just as I have only truly ever been a God of Light. It is the duty of the light to dispel the darkness, and that is what I have always done."

The Fallen One placed his hand atop the head of his defeated adversary and squeezed hard, causing silver pools to form in the dimples made by his fingers. The other cried out in agonizing pain, right up until his head was cut from his body, covering Lio in a spray of the silver liquid. He licked it off of his lips and wiped the rest on his hand. Instantly there was a shift in the Divine Plane. It was as if his surroundings had gotten slightly dimmer and his eyes had lost focus. He stood, not at all alarmed, as he knew that he would be seeing this phenomenon several more times in the coming days.

*The others will all know that something has happened. Now that I have their attention, it is time that I finally converse with my new companions.*

Sheathing his sword and carrying the severed head of the Grey God, the Fallen One made his way back toward the molten rivers of Infernaak.

# CHAPTER 13

On the Mortal Plane, Aenna, opening to the world above, dimmed in response to the Grey God's death. It was an almost imperceptible change that few would directly notice, and those that did would simply think that they had imagined it. This was not so for the small party of dark figures looking up to the sky with watchful patience. The Herald of the Fallen One was looking for just such a change in the heavens above, a sign that it was time to begin. Aenna had faded just as the Fallen One said it would, the opening reflecting the state of the Divine Plane above. The creature's face split wide in a grim smile, his razor teeth glinting in the afternoon sun. Everything was falling into place just as they had planned.

The Herald turned and nodded to the seven Demons standing behind him. They silently responded by dragging the small screaming woman over. Her face was mottled with cuts and bruises from her capture at his hands some days before. She had remained in a mostly catatonic state after the Herald had dealt with her final Paladin protector, but it was clear that the frightened creature knew that her fate was about to change yet again at the hands of her captors. He could still make out the curves of her body underneath her night clothes. In another life this would have stirred in him some kind of physical response, but he had been far beyond that for several hundred years. Her scent wafted up to his nostrils, reminding him of why he had been drawn to her in the first place. Now the lovely smell was mingled with that of fear and excrement, but it still made him hunger for her.

His fascination with humans had existed as long as he could remember, their delicate little lives giving him the utmost joy to snuff out in an instant. As for himself, he could not even remember being an Accursed, let alone a mortal man. He knew that he had been one once, perhaps hundreds of years before darkness took hold over him. Perhaps it was possible that he was one of the first, although this seemed to him to be unlikely. His memories only went back so far as to when he was a Demon, and even then a hazy pall hung over everything that had happened to him before his ascension to the rank of Herald. He had even named himself since then, although he had mentioned it aloud to no one, not even his god. It seemed as if being the dark counterpart to the Seraph was the role that he was meant to play from the moment that the High God created his spark, if such a thing even truly existed. The creature was vaguely aware that there had been hundreds of Heralds once, before the Pact when the gods walked the Mortal Plane and the Divine Beasts were not trapped within their seals. Since that time there had been just dozens of the winged creatures, an unbroken line of servants to the Gods of Darkness, each taking over for the last when they were killed in battle. And yet this was all so long ago that he paid it no heed; all that mattered to him now was his duty to the Fallen One.

They stood at the edge of a large flattened circle in a rocky outcropping. The clearing was several hundred feet across, and held not a stray stone upon it, a stark contrast from the uneven wilderness around it. He gripped the girl with one black claw and began to drag her to the center of the site, barely taking notice of the blood that flowed from where he had punctured her. She screamed and beat her hands against his body, the most resistance she had shown since he had killed her brother before her eyes. Underneath his tattered red robes and oily skin was taut muscle, preventing her feeble attempts at causing him harm or even drawing his notice.

Finally they reached the center of the circle, where he lifted her into the air like some doll to fully look her over. Her crying became louder shrieks now, which grated upon his ears. No doubt she found his appearance abhorrent, for his resemblance to man now only existed in his vague outline, and certainly not in his altogether reptilian face. His skin was an unnatural shade, as if he were a hole in the world that no light could penetrate. Below the wicked horns that sprouted downward from his temples were his large milky white eyes, each slit with a snake-like pupil. No, the resemblance to man was only in general description, at best.

"Shh," he rasped to her, making a weak attempt at comfort. "I will not harm you. You are only needed for a few more minutes to aid my master in something. You won't run, will you?"

They both knew that he was lying, but he had hoped that what she had witnessed in the village would be enough to keep her obedient for just a few minutes more. She failed to respond, but instead began to sob and make irritating gurgling noises. The tears running down her face mingled with the mucus running out of her nose to form a torrent that streamed down her neck. The look in her eyes was such a wild fear that he knew she would surely run as soon as he lowered her to the ground, and he couldn't have that.

Pulling her close he whispered to her one last time, as if by some compulsion. "My name is Enoc."

The Herald threw the girl to the ground with such a force that he heard the sounds of her legs breaking in a satisfying crunch. Her sobbing intensified, and she began to shudder uncontrollably from where she lay, both her clothing and the ground turning red with her blood. His favorite smell now mingled with her other scent, but it wasn't enough to make him wish to withstand her pitiful sounds any longer. The Herald spread his great leathery wings and flew back to the side of his Demons, removing himself from the annoyance of the sounds that the woman was making.

"Begin," he commanded.

They did so, silently.

Demons retained the power of speech, and yet perhaps their greatest trait was that they often refrained from using it. The Herald could only remember that his predecessor ruled through an absolute fear that he had instilled in his Demon commanders. This was a method of leadership that he had emulated early on once he had ascended to his current role. Accursed were mindless, doing nothing at all when not following orders. The only sensations that they knew where based upon pain. Demons, on the other hand, were possessed of a sharp cunning that often made them unpredictable. They did as they were told because they followed strength, not because they had no other choice. It was for this reason that the seven he had chosen for this crucial mission were his most trusted commanders, the very same group who had slain the last Seraph twenty years before. They walked toward the girl, spreading out into a large circle as they approached. From this vantage point she looked like a small child, not the grown woman that she nearly was.

*Soon all will be as he foretold. He will rule the Divine Plane while I will rule here, a god among the mortals.*

The Herald surveyed the area within which the ritual was about to take place. They were deep within the wilderness, not far from where his army gathered near the Great Chasm. This flat circle was one of many such sites, placed by the Grey God in a time long before the Herald could even contemplate. Its surface was completely smooth, somehow having remained unmarred in the intervening years since its creation. What little life existed this far to the west stayed clear of this place, for it gave off an unnatural aura. The true purpose of these circles was lost to all but the gods and the few that they deemed worthy of the knowledge.

That would change in the next few moments.

The Fallen One had spoken to the Herald of these sites early on in their partnership, using the knowledge of their power to tempt him into action.

*The seals.*

The circle of Demons finally closed in on the sobbing lump of a girl and raised their crooked blades. Weakly she lifted one of her arms to shield herself from their attack. It was in vain. The blades came down savagely upon her again and again, reducing what was once a woman into a red mess of torn clothes and loose flesh upon the ground. Even from this distance he could see that the Demons were now covered in her blood, the bulk of which had fountained into the air. The sickening sight would have driven any human mad, but it merely brought a cold satisfaction to the Herald. His bright red tongue flicked across his teeth as he watched, thinking to himself that her scent would never be the same. When there was nothing left of her but a scarlet lump that no passerby would ever know was once human, the Demons stopped their brutal assault. The armored figures turned in unison, each heading in a separate direction away from the body, the blood of which was no doubt already seeping into the earth. Once they reached the outer edges of the great circle they planted their blades into the ground in a perfect ring, evenly spaced about the clearing. Finishing that, the Demons left the newly bound seal and walked back to a safe range as the Herald had made clear to them earlier.

*What a pleasing sight this will be.*

He launched himself high into the air, only opening his wings when he felt the pull of the ground finally take sway over the momentum of his jump. Calmly he glided to the center of the great circle, only stopping when the distant red smear was directly below him. These seals had been made with the power of Divine Blood, but it was mortal blood that would break them. The Grey God had thought that in this way none of his fellows could circumvent his power. Not that it mattered while he lived in any case. But he was no longer living, and his power would already be seeping from the world.

The Herald closed his eyes as he filled himself with power fed directly to him from his god.

It had been a pleasure serving the Fallen One alone. Vardic and Rhenaris had long ago ceased communications with their servant, leaving him to oversee the forces of Darkness by himself. In the beginning he didn't mind the freedom that he had been given, choosing to raid villages and attack supply trains at his leisure. His joy came from the little pains that he was able to inflict on the weak humans who lived outside of their precious city. Soon he began to feel an emptiness in his existence, however. An emptiness that was quickly replaced with fear. In those days the forces of Light would march out from Illux and hunt down his troops, leading him to think that he had been forsaken by his gods to face the agony of defeat and the nothingness that would come after. But then a voice had spoken to him in the blackness of his mind, and it had promised him that the war between the Light and the Darkness would soon be over. All that he needed to do was serve, and one day he would rule. Ever since he had first heard that voice he had been filled with a feeling that could almost have been called joy.

The Herald focused the energy that filled his body down into his large claws; they crackled with red flame at his command. It was then as if all of the light were being drained from the sky, leaving everything in darkness except the twin red suns that floated just above the circle. The feeling of power that washed over him was invigorating, the Fallen One feeding him more energy than his own small portion of Divine Blood would naturally allow. It was a glorious feeling, and he knew that if he weren't careful he could be lost to it. Then a crack of thunder shook the countryside as the red flames exploded from his claws into all seven of the swords, setting them ablaze with a scarlet radiance. The light continued to leave his arms and pulse into the blades, a torrent of fire that lived at his command. Over the sounds of the humming energy, several loud cracks could be heard as the ground shook and split in the heart of the circle. Once the earth began to tear asunder he released the last of the flames, light returning to the area around him. First the cracks shot outward from the swords, converging under the remains of the girl. After a few moments they quickly spread over the seal in all directions until its surface was so thoroughly marred that it resembled the shell of a broken egg. The Herald returned to the earth some distance away from the circle just as the ground gave way and collapsed in on itself, falling into blackness. Smoke and dust rose out of the hole, blocking out the sun and Aenna both, in a dusty haze.

"Rise Akklor the Unbidden, you are no longer chained!" he cried out, his voice echoing into the depths of the chasm.

A deathly silence hung over the land, as if the entire Mortal Plane held its breath to see what would rise from within. The Herald knew not what to expect, only having received details on the power of that which he summoned, not the physical characteristics. Then the silence was broken by a loud scraping sound, followed by the beating of two great, leathery wings. A titanic shadow rose from within the chasm and launched itself high into the air, blotting out what light remained in the sky from the rolling dust and smoke. The shadow let out a roar that split the heavens and could be heard for miles around as a crack of thunder.

The Herald finally was able to take it in as his eyes adjusted to the darkness that it had caused. It was a wretched thing, covered in hair and scales both, a remnant of the world from before the Pact. Surely this would be a weapon that the Light would never see coming.

"Get word to the others that the time has come," he said to the Demons at his back. "Raid the villages, capture as many as you can. Once more of the seals are broken the war can truly begin."

He would again gather the next victim himself, for there was another target that needed the special attention that only a creature such as this could provide, and it needed it soon. He could not wait for the Demons to return from the villages, if they returned at all. Now that Ravim was dead and Aenna faded, their plan would be in the open. It would not take long for the forces of Light to muster themselves and prepare for a siege on their city. While contemplating the implications of what he had just unleashed, the Herald took to the air again and leveled himself with the colossal beast.

"Akklor, I know that you thirst for the destruction that has been kept from you for the last thousand years, but you must wait until more of your brothers are free before you make your presence known. I promise you that once our army strikes the walls of Illux, you will have your fill of Paladin blood."

The creature known as Akklor the Unbidden opened its gaping maw and screeched again, this time even louder than the last. The Herald had been told by his master that these creatures were possessed of great intelligence and the power of speech, yet this thing said nothing. For several moments he hung in the air, waiting for some kind of response. After a time, he began to fear that the Fallen One had erred in commanding him to awaken this one first of its brethren. Akklor was not said to be one to favor the service of the Fallen One of all the Gods of Darkness, for it was he who had killed its true master in the days before the Pact. It had only been chosen first because of its unmatched ferocity in battle. Finally it spoke, answering the Herald's anticipation.

"For too long have I slumbered beneath the earth, trodden over by both man and beast. Yet still you bid me wait." Its voice was thunderous, as if a very force of nature spoke rather than a winged caricature of life. "You who are but an insect before my eminence. I was first of the servants to great Xyxax."

"Your god bids you wait," the Herald said, and with that pronouncement he pointed one clawed finger at Aenna above. This was the moment that would decide his fate. Hopefully his master had been right.

He sensed the hesitation in the great beast as it hung in the air, beating its massive wings with such force that the Demons below struggled to stand. The creature could clearly tell which of the Gods of Darkness now commanded it; indeed, his master most likely spoke to it even now. Its imprisonment had happened shortly after the God of Light had been cast down, but even then Akklor had witnessed the death of its master by the Fallen One's hand. There was no doubt that it was not yet sure that it should be commanded by a god such as this, a god who had, not so long ago by its reckoning, been a foe rather than an ally. Finally it nodded its great head in submission.

"Go with these Demons to the place where our army gathers and wait," the Herald said. "I will return to you shortly. The last servants of our enemy that chained you require the attention of one of your brethren. Once they have been seen to, we will commence our attack on the City of Light."

"As the Gods of Darkness command."

The great winged beast lowered itself to the ground, allowing all seven of the Demons to climb upon its large back once they had retrieved their blades from the edges of its prison. They were able to grab hold of large tufts of hair and hang in place as it returned to the air. Within moments Akklor and its new passengers were headed in the direction of the Great Chasm and the army that waited nearby.

Without wasting any further time, the Herald followed suit and disappeared into the distance, leaving the gaping hole behind him. He knew of at least three more such sites, and was sure that his god would reveal the location of all of them to him in time. A feeling of dissatisfaction washed over him for a brief moment as he realized that he would no longer be the only servant of the Gods of Darkness with Divine Blood in his veins. He pushed this feeling away almost as quickly as it had arrived, remembering that he alone still held the ear of the gods.

*No, not the gods. The Fallen One alone. My master was correct; the seals are failing.*

# CHAPTER 14

When it happened, the change had been almost imperceptible, and yet Arra had known at once that something was wrong. The forest around her, though always ephemeral, had faded slightly, losing some of the luster that it had known just moments before. The wildlife in the area had gone silent, no doubt frightened by the portentous change as well. This had only happened one other time in all of existence, and it had happened when a god had been killed. There was no denying that such a tragedy had happened once more. The very existence of this realm was tied to the lives of its primary denizens; if there were no gods, there would be no Divine Plane.

At first she had simply stood in place, shocked at what this could mean.

*Who could it have been? Which of the other gods has died this day?*

The death of a god saddened her even more than the death of one of her beloved mortals. When a mortal died it was said that they would return to the High God, their spark journeying to the Astral Plane beyond the realms of creation. A god had no such soul, only blood. And once blood was spilled, it could not be saved.

Her first thought was that perhaps something had happened to either Samson or Luna, reducing the strength of the Light yet again. It was possible that her earlier uneasiness had been correct, and that the Gods of Darkness had launched some kind of surprise attack against them. That would explain what her Paladins had found in the wilderness. Arra's mind raced at the implications of what this could mean. Any death would have to be answered by Ravim. The Grey God would once again find himself embroiled in their war. He would have to right the scales and kill another god to answer the death of the first.

*That would make three of us that have been killed since the start. He will never forgive us now.*

She knew that she must return to Ayyslid, as much as she wished not to. Arra had to ascertain whether or not something had happened to Samson or Luna. As much as she loathed them, she couldn't hide in the forest while their enemies brought death to their door. She had loved them once, before time and the ways of war made their differences more apparent. Even so they fought for a common cause, and she would answer blood with blood if she had to, as much as it pained her. Instinctively she reached for her greatsword, a motion that gave her pause. It would feel good to let it bite into the flesh of her enemies again; to cut down the wicked and bring her righteous fury to bear. But that was another time. And those were the thoughts that had brought Lio so low.

As she walked through the towering trees her mind wandered back to the beginning of all things, long before the events that now shaped the world had even been considered. Her eyes had opened upon a paradise, inhabited first by mortals of all kinds. The men and women before her had come in all colors, a tapestry of human life. She had known at once that she loved all of them before she even knew why. The High God had been standing before them in his radiance, and he had made her cause for existence clear. And so she had made herself into a champion of justice, a Goddess of Light.

But soon darkness had crept into the souls of men, brought forth by her enemies who had cowered in the wilderness just beyond the paradise. It had not been long before war broke out between the two factions, and since that moment it had never stopped. In those early years the gods still walked the Mortal Plane, fighting alongside their servants in glorious combat that tore the realm asunder. Lio had been her greatest friend then, his love for her second only to his love for Daniel, favored son of the Seraphs.

*Daniel. I loved him too, in my way. He deserved a better end.*

It was Xyxax who had shattered their happiness. Xyxax who had brought this madness upon them. But she knew that that wasn't the whole truth. Lio had made a promise to the High God, a sworn charge that they had all taken up. They were to give mankind the choice between good or evil, not to destroy one another in anger. They were to lead by example, not rule through their great power. What Xyxax had done to Daniel was monstrous, but the reckoning that Lio brought upon him was born not of justice but of hatred. His choices made him an outcast not just among the Gods of Light but the Gods of Darkness as well. Even she couldn't stand to look upon her greatest friend once he had found himself cast down. She hated herself for that, even now. Arra imagined that his new companions were no better, showing him even more scorn than the Gods of Light had.

*What if it is Lio who has been slain? His crimes finally being answered by Vardic and Rhenaris?*

It was not at all unlikely. Xyxax had been the greatest of their number, a natural leader to the others just as Lio had been. Losing him had probably been just as painful to them as losing Lio had been for her. The thought of him dying even now brought her more pain than she would have thought possible. The god she had loved and called friend had died the day he cast Xyxax into the earth. What remained was nothing more than a shell wearing his face, and yet she still couldn't bring herself to fully abandon him to her memory. There had to be a part of what he once was in there somewhere. Unlike the end that mortals faced, the death of a god was a true death, and she could wish that upon no other. If Lio had truly met the same fate that he had bestowed upon Xyxax then she would find no joy in his passing.

Her thoughts were interrupted by a deep and guttural growl from within the growth behind her. The sound cut through the silence of the wood, reminding her that she walked through a living forest that had only recently gone silent. The sound was meant to alert her to the other's presence, not to intimidate her or warn her away. Smiling, Arra turned to find her only remaining companion, Divinity, stalking out of the underbrush of the trees. She was a great white cat, covered in a thick fir that was soft to the touch. Black stripes adorned her body, allowing her to better blend in with the shadows and bands of light that cut through the trees. The tigress was just one of the many animals that were native to the Divine Plane, created to mimic the paradise below. She had been a near constant companion to Arra ever since the two stumbled upon each other during one of Arra's many walks through the forest. How long ago that actually was she could not remember. Divinity was not a flesh and blood creature like those found on the Mortal Plane, nor was she wholly Divine like Arra herself. The native creatures of the Divine Plane were something in between, the full details of which were known only to the High God.

The great cat sauntered up to Arra and rubbed her head upon the goddess' hand, licking gently at her fingers. The ticklish sensation that Arra felt upon her fingertips was one that she never tired of, even when in the foulest of moods. At moments like this Divinity seemed a docile friend, and not the fearsome beast that she appeared. Yet Arra knew that Divinity was a force to be reckoned with if threatened, even though she didn't actually hunt to survive as mortal animals did. The creatures of the Divine Plane were made from the same material as the trees and the earth and the sky. Their life was connected to the gods just as the realm was.

Divinity often prowled through the forest alone for days at a time before returning to Arra's side. Where she went when she was alone Arra could only guess, but she knew better than to follow her companion when she didn't wish to be followed. After petting the large cat, Arra studied her for several long moments, noticing a general tension in her frame that wasn't normally there. Even though she seemed relaxed around the goddess, the hackles on her shoulders and back were pricked up ever so slightly. She could sense the changes in her home just as Arra had, and she knew that something very wrong had happened. The goddess suspected that every living creature on the Divine Plane felt the passing of a god even more deeply than she would, for that meant part of them had died as well.

Arra stood from the slight crouch that she had placed herself in and resumed her walk toward Ayyslid, the white tiger following close behind. The soft padding of Divinity's feet was all but drowned out by Arra's own steps. In comparison she felt as if she were crashing through the underbrush like some great oaf, making enough noise to rouse the Grey God from his meditations. Around her, uneasiness permeated the wood, seeping into every root and branch like a plague. The usual sounds and movements of the forest had stilled, replaced instead with the silence of death that only her walking disturbed. Even the smells were wrong. The entire Plane cried out in silent anguish at some misdeed that the goddess could only guess at.

The walk was taking her longer than usual. This time when she had left Ayyslid she had planned to never return. After her visit to the Basin she had entered the forest and begun walking as far away from the place as she could. Her thoughts drifted back to Trent and Devin and what they had stumbled across in the wilderness. After sending them all of the power that she was able to give to a single mortal she had watched them for a time, trying to determine just what it was that they had found out there. After several hours it seemed as if they would never wake, and had she not sensed their breath she would have assumed the worst. Something beyond the single band of Accursed that they had encountered had troubled them greatly before they lost all consciousness, but what?

Arra had used the Basin to scan the immediate area, hoping to gain some sense of what had happened, but without knowing exactly what or where she was looking for the effort become too aggravating and she gave up. Seeing that she would have no luck determining what had sent her champions running, and that she could do no more to help them, she stormed away from the Basin in the darkest mood that she had felt in a hundred years. Against her better judgment she refrained from contacting Ren, thinking instead that she would no longer involve herself in whatever was transpiring below. Rather she decided to confine herself to the solitude of the forest and begin her hermitage. Arra had finally fallen into the same rut as her fellows with the cold realization that all of her actions were ultimately futile.

Her uneasiness about what the enemy had been planning had not been entirely unfounded, it seemed, and yet she had dropped the matter and gone into exile. It wasn't until the dimming of the Divine Plane that she realized just how mistaken she had been. In her heart, Arra knew that whatever the Paladins had found was connected to whatever had killed one of the other gods. It was for this reason that she turned and began the long walk back to her home, for no matter how hard she tried she could not forsake her duty. Arra knew that dropping her suspicions as she had, even for that short amount of time, would haunt her for the rest of eternity. There could be no absolution for a god.

Finally the forests thinned and the fortress of the gods again rose above her, crafted from the living wood of her surroundings. Even here all was still, as if death itself had approached and gained entry to her sacred home. Arra stopped and gazed about the clearing, looking for any sign that unwanted visitors had made their way within. Beside her, Divinity sniffed at the air cautiously, but otherwise showed no signs of distress. Arra trusted the big cat's senses more than her own, and, as such, made her way toward the wooden keep. The walls of Ayyslid parted as she approached, giving the Goddess of Light entry once more. The white tiger chose not to follow, instead deciding to lope off into the trees where she quickly faded into shadow. Arra knew that Divinity would be nearby in case she was needed.

Within seconds of entering, Arra found herself facing an arrow nocked in Samson's bow. The point of the weapon was so close that she could see the grains of the wood on the shaft. Upon recognizing her, Arra expected her fellow god to lower his weapon, but he did not.

"Why have you returned to us, dear Arra?" he asked through gritted teeth.

"Yes, I believe we told you never to come back." Luna no longer sounded musical. She stepped out from behind a corner, her hammer gripped tightly in her hands.

For several tense seconds Arra considered reaching for her sword, thinking she had walked into some kind of ambush. She had never considered that perhaps she was in danger from her companions as well, especially if it had been they who had attacked first. The notion that her fellow gods had struck the first blow and not the other way around began to truly take hold until she noticed something in Samson's eyes. It was a look of confusion, not anger. This realization finally made her speak.

"I had to ascertain if you two yet lived. Surely you felt it too."

"Of course we felt it, you fool," Samson snapped, lowering his bow. "The entire Plane felt it. Once again one of our number is dead, bringing the remaining count of gods down to six."

"But which one of the others has died?"

"We were hoping you would have some idea." Luna lowered herself into a wooden chair that rose to meet her, dropping her hammer harmlessly onto the floor.

"I don't, but I fear something terrible has occurred. The two Paladins discovered something in the wilderness."

Samson looked more curious than concerned. "How do you know this? Ren has mentioned nothing."

"I doubt that she yet knows. Trent and Devin were fleeing from something when I spied them in the Basin. They were ambushed and called upon me for aid."

Samson turned and sat next to Luna, making himself comfortable. The proud god reclined in his seat, his look becoming quickly disinterested until Arra finally moved in from the doorway and sat opposite them. She could tell that her sour look displeased her hosts.

"That could be an interesting change, could it not?" Luna's voice had regained its usual cadence.

"Yes would be. But not yet a cause for concern. It seems more and more likely that one of the fools has finally gained power over the others. Perhaps they are asserting their control over the Mortal Plane as well. That would also explain the death."

"So you think one of them has killed another?"

"Clearly. The Grey God certainly didn't disrupt his precious balance on a whim. Ravim is far too boring for anything like that now. No, I think Vardic has finally decided to pick up where Xyxax left off, just as he has always wanted. If I had to make a guess, it was Lio who was finally killed, and now the Darkness is united in purpose again."

Arra noticed a slight change in Luna's expression when Samson mentioned Lio by name. There was a flash of discomfort there that she almost didn't notice. It was gone before she was able to fully decide what it could mean.

"You say this as if it is of no consequence." Anger began to filter into Arra's voice. "Think of what this means for us! What if they plan to strike at Illux! Clearly there is more going on here than we know."

"No there is not," Luna interjected. "As usual, you find yourself beholden to fear. We know nothing about what has transpired, but that doesn't mean that we have to suddenly fear for our safety or the safety of our people." She paused for a moment. "Why should the death of one traitor cause us any concern at all?"

"That traitor was our brother once. And even so, do you really think that Ravim will ignore this change? Do you really think that he will allow us to outnumber them now? What happens when he comes to kill one of us?"

"It sounds as if this war has finally gotten interesting again." Samson smiled as if laughing at some private joke. She imagined knocking the teeth from his golden head.

Arra could feel the wood recoiling underneath her iron grip. Her mind raced through all of the possible scenarios that could have led to the death of one of the Gods of Darkness. She even allowed herself the briefest moment to contemplate whether it might have been Ravim himself who had died. Arra didn't want to give in to the fear, as Luna accused her of doing, but she couldn't ignore the obvious threats that they faced. Before she had arrived, those two had clearly been cowering within Ayyslid, afraid that they would be next, but now they hid behind their bombast and false confidence. It wasn't fitting for a God of Light to show fear.

"What do we do then?" she asked them.

"We do nothing. We wait for the Grey God to contact us," Samson replied.

"I cannot just sit idly by! Something must be done. We must go to him!"

"No." Samson sounded firm now. He sat upright before continuing. "We will wait for him to come to us. I do not believe that your fears are founded. But suppose that they are. Do we want to be caught unawares and in the open? Do you want to walk into some kind of trap? We must wait here until we know more, or else we risk compromise."

Although she disagreed with inaction, Arra had to admit that, for once, his logic was sound. Waiting for Ravim was possibly the wisest option available to them at the moment. If there were danger brewing in Infernaak, they needed to stay as far away from there as possible until they knew more. Her thoughts turned quickly to Divinity for a moment, the tigress stalking the woods around Ayyslid alone. Arra doubted that any harm would come to her dearest friend without it being returned in kind. The same could not be said of her wounded champions on the Plane below.

"And what of the Mortal Plane then?"

"The Paladins don't seem to have returned to Illux yet," the God of Light told her. "I want them to bring word to Ren themselves before we warn her that they may have found something. I wish to see how she will react."

"Delicious," Luna cooed.

"You would risk allowing harm to befall Illux just so that you can test your servant?"

"I simply wish to see what this champion you have chosen is really made of. This could be the event that defines her rule over the Mortal Plane. Will she rise to the challenge or cower behind her walls? I know how Castille would react, but what of Ren?"

"Castille is not the Seraph! I know that you whisper to him in his heart about how much he is truly favored by you, but he is not our vessel!"

"Not yet."

The other two gods stood and made their way toward the level above, leaving Arra alone to sulk in the lower reaches of Ayyslid. She was grateful for once that the only Mortal whom they could truly monitor and communicate with was the Seraph. Otherwise, who knew what kind of influence they would have on Castille. Even so, she knew that they had planted a seed in his dreams that caused him to think he was far more worthy than he was. The hearts and minds of some mortals filtered up to the Divine Plane stronger than others, and in these glimpses Arra had seen enough of the veteran Paladin to know that he would never have her favor in the way that Ren had. Ren had earned her place without ever seeking the power that she wielded. She was just as worthy a Seraph as any before her. And yet doubt clawed at Arra's mind again as it had about everything as of late.

*Don't fail me...*

# CHAPTER 15

Some four weeks after they had set out from Illux, Trent and Devin returned to its golden gates. They came upon the city of Light in the early morning, nearly crawling upon the road. Trent could feel the cracks and fissures in his dry lips, and his mouth had lost all sense of taste. The path they had taken had led them away from any village, and they hadn't dared risk wasting the time to try and find one.

As they approached, the golden gates ponderously swung open in response to their presence. Clearly word had been spread to keep an eye out for their return.

When the grinding of the opening doors finally stopped, a retinue of City Watchmen approached them. At the head of the small column was a familiar face—a face that Trent had almost forgotten.

"Edmund!" he cried out, nearly stumbling over.

The onetime Paladin recruit rushed to catch the falling warrior, holding him upright. "Gods have mercy, what happened to you two?" he asked.

"There is no time," Trent said. "We need to speak to the Seraph at once. Send word."

Edmund nodded in agreement and barked orders to the men at his back. Runners were dispatched to the Fourth Spire at once while Trent and Devin were hauled inside the city. The gates swung shut behind them as they were led into the base of a watchtower near the entrance. The walk from the street into the small room was a blur to Trent, who struggled to maintain consciousness throughout the short journey.

A basin of water was fetched so that Edmund could begin washing the blood and dirt from their skin. At first Devin struggled against the unfamiliar hands, but quickly relented, overwhelmed with fatigue. Trent tried to laugh at his companion but could only manage a wheeze. Fellow Paladins stationed at the wall arrived shortly thereafter and began to feed them healing energy, bringing them back from the brink of death.

"Bring us some wine. We haven't had a drink in days." Devin was finally able to speak, and it appeared the magic was returning his thirst, at least.

Water and wine entered their lips and spilled onto the floor around them. By then a small crowd of watchmen and Paladins had formed to see what tidings the veteran rangers had brought from the wilderness beyond. When he had had his fill of wine Trent waved most of them away, telling them that the news he brought was for the Lady Ren alone. Soon all that stood with them were two Paladins and Edmund.

"I see that you decided to keep with the watch," Trent commented once the audience had dispersed.

"Aye," Edmund answered, pulling a wooden stool up next to where Trent sat. "I was given some good advice, and I decided to follow it."

"I meant what I said. These people need a man like you."

"I will always do my best to serve. You two get some rest; we can catch up after you speak to the Seraph."

Edmund stood and walked from the room into the city beyond. Trent watched him go before allowing his vision to darken. He had known that sleep was imminent once they had sat him in the rather uncomfortable chair. The last several days of traveling had been some of the hardest days of his life. They had almost never stopped to rest, and once their water skins had been emptied they hadn't bothered to refill them. The fear of what would happen if the news of what they had seen didn't reach Illux in time had been too great. Thousands of lives depended on the tidings that they brought.

Trent's mind drifted off from these thoughts in a matter of minutes as sleep finally took him. The last thing that he heard was Devin's deep breathing, telling him that he had done the same.

When he awoke he had no idea how long they had slept. Judging by what little light filtered into the small guard room from the shadow of the wall outside, he guessed that it hadn't been more than an hour. There were several more Paladins in the room now, gathered about the two warriors in a tight cluster. In the center was the Lady Ren herself. When she noticed that her two champions were finally stirring she sent the rest of the Paladins outside where they could not hear the words that would be spoken. It seemed to Trent that she was glowing more now than she had ever been. A small smile crossed her face when she saw that he was waking. Trent tried to stand but stumbled back down, causing her smile to quickly turn to a look of grave concern.

"What in Arra's name happened to you two?" she asked as she knelt between them, feeding each of them some of her own energy. "They told me that you were weak and weary but I didn't expect this. You look as if you crawled back from the afterlife itself."

Trent looked toward Devin, who was now also awake. His companion gave him a short nod signaling him that he could be the one to speak.

"There are thousands of them, my lady," Trent finally forced out. "Thousands upon thousands."

Ren kept her emotions surprisingly under control. She searched Trent's face to be sure that what he said was true before looking at Devin, who nodded in silent agreement. Trent could see fire behind her eyes when her gaze finally fell back to him.

"That cannot be. Where did you see this?"

"I'm afraid it is, my lady. We journeyed south for days without any signs of Demons or Accursed. Finally we came across a band that was headed west and we decided to track it."

"We followed them for several days," Devin broke in, his voice still hoarse. "With each passing hour their numbers grew. Each roving band fell in line with the last until we were following a group of hundreds, and still they kept heading west beyond the range of any village. Finally, we saw why. They are gathering by the Great Chasm, more than we could possibly count."

"Was there any sign of the Herald?" she queried.

Both men shook their heads. There had been no sign of the dark god's messenger for many years, not since the previous Seraph had engaged him in battle on one of his ranging missions away from the city. Since then, none had heard what had become of the creature and it had almost faded from memory. Trent knew that the Herald must have been active again if this many of their enemies were gathering together. No simple Demon could hope to command such a force.

"It was on our way back that we encountered another band of Accursed," Trent continued. "Thankfully it was small and only led by a single Demon. Even so, we had traveled so far and with so little rest that we were almost killed. Had it not been for Arra's aid we surely would have been."

Devin was again remaining silent during Trent's retelling of events. It seemed as if he didn't wish to relive his near defeat this soon after returning to safety. More than his pride had been crushed by their battle.

"This force gathering now is no coincidence," Ren said. "While you were on the road did you notice Aenna dim?"

"I thought I saw something, but we weren't sure," Trent said.

"Do we know which god has fallen?" Devin asked, breaking his silence.

"No, we do not. I have been told that none of the three have been injured, but they have yet to learn who from among the others has died. They are waiting in Ayyslid until the Grey God contacts them about the Gods of Darkness."

"And what if it is the Grey God who has died?" Trent questioned, sounding slightly alarmed.

"Then we are indeed in danger." Ren stood up slowly. "I am glad that you have returned to me safely. This is grave news that you have brought. The world is changing around us faster than we had realized. War is coming to our gates and we must answer it. Castille and the others must be gathered so that we can discuss our next action. Meet me at the Fourth Spire within the next two hours. We will not discuss it until you arrive."

"And what of the villages? We must evacuate them."

"I will send riders to all of the western villages. If it comes to that, we will send for those to the east as well."

Ren turned and made for the door, only stopping to look over her shoulder just before the threshold. She gazed back at her champions with a look of the most sincere regret before she was able to speak again.

"There is one other matter. While you were gone we missed a shipment of crops from one of the southern villages. One of our riders returned just before you did. The entire village was razed to the ground. There is nothing left but ashes and bone. There were no survivors."

Devin sat bolt upright beside Trent, his fist clenched so tightly that Trent could hear the metal of his gauntlets creaking. They both feared the same thing.

"Which southern village?" Devin growled, all niceties having fled his voice.

"I'm so sorry. For both of you."

Trent fell back in his chair in shock, nearly deafened to the sounds of Devin's cry. It sounded as if his soul had been torn from within his breast. In a blur the distraught warrior was standing and throwing his chair against the wall, pummeling the stone with his fists. Trent looked to Ren for support, but behind her eyes he saw only grief.

"I fear there will be more to come."

She finally exited the room, leaving Trent and Devin alone in their despair. Trent looked on in horror as his closest friend beat his hands bloody upon the wall. Gil, his friend and lover, had been killed. Gil, with whom they had shared so much. Together the three of them had become Paladins. The three of them had killed Demons and Accursed. Together they had stopped bandits and blood cults. And now one of them was gone, and they hadn't even known.

Finally Devin's exertions proved too much for him and he nearly collapsed onto the floor. Trent was there then, catching his brother before he fell to the stone. He held his friend, the larger man sobbing openly now like Trent had never before seen. His own eyes were hot and blurry, the tears dripping onto his breastplate with a small tinny sound. They must have missed the slaughter by mere days.

*What if we had been there? Gil might yet have lived.*

"We will answer this with blood," Devin said through gritted teeth as he straightened himself. "I will cut down any who stand before us until I have broken the skull of his killer with my own hands!"

"And I will be there with you, until we both meet him again."

It was then that Devin laughed, a harsher sound now than it had ever been.

"I'm sorry," he said.

"For what?" Trent was confused now.

"I never should have stopped you from killing your father. I can see that now."

Trent had no response. He simply looked at the open doorway to the slums beyond. In his mind he saw Terric cut down again, falling into the snow. Beside him Gil lay dying as well. His life had been defined by the loss of a brother, and now it seemed that the same grief was upon him again. He looked back at his friend, who nodded at him in response. Without another word they gathered up their belongings and walked from the room into the city.

As they left the wall behind, men of the Watch attempted to approach them, but all who saw the rage in their eyes wisely retreated to a safe distance. There could be no peace for them now. Not ever again.

At first, the walk did little to clear Trent's head. Memories of himself and Gil flooded his thoughts, nearly bringing him to his knees. They had grown apart in recent years after Gil's reassignment, but he had never stopped loving the man as a brother. It had been the three of them together that had risen through the ranks and first gained the attention of the Seraph. It never would have happened without Gil.

*Why has this happened? That village was nowhere near their army.*

Trent cursed silently to himself and made one final attempt to banish all thought of his fallen friend from his mind. He took in the sights and sounds of the city around him instead in an attempt at preventing himself from being alone with his dark thoughts. The sun overhead had begun to beat down on the two Paladins, causing Trent to sweat in his heavy plate. He looked above at the great yellow disc, shielding his eyes from it so that he could better study the other light that sat beside it. Aenna was still present, but not as bright as it had been. The window to the heavens had been darkened by some cold deed.

*Which god could have died? And why?*

Whoever it was that had fallen, it didn't look good for the forces of Light either way. The Pact had made them grow complacent; they had believed that the balance could never again be upset. They were now paying the price for that lack of vigilance. Ren's focus on the defense of the city during her tenure as Seraph might prove to be the only reason that they would survive the coming conflict. And yet it may have been for this very reason that the forces of Darkness had been able to grow unchecked. They would find out soon enough, for there was a battle coming. Of that he had no doubts.

*May the High God have mercy on those who stand before us in our wrath.*

They kept a brisk pace, mindful of the impending doom that bore down upon them, but they were still held back by the remaining effects of their fatigue, both physical and mental. Trent wished that he could have a few days to recover, but somehow he knew that it wouldn't be so. Soon the spires of the Cathedral rose above them and they were entering the plaza that surrounded it. The normal bustle of activity was amplified with an expectant energy. Paladins and common folk alike brushed past them this way and that, all looking at the two as if they were looking upon death. Surely the news of the approaching army had not yet reached the general populace, but perhaps the word of an entire village being wiped out had? To make matters worse, the riders had been sent out nearly an hour before, and in such a fashion that it would have been hard to deny something was very wrong.

A rough-looking man in ill-fitting clothes approached them. He seemed to recognize them from somewhere, though Trent couldn't place him.

"What word?" he asked as he got closer. "Riders have been sent forth, and they say a village has burned. Surely you know what is going on?"

"It is for the Seraph to make that known," Trent replied, pushing past the man without another word.

Others came with similar questions, some Paladins, some not. All were given the same response and sent on their way. It would do no good to incite panic among the masses before a course of action could be decided. Even so, Trent had to resist the urge to tell every living soul what was coming. Especially after what had happened to Gil. Death marched for Illux, and they needed to be ready for it.

Finally, they reached the training grounds and made their way directly into the Fourth Spire, choosing to forgo the side entrances into the center of the Cathedral. The stairwell that they entered was at the side of the small chapel where the initiation had taken place over a month before, a small alcove that housed the door to the passages above. The large spiral staircase was choked with Paladins moving up and down, a flurry of activity that mirrored what was going on outside. Those who recognized them nodded in greeting but said nothing. They knew better than to question men on their way to see the Seraph and her advisors.

At the top of the steps they entered into a wide passageway that split off into several smaller halls and rooms. Directly across from where they entered was a large oak door that hung open, giving a glimpse of those gathered inside. Within, Trent could see Ren and Castille, along with some other Paladins of note, standing around a large table. Seeing their destination that close, the two men quickly vaulted into the opening and shut the doors behind them.

The room was a large circle with few windows but many torches. In its center was a large table upon which sat a map of the Mortal Plane. Castille and his retinue looked at Ren with clear impatience that only slightly abated when Trent and Devin entered the room.

"Ah, now we can finally find out what we have all been waiting so long for," Castille said with clear disdain. "I am glad that you felt the need to use the necessary haste to get here quickly. From what I hear of the villages, lives are on the line."

Devin tensed at this last remark but attempted to hide his mourning behind a smile. "Anticipation adds to the pleasure, Castille."

The older Paladin glowered back at them, but just when it seemed he would speak, he was silenced by a sharp look from Ren. Trent and Devin stood opposite him, taking their places next to the Seraph.

With the entire known world spread before him, Trent couldn't help but study the Mortal Plane in silent awe for a few brief moments. From this vantage point the lands that mankind had actually explored seemed relatively small, assuming that there was anything that existed beyond the known wilderness. None had been north of the Rim or west of the Great Chasm in recorded history, or if they had they had not returned to tell of it. As for the east and south, it was easier for expeditions to explore these regions, but there was little of note for them to bring back.

*What little of creation we have explored and fought over. Perhaps the High God spends his time out there, just beyond our sight.*

"Trent, tell the others what you have told me," Ren said, just loud enough for everyone to hear.

Trent retold the tale just as he had related it to Ren some hours before. He pointed at the map spread before him to explain where he believed that the army was camped, just near the Great Chasm. He faltered for a brief moment when his eyes drifted to that most southern of villages that he knew was now nothing more than a charred husk. Devin interjected only to agree with what Trent had said or to clarify something that he had left unclear. Surprisingly to both of them, Castille remained silent through the entire tale, his brow furrowed in deep thought.

But once it was over he could stay silent no longer.

"Are we supposed to actually believe this?"

"Why wouldn't you?" Ren asked, unable to hide her dissatisfaction.

"To start, there has never been an army the size that they describe since the Pact was taken."

"That's not entirely true," Devin replied. "When the Balance Monks massacred the city, it was only after the Light crushed a force nearly the size of the one that we saw."

"That was a force that had responded to our actions, not the other way around! Do not lecture me on history. I am nearly twice your age."

"Enough!" Ren bellowed as she slammed her fist upon the table. The small mutterings that had begun were instantly silenced. "I will hear no more of this. I trust their senses, and believe what they saw. Something is going on beyond our walls, we cannot doubt that now, not after what has happened. And something has changed on the Divine Plane as well. We cannot waste time arguing, we must act as if the Forces of Darkness are gathering to strike at us, for they may well be. I have already taken the necessary precautions to have the western villages evacuated. Now we must gather our own troops."

"And then you suggest that we hide behind our walls while this so-called army ravages our farmlands and burns our villages? It seems that they have already done so, and yet we don't strike back?" Castille snorted.

Trent prepared to speak in Ren's defense when Devin again opened his mouth first. "For once I am in agreement with Castille. I demand justice for what has been done already!"

"I never said that we would hide behind our walls."

"No, but based upon the choices that you have made since being made Seraph, I can guess," Castille shot back.

The old man had finally gone too far. Trent looked to Ren and saw a rage boiling inside her that he had never before witnessed. "You dare talk to me that way? My choices are not my own, I speak with the voice of the gods."

"Interesting that the gods chose to take a less aggressive course once you were chosen. Your predecessor—"

"That's enough!" Trent yelled as he stepped forward with his hand on his sword.

Even though he had sided with Castille a moment before, Devin could not allow such insolence against Ren either. His axe was already unclasped when he spoke. "Allow me."

The look on Castille's face changed from its previous mocking expression to a look of true fear. His hand dropped to the pommel of his blade, as did those of his retinue behind him. The gathered Paladins all froze in place, none daring to make another move. Ren forcibly pushed her way between the two groups and spread her wings, causing all of them to step back.

"Enough!" Before Trent had even seen her move she held Nightbreaker aloft, pointed at no one in particular. "This is not the time to bicker amongst ourselves. One of our villages has been burned, and more are sure to follow. We are not hiding behind our walls while our people suffer and die, no matter what you may think of me. We are marching out to meet them before they even step foot in another village."

Stunned silence spread through the gathered Paladins like the passage of a plague. None gathered would have imagined that such would have been her response. Trent couldn't help but smile at the Seraph's newfound boldness. He had never doubted her, and now she showed him why that was.

"I want all of the troops ready to march by the end of the night. Send word that every man or woman in the army is to be ready by daybreak tomorrow. We leave for the Great Chasm at dawn. Draw off half of the City Watch, and leave behind only a token force of Paladins. We will need as many fighters as we can bear."

"My—my lady," Castille stammered, no longer confident. "This cannot be done. It is impossible to gather the troops in this amount of time. And the army itself is merely a token force; none of its members have ever marched into battle; they are more unprepared now than they have ever been. We haven't had a serviceable military for nearly twenty years."

"If you can no longer maintain your command over the army then you are relieved of your post," Ren said, her eyes twin coals burning into Castille.

Regaining some of his composure due to his indignation, Castille replied. "Who then will command them? What man here can stand above me?"

"I will command them myself, as every Seraph before me has. As for your replacement, Trent and Devin have been recently promoted because of their loyal and unquestioning service. They shall now answer to no one but me."

The look upon Castille's face gave Trent the greatest joy. He imagined that he could hear the older man's teeth grinding in his head even over the raucous laughter from Devin beside him. Through it all, Trent and Castille never unlocked eyes, even for a moment.

"I will not be commanded by the likes of these! They are more green boys than men. They have only been Paladins for less than a decade!"

"You won't have to answer to them. I am leaving you here in charge of the city in my absence."

Seizing the opportunity to question her again, Castille slammed his fist on the table as he growled, "And yet you leave me with no army and half of the city watch? How many Paladins then do I have to stand with me?"

"The contents of this room," she answered coolly, challenging him with her icy stare.

For a moment, Trent thought that the challenge would be answered. He found himself gripping his own sword so tightly that it made his hand ache. Castille's eyes flitted about the room, looking over his fellow commanders of the Paladin order, all of whom were more loyal to him than to Ren. When his eyes finally returned to the Seraph, Trent saw a hatred in them not unlike what he had seen in any number of the bandits that he had killed over the years. Finally, it seemed as if Castille had thought better of doing anything more, and he bowed to Ren in mocking deference.

"As my lady commands."

"Then leave us. Send word that my orders are to be carried out; the army is to be ready by dawn tomorrow," she said curtly, moving aside so the veteran warrior could make his way out the door. As he was in the threshold she spoke to him one final time. "Castille, if you ever challenge my god given authority again, I will kill you where you stand."

The Paladin commander didn't even stop to acknowledge her, choosing instead to continue into the halls beyond. Trent watched him go, listening to each receding footfall with an intense satisfaction. After Castille's men filed out behind him, Ren, Trent, and Devin were left alone in the room staring at the map upon the table. Exasperated, the Seraph let out a long sigh. She took a brief moment to regain her composure before she began addressing her new commanders.

"I want my orders carried out in full. I leave it to you two to see that it is done. We can no longer trust Castille to do as he is commanded. I fear that before this conflict is over he will move against me."

"We must strike first then. It is clear that something must be done to stop him from turning against you," Trent said, moving closer to her. Devin shot him a knowing glance.

"I need his experience now more than ever. We cannot take action against him until this crisis is averted. By the end, we will deal with all of our enemies, even Castille. One way or another he will answer for his insolence."

"You know that you will always have my support," Devin spoke up as he dropped to one knee.

Ren's eyes met Trent's and her mouth curved upward in a small smile.

"I know that I can always rely on both of you, which is why I want you by my side when we ride to face this enemy head-on. There have never been two other Paladins whom I could trust without question. Ever since the situation with that cult, you two have been an indispensable asset to our cause. For that, you have my gratitude."

For a brief moment Trent's pride was overshadowed by painful memories that passed through his mind. He remembered the event of which she spoke, and the men whom he had killed. Even harder for him to bear were the thoughts of the others who had stood by him. The Paladins had discovered a group of bandits that had styled themselves as a cult worshipping the Gods of Darkness. None had escaped that bloodbath.

*It wasn't just the two of us that day. Gil was there too. And now he is gone.*

Devin stood back up and nodded his head; Trent simply forced himself to return her smile. Her rank deserved respect, and their love for her deserved an undying loyalty, just as they had felt for each other. Trent knew that either of them would die for their Seraph, and the thoughts of Gil made him realize that by the end, one of them might have to.

"During the battle," she said, more softly now, "the gods will be busy lending us their power wherever they can, but it will be dispersed among many of us. Surely they will also be flooded with prayers, as is the case whenever there is such violence. I have been told that this makes it hard for them to discern what any single mortal cries out for, like trying to speak to someone in a crowded room. Do not rely upon Divine aid to give you strength and to heal your wounds, for it may not come."

"What do they have to say about this gathering of troops?" Trent asked.

"Samson and Luna are of a mind that one of the Gods of Darkness has taken charge over the others, and in the process slain one of them. They believe that this would account for the dimming of Aenna and the Divine Plane."

"And the Lady Arra?"

"She harbors doubts. Arra fears that plans are in motion that we cannot even guess at. She knew that you two discovered something out there, and the fear of it has troubled her for some time. Her fears are scoffed at by the other two, who have forbidden her from leaving Ayyslid to see which god has fallen."

"So they experience discord?"

"They do. Much as they always have. The hubris of the gods is a well-known trait to the Seraphs, although it is kept out of the religious services in the Cathedral. Discussing the weakness of the gods doesn't often go over well among the faithful. They bicker just as we do, and often in our times of greatest need. Now more than ever, we must know what we face, on the Mortal and Divine Planes both. Unfortunately, it appears that we must act with only the information that you two have brought. The only thing that the gods and myself agree on is that we must act somehow, and that we cannot allow an army to reach Illux."

*If even the gods don't know what to do, then what chance does man have?*

"Once the battle is met, we must try and draw out the Herald at all costs," the Seraph continued. "His death is the key to our victory. Like a Seraph, he can be replaced from within the ranks of the Demons, but this process takes time, time that we can use to crush their forces while they struggle with no leader. It is only during this window that we will hold any advantage. The Herald possesses powers that rival my own, so we must use extreme caution. Be thankful that the Divine Beasts no longer walk the Mortal Plane or this battle would go far worse for us.

"Now, go and ready yourselves for the march ahead. Once the army has begun preparing, you two will both need rest. I wish that you could have had more time to recover first, but we don't have that luxury. I will send for you at dawn when it is time to begin. Remember, you are both commanders now; act accordingly."

Trent and Devin nodded in acknowledgement and exited the room, walking through the halls of the Fourth Spire. So much had happened during their meeting that Trent found it hard to process it all. He was a young man, and already held the highest rank one could achieve under the Seraph. There were dozens, perhaps hundreds of men and women with more experience and right to lead than he, and yet it had fallen to himself and Devin. Finally, deciding that he needed Devin's opinion on the matter, he spoke.

"So, we are commanders now," he said. "Could you ever have imagined?"

"I have, and frequently!" Devin roared, laughing again. "We are smart, brave, and loyal. What else could a commander have that we do not?"

"Experience."

"Experience be damned. And we've got that too, just not as much as some. Besides, it's the experienced ones you can't trust. They think they have seen it all. They haven't, none of us have."

Trent reflected on the implications of what Devin was saying as they left the Cathedral behind and walked into the practice yards. Once they had returned to the light of day they were greeted by the sight of hundreds of armored men and women running in each direction; the preparations for war were already underway. One group of Paladins that was running past slowed as Trent called out to them. They turned and approached, each taking a knee before the two men as they did so.

"Commanders," a woman said, clearly the highest ranked of the bunch.

*Word of our rise has spread fast. I didn't think Castille would talk of it gladly.*

"What of your orders? How go the preparations?" Trent asked.

"My lords, we are gathering arms and armaments for the fighting. The army has been alerted and is forming beyond the western wall. They shall be ready by dawn."

"And what of those who are staying behind?" Devin asked.

"The City Watch is preparing the slums to take in the refugees from the outer villages. We have had orders to leave two hundred Paladins to help them."

*Castille.*

"Those orders are incorrect. Spread the word from your new commanders and the Seraph herself, only half of the City Watch stays, and no Paladins other than Commander Castille and his closest companions."

"My lords."

It took the better part of two hours to correct Castille's purposeful mistake. Word of their ascension had not actually spread as quickly as Trent had at first thought. Once the two men had established their rank, they were able to correct the miscommunication and get the preparations truly under way.

Gathering a force as large as this on such short notice was nigh impossible, just as Castille had said. But it had to be done if they wished to meet the enemy anywhere but on their very doorstep. Word spread quickly once the army was being assembled that any who wished to join the battle was free to do so. They hoped that they wouldn't need to resort to forced conscription yet. Men who didn't wish to fight rarely fought well.

Food was collected from all over the city and stored in a large supply train that was assembled from the various carts and wagons normally used to ferry food from the villages to Illux. Word had been sent to all of the villages that were not yet being evacuated to send what goods they could spare to meet the army en route. The city would soon have more mouths to feed, and what little food they had left wouldn't last long, but the army needed to eat if they were to fight, and that took priority.

*What is a worse fate? Starvation or being overrun by the enemy?*

Trent feared that his actions were condemning some in the slums to die a slow death over the coming weeks, but he knew that if they did not act, everyone in the city would fall. He toyed with possible solutions as they made their way outside of the city gates to survey the gathering army before settling in for the night. Many of the men and women there had never experienced real combat before, and a few had never even been trained in the use of the sword or bow. As they walked up and down the lines, those who recognized them bowed in greeting. It was an odd feeling.

Devin noticed several children in ill-fitting armor standing proudly within the ranks of real fighters around them. It was clear that their call for more fighters had brought less able bodies than they had hoped. Devin left Trent's side and spoke with the children for a while, convincing them to return to their homes. It seemed that most of them didn't wish to fight in the first place, but had been sent to do so by family. Trent sent word to the troop commanders that any child under the age of fourteen was to be sent back to Illux without question.

Arms and armor were in better supply than Trent could have hoped, the city having stored away a steady stockpile in case of a need such as this. Trent mused that perpetual warfare did have its advantages. In ages past, the people of Illux had been hardened for situations such as this, but in recent times they had grown softer than their forebears. The mettle of everyone standing before him would be tested many times in the coming days.

When they were satisfied that they had done all they could, the two Paladins returned to the barracks. Just before they reached their destination, Trent thought of one more thing that he must do.

"Go on ahead of me and get some sleep," he said. "I have to do something else first."

"Elise?"

"Yes, I can't leave her unprotected."

Devin turned and entered the mostly empty barracks, leaving Trent alone in the dim light of the setting sun. The Cathedral at his back still sparkled from the little light that illuminated it. It was a symbol of what they fought for, but it didn't bleed or feel pain like the people of this city. It was they who really needed them to fight.

Trent quickly found a member of the City Watch who pointed him in the direction of the man he was looking for. Within a few minutes he was inside of a large room filled with high ranking members of the Watch.

In back, deep in conversation, stood Edmund.

When his eyes met Trent's he broke off what he was doing and quickly approached the new commander. "What news, my lord?"

"There is no need for that. I have come because I need you to do something important for me."

"Anything. I owe you that much."

Trent paused for a moment before continuing. "There is a woman in the slums near the southern gate. Her name is Elise. She washes the clothes for all of her neighbors; you shouldn't have trouble finding her."

"Aye, you want me to relocate her somewhere safer?"

"No, she is too stubborn for that. But I do want you to keep an eye on her. If the city is breached, keep her safe. She is like a mother to me, and I can't bear to leave her unprotected."

"I will see it done personally."

"I knew you would."

Trent left without saying much else, briskly returning to the barracks so that he could finally sleep. Part of him wanted to see her one more time before he marched off to what could be his death. But he knew that the pain for both of them would be too much. Edmund would watch her, and that would have to be enough. When he finally returned to his room, the weary warrior fell upon his bed.

SQUAWK.

*The Vulture again. But this time it didn't have the white bird clutched in its cruel claws. It was flying overhead in wide circles, slowly descending from the upper atmosphere. Behind the bird he could see that Aenna was flickering like a candle just before it is blown out. The wide arcs of the bird were almost mesmerizing to stare upon, the only thing keeping his mind from spiraling into blackness.*

*Squawk.*

*He was lying flat on his back, his pigeon body still without any wings. Fear clutched at his heart as the Vulture got closer and closer to him. He craned his neck around to see where he was. All around him lay the lifeless bodies of scores of other wingless pigeons, necks and legs splayed out at odd angles. He was on a killing field, ready to be feasted upon. In the distance he saw the body of a Paladin, lying in a pool of blood. His face.*

*Gil.*

*He blinked and the body was gone. Only a severed arm lay there in its place.*

*-Trent.-*

*As the vulture got lower it cast a large shadow on the field of dead birds. The winged shadow was large and cruel, but he somehow felt that it didn't belong to the wicked bird that squawked above him. He felt that the shadow was something else. Trent watched in horror as the shadow began to move across the bodies of its own accord, freed from its connection to the bird over him.*

*Squawk.*

*Now the Vulture was just above him, its black beak splitting wide to tear into his flesh. Black blood dripped from its eyes and burned his skin. It was on top of him then, ready to rip the meat from his bones. A white shape rocketed into its side and sent it spiraling away. It was the white bird: The Dove. The Vulture and The Dove battled in the air now, ripping and tearing at each other's wings. Trent still couldn't move a muscle, couldn't try to save The Dove when her throat was torn open and she was forced to the ground by the Vulture.*

*-Trent.-*

*She called out to him. He must act. This time he could not allow her to come to any more harm. She had saved him. He must. Trent forced himself to move, lifting himself up and making his way toward the source of the squawking. The two birds had landed on the far side of a great chasm which had split the field of death in two. The Vulture was seated upon the body of the lesser bird, his beak already full of flesh from her neck.*

*Her eyes pleaded with him.*

*-Trent.-*

*He tried to clear the chasm, but he couldn't, he had no wings. He fell just as he always fell. Above him he could see Aenna flicker like a candle, and then, just like that, it was extinguished.*

Trent awoke covered in sweat, a light rapping sound on his door. It was a messenger from the Seraph. The sun was rising; it was time to march.

# CHAPTER 16

It had finally begun the day before.

The siege on the Grey Temple had started just as his master had enacted the first stage of their plan. With Ravim dead, their greatest enemy on the Divine Plane was no longer a concern, and now it was up to the Herald to remove his forces from the Mortal Plane as well. He had gathered a contingent of Accursed and Demons at the base of the Rim and given them express orders to destroy every trace of the monks by nightfall. Even with their deity dead, however, the Balance Monks had put up a stronger resistance than he had anticipated. The monks had been disoriented in the beginning, but they had somehow pulled themselves together as the day had worn on.

But that had been yesterday. The Herald hadn't been to the Temple in person yet. And he still had one piece to play.

The monk was lying on his side, fluids running out of the large wound in his shoulder; his lifeblood slowly leaching into the ground. The coppery smell of it was almost lost amidst the other smells of this place: smoke and dirt and something far older. He was lying in the center of a large clearing, a perfect circle of trees in which the earth was completely smoothed over. It was another ward meant to hold a Divine Beast within. The Rim of Paradise held more of these sites than anywhere else on the Mortal Plane, which was no doubt the cause of the uneasiness that the place exuded. It must have been for this reason that the Grey God had bid his followers to build their temple here a thousand years before.

*That was their undoing.*

With the seals on the Divine Beasts fading, the Herald alone held the keys to freeing them and using them to finish the war in one decisive strike. He was grateful that his master had given him this power by illuminating this ritual to him, but in a way he felt that he was always meant to be the one. Who else but he was great enough to usher in this new age? The Fallen One had sensed his greatness, but he had not created it. The Herald had always been destined for such things.

The proud creature continued to fly in wide circles around the site, diving and soaring back up like a great bat, never once taking his eyes off of the wounded man at its heart. From his current vantage point it seemed as if it was so simple a task to free yet another weapon for his master's war, so small seemed the dying monk. In the distance, smoke was still rising from the fires his soldiers had started the previous day, the last defenders holding out in the Temple just out of sight. The fact that the Temple hadn't already fallen by the time he had arrived had caused him minor irritation, but that mistake was to be rectified in short order. The monk had been dragged from the field of battle, still clinging to life, and deposited here just minutes ago.

The Herald stopped flying and hovered directly over the center of the circle, signaling for the Demons on the outer edges to begin. Just as had been done with the girl, seven of the armored giants walked to the wounded monk and butchered him as if he were an animal. No cries escaped his lips as they did so; whether this was a sign of his resolve or of the severity of his prior wounds, the Herald couldn't say. One thing was certain: these were no whimpering children that they faced.

Once again when the bloodied blades were jammed into the rocky earth at the edge of the seal he lanced red-hot flames from his arms into the swords. A now familiar rumble greeted his ears as the light drained from the sky and the ground began to crack. Each fissure formed from his magic was met with another shudder and groan from beneath the surface. This prisoner wished for freedom more longingly than the last.

But that was to be expected.

*He must be hungry.*

Finally, the last cracks on the seal formed, but rather than collapsing inward to form a crater, fragments erupted into the air as the Divine Beast within shattered forth, showering those gathered nearby with debris. The dust that billowed forth did little to hide its countenance, a sight horrific enough that even the Herald paused. It was a terrifically misshapen monstrosity that pulled itself from the pit. Multiple legs clawed frantically at the earth, lifting its lizard-like bulk to the surface. Upon sighting the gathered Demons, the great creature lunged forward, engulfing two with its forked tongue while pinning the rest beneath its hooked feet. That was when the scent of the thing finally wafted up to the Herald, taking his focus momentarily away from the surprising sound of Demons crying out in fear. It was a fetid odor, like a corpse that had been left out in warm rain.

When it was done feasting, the Divine Beast swung its massive head upward and attempted to catch the Herald, who moved just out of its reach. The forked tongue flashed past him, faster than he would have guessed was possible, bringing with it that familiar stench. The Herald had assumed that something like this might happen, so he had made sure not to let his guard down; but the insolence of the thing below him still took him aback. The creature was punished for its mistake with a barrage of flames that licked at its vulnerable eyes and scorched the soft flesh of its tongue. It moaned in response and returned all of its great legs to the ground, once again looking for prey.

*A hunger that can never be satisfied. A weapon that can never be stopped.*

"Gaxxog!" he cried out, anger leeching into his usual rasp. "Heed your master. I have freed you from your prison. Obey me or face the wrath of your god!"

The powers of speech seemed to have eluded the Divine Beast, which simply roared skyward in an act of defiance. Ignoring any further communication with the Herald, it turned and began making its way toward the smoke, just as he had thought that it would. His master had warned him that there was little hope of controlling this one, or even attempting to reason with it. Cursed by its creator with an insatiable hunger, the beast had most likely been driven mad by a millennium of imprisonment with no sustenance. Even so its attempted attack angered him, and he considered punishing the great beast again, but thought better of it. A weapon such as this didn't need to be controlled, only pointed in the proper direction.

The towering pines of the mountain wood gave way before the behemoth as it lumbered toward its target, angrily shattering what trunks didn't simply give way before its bulk. What it hoped to find beyond the smoke he could only guess at, but that mattered little as it would find a feast laid out on the mountain plain, waiting to be devoured. Within a few hours it would carve a direct path to the Temple, wide enough for hundreds to march up and down the slope. Not that any more troops would be needed after Gaxxog arrived.

The Herald kept to the air just out of reach of the beast, ever mindful that it carried Divine Blood in its veins just as he did. His thoughts turned to the other seals that he had been shown, each holding within it a creature more deadly than the last. Some he would avoid unless commanded otherwise; these contained creatures whom even the gods had come to fear. He knew of at least one such beast that currently slumbered beneath the sea. Others held servants of Light, monsters that would attempt to destroy him if he made the mistake of setting them loose. Perhaps one day when the Mortal Plane was his alone he would free them just for the sport of watching them do battle with their kin. Again, he looked ahead at the swirling smoke before them. Once Gaxxog reached the Temple, the monks would be destroyed and he could focus his efforts on the armies of Light.

*Will they muster their strength or will they hide behind their walls?*

It mattered little.

The forces of Darkness had been slowly building in purpose ever since the Purge of Illux. They had nearly been wiped out by the forces of Light those centuries ago, down to the last Demon. But now, under the careful guidance of the Fallen One, they outnumbered their enemies three to one. They had operated slowly, taking just those that they needed to build up the ranks, carefully planning raids and attacks so that they didn't look suspicious. It had not been until recently when they had begun gathering their forces together that they had fully stopped reminding Illux of their presence. And now, with the Grey God dead, it was only a matter of time before the other gods followed, and then the Herald would rule over the Mortal Plane while his master ruled in the Divine. It would be glorious, just as he had promised.

Even with its insatiable hunger gnawing at its belly, the Divine Beast moved at too ponderous a pace for the Herald, who quickly tired of watching it tear its way through the forest. There were still too many preparations to be made for him to be wasting time making sure that every man and woman in the Temple above met with the sword. There were still scouts that he hadn't heard back from yet, and more beasts to unchain. And yet he couldn't bring himself to leave without enjoying the carnage, at least for a time. Balance Monks were a delicacy when it came to killing, for they rarely stirred themselves to enter the world below. He couldn't miss what would be his final opportunity to hunt them. His mind quickly flashed to the Paladins whom he had toyed with in that village some days before. The Herald still felt a pang of disappointment that he didn't stay long enough to see the blonde one who had been protecting the girl die. He had placed his duty above his own pleasure, and now he regretted it. That would not happen again. With a wicked smile upon his face the Herald flew straight for the Temple, leaving Gaxxog well behind.

Smoke choked the upper airways that he glided through, pockets of heat from below pushing him upward above the mire. His nose detected more than the smell of burning wood in the swirls of black that engulfed him. When he finally emerged from the acrid smoke, his eyes were greeted with a most glorious carnage, greater than any he had yet seen. The outer walls of the temple were blackened and crumbling, bodies piled up against them like so many scattered dolls. Blood ran in a torrent down the gradually sloping plain into the trees beyond. Demons and Accursed milled about like waves, occasionally breaking upon the walls of the temple before being forced back by a weak counterattack staged by those corralled within. The monks would surely fight to the last man to defend their sacred temple, the thought of retreat never even crossing their minds.

*Fools. What hope do you have with no god to protect you?*

Wheeling about, the Herald could see a small cluster of monks surrounded by Accursed, only just saving themselves from being overwhelmed. It wouldn't be more than a few more minutes before they found themselves overcome and destroyed. Surely these monks had found a way to sneak out of the temple and thought to bring the attack to their enemy from the rear. Perhaps if the Herald had only sent a token force this would have worked, but he had not. While only several hundred strong had marched up the mountainside, he had sent a greater number of Demons among them than usual. He had hoped for a quick end to the slaughter, which would have freed these forces to join up with the bulk of the main army that gathered in the wilderness. Once they were all gathered in one place, they would be ready to strike at Illux and end the war with one blow of the hammer. Seatown and the lesser villages would fall with little resistance once their mother city burned. Still, the resilience of these grey monks had proven to be more than he had anticipated.

But that was where Gaxxog came into play.

In the distance, the swath that the great beast was cutting through the forest was yet obscured by smoke, but he knew that it was only a matter of time before the conflict was over. Most of those loyal to him on the ground below would die as well, victims of the Divine Beast's insatiable appetite, but this was the price that had to be paid in order to accomplish that which he had set out to do. He wouldn't have had to resort to such drastic measures if those he had sent hadn't failed in the first place.

He focused again on those monks that struggled for survival below him, unaware that their death now came from above. The Herald dove like a scavenger to a carcass, his black wings tucked tight against his body, red cloak fluttering wildly during the descent. The monks only just noticed his approach as he struck into one of them, shattering the man's insides while sending him careening backward into the conglomeration of Accursed gathered around them. The monk wasn't quite dead as the horde of monsters began tearing him limb from limb. The Herald gained his footing and spun about, casting his wicked grin upon the bewildered defenders who quickly took defensive stances against this new threat. After finishing with the wounded monk, the Accursed reacted to the presence of their master by slowly retreating to rejoin the siege on the temple proper. Even these mindless servitors of darkness knew better than to come between the Herald and his sport.

With the Accursed gone, the monks quickly fanned out, circling the new arrival as they prepared to attack. He studied them in the intervening moments as they surrounded him. They were an assortment of females and males of all colors and ages. Each was covered from head to toe in swirling grey tattoos that seemed to match their now torn and disheveled robes. Most were unarmed, he noticed, although a few held staves made of solid wood. He knew that they were more of a threat than they seemed, but with the death of their god, none of them would have any reserves of Divine energy to call upon. And these battered few seemed tired. Even so, each locked eyes with the Herald; their steely gazes showing no hint of fear.

But he could smell it on them.

It was a woman who struck first, her staff lithely glancing past the Herald's face, each following blow narrowly deflected by his claws. She was probing his defenses, testing his reaction time and awareness in order to formulate her strategy. But he was no sparring partner whom she could learn from and then best. He was one of the most powerful entities that walked the Mortal Plane. He moved far slower than he was actually capable of, leading them to think him less powerful than he was. The monks would be in for a nasty surprise when they moved in closer.

Finally, one of them did, a man jumping at him from behind, attempting to take advantage of the Herald's distraction from the woman. He could hear the blades of grass part as the man launched himself into the air, sensing him flying through it as if he were louder than the sounds of combat from afar. The monk quickly found himself impaled on an outstretched arm, which now protruded from his back between the shoulders. When his cries of anguish faded and his head drooped, the rest of the group charged in unison, hoping to overwhelm their adversary with their superior numbers. Dropping the dead monk to the ground, the Herald began spinning about, matching blow for blow with his own. Within moments a monk recoiled in pain, clutching at her bloodied arm as her hand fell to the ground.

This flurry of attacks and counters continued after that for some time with neither side gaining the advantage. The Herald gained no victories after the first several injuries that he had doled out, but he had received a few of his own. He quickly realized that if he didn't change tactics soon his little game might have a chance of failure due to their greater numbers. Surely they would tire before he did, but what if they broke through his defenses before then? Spreading his wings, he returned to the air, knocking several of the monks to the ground as he did so. Once above them he spun and bathed the monks in red flame, turning those who couldn't stand quick enough into cinders. When the small batch of smoke cleared, he could see that only three of the monks still lived. The survivors were beginning to spread themselves out, hoping to prevent another single barrage of his fire to end the struggle.

His first target was the woman with one hand; the bloodied stump tightly wrapped in now scarlet robes to stanch the bleeding. Her eyes locked with his again, daring him to bring what she knew was coming. The woman never flinched, even when he was upon her, tearing her apart in a flurry of motion. Streaked in gore around his mouth and on his claws, the beast turned to face the remaining two monks who now approached him from opposite sides.

The first thing that he noticed was that this was the same woman who had probed his defenses with the staff earlier. Now the weapon was in the hands of the man, however, and he seemed to wield it even more comfortably than she had. They moved in unison, somehow in communication with one another. He could tell that these two were connected somehow, making it all the more fitting that they would be the final two left standing. This brought the Herald a small amount of amusement, as he knew that this simply meant that they would feel even greater pain when he killed them, each knowing that the other was dead.

The man took off the upper portion of his robe, revealing his tattooed and muscular physique. He carried the staff aloft as he slowly approached, his companion doing the same on the reverse side, keeping her hands poised to strike. Around them the Herald was dimly aware that an audience of Demons had begun to form, leaving the Accursed to mill about ineffectively, the walls of the temple still unbreached. This caused him minor annoyance, but he accepted that he would just have to make quick work of the remaining two monks before the Demons again attempted to make entry.

*It matters not. Nothing will stand once Gaxxog arrives.*

The monks charged in perfect unison, reaching him at exactly the same moment. Each struck at the holes in his defense that the other had opened; a flurry of blows from the fist and staff landing on his torso and wings. They worked far better together than the entire group had earlier, a feat that shocked him more than he would admit.

Each swipe of his great claws was turned away at the last moment by a deft movement of the wrist or a sharp jab of the staff. Perhaps these two would be able to embarrass him in front of his forces, something that he could not abide. The Herald finally caught the staff with one hand, yanking it free from the monk and swinging it into the head of the woman, shattering her nose and sending her stumbling away. He released the wooden weapon and followed her retreat with a torrent of magic; flames licking at her heels as she tried to escape, blood covering her face.

Without realizing it the male was upon him, landing blow after blow upon his exposed back. Even without his staff the man fought with a fury that was only counterbalanced by his outwardly calm demeanor. To his surprise the Herald felt one of his wings snap, and the membrane was torn within the man's claw-like grip, causing silver and black blood to spray from the open wound. Roaring in agony, the Herald was able to spin and scratch the monk across his exposed chest as he jumped away, his flesh tearing as it made contact with the Herald's claws. Rage flowed through him as he reset his broken wing and spent the next few moments healing it, keenly aware that the eyes of his followers were now intently upon him. The two monks rejoined each other and had already prepared for another attack. His wounds would be healed and theirs would not. The end was finally upon them.

*Now I have them.*

His thoughts of victory were interrupted as the temple doors were thrown open and dozens of the surviving monks rushed onto the field, easily killing the Accursed where they stood. By the time the Demons had realized what was happening their line was broken and the monks had begun to push the invaders further from the temple. It didn't take long for the Herald to realize what was happening. The group that he had engaged was simply a distraction, meant to draw off as many troops from the temple as possible so that the monks inside could flank the invading force. This strategy had been mostly unsuccessful until he had engaged them himself and made a spectacle for the Demons to watch. His own arrogance had placed his entire plan in jeopardy, a fact that filled him with white-hot anger. His wrath would see those final two monks dead if it was the only victory he could achieve here. Already Demons had begun to fall, still not fully recovered from the surprise strike. Desperately he looked about for his own targets, but they were gone.

The two monks whom he had engaged had disappeared into the onslaught, fading into the mass of charging and retreating combatants like ghosts. They may have been brave, but they were smarter than to engage him again now that he was fully healed and they were not. This angered him even more as he felt his vengeance being pulled from his grasp. What he had thought was a carefully orchestrated siege was unraveling before his very eyes. The Demons quickly rallied the Accursed to them and held against the reinvigorated defenders, but by then the damage had already been done. For each monk that fell, countless Accursed were already upon the ground, followed soon after by their Demon commanders, overcome by the inhuman fury with which the monks fought.

Angrily, the Herald took to the air to look for the two monks who had escaped him. From his new vantage point he could see how much danger they were truly in. All across the field it looked as if the monks might yet be able to defend their home against his troops. More of them lived than he had been led to believe, his own surprise strike having taken fewer lives than he had anticipated, it seemed. If the monks were able to successfully repel them and join up with Illux, the coming battle would be harder to win. If he failed here, the Fallen One would never entrust the Mortal Plane to him. Winning the battle no longer held meaning for him now that he knew how he had been cheated. Killing those two monks who had made such a fool of him was his only goal. He tore through air over the battle like a mad beast, circling this way and that, scanning the grey robed figures below hoping to find any sign of his quarry. Within a few minutes he spotted the pair battling in the center of the mass, felling Accursed and Demon alike. Quickly he descended again, hoping to finish the pair and then figure out how to salvage this siege. He had almost reached them when the trees at the edge of the clearing erupted in a torrent of shards. From behind he could hear an earthshaking roar.

He had almost forgotten.

*Gaxxog.*

# CHAPTER 17

It was not long after the march had begun that the rain started to fall. At first it was just a thin drizzle, but by midday it had become a torrent. Visibility became limited, and the army grumbled as they continued their march through the mud in wet armor and underclothes. The heavy drops struck numb skin like blades cutting into the flesh. Trent found himself removing his wet hair from his face more times than he would have wished to.

*The High God's tears fall upon us this day.*

Trent and Devin rode at the front of the train beside the Lady Ren, each seated upon an armored horse. The two Paladins had rarely fought from horseback, choosing instead to dismount when the battle was met, as they hoped to do this time. The rest of the cavalry, all of whom would be engaging the enemy while horsed, rode behind them. These were made up of Paladins and normal men alike, the elite members of the army who had received the most training. Horses had once been plentiful in the wilderness, but their numbers had slowly dwindled since the creation of all things. Behind the cavalry marched the foot soldiers, with the supply carts and pack animals bringing up the rear. The trail of men and women marching toward the unknown stretched back almost as far as Trent could see.

It was the greatest force that had been gathered in his lifetime.

The red-haired Paladin found himself shivering in his armor, the cold biting him in even the most covered of places. It wasn't the normal rainy season, so they expected the showers to pass by sometime in the afternoon. When even that came and went without any sign of the rain slowing, Trent began to see it as more of an omen than a natural occurrence. Horses slipped and threw men into the mud, supplies were ruined and boots got sucked into the muck. Some even whispered of turning back before they were silenced by sharp looks from the Seraph.

It was just past the middle of the day when they finally came across the fleeing throngs of villagers from the west. They came carrying everything that could fit upon their backs, leading horses and carts filled with what food they could gather on such short notice. Once the army met them, those without children were conscripted, and extra foodstuffs were added to the supplies.

"I won't fight!" a man pulling a cartload of turnips yelled as they tried to place a sword in his hand. "Why would I fight for the lot of you? When did Illux fight for us?"

Ren nodded and the man was placed in irons, while his cart was taken to the rear of the column.

"All those who are able must join our cause!" she boomed, her voice supernatural. "If you do not choose to fight now, you will be forced to fight when the time comes."

The man was dragged off toward the back where he would be forced to march with the rest of the troops until the time came to remove his shackles. Trent looked to Devin who merely shrugged and continued looking ahead, seeming to take no notice. Not all of the fighting men and women of the city had been forced to come, so why must it be so now? He knew that should they fall, the city would still need defenders; why couldn't these villagers be among them? The only answer that satisfied him was that the Seraph was afraid. It was clear that she didn't think the original force that she had gathered would be enough to keep her city safe.

The Paladins who escorted the villagers this far fell into line while the remaining refugees made their way to the city. Soon they would filter in and find that even with every third citizen marching forth in the army there would be little room for them.

*The slums will be filled to bursting soon. It won't be long before they run out of food and Castille has chaos on his hands.*

This grim realization gave Trent all the more reason to wish the battle lines were drawn so that all of this could be over. His mind strayed back to Elise for the briefest of moments, and he found himself hoping that he could rely on Edmund to keep her safe when the time came. They could not make any assumptions about what exact fate would befall them once the enemy was met. Even the large force that they had rallied would be hard pressed to stand long against the multitude that he had witnessed gathering in the wilderness.

Beside him Devin rode with confidence, sitting tall even against the downpour that plagued the army. He remained unfazed against the forced conscriptions Ren had placed on the villagers, oblivious to the discomfort of those around him. His large smile seemed to have returned permanently, as if nothing could break his spirits now that he was healed and on his way to another battle. Trent admired him for this, but he also respected caution, which his good friend often lacked.

Trent's eyes fell next onto the Lady Ren, who looked anything but comfortable. He could see in her eyes that forcefully conscripting the villagers brought her no pleasure, but she was a woman of duty, a duty that could not stand aside for acts of kindness. Her grim countenance was framed by her snowy white hair, which was plastered across her dark face. Even now Trent found her beautiful, and intended to stay as close to her as possible in the coming battle. She was the sword, and he would be her shield.

By the end of the first day the rain had not abated one bit, seeming almost like a malevolent force bent on enforcing its will upon them like an incurable plague. The army was forced to make camp just beyond the first village in a mire of thick mud. Slowly tents were erected on the uneven terrain, crushing crops that had yet to be harvested. The village itself was behind them now, no longer in sight of even the rear of the march. It might have been wiser to take shelter in the abandoned homes of the small emptied community. But as they had passed through it Trent had felt an uneasiness at seeing so many empty homes in one place.

*Gil.*

The tents only served to keep the rain from falling directly onto one's face as one slept, for it was far too late to stop the cold that had crept into their armor or to remove the sludge that caked their skin. Before retiring for the night, Trent and Devin helped the rest of the troops dig latrines at the edges of the makeshift camp, oftentimes relying on preexisting channels for irrigation as an easier alternative. It would be months before the fields here would recover from the damage that an army of this size would cause. A watch was set and the two commanders returned to their tents and fell upon the wet ground to sleep. As far as Trent knew the night passed without incident, for nothing awoke him from his fitful dreams.

The next morning they broke camp just before dawn. The rain had finally abated, but left behind a thin mist that clung to their clothes and the ground beneath their feet. The smell of the damp earth greeted Trent's nostrils like an old friend, reminding him of better days from his childhood. He had always loved that smell, and for some reason it now brought him some small comfort.

After they'd fed the horses, the march resumed through the mire, slower now than it had been the day before, but never stopping. By midday the rain had returned and the journey entered into an endless cycle of cold and mud.

After several more days, the grey march passed the final shell, marking what had been the limits of human habitation just a week before. The small ramshackle houses of the final village seemed to jut out from the earth like tombstones, marking the place where something ancient was buried. Surprisingly, none of the villages to the west had reported any incident before they fled east toward Illux, even though they had been the closest to the gathering storm. Trent imagined that this had been to prevent any word from reaching the city of their enemies' location. It was clear that the forces of Darkness had not counted on two Paladins stumbling across that valley and living to speak of it. Even so, the air in the empty town was toxic, a thick miasma that choked all hope from the soul. Trent knew that it was more than just the fear that had emptied the village that he felt. They were nearing the Great Chasm now, and its taint would never be removed from the land.

Again, they camped just beyond sight of the village, none wishing to stay the night in the uneasy place, even if it meant shelter from the rain. The next morning, when the march resumed, the terrain began to gradually change from grassy farmland to harsh stone. A sickness began to creep upon Trent as he recalled his previous journey to this part of the world just a few weeks before. The land here gave way to taint quicker than it did in the south due to its proximity to the Great Chasm. Marching ever toward the evil place began to make the army restless with fear. It seemed that a sense of expectancy hung thick in the air; surely today they would do battle with their foes, for what other end could come of entering such an evil place? There was little mud here among the stones, and the rain finally seemed to have subsided for good by the early morning. This made Trent feel even more ill at ease.

*Even the High God stays clear of this place.*

Ren gave the order and riders were sent out ahead of the army to make sure that they didn't stumble across the enemy unawares. The fastest horsemen were chosen and sent out in varying directions. They were instructed to report back after only traveling one or two miles at most to make sure that Ren knew that nothing had happened to them. Trent wished that he could have been one of the men chosen, for who was more familiar with such ranging than Devin or himself? But he knew that his value in this mission was as a leader in the battle, not as a scout, a fact that he still couldn't believe.

For the first half of the day the riders brought back the same report: no signs of the enemy. They found no fresh tracks, nor any sign of a large force having stayed in the area.

Shortly after midday there was a frightening change: one of the scouts didn't return.

Ren sent others in the same direction to discern what had become of their companion, but they disappeared as well. Once they were certain that none of the riders were coming back, Ren called the entire march to a halt. All of her commanders gathered about her to decide what must be done. Battle lines were drawn for the rest of the army's advance forward. The cavalry was to keep to flanks on either side while the infantry held the center. Scattered about the regular troops were Paladins, acting as unit commanders and Demon counter forces. Ren and her two commanders dismounted and remained at the center of the line, choosing to lead the engagement from the front where they would inspire the most confidence in those they led into battle. There could be no hiding for the Seraph if she wished to draw the Herald out and finish him quickly.

They continued on in their battle formations for well over an hour, the initial surge of adrenaline wearing off as signs of the enemy remained nonexistent. Somehow the air was still about them, and the sounds of their advance were muffled. Thousands of armored boots walked upon the flat stone, and yet, to Trent, it sounded as if they walked through cushioned grass. To either side of the advance stood rocky defiles that marked the entry into a gradually sloping valley, the edges of which rose up like a blackened crown. Trent looked over toward Devin, who nodded in solemn agreement: they were nearing the place where they had initially seen the enemy camped. It was from those very cliffs above them that the two warriors had seen the forces of the enemy sprawling across this plain.

There seemed to have been no signs of them, almost as if they had never milled about in this place, planning to strike at the light beyond.

Trent's uneasiness grew until he felt that he could barely contain it. Sweat had begun to run between his shoulder blades, causing his armor to chafe.

Then he heard the sound that he had been waiting for, and fear was replaced with an iron resolve. From somewhere in the ranks of the cavalry a horn blast sounded. The enemy had been spotted. Just on the horizon a black smear came moving swiftly in their direction. Ren barked orders and the army was wheeled about to face the charging army head-on. Prayers were said to the gods and steel was drawn.

*This makes no sense; they haven't moved since we saw them last. Surely they would have marched closer to Illux by now.*

The sickening feeling returned as a sudden realization washed over him. He swung about and addressed the Seraph, barely keeping his voice from wavering. "This is where we saw them before. They wanted to draw us out from the city!"

Her expression hardened. "I began to suspect as much this morning," she said. "They must have some trap that they plan to spring upon us if they would rather risk open loss in the field rather than simply trying to starve us out of Illux."

"Then we had best kill them before they can spring it!" Devin bellowed, raising his axe into the air.

"Hold the line!" Ren shouted, her voice taking on a supernatural volume.

The black mass rushing toward them slowly began to take shape, Demons and Accursed alike running forward with an unstoppable momentum. When the enemy forces were finally close enough that individuals could be made out from the whole, Ren gave the order and arrows were loosed. The sky was darkened with the flying shafts, felling hundreds in the front lines, yet still they came on, trampling those who had fallen. Their own archers returned the favor, sending volleys of crossbow bolts at the defenders.

"Shields!"

The cry went up and the sound of metal punching through metal echoed across the field. Ren shouted again and another volley came down, this time seeming to make even less of a difference. Their enemies easily outnumbered them by half, a conglomeration of hate that existed for one purpose alone. As they came closer, Demons could be heard howling battle cries while the Accursed silently stumbled ahead as fast as their broken bodies could carry them. All along the ranks, men began to cry out in fear, with some turning to run. The Paladins stationed near the cowards tried to stop them when they could, but none dared to take their eyes away from the death that made its way toward them.

Finally, Ren drew forth Nightbreaker and raised it above her head, letting out her own cry. "With me! With Nightbreaker! With your gods!"

The cry was answered by her troops, who broke into a sprint, following her advance with what speed they could muster. Trent and Devin ran as fast as they could to keep with the Lady Ren as she soared ahead, flying just above the ground like a hawk before it takes a mouse. Their blue cloaks billowed behind them as they ran, their white armor glinting in the shattered rays of the sun. Each step was like a hammer blow on the rock, shaking Trent to his core. Beside him Devin laughed loudly, lifting his great axe above his head. Trent only took a passing notice of these details, his mind too firmly bent on keeping pace with Ren. He promised himself that he would not be parted from her during the battle unless he had no other choice.

Then the lines met.

Accursed and human, Demon and Paladin, all were thrown together in a great flood of steel and iron. Ren flew up and down the line, hacking and hewing skulls and helms. Finally, she doubled back and landed among her men near her commanders, her presence bolstering the assault.

Trent and Devin slammed into the wall of fetid warriors with a ferocity that was unmatched in either line. Sword and axe swung side by side, biting into flesh and bone. They could not disarm their opponents without removing limbs, causing them to aim their attacks at exposed joints. For each Accursed that was felled, another stumbled forward to take its place. Through the haze of dust thrown up by the battle, Trent could just barely make out the cavalry on the wings harrying the flanks of the enemy force. The forces of Darkness as of yet had no answer to the cavalry, an oversight that might yet win the battle for the people of Illux.

"Forward, men!" Ren cried out, her voice full of thunder. "If we can split their center, they are done for!"

Nightbreaker sang a deadly song as Ren hacked back and forth, cutting a broad swath forward. Trent could smell the rotten blood that sprayed on her face from where he stood, fountains of ichor that were released by her strikes. She parted limbs and swords from the Accursed at a faster pace than even he could hope to match. The enemy stood no chance against her, and yet they came on with a mindless intensity. All about them men and women cried out in pain or choked out their last breaths as they fell before the onslaught. The sounds were deafening.

The first Demons that the trio encountered waded through the throngs of lesser fighters, moving with purpose to surround the Seraph. They shouldered through Accursed and cut down the soldiers of Light without ever removing their gaze from Ren. Trent noticed their approach first. He quickly gained Devin's attention and the two Paladins moved to either side of their Seraph, challenging the Demons head on. A prayer played across Devin's lips before he leaped through the air roaring like an animal. The large Paladin brought his axe down onto the helm of the foremost attacker, splitting it in two. The smoking shell of the armored behemoth fell to the earth a black ruin.

"Who else wants to try their luck?" Devin bellowed at them, lowering himself into a crouch.

*But whose luck will they be trying?*

It was not easily that Demons fell. Devin had killed the first with little trouble, but Trent doubted that would happen again. He rushed past his friend, engaging the next closest of the Demons, matching its attack swing for swing. This adversary was more prepared, refusing to fall as quickly as its predecessor had. Around them Accursed poured past, driven away from the smaller skirmish by the advance of the foot soldiers behind Ren. The humans continued to press their advance, engulfing the embattled Demons and Paladins in their wake. Ren engaged two of the Demons at once, easily blocking their attacks while answering them with her own. When the red energy began to crackle around their hands she responded with her own offensive magic, lancing blue fire from Nightbreaker and turning one of them to ash. The second was able to withstand the barrage and make it to her, his sword biting deep into her left wing before she was able to throw him back. She grimaced in pain but never slowed her attack.

The Demon with which Trent struggled had proven even more competent than he had realized, causing him to lose his shield in the mass of fighting warriors to his right. Unfettered by the heavy bulwark, he launched himself at the beast with all of the strength that he could muster, swinging again and again at the black sword that it held up to protect itself. Each blow vibrated his entire arm, but still he pressed on, thinking only of rejoining Ren to prevent her from receiving more harm. When the Demon finally returned an attack of its own Trent twisted to the side and rolled behind it, picking up a fallen sword as he did so. Then he quickly turned and stabbed the sword through the blood red cloak of the creature, pinning it to the dirt. Watching as the Demon struggled to free itself, Trent unhooked his own cloak and sprung into the air, lowering the point of his sword directly at the back of the Demon's head. It finally tore itself free and spun around just in time to see death descend upon it. Steel punched through its helm just where the eye would have been, causing it to collapse upon the ground.

Trent looked back at Ren to see that Devin had aided her in dispatching the last of the Demons. Freed from this immediate threat, Ren and her commanders again moved to the front of the line, leading their forces deeper into the center of the larger army. They stood at the point of a wedge that had slowly begun to pierce the heart of their enemies. Even so, Paladins and soldiers alike fell in numbers too great for them to keep up for much longer. If they could not gain the advantage that Ren hoped by cutting the enemy forces in half, then their losses could turn out to be too many for them to be victorious in this battle. The Accursed fell by the score, but their near limitless numbers still made them able to overwhelm the holy warriors.

Over the clamor of the fighting, Ren turned back to Trent. "There is still no sign of the Herald," she said. "I must make my presence known to draw him out. We cannot allow him to strike at us when we are not ready."

"Be careful my lady," he cautioned as she healed the wound to her wing and took to the air.

Ren flitted back and forth just over the tops of her enemies, attacking here and there before returning to the safety of the upper air. Trent reclaimed his shield and pushed ahead in her place, leading the wedge deeper into the midst of the enemy. Devin joined him, laughing again as he cut down anything that moved into his path. Slowly, they were gaining ground as Accursed and Demons either fell back or were cut down. Even with their losses, it had begun to feel like they had finally gained the upper hand that they desperately had needed. The scent of death hung heavy, wafting among the thick haze of blood and dust that choked the air. Even so, Trent could see the Seraph flying higher and higher now, spreading her wings as wide as she could to make herself visible across the entire battlefield. After several minutes of doing this she dropped back down again, falling like a stone before she lifted up at the last moment, killing several Accursed in her wake as she did so. It was a magnificent sight to behold, giving her troops on the ground the needed boost to push onward.

"For the Seraph!" Trent cried. "Forward, make a path for your lady!"

Trent and Devin's position at the front of the wedge was bolstered by several more Paladins who sprinted forward to join their commanders in the thick of the enemy. But once they were at least ten strong, Trent noticed something odd. It seemed as if most of the Demons were keeping away from the center where the Paladins had begun to cluster, as if they were purposefully avoiding battle with their chief rivals. This flew in the face of every normal behavior that a Demon possessed.

*Why do they not swarm us here? Do they simply wish to do more damage among the normal troops?*

"Where are the Demons?" Trent yelled to Devin.

The large Paladin turned, his white armor blackened with mud and blood.

"I do not know. They must realize that you and I will send them back to the High God before their time!"

With that pronouncement he launched himself back into the thick of combat, causing the wedge to split the Accursed even more than it already had. The other Paladins quickly followed in his wake, spreading out and cutting down the Accursed in an even path in all directions. Overhead, red flames arched across the sky, each aimed at the winged figure that spun and dropped to avoid them. She launched back blue flame and white hot energy of her own, cutting down those who dared to attack her.

*So she has been noticed. But still no sign of the Herald.*

Ren finally returned to them, thinning the ranks just ahead of the wedge as she did so. She landed just to the side of Trent, making quick work of the Accursed that he was battling with before pulling him back from the front. At her command, several other men rushed forward to fill the gap that they had created, allowing her to speak to her commander away from the fighting. All around them they still gained ground in a steady advance, now making regular progress even faster than they had been before.

"Something is not right here," she whispered to him. "There has been no sign of the Herald, and our wedge makes too much progress too quickly. We have almost cut their forces in two already, and yet they still outnumber us by half. Our cavalry does well on the flanks, but we have suffered our heaviest losses just on the edges of the wedge, far behind where we now stand. That should not be."

"I have noticed that the Demons have kept away from this position as well, even though they would be the most able to halt our advance."

"I don't like this at all. I am returning to the sky to gain another look. If nothing changes then when I return, we must reform the line."

"But that will give them ground."

"It will, but we cannot allow ourselves to be cut off and fall into some sort of trap. I will return."

Ren again took to the air, this time flying far afield of where they fought in the center of the battle. Trent tried to push Ren's uneasiness from his mind, removing any further distraction that it might cause as he made his way back to the front beside Devin. Shouting over the clashing of swords and the cries of pain all around them, he tried to pass on the misgivings of the Seraph. Devin's face never lost its smile, even when he nodded his head in agreement that something strange was going on. The two friends continued to fight side by side for a time, slowly feeling the fatigue of the hours of battle setting in. It would not be long before they would have to remove themselves to recover from the near endless exertion. The enemy would not tire, which put them again at a disadvantage.

Ren was returning to them when cries of fear and shock were taken up over the entire line. Men and women stopped fighting and pointed to the sky beyond the Seraph. She spun round to face what it was that those below her had seen. Around Trent men were cut down in a renewed frenzy, the Accursed not needing to halt to see what it was that had given the humans pause. He pushed his enemies back with his shield so that he could catch a glimpse of the thing that had filled his comrades with such dread.

On the horizon a great black shadow moved through the air, winging its way toward the gathered armies. Trent could tell even from this distance that the creature was a giant, easily the size of any building in Illux. It moved with a speed unlike anything he had ever seen. As it got closer it let out a near-deafening roar.

"What in the High God's name is that?" Devin called out.

In the back of Trent's mind a vulture squawked.

*Our doom.*

# CHAPTER 18

*The world is out of balance, and only chaos reigns.*

So mused Teo, one of the last Balance Monks left in the world. He had been bracing a wooden door that kept the Accursed from pouring into the room in which he and the others had barricaded themselves. So many pressed against the solid oak that he could smell their rot through it, an odor that made bile bite at the back of his tongue. The door had begun to buckle under their advance, but somehow he still held firm. There was no longer any hope for survival. All they could wish for was a few more minutes that Teo could hold the door to delay the onslaught that would rejoin them with their fallen god. Perhaps they could use this time to return their minds to the balance that had been taken from them hours before.

*The Grey God is dead, and there is no way that we can continue alone.*

The initial realization had come when he had tried to reach out to his deity after discovering the surprise attack on the fields below. He had quieted his mind and reached out to his god just as he had done thousands of times since he had joined the Balance Monks. Immediately, he had had known that something was terribly wrong. He'd cleared his mind and attempted to contact the Grey God again, hoping beyond hope that the problem lay with him and not his master. All sensations of the smoking farm and the burnt corpses that surrounded him had melted away, leaving Teo alone with his now tenuous link to the Divine Plane. Then the link had been cut and the world dropped out from under him.

His eyes had snapped open and looked to the sky. Already he'd been able to see that Aenna was dimmer than it had been before. His cries of anguish had been answered by every monk in the temple, each having felt the loss just as he had. Tears had rolled down his cheeks and a pit had formed in his stomach. He'd known even then that all was lost.

Rella had returned to him within minutes, barely holding herself together. She'd pulled Teo to his feet and the two had decided to return to the temple and do what they could to help the others. Even with Ravim dead they had to maintain balance on their own, no matter the cost.

But that was nearly two days ago now, and much had changed since that moment. The Balance Monks of the Grey Temple had been massacred by the forces of Darkness, nearly down to the last man. There were several holdouts within the temple, such as the group that Teo and Rella found themselves huddled together with now, but not many.

The others had been caught almost completely unawares, still reeling in shock at the loss of their god. Rella and Teo had been too late to warn them, and most had died in the open before they had even known what was happening. By the time the pair had reached the clearing, scores of their brothers and sisters had already lain dead upon the field with a wave of darkness washing over the refuse. Through sheer luck they had been able to make it inside the barricaded fortress and organize a counteroffensive. Teo and Rella had found themselves leading a small group at the flanks of the attackers, hoping to draw off enough of them that those inside could charge out and catch the rest with their backs turned. Below them the forest had caught fire from the burning crops, black smoke and red flame covering the mountainside.

The plan had failed at first, bringing only a token force of Accursed into their trap. The monks had also allowed for their rage to boil over their usual battle calm, causing them to lose their edge. It had seemed altogether hopeless until the Herald had arrived. The black messenger had taken notice of the fighters and begun slaughtering them himself, drawing more invaders to them than the monks had been able to alone. Once enough of the Demons were distracted, the gates to the temple had been thrown open and the field again plunged into chaos, but this time the Balance Monks had had the upper hand. Teo and Rella had barely escaped their battle with the Herald alive, Rella nursing a shattered nose and Teo with deep rends across his chest. Even so it seemed as if they had turned the tide of the siege in their favor—until the creature had arrived.

*Gaxxog the Incorrigible. One of the Divine Beasts.*

It was in the shape of a great lizard, large enough that it had to fell the trees in its path rather than fit between them. Its great scaled hide was a mottled mixture of sickly greens and rich purples. Spines covered every inch of its body like a phalanx of pikemen. Six great legs pulled it along, a tail tipped with an edge like a razor trailing behind it. The beast had emerged from the flames of the forest at the least opportune time, and it immediately began feasting upon the attackers and defenders alike. Teo knew that it was possessed of an insatiable hunger that it yearned to quench at any cost, but would never be able to.

As part of the Pact, each of the Divine Beasts was imprisoned by the Grey God beneath the earth. It was his decree that the Mortal Plane would never again be ravaged by the bearers of Divine Blood. It was clear that with his death, the seals under which he had shackled them were fading. Teo had known what this great creature was as soon as he had laid eyes upon it; his knowledge of the contents of the library was unmatched. One of the tomes located therein was an illustrated catalogue of all of the Divine Beasts, as dictated by Ravim himself.

*Now it is only a matter of time before they are all lost.*

They had gathered in the library, toppling shelves to bar entry from all of the windows and doors save the one Teo held firm. For some reason he wouldn't allow them to brace this final entry point. But why? Did he hope that they would still be able to escape? Or did he secretly wish for a quicker end to the misery that he now found himself in? Everything that had kept him sane after the horrors of his previous life had been taken from him, and he felt even now his old nihilism creeping in. Behind him he knew that his fellow monks were looking through what books they could in an attempt to gather the most important of them in case they found an opportunity to escape. Somewhere outside, Gaxxog climbed the exterior of the temple, tearing at the grey stones with its claws, looking for more sustenance hiding within. Outside the door Teo could hear the scraping sounds of iron against iron as the Accursed struggled to force their way through.

Rella stood at his back, holding her hands out in a battle stance. He didn't dare turn from the door, so he pictured her determined face in his mind as it was before all of this began. He knew that she looked different now, her nose broken and her eyes hollow. Finally, most of the other monks began to meditate, making a last feeble attempt at restoring their concentration before they faced what lay beyond the door. Teo had given up on such foolishness. He slowly watched as his training and hours of meditation slipped through his fingers, and yet he did nothing to reach out and catch them. It was too late for that. The Grey God was dead.

*Teo.*

The voice cried out to him, echoing through his mind, a stone dropped into an empty well. He immediately became alert, further bracing the door, which had become loose as his concentration had waned. The voice was familiar and comforting, but not quite his own. It had come from deep within himself, perhaps from some hidden wellspring of calm and courage that he had secreted away. He closed his eyes and let his mind reach deeply to the source of the voice. Teo felt a reassuring strength that he had thought he would never feel again. It washed over him as the voice spoke once more.

*You must bring balance.*

Suddenly his eyes snapped open, his focus restored on the task at hand. The old Teo was dead, and he would never again control the actions of the new. It mattered not if the voice was his own or that of another, but he must act to restore the shattered balance of the world; he knew that now. To do that he must survive this battle at all costs. The histories must be preserved, and the Balance Monks must go on to carry out the task that was assigned to them by their fallen god. Teo finally looked over his shoulder at his comrades and began to speak to them in a commanding tone.

"Brothers and sisters, we must prepare ourselves. There is no time for fear or meditation any longer. This door will not hold for more than another few minutes, but our order must go on, our histories must be preserved. We have a charge with which we were entrusted, and to fulfill that charge we must fight our way out of this temple, no matter the cost. So long as one Balance Monk survives this day, we are victorious."

Rella let a small smile cross her face. Teo's words were answered by murmurs of agreement as the other monks pulled themselves to their feet and prepared for battle, raising their staves or forming their bodies into the battle stance required for hand-to-hand combat. Rella walked over, picking up Teo's staff where he had dropped it upon the ground. She nodded to him and he jumped backward from the door, catching the weapon as she threw it to him. Outside, the sounds of the Accursed became a maddening frenzy as the door finally splintered and buckled inward. Within seconds it blasted off of its hinges, allowing the multitude of the wretched things to pour through the opening. The Balance Monks never moved, instead holding their ground and allowing their enemies to come to them.

The rushing onslaught of corpse warriors filled the room,

surrounding the outnumbered defenders. Teo swung his staff with controlled ferocity, smashing open skulls and rendering their weapon arms useless. The sounds of bones breaking became a deafening roar in the small library, bouncing from wall to wall. No blade could reach him; each was batted away at the last moment as if he were engaged in some beautiful dance of death with a dozen partners. Rella fared just the same, using her hands to catch the flat sides of the swords to turn them away from herself before twisting a neck or pushing a gore covered fist out the back of a rotted torso. The small group was able to fend off nearly three times their number before the tide of enemies slowed. Outside, the cracking of stone and near earthquake like rumble of Gaxxog could be heard. Around them the tapestries either fell or had been shredded by the fighting. Fissures had begun to form in the fresco of Aenna above them.

At a motion from Teo, Rella and the other monks grabbed the knapsacks of books that they had made and tied them to their backs before exiting the room. They ran down the halls of the temple in a tight cluster, easily dispatching any enemy that they came across as they made their way toward the large central chamber. Teo knew that it was a gamble to leave through the main doors, but other routes seemed too far from them now, and those they had passed had been covered by rubble from the beast that clung to the shell of the temple.

Upon gaining the large opening of the central chamber they were greeted by no fewer than three Demons, who quickly drew their weapons at the sight of their approach. The monks fanned out to surround this new threat, keeping their eyes open for any Accursed that might be lurking nearby. High overhead, light streamed through the many new openings in the vaulted ceiling. A great green tail could be seen slithering past a sizable hole.

This time it was the monks who took the charge to their foes, for they could not allow the Demons to gain the upper hand. Sprinting side by side they cleared the distance to the creatures in a matter of seconds, never losing the composure that they had spent their lives maintaining. The first monk to reach the Demons was slightly ahead of Teo, springing into the air and bringing his staff down upon the creature's thick armor. His attack was blocked by a ferocious swing of the Demon's blade that shattered the wood into a thousand tiny shards. The strike continued clear through the man, nearly splitting him in two. The unfortunate monk was tossed aside, leaving a pile of entrails in his wake as he skittered across the tile.

*We cannot allow them to use magic. With the Grey God dead, we will have no way of countering it.*

Teo twisted his body at the last moment as he reached the first of the horned brutes, barely dodging its attack before delivering a flurry of his own. Each blow that he landed left a dent in the onyx armor deeper than the last. And yet the creature never slowed, as if it didn't even notice the small amount of damage it was sustaining. The other Demons had begun to engage the remainder of the monks, and it seemed as if they would overcome them in short time, their armor protecting them from any reprisals. Teo knew that he would need to rely on his speed to bring the Demon down. He rolled under the behemoth's great legs just as it turned to strike at him, sending it staggering from a harsh thrust to the back of its helm. He could feel the metal give slightly, but he didn't have the strength to cause any real damage. The head of the thing turned and glowered at him, even with no holes for eyes to see from. The lone monk lowered his staff and stood completely still, closing his eyes as if to meditate, even in the thick of battle.

The Demon took the bait.

It hissed and raised its sword high over its head to bring it down in one final, crushing blow. Lightning fast, Teo struck, thrusting the staff just into the small gap where the helm meets the breastplate, shattering whatever flesh and bone hid therein behind the thin gorget. The Demon stood as if it were stone, transfixed in place with the sword still above its head. Teo withdrew his staff and jammed it in again and again, each time getting deeper and deeper into the creature beneath. Finally he saw the staff protrude from the back of the Demon's neck, at which point the sword dropped from its hands and bounced across the floor. Once he pulled his staff free the armored brute fell facedown, never again to rise.

Teo turned to see the progress of his companions; most lay dead or dying, as did the second Demon. The third had begun to back away from the survivors, who had started to encircle it. Rella led the way, covered in blood both red and black. She stepped toward the beast, clutching the sword of its fallen companion in both hands. Teo knew that only she out of all of them would be able to use such a weapon effectively. He began to make his way toward the group when the Demon suddenly roared and savagely sent lances of flame flying from its mailed fists. Stone and human debris exploded from the floor where the attack struck, leaving nothing of the monks who had stood in its path. Rella had barely avoided the new onslaught, dropping her newfound sword and returning herself to her combat stance just to the side of where the attack had landed. Even her speed might not be enough to overcome this Demon if it relied wholly on its magic. The sounds of the attack bounced off of the walls of the chamber and down the halls connected to it. Within moments more Accursed and Demons poured into the room, leaving behind whatever tasks they had set themselves to in the rooms beyond.

All of the monks held their breath, afraid to face whatever new occurrence would plague them next. Teo felt that their chances at escape were again slipping away.

But before any of the new attackers could reach the remaining combatants, they were covered by a sudden avalanche of stone and mortar pouring from the ceiling overhead. It seemed as if the entire roof of the temple had been shorn off so as to allow the great girth of Gaxxog entry. Many of the running Accursed and Demons were crushed instantly, the survivors making for the walls where they were well away from the open maw of the Divine Beast. Gaxxog quickly pulled its weight down into the chamber and began to feast, bringing several of the walls collapsing inward as it did so.

In the confusion, Teo and Rella made for the front door of the temple. It hung open on twisted hinges ahead of them, the last barrier to freedom just within their sight. The Demon that had inadvertently summoned Gaxxog had disappeared under the rubble along with the remaining Balance Monks. One man made it free from the vortex of dust and death to fall into line just behind the fleeing pair. From the corner of his eye, Teo could see that it was the initiate with whom he and Rella had sparred several weeks before. Surely his skills had improved if he had lasted this long. Perhaps he was the key to starting the order again once they were free of this place.

The trio ran through the door just as the great lizard caught sight of their frenzied flight, launching itself in their direction. The remaining wall of the temple halted its advance for a few brief moments, giving the three monks time to gain access to the smoke-filled clearing beyond.

Just as they had thought themselves clear of danger, one long reptilian arm emerged from within the open doorway and came crashing down upon Rella. The initiate threw himself into her, sending her careening just beyond the razor claws as the foot smashed him like a man smashes an insect. He remained conscious for only a few more seconds, looking at Teo with pleading eyes before he was dragged back into the ruins of the temple. Lying on the ground next to where he fell was his knapsack of books, which Teo grabbed before pulling Rella to her feet and running through the smoke into the ruins of the forest. They never once looked back at what remained of their home.

The two monks continued running down the mountainside for hours, narrowly avoiding trunks that still burned and patches of smoldering earth that surely hid enough coals to end their escape. The loss of his newfound companion caused him great pain, but there was no way that he could bring himself to stop running, lest his death be in vain. Beside him he could see that Rella's eyes were watering from more than just the smoke that choked their vision. Soon they passed the remains of what had once been their fields, still strewn with the bodies of their fellow monks. So far, it seemed they were the last.

Finally, Teo and Rella found themselves near the base of the mountain, some hours after they left the shell of the Grey Temple. There was a stream at which they stopped to clean their wounds, neither choosing to break the silence with anything as pointless as speech. It seemed as if after what had just happened, no period of silence would be long enough to honor the fallen.

After finding nourishment in the surrounding wood they both sat down and attempted to meditate, Teo hoping that he would be able to clear his mind and gain some insight into what they should do next. When all of the world around him had slipped away, the voice that had spoken in his mind earlier finally returned to him.

*Teo, your god has need of you.*

# CHAPTER 19

One hand firmly gripped the black cord that hung from the bell, the other still clutched the severed head of the Grey God. The Fallen One quietly stood on the center isle of Infernaak, listening to soft murmuring of the liquid fire as it meandered past. It had been days since he had killed the main obstacle to his plans, days that he had spent wandering the abyss that separated the light from the dark. He was looking over all that would soon be his and his alone, all the while biding his time. Lio had waited to summon the others so that all of the proper pieces could first fall into place. Now he simply had to wait for the right time and he alone would walk the Divine Plane.

Lio knew that the others would have sensed Ravim's death, but neither would have any idea of who it was that had actually fallen. It was likely that they had chosen not to communicate with one another; rather, they would wait to be contacted by the Grey God himself. What fools they were. Cowardice was at play here more than caution —cowardice and apathy.

*That will give me the edge I need to deal with them.*

The bell hung silently, commanding Lio to ring it and call forth his companions. He could easily slay them both before they even knew what had happened. Even at the peak of their power they wouldn't have been a match for him. Only Xyxax had come close, and even he hadn't stood a chance. These two were like children compared to Xyxax, just as Ravim had been. It would be so satisfying to see the mocking grin on Vardic's face turn to pain and fear. The thought made the Fallen One lift the head of the Grey God to study it.

*Something like this expression right here.*

Part of him wished to wait here for days, just to see how long it would take for them to venture forth on their own. He knew that it would be a millennium before that happened. The fires of war burned so low in their hearts that it was hard to even tell that the two sides opposed one another. This lack of interest seemed to him to be more akin to cowardice than anything else. Ever since Xyxax had died, all of the gods had begun to fear for their lives like they never had before. He could stomach it no longer. His grip tightened on the cord even stronger.

"I will be certain that both of you know that it was I who did this before I take your pitiful lives," he snarled. "You will no longer mock me after this day."

The tolling of the bell shattered the silence of Infernaak, bouncing off the black walls and returning to the ears of the Fallen One. He pulled the cord again and again, the loud clanging becoming almost musical to him. How long had it been since he had heard that sound? Far too long. Each descent of his arm caused him greater fury, sending him closer and closer to the madness that he often tried to keep at bay.

*They will answer my summons or I will kill them in their keeps!*

Finally, he pulled down on the great cord with such force that the entire bell came crashing down onto the stone. He drew his blade with his now free hand and began roaring at the two fortresses like a wounded animal. It seemed to him that his bestial snarls echoed even louder than the bell before them had. With each passing moment that his summons remained unanswered he clutched harder at the skull of the Grey God, threatening to crush the head like an egg in his palm. On the ground beneath the macabre trophy a pool of silver had begun to form, fed by the rivulets that drained from where the Fallen One dug in his fingers.

Then a door opened.

It was the keep to the left of him that emitted the solitary form of a woman. Rhenaris. She exited the tower with no great urgency, coming out as if she were on a simple stroll. Even from this distance he could see her grey skin as it was illuminated by the fires below. He hoped for a brief moment that once she reached the bridge her pace would quicken and they would be face to face all the sooner, but she denied him even that. Lio actively forced his rage back into check, for if he did not there was no telling how he might respond to the goddess.

*No. Not yet. It's too soon. Where is the other? Where is Vardic?*

Rhenaris finally made it across the bridge and came to a halt some distance from the Fallen One, keeping her eyes on the blade that he still held aloft. If the blade alone was not enough to give her pause, then surely the look of madness in his one good eye was. He wasn't sure if they had ever truly feared him before, but after today that would surely change. He locked eyes with her, waiting for her resolve to crack, but she said nothing. There was still no sign of the other member of their pantheon, a fact that nearly caused Lio to lash out at his new visitor. She must have sensed his intentions, for her hands twitched, almost imperceptibly, toward her own weapons: twin flails with skull-like heads hanging from black iron chains. The dark spines upon her head and neck bristled.

"Why have you summoned me here, cretin?" she hissed finally, shifting her body to a more defensive stance.

It was Lio now who remained silent, choosing instead to study her rather than respond. He had almost forgotten the sight of her voluptuousness in the intervening years of his exile. The armor that she wore was light, barely covering the vital parts of her body. She preferred instead to show as much of herself as was possible, luring many a mortal to give his soul for a chance to see more of what lay beneath. A longing for her grey skin crept over him and filled him with a revulsion that dominated every other emotion that he contained. Her look of seduction was not meant to cause pleasure, but madness, something that he had to remind himself. Even so, he had never loved another before or since his Daniel, and no god or goddess could fill that void.

The long black spines flared again when the minutes continued to drag on without a response from him.

The Fallen One smiled at her once he noticed that her eyes had finally drifted down to the prize that he so desperately clutched in his off hand. Her eyes opened wide and she let out a terrible scream, drawing forth both of her flails. Distantly he watched as the exposed muscles of her abdomen clenched, her entire body preparing itself to strike. Even more curious to him was the way in which she seemed to quiver now. Finally, she saw him as the threat that she should have from the beginning.

"What have you done?" she demanded angrily, her spines bristling in all directions.

"I have brought nothing more than a gift for my companions, a sign of good will. And yet you reject my summons and address me with disrespect."

He closed his good eye for several long seconds, struggling with the weight of what he must do. It seemed to him that he had never undertaken so insurmountable a task as facing down these two dark gods. All the while his white orb looked on, unblinking as always. The smell of sulfur finally began to overwhelm his other senses as he drifted into the recesses of his madness.

*Still, I need the other.*

"Where is Vardic?" he asked, keeping his eye still closed.

"I am here, Fallen One, though I know not why you have called us forth," said a new voice, this one confident and deep.

Lio slowly opened his eye, seeing that his second companion had finally joined the first. Even for all of his bravado, Vardic kept a safe distance from his crazed summoner, and, it seemed, his female companion as well. He looked just as he always had, his mocking grin showing that he held no respect for his onetime enemy. His own armor was large and bulky, not unlike that of the Demons that served them, but he wore no helm upon his head, preferring instead to show off the large horns that sprouted from the sides of his temples and curved inward like the horns of a bull. He had always been the vainest of them, as could be seen by the red ribbon that bound his jet-black hair where it fell behind his shoulders.

Before Lio could address him, Rhenaris pointed at the dripping head in his hand, quietly hissing as she did so. Vardic only let his own shock show for the briefest of moments before the sardonic smile returned. His expression did little to hide the fact that he now held his spear with its multitude of barbs slightly in front of himself rather than keeping it at his side.

"So you kill another of our members, and still expect to call yourself one of us?" he spat, motioning with the spear.

"Ravim had not been a God of Darkness since I slew Xyxax."

"His new position made him no less one of us than yours made you any less a God of Light."

*He never considered Ravim to still be a God of Darkness. He only wishes for a reason to kill me and take my place as the lone god.*

"I am what the High God made me. As was Ravim. He cared not for you any more than you did for him. You are not actually angry that I killed him, but fearful of what that means for you!" Lio couldn't keep his rage from bleeding through again.

"Why have you done this?" Rhenaris asked, her eyes never leaving his face.

"I have done this because it is the only way that the war could continue. While the Grey God lived, we feared him and his retribution, so we failed to continue our task and try to extinguish the Light! For what other purpose do we exist than to defile and desecrate that which is sacred?"

"We may have lost our taste for the war, but never did we abandon our stake on the hearts of mankind. Men still kill and steal and rape and cheat on the Mortal Plane. This is our doing, Vardic and I."

"They do not need us for that. Mankind is weak! This is why he must be subjugated by the Darkness. He doesn't need your infernal whispers to stain his heart, for it is already black. What have you done of late besides that farce with the bandits and the blood sacrifice? Nothing. We must crush them or lead them, not play games with them."

"And why should we believe anything that you say now? Why should we trust you? You who have killed two gods now, and broken the Pact?"

"Because you still wish to destroy the Gods of Light as I do."

"What then is your plan? Enlighten us." Vardic lowered his spear, but never dropped his condescending tone.

*I will kill you first, once your guard is truly lowered.*

"Already I have marshaled our forces on the Mortal Plane. All of our servants are converging to form the greatest army that we have ever mustered. Once Illux gains word of the threat they will march forth and be annihilated."

"How are you so sure of this? What if they wait behind their walls?"

"Our Herald has already begun awakening the Divine Beasts. They will be used to crush the forces of Light and then the city itself. Where they decide to make their final stand matters little; their doom is inevitable. The Grey Temple has already fallen to one such creature. Or were you so distracted by your plots that you didn't sense the awakening of Akklor or the hunger of Gaxxog?"

Rhenaris said nothing, but a flicker of doubt passed behind her eyes. Vardic almost looked as if he genuinely held some admiration for Lio after what he had just been told. The Fallen One knew better. Vardic would never respect him, not even once the knife was plunged into his heart.

"The other gods do not yet know of the Grey God's death. Like you two, they are cowering in Ayyslid thinking that the dead fool will contact them about which one of us has died. This gives us the time that we need to strike."

*And then I will kill you both.*

The other two Gods of Darkness exchanged furtive glances before looking back at Lio. Rhenaris lowered her flails, smiling as her spines dropped flat. Beside her Vardic struck his spear into the ground, cracking the stone. They were playing right into his hands, just as he had known they would.

"When do we begin?" Rhenaris asked.

The Fallen One loosened his grip on the head.

*It is only a matter of time.*

# CHAPTER 20

As the shadow moved closer, a second, smaller shape broke away from it and flew lower to the ground. This other thing soared directly over the enemy troops, causing a new furor to wash over their ranks. Without a doubt Trent knew this lesser creature to be the Herald, the absence of whom was now perfectly explained. Whatever the larger beast was, it sent chaos through the ranks, causing some men to flee in fear while others who had been distracted were cut down by the Accursed. Trent felt a chill as he realized that the entire tide of the battle had just changed.

The great beast finally swung close enough that Trent could make it out in its entirety. It was a wicked looking thing that seemed to him to most closely resemble a bat, if not altogether twisted into some cruel mockery of such a thing. It was covered in tufts of brown hair intermixed with black scales and spines. At the apex of each leathery wing was a clawed hand, the fingers of which ended in curved yet altogether human-like talons. Likewise, the feet held the same monstrous appearance, behind which followed a hair-covered tail. It banked hard left and then right, blocking and unblocking the sun in a sweeping motion, sowing madness wherever its shadow fell. An unnatural roar emitted from the great maw that split the beast's head in two. Above the mouth and flat nose were two red eyes that Trent felt every time they passed over him. Within its brown mane he could see that it possessed large ears that were cupped in a way to better take in the sounds from the ground beneath it.

Trent could see the Lady Ren returning to their position now with a greater urgency than she had before. It seemed as if the heavenly glow which usually surrounded her had been extinguished, for even Aenna above was blocked by the dark shape that made its way toward them. It was more important now than ever that she rally her troops, lest the forces of Light break into a full retreat. Already the line to the left and right of Trent was almost shattered, and the forces of the enemy pressed their considerable advantage. Soaring low and high while still dodging a barrage of enemy crossbow bolts and Demon-fire, Ren landed just behind the front, immediately barking orders in her commanding voice.

"With me! We cannot falter now! Do you want that beast at our door? Do you wish for it to attack our homes and devour our children? With me!" Her voice thundered over the clamor of battle and the sounds of a frenzied retreat.

With those words she charged ahead, attempting to help force the line back into position. Any man that turned to run was quickly righted when she threatened him with her blade, which was black and red with blood. The line would hold, or all was lost—that much was clear. The wedge needed to cut the enemy forces in two, and quickly before the great bat-thing was able to break the ranks. Ren's earlier premonition was correct, and they had fallen into a baited trap.

Trent slew an Accursed that barred his way to her, cleaving through to the bone at the shoulder in a splatter of black gore. Others he shoved from his path or cut down where they stood. He needed to know what they were up against and how they were supposed to deal with it.

*If she doesn't have a plan, we are lost.*

"What is that thing?" he cried out, leaning close enough for her to hear.

"It must be a Divine Beast," she replied, hacking into the head of an enemy that strayed too close. "I have already spoken to the gods; they have no idea how the seals holding them have failed."

"Do we know which one it is?" Devin panted, having fought his way to his friends without Trent noticing.

"Arra says that it must be Akklor the Unbidden. He was a favored servant of Xyxax before his death, and one of the most fearsome of the creatures."

"Must be? Are the gods still not watching the battle through Aenna?"

"No, they hide away in Ayyslid until the Grey God summons them."

Devin blocked a blade from reaching the Seraph before decapitating the attacker. "I think it is safe to say that if his seals are failing then he won't be summoning them. How do we kill it?"

"Like any other creature. With steel."

Devin began to laugh at the Seraph's answer but he was cut off by another ear-splitting roar from the Divine Beast. By now Akklor was almost directly overhead, and it was making its way straight for the wedge. Ren nodded to her companions before launching herself into the air at the thing. Trent felt his stomach tie itself in knots as he watched her small form race ahead toward the larger flyer. Even far below where he and Devin stood they could hear Ren cry out to the gods above as she brandished Nightbreaker above her head. The two collided in a matter of seconds, the great beast attempting to grab the Seraph with its winged arms or lash at her with its taloned feet. The sun backlit the duel, turning the fighters to shadows that stained the sky.

Feeling helpless, Trent grabbed the nearest soldier that he recognized, a woman named Tess, commanding her to make her way to back of the line and bring forward every archer that yet lived. They were to fire upon the beast only when Ren was a safe distance away from it. She nodded and turned, pushing her way through the throngs of men who were not yet in the thick of battle on the edges of the wedge. Trent knew it would take her a good while to do as he commanded, for it would be no easy task to push against the tide of fighters that made its way toward the enemy. Still he hoped that she would return in time to make some kind of a difference. He returned his gaze to the sky just in time to see Ren deftly fly underneath one of the beast's wings, cutting a long red tear as she did so. Black blood flecked with sliver fountained forth and landed among the fighters on the ground. The smell of it filled the air, somehow stronger and sweeter than the smell of decay and death that had previously covered the earth upon which they fought.

Akklor cried out in pain.

"You will pay for that transgression, witch!" its inhuman voice thundered, drowning out all sounds of battle across the field. Even the mindless Accursed were distracted for the briefest of moments as they gazed skyward.

Ren twisted and dove, easily out-flying the much larger creature as it tried to retaliate against her. Suddenly it swung its arm, catching the Seraph across the chest, sending her spinning away like a rag doll before falling like a stone. Trent was far from the only warrior in the line to cry out in dismay. A blow like that would have killed any who did not have Divine Blood, and even the Lady Ren must have suffered serious injury. Desperately, Trent scanned the skies for signs of the Seraph, but saw no trace.

Then the line broke.

The shock of seeing the Seraph fall had given the forces of Light just enough pause that they had been overrun by the attacking Accursed. The rotting warriors flooded through the front lines, tearing into the men and women who had been up until now safe from direct assault. The wedge had failed, and within moments it became intermixed with friend and foe alike.

It was then that Akklor resumed his attack upon troops along the ground. The Divine Beast swept low, raking the earth with its talons, sending rock and warrior flying into the air in a flurry of dust and blood. Once he had gone beyond the wedge he turned again for another pass, this time splitting it right up the center. His path intersected directly with Trent and Devin, who found themselves jumping to safety beyond the line of Accursed.

As the Divine Beast flew off to attack the cavalry on the sides of the army, Trent and Devin became surrounded by enemy warriors. Accursed came at them with sword arms swinging wildly, their empty eye sockets filled with impossible hate. The two Paladins quickly fought their way toward each other, dodging crossbow bolts and iron blades that whistled through the air. They backed up to one another in a crude attempt at prolonging their struggle, forcing the Accursed to form a tight ring around them. The once clearly demarcated line of fighters that had formed on the edges of the wedge had begun to recede from their location; the overrun men and women fell back in a barely controlled retreat. At the edges of Trent's vision, he could see Akklor laying to waste the men on horseback, tossing riders and mounts into the air to be caught in its gaping jaws.

Desperately, Trent began to pray, hoping beyond hope that the goddess Arra could afford him some measure of support. Her response never came and he was left with only Devin at his back.

*That is all I need.*

"We have to make for the line. We cannot stay here," he gasped over his shoulder.

"I figured you wanted to kill them all from here. Now that I know otherwise, we should run."

Trent couldn't help but smile, yet he knew that they were running out of time. The battle had been raging for hours now, and even their energy reserves would fail soon. Exhaustion, more than any other foe would be the death of them. Seeing a small opening Trent yelled to Devin to follow before he started running, pushing Accursed out of his path with his shield and hacking others with his sword. Devin followed closely behind, bellowing a great war cry while rending his foes with his battle axe. The two warriors cut a path back toward salvation in even less time than Trent could have hoped.

Just when they thought that they would regain the safety of the line, the ground underneath them exploded in a flash of red flame. From behind them a lone Demon approached, throwing its minions aside when they found themselves in its way. Trent shook his head to free it of the ringing in his ears. He could feel that the hairs on his face were singed, but he was otherwise unharmed. Beside him Devin had already pulled himself to his feet and was preparing to face this new threat. Trent pushed up from the blackened stone and attempted to do the same.

*Where have you been hiding?*

The Demon came on slowly, not with caution but a clear arrogance. It seemed as if the armored behemoth felt like it had all the time in the world to dispatch the two Paladins. It was as if they were cut off from the rest of the fighting, and battled this new aggressor in an isolated arena. Infuriated by the attitude that the Demon presented, Devin charged ahead, swinging his axe wildly with no care for aim. Trent quickly chased after him, not wanting his friend to become overwhelmed while facing the creature alone. The Demon easily parried each blow, barely even bothering to return any of its own. As this continued for several minutes, Trent could feel the sweat that soaked through his underclothes from the ceaseless exertion. He soon realized that he and Devin were slowing down while the Demon seemed altogether unfazed. Anger and fear alike washed over him.

*Most of the Demons stayed back during the early fighting. They will all be at full strength like this one, just now arriving to clean up those of us left.*

As his endurance slowly began to ebb, he knew that there was nothing that he or Devin could do to outright overpower the creature. It would simply wait until they either made a fatal mistake, or were weak enough that it could batter through their defenses and finish them with little threat to itself. Any use of magic by either Paladin at this point was likely to be a death sentence for the caster, using what little life-force he had left. Even so, Trent decided that this was truly his only option. The Paladin stepped back from the range of the Demon's blade and cleared his thoughts, preparing just enough energy to heal his companion. He did not have the strength left to attack the Demon directly with magic, but he hoped that he could give Devin enough of his strength back to finish the beast on his own terms.

The ground shook beneath their feet.

From behind them men and women began to scream in fear, screams quickly answered by the sounds of death. A great roar split the sky, again causing men to cover their ears in anguish. Trent allowed himself one glance over his shoulder. Akklor had landed amidst the remnants of the wedge and had begun feasting on the remaining troops there. The Divine Beast was covered in arrows, and yet it seemed completely unhindered. Even the bloody wound that Ren had left behind in its wing seemed to give it little discomfort. The forces gathered around the beast ran in all directions, fighting madly to get away from its monstrous reach. It was this push that moved the line closer and closer to the beleaguered Paladins. The Demon used this confusion to press his advantage, knocking Devin back and quickly disarming Trent. Left with only a shield, all he could do was grip it tightly with both hands and try to fend off the savage assault. Each clash of blade and bulwark rattled Trent to the bone and brought him closer to failing. When Devin tried to intervene he was again knocked backward out of reach.

*Gods, help me.*

Soaring out from the haze above came the Lady Ren, bloody but unbroken. Nightbreaker ever clutched in her hand, she swooped low and made straight for the slaughter happening just around Akklor. Upon seeing the fate of her two trusted commanders she abruptly changed course and dove directly into the chest of the Demon, punching through its breastplate before it even knew she was there. It was over before Trent had even realized what was happening. She followed her initial assault with an outpouring of blue energy that incinerated the Demon completely, leaving only ash in its wake. He could see that the expression upon her face was of the utmost rage. Without a word she laid her hands upon both her champions and filled them with healing energy, energy that Trent knew she could not do without. Her own wounds still looked fresh, and blood had begun to turn her white hair crimson. Meekly he tried to protest her actions, but a stern glance silenced him.

"Come. One way or another, we must end this," Ren said. "That beast dies now."

She returned to the air and flew just along the heads of her enemies, cutting a swath for her men to follow. Trent and Devin ran through the pathway she had created, desperately trying to keep pace with their Seraph. She had renewed large quantities of their stamina, but Trent still feared that it might not be enough. Ahead of them, Akklor continued to rip men from the ground and bite them in half, throwing the discarded parts into the sea of fighting below him. Its earth-shaking roars were intermixed with sounds that could have been construed as laughter. As the commanders ran on, they gathered a mix of Paladins and soldiers who clung on to what little courage they had left, their strength renewed by the determination shown by their Seraph.

Finally, the Lady Ren and her forces reached the clearing of corpses that had formed around the Divine Beast as it thundered about the killing ground, crushing and clawing at any survivor that caught its eye. At her sharp command the fighters fanned out in a wide arc to avoid being easily crushed all at once by the bat-creature while Ren flew up to eye-level. Her fury was almost palpable as she called out to it, causing Akklor to turn and rest its wicked gaze upon her.

"I will crush the life from you," it roared, lunging forward but never leaving the ground.

The Seraph dodged its attack, swinging her sword at the side of its face, causing it to screech in pain.

"As long as one servant of the Light yet lives this day, then your wretched life will surely end," Ren said.

"Then I will crush them all!"

Akklor suddenly took notice of the warriors upon the ground, many of whom had reached the base of the monstrosity and were attempting to hack at its legs and tail. Trent dug his sword deep into the tail of the beast and started to climb, hoping to gain a position where there was softer flesh to attack. Being this close to the thing brought forth a foul stench that nearly caused him to retch, and the feeling of its matted hair made his skin itch. Devin was still upon the ground with the others, striking directly at the monster's talons, which seemed to do little at all. Sensing the danger, Akklor swung its great tail, shaking Trent loose and sending him careening into the earth while his blade stayed firmly embedded between two black scales. The tail swept along the ground, crushing several Paladins in its wake. Above, Ren still circled it, flying in close to attack at its neck and face. Trent gazed helplessly at his sword from the ground, still lodged in the upper reaches of the tail.

Ren dove under the undamaged wing and sliced another long rent to match the first. Just as before, silvery blood rained upon the battlefield, sizzling where it landed amongst the corpses. As if it suddenly realized that it could never outmaneuver her from the ground, Akklor lifted itself into the air, its great wingbeats driving the remaining attackers into the stone. Trent dazedly realized that the Accursed seemed to be making their way toward where he lay upon the earth, but he still struggled to pull himself upright against the gusts that the flying beast generated. Ren and Akklor dipped and rolled around each other in the air, leaving those below to stare upward in awe.

Trent finally pulled himself up and joined his haggard group that had all done the same. Arming himself with a stray sword that he nearly stumbled over, the dazed Paladin stood shoulder to shoulder with his brothers in arms, Devin chief among them. The forces of Darkness began to close around them, forcing the soldiers to begin a hasty retreat, keeping their eyes ever on the aerial fight above them.

Then out of the swirling smoke and dust a dark shape slammed into Ren, sending her spinning away from the Divine Beast in the blink of an eye.

*The Herald.*

Freed from his sole opponent once again, Akklor returned his sights to the men gathered just below him on the ground. Within moments he was in a dive, his shadow covering the small group who scattered to evade his strike. His claws raked the ground with a deafening crack, killing half of the group in a single pass. The Divine Beast spun in the air and returned for another blow. The others ran in different directions, leaving Trent and Devin to stand alone. Trent knew that they wouldn't be able to run from it this time, and it seemed to him that Devin knew this too. The large Paladin unhooked his shredded cloak and readied his battle axe. Trent looked at him quizzically, for the situation was hopeless and yet his friend still prepared himself. Devin merely shrugged and began to laugh.

"It had to end sometime," he mused mirthfully.

Trent nodded and readied his own blade. "I will look for you by the High God's side."

"I suppose you will, but not this day." Devin pushed Trent down to the ground with the butt of his axe before launching himself into the air as high as he was able.

Trent cried out to stop him, but it was too late. Akklor had swooped low, and now slowed its flight to roar at the speck that flew into its view. The great beast snatched Devin out of the air with one of its winged hands, nearly crushing the large warrior as it did so like an insect in its palm. It held the Paladin before its face to study him for a brief moment, all the while keeping itself suspended in the air. Devin never stopped laughing, even as he pulled his axe free with one hand and threw it directly at the face of Akklor. It spun end over end, passing through the short distance between them as if it were carried on the wind. The Divine Beast tightened its grip, crushing Devin and cutting his laughter short. Moments later the axe buried itself deep in the beast's eye, causing it to roar in anguish.

On the ground below, Trent answered its cry with one of his own.

# CHAPTER 21

The air had been knocked from Ren's lungs and she was spiraling out of control, wrapped in the treacherous embrace of her winged rival. His presence enveloped her completely, from his iron grip to his musky scent. The smell of this thing was different than all of the other dark creatures gathered this day, more perfume than rot, yet it still made her skin crawl. During her attempts to kill Akklor, she had almost completely forgotten that the Herald had yet to show himself, and now she chided herself for it. She knew that without her, the soldiers that she had left behind would stand no chance against the Divine Beast. Even if she could free herself from her assailant, did she risk giving up her chance to kill him by returning to save the rest of her forces?

*Even Trent and Devin? Those whom I care for the most?*

The voices of the gods filled her mind, responding to her thoughts as if she had spoken them aloud:

*The Herald is the key; you must strike him down no matter the cost.*

*Do not fail us Ren.*

*No! Finish Akklor! Without our own Divine Beast, he will wreak untold havoc!*

There was the voice of Arra, always set apart from the others. It was only because of the wishes of that goddess that Ren had even been appointed Seraph. If Luna and Samson had gotten their way the position would have gone to Castille instead, a fact of which they were quick to remind her at every opportunity. The old man knew it too, and never forgave her for it. In her times of weakness, she thought that maybe he would have made a better leader, more akin as he was to her predecessor. At the very least, her life would have remained simpler if she were a Paladin and not the voice of the gods. But this was no time for weakness, so she did as she always had and pushed her doubts aside to focus on the task at hand.

*I will not let this creature best me, nor will I allow Akklor to destroy my friends.*

They were still flying, the Herald's claws digging through her armor into her flesh. She could feel her energy slowly fading from the constant flow of magic that he was feeding into the open wounds, preventing her from healing herself or gaining the strength to break from his parasitic embrace. Nightbreaker was still clutched in her hand, but she could not bring her arms to bear. She needed some other way to loosen his grip so that she might escape. The Herald's head was just within reach of her own, the horn-covered countenance looking at the ground rather than its quarry. Seeing that this would be the only opportunity that she would be given, Ren bit down on the scalp of the creature, just above the base of the horns, and tore upward. Flesh and sinew gave way, spurting black and silver blood onto Ren's face and chest, leaving her hair stained the color of onyx. The Herald roared in pain, jerking his head upward, one of his horns slicing open her cheek.

Her face was burning from the contact with his tainted blood, but the lapse in focus was all she needed to break free of his bonds and kick him away. Finally it was her own wings that kept her aloft rather than those of the enemy, bringing her close to him again as she readied herself to attack. Nightbreaker flashed before her, tearing through cloth and flesh on the beast's chest, sending him spinning backward in agony. The wind that rushed past her ears was almost deafening as she continued her assault, flying directly into him while bringing sword and even fist against him.

Slowly regaining his composure, the Herald parried each of her blows with his claws, his reptilian eyes following her every movement in his attempt to outmaneuver her. The two remained locked in this dance while staying aloft, spiraling and diving around one another high above the fighting below. In the distance Ren could vaguely make out Akklor rising through the air.

*I have to speed this up, or it may be too late.*

Ren pointed Nightbreaker at the Herald, sending a blast of blue lightning down the blade and directly at the creature. His response was swift, meeting her own attack in midair with a barrage of red flame. The two competing flows of magic illuminated the battlefield for a brief moment before Ren's sputtered out, her own energy wavering from fatigue. The fire from the Herald slammed into her body like a stone, sending her backward and downward, hurtling toward the earth below. Nightbreaker fell from her hands and dropped even quicker than she, disappearing from her sight.

*I can't let it end like this. Gods, give me strength.*

The energy that they fed to her was small, just enough to give her mind clarity again. The world around her was spinning faster and faster as she came closer and closer to reaching it. At the last possible moment before splattering upon the ground, Ren spread her wings. They caught the air so forcibly that they almost tore free from her body, causing her to cry out in pain. She could feel the fractured bones within them, and the blood that now flowed without. Ren collapsed onto the earth, broken but alive. Above her the Herald was descending, a triumphant smile splitting his dark head. Her intense focus on the figure coming toward her made his leathery wingbeats sound deafening in her ears.

When he was just overhead he spoke in a whisper-like hiss. "You disappoint me, Seraph. I had hoped for more of a challenge, but after all, we killed your predecessor to have an inexperience foe. Surely he would have fought better than you."

The muscles in her neck tightened as she choked back a retort.

*I will not give in to him. Where is my blade?*

Desperately she scanned her surroundings for Nightbreaker. They had landed just to the edge of the battle, the bulk of the fighting happening some way off where her forces moved out of range of the Divine Beast. Nearby the cavalry attempted to regroup and regain command of their mounts after the madness that Akklor had caused when it had landed among them. They all seemed so far away from her now, as if they fought in another realm that she could only see glimpses of. Some distance away from her she saw the familiar glint of a sword stuck into the earth. The Herald followed her gaze to the blade and let out a mocking laugh. He began to angle his slow descent toward Nightbreaker rather than Ren.

*I'll kill him, even if I have to crush his face in my hands.*

Then the battlefield was torn asunder by the cries of Akklor. This roar was unlike any sound that the beast had previously uttered, a mix of pain and terror that was unbecoming of such a creature. Ren looked in the direction where she had left the winged thing and saw that it was now flying madly in her direction, bobbing and weaving through the air as if it had lost its mind. Again and again it roared, causing the nearby cavalry to lose control of their mounts once more. Blindly it lashed at the earth, sky, and even itself, raking its claws across its face and back where it could reach. From this distance Ren could not make out what ailed the beast, but she knew that she would soon find out.

The Herald turned in the air to see what had caused his pet such pain, giving Ren just the chance that she needed to spring forward and sprint for the blade. Ignoring the pain in her wings, she threw herself upward and made for her salvation. Hearing her footfalls on the stone, the Herald retrained his attention on the matter at hand, diving for Nightbreaker himself. From behind him the thunderous approach of Akklor could be heard getting nearer and nearer. Surely by now the crazed thing was just above them, ready to fall and crush both Divine messengers in one fatal blow. At the last possible moment, just as Ren reached the blade, the Herald pulled back and rained fire down upon her. Stones were blown from the earth in a cloud of dust and debris. Ren was barely able to throw up a barrier of energy for herself as the attack struck, only just saving her own life.

It was then that Akklor soared overhead, creating a gust of wind that sent the Herald careening to the ground and the Seraph to her knees the moment she allowed her barrier to fall. Ren was able to catch a brief glimpse of the Divine Beast's face contorted in rage. Its left eye was gone, replaced instead with what appeared to be a large axe. Upon its back she could see the shape of a lone figure, armored in white, striking repeatedly at the base of the neck. Akklor shuddered from the blows, sending showers of blood and hair below with each convulsion. It finally came crashing down just some distance from where she was crouched, shaking the earth so furiously that she again lost her footing. The cloud of debris thrown up by the collision with the stone would block out the sky for several minutes.

*One of my Champions. I must go to his aid.*

*Ren, the Herald! You cannot falter now.*

It pained her, but the gods were right. Her foe must be dispatched before he had time to regain his advantage. The fate of her friends and confidants would not matter if the forces of Darkness continued to crush their army. With the beast behind her dead the opposing army had lost its greatest advantage, but with the Herald they still could maintain the order needed to press their attack. Order was what would win this fight now. In the distance she could barely make out the shapes of her men and women who it seemed had begun an open retreat, the Accursed chomping furiously at their heels. Even with the Divine Beast taken down, the battle had been all but lost.

Scanning the haze, Ren saw the Herald running toward her, his right wing badly crushed. Summoning the remainder of her strength, the Seraph took to the air, flying past the red flames that now licked at her face. With an earthshaking cry she swung Nightbreaker before her, striking the Herald in the chest with blade and magic both. The crackling blue lightning sent the creature flying backward with an inhuman cry before he landed sprawling upon the earth. Ren landed and cautiously approached the fallen figure, her legs barely keeping her upright. She would end his pitiful existence and make her way back to what was left of Akklor. The Herald lay upon the ground clutching at his broken wing, the membrane of which was shredded and bloody. His chest was still smoking from her assault.

"You wanted a challenge?" she cried to the beast, her dry throat causing her voice to crack. "I would have found a way to kill you if my every limb had been torn from my body."

His eyes locked with hers, the reptilian orbs looking her over not in fear or even respect, but curiosity. She knew that he had finally realized that she had been underestimated, and that gave her some measure of pride. Ren raised Nightbreaker over her head and brought it downward, straight for the heart of her enemy. The Herald spread his wings and launched into the air, knocking Ren backward as he did so. She collapsed onto the stone, but this time kept her blade tight in her grip. Her enemy winged his way back toward the rear of his troops, disappearing into the distance.

She could feel the hot sensation of tears welling behind her eyes as hopelessness began to take hold, but she pushed it away as she knew she must. Cursing herself for allowing her enemy the time to heal his wing, she pulled herself upward and turned toward the small crater that had formed where Akklor had fallen. She could sense the dissatisfaction of the gods, but none chose to speak to her. Moving with all the haste that she could muster, Ren made her way to edge of the pit. The Seraph knew that she could waste no more time in pondering her previous mistake, for now she feared just what she would find within the earthly scar before her.

*Please be alive. I cannot bear to lose either of you.*

Ren innately knew that it was either Trent or Devin that brought the creature down. The axe that she had seen buried in the beast's eye had to have been Devin's, and the great Paladin would have been hard pressed to abandon the weapon. What that meant for himself and Trent she could not be sure. Perhaps there had been two figures upon the creature's back?

Reaching the lip of the crater she peered over the edge, taking in the horrific sight all at once. Lying upon the earth at its center was the still twitching body of Akklor the Unbidden. The Divine Beast was covered in silvery black blood and his head lolled to the side as if the tendons holding it in place had been severed. It appeared that the base of its neck had been torn open by some enraged beast many times its size. Wondering with what inner strength could have brought forth this attack on the creature, Ren caught sight of the crumpled form of a Paladin lying some distance away from Akklor. The cloak and armor of the warrior was blackened and crumpled, and he lay in a pool of blood both red and black. Recognizing the long red hair, she cried out and ran to him.

"Trent!"

She reached his side, cradling his head in her lap. The back of his hair was sticky and matted from blood. His breathing was shallow, but he yet lived, though he already smelled of death. Probing his body, Ren could tell that many of his organs had been damaged, and several of his bones had been broken. He would die within minutes if she did not act. But could she? She barely had the strength to go on herself, let alone to provide the extensive healing that Trent required. With her troops in full retreat, her presence was needed more than ever, especially since it was her mistake that allowed the Herald to escape. Even if she could muster the strength to save Trent, it could very well mean her own life.

She brushed the strands of hair from his face and studied it; his expression was almost serene. How different he looked now than when she had first seen him all those years ago. It was possible that he had never looked this peaceful in all the time that she had known him. Ren had cared for him from the first, the small boy who had thrown himself into Paladin training to avenge his dead brother. He had taken to the training quicker than some of the other recruits nearly twice his age, ruled by an anger that most of them could only imagine. Still, she had seen something in him that others could not, some piece of that little boy whose innocence had never completely been snuffed out. Over the years, the motherly compassion turned to an outright respect for the skilled warrior and ranger who had become unflinchingly loyal to her. He had surrounded himself with friends to replace his brother, but it was something else that had drawn him to her. Even when Ren found herself scorned by her commanders or the gods, still Trent and his friend Devin had remained steadfast. She respected the bombastic Paladin the same as she did Trent, but as of late something else had begun to stir in her breast, a feeling that she knew as Seraph she must suppress. Laying here in her arms, it was impossible for her to deny the presence of those feelings that she had for him.

Looking away from Trent, Ren again studied the now-still body of the Divine Beast. The axe that had been buried in its eye was surely the one wielded by Devin. The glassy orb had been cut open and drained of all fluids, leaving the weapon lodged into the weak flesh beneath. Of the warrior himself there was no other trace. Ren felt ill when she realized what that had to mean. Only his death could explain the savage wounds on the back of the creature's neck. Trent wasn't just killing Akklor, but the beast who had killed his friend, the Demon who had killed his brother. She looked down at him again, finally at peace. Would saving him be the crueler fate? Had he not suffered enough? Terric, Gil, and now Devin?

*No. I will not lose you both. Gods, give me the strength to save your champion.*

The Gods of Light did not answer her prayer. She could still sense their presence, but they refused to speak to her. Her failures against the Herald had made them turn from her, even now in her time of greatest need. Only Arra gave the slightest response, and even that was only a feeling of deep regret. Enraged at her abandonment, Ren cast Nightbreaker aside and cradled the dying warrior against her chest. Behind her horns blew, confirming that the retreat was absolute. It was very likely that the troops assumed their leader dead, or simply no longer cared and were acting accordingly.

A tear ran down her cheek as she began.

Ren fed all of the healing magic into Trent that she could, taking away from any lingering attempt by her body to repair itself. All of her old wounds began to slowly reopen, no longer receiving the attention that they demanded. She could feel the broken bones and damaged organs inside Trent begin to heal, each returning to the fallen Paladin a measure of strength. His breathing finally returned to normal and he began to stir. Still Ren kept on, refusing to stop even when she tasted blood in her mouth.

Finally, it was done. She was barely conscious of Trent opening his eyes below her, staring up in wonder.

"What?" he asked, confused.

Ren couldn't get any words out, but forced a weak smile. Trent sat up and looked around at the carnage, clearly in awe of what he had wrought. The Seraph could feel herself slump over onto his chest, her energy finally giving out all at once. Vaguely she could hear her champion shouting her name, but it was drowned out by the sound of the horn.

*We have lost. I have failed.*

# CHAPTER 22

"I can't wait any longer!"

Arra slammed her fist on the branch beneath her, the living wood recoiling from her attack. She glowered menacingly at her companions, each reclining on curved chairs made from moving branches. There the three had been sitting for the past several hours, witnessing the battle on the Mortal Plane below through the mind of the Seraph Ren. They had taken turns answering prayers and sending energy below as well, although that had stopped sometime after Akklor had arrived. It was difficult for them to intervene more than they had without directly seeing the action through the Basin, but until they were contacted by the Grey God, they had all agreed it was too dangerous to yet leave Ayyslid.

"But you must wait, dear, for it would be unwise to leave Ayyslid until we know what is really going on," Luna cooed.

"We may wait here for an eternity if we expect Ravim to come and summon us. A Divine Beast has been awakened, which means his seals upon them have either failed or been circumvented, neither of which would have happened if he still drew breath."

"If you truly believe the Grey God to be dead then all the more reason to remain here, lest you walk into a trap and meet the same fate." Samson stood, anger playing across his face. "We do not know that he is dead. Perhaps he chose to allow them to free Akklor since one of their number was killed by the others. In this way balance can be maintained without striking one of us down."

"You don't really believe that," Arra spat, standing herself. "Neither of you believe that. You have only refused to leave until now because you are afraid!"

"Afraid of what?" Samson asked. "Those cretins in Infernaak? We could crush them at any time."

"You fear death, as all of us do. There is no afterlife for a god, and that scares you!"

"If you wish to run to your own doom, then leave!" It was Luna who sounded angry now. "We have no more use for you here."

"The champion that you forced upon us as Seraph has failed, and our armies are routed," Samson said. "She disobeys our commands at every turn. She will fall soon, and then Castille will ascend to her place."

Arra walked up to Samson, her eyes never leaving his own. She rested her hand upon the greatsword at her back, her fingers brushing across the snarling tiger on the pommel. At this range his bow would be almost entirely ineffective if she chose to strike. This would be the first time in this war that blood had been spilt between two gods of the same pantheon. Would she really be the first to commit such a sin?

*Unless we are right about the Gods of Darkness turning on each other. How are we any better?*

From the corner of her eye, Arra could see Luna standing and drawing free her warhammer. There was no way she could win against them both. Samson knew this, which must have been why he showed no real signs of fear. Arra thought he was being foolish, for he would surely die before Luna could come to his aid. How perfect would that be for Samson and herself to die this day, leaving Luna to sulk alone for all time? Or would the High God return Lio to his rightful place to fill the void? Could this moment right old wrongs?

She doubted it. Arra lowered her hand back to her side.

"If Ren falls I will hold both of you personally responsible. What kind of a god wishes destruction upon their own? How are either of you better than Xyxax or Lio? How are any of us better than them?"

She sighed. "I am going out there to see just what it is we are up against. With our army having failed, we need a new plan to ensure that we aren't wiped out, an outcome you seem to be ignoring. Don't expect me to return."

Arra strode past them both, making her exit through the walls of the keep. Behind her Luna and Samson stood speechless as they watched her go. How many times had she left them like this over the millennia? But this time she didn't intend on returning unless she was dying. Arra heard the walls of living wood close behind her for what she hoped was the last time. Rarely had she gotten along with the others, but ever since Lio had fallen she had remained apart intentionally, blaming herself for the rifts that had formed.

*What have we become? I could look upon the Gods of Darkness and see no difference any longer.*

Arra continued through the forest, slower and more cautious than usual. With a quiet growl Divinity returned to her, the great cat stalking just ahead, never completely out of sight. With her last true companion at her side, Arra felt that she would be far safer than she had been hiding in Ayyslid. Like her companions, she had thought that it had to have been one of the Gods of Darkness that had fallen, but as the battle was met between their forces she had grown more and more unsure. After the appearance of a Divine Beast on the Mortal Plane she was certain that something had happened to the Grey God. No amount of posturing from Samson and Luna could convince her otherwise.

Prayers filtered up to her ears from the Mortal Plane below. Never before had so many cried out to the gods for aid since the cleansing of Illux by the Balance Monks some five hundred years before. When Akklor had arrived the cacophony had almost been deafening, and now it slowed, not due to a lack of need but a lack of hope. The power that the gods could extend to their followers on the Mortal Plane came from their Divine Blood, and as such even it had its limits. The amount of blessings that she had already bestowed upon her champions during the course of this battle had been too much to replenish. It would be another day before Arra was back to full strength. She could not even help those whom she favored the most, which is why she had accepted that Trent would need to begin his journey to the High God. And yet her Seraph had disobeyed her orders and expended much of her own life force to save the Paladin.

*This is why she was chosen. She never puts herself, or even her gods, before her people.*

But now it was possible that both would perish because of the Seraph's choice. The army was in full flight from the battle, with the forces of Darkness nipping at their heels. They wouldn't make it far before they were forced to again turn and fight, at which point they would be slaughtered, even without the presence of Akklor. Ren was too weak to lead, and due to her failure to kill the Herald the forces of the enemy were still unified. They had played right into a trap that it seemed to Ren was years in the making, and none of them had had the foresight to see it coming. What had happened to Ren and her army fell onto their shoulders as well.

*If only we could find our own Divine Beasts and free them. Then they might stand a chance.*

She knew that would not happen. It was only a matter of time before the army would find itself crushed. Then it would be up to Castille and his paltry forces to hold Illux against the deathblow that hung over it. In the past they could have expected help from the Grey Temple or even Seatown, but if her fears were at all correct then no help was coming. The forces of the Grey God were most likely in just as much disarray as the army of Light, and those in Seatown had most likely seen the opportunity to take the independence that they had been craving. It would take a miracle for them to withstand the attack that came at them now. Once their people were defeated, what purpose would the Gods of Light serve? How long before they too fell to the Darkness of Infernaak?

*And my companions don't even see it. None of us saw this coming. How could we be so blind?*

As she walked behind the great white tiger she contemplated which of the three Gods of Darkness had conceived of this masterful strike against the Light. Surely it had not been Lio. The Fallen One had remained an enigma to Arra ever since he had been cast down. The scorn he had received from his brethren would surely have given him cause to hate them, but even he must have seen that it was by his own hand that he had fallen. But now she was not so certain. Surely he did not wish to eradicate the Light as his newfound companions did? After all, the god had not changed, only his position.

That left Vardic and Rhenaris as her only choices. They could have planned this attack together, but she deemed that unlikely. The Gods of Darkness had rarely worked in tandem since the death of Xyxax, and before that it was only in fear of him that they worked together at all. Vardic might have been the more dangerous foe, for he was the bravest and vilest, but Arra felt that this was most likely the work of Rhenaris. The attack had been somewhat deceptive, with the forces of the enemy assembling in secret and the Divine Beast being used only at the most opportune time. It fit the style of the dark goddess more than her male counterpart. It had been decades since she had actually seen either of them, but their ghastly countenances still burned in her mind's eye.

Divinity slowed and returned to her side as the trees began to thin ahead and the white stone became visible in the distance. She would know the answer very soon one way or another, of that she was sure. Once she stepped upon the smooth white surface she turned to the great cat and stroked her cheeks. Her companion rumbled in response, the intelligence in her eyes urging caution.

"You should stay here," Arra said. "You are at home in these woods, not where I must go. Watch for my return."

She wiped the tear that formed and continued on ahead, scanning her surroundings vigilantly now that she was again alone. Her enemies surely wished to catch her here in the open and remove one more obstacle to whatever plan they had crafted. And yet she did not lower herself to the ground, or attempt to hide her approach in any way. The goddess walked with a confidence that masked the doubts which plagued her mind. She couldn't allow anyone to think that she had lost control of the situation.

Her footfalls on the hard stone echoed in the silence in a way that she didn't recall noticing before. Each step reminded her that she walked toward an empty seat. Ahead it loomed, the Throne of the High God. As she neared it she noticed something that made her stop short and let out an almost inaudible gasp. The great stone chair was, for the first time in over a thousand years, unempty. She quickened her pace to see who it was that actually sat upon the sacred throne.

*Could it be? Has he returned in my time of need?*

Arra got within range of the High God's Throne and stopped, appalled at what she saw. Seated upon the carved throne was the god whom she had not seen in any capacity since he had been cast down from the Gods of Light. Lio, the Fallen One, sat as if in deep thought, with his grey head resting upon his mailed fist. His greasy, yellowed hair covered his good eye—leaving only the dead white orb to greet her. Cradled in his lap was an object that she couldn't quite place. Anger seethed through her at his gall to defile the most sacred site in all of creation.

"By what right do you defile the High God's Throne?" she exclaimed, drawing forth her sword.

The Fallen One lazily looked up from his perch as if he had not a care in the world. Upon seeing the angered goddess who addressed him, a smile crossed his face.

"My eye has not gazed upon your beauty in some time, Arra," the Fallen One said. "I have missed my closest companion."

"I will ask you again, *Fallen One,* why do you sit thus?"

His genial expression was replaced by one of rage for a brief moment. His smile then returned before he began to speak. "I sit here by the Divine right of godhood, bestowed upon me by the maker of this throne himself."

"You taint the very stone."

"I am as I was made. Tell me, why have you come here, old friend?"

"You are no friend of mine." She gripped her blade tighter.

"I almost forgot, you abandoned me with the rest of them. I would have expected as much from Samson, and even Luna, but never from you. You, who were my closest friend before I was unjustly cast down." His voice had turned cold.

"You were cast down for your crimes against creation."

"My crimes?" The rage returned to his face. "What of Xyxax's crimes? Would the High God have punished those? I was merely meting out justice to a depraved monster. I was fulfilling the charge given to me by my creator. What of the rest of you?"

*Has he gone mad?*

"Your charge was to protect creation and spread the Light, not to destroy our enemies and ruin the Mortal Plane!" Arra cried.

"You are no different than the rest of them, are you?" he asked, almost to himself.

"I am very different. I am perhaps the only one of us who actually wishes to fulfill her charge."

"Yes, you are ever loyal to our creator. The rest of us are below you, as we have always been. It is truly too bad, then, that you have failed in that charge. Your people are dying, slaughtered at my command, and you have done nothing to save them. Even now your Seraph has fallen."

*So it was you. It was I who has truly been blind.*

"How could you turn against your own so easily?" she asked, her voice losing its confidence.

"Because you could abandon me so easily. Look into the Basin. Show yourself how it is that you have failed so miserably, Arra."

She could see the surface of the Divine Blood begin to shimmer and change, showing an image of the Mortal Plane below. Yet she chose not to look, unwilling to lower her guard and play into his hands.

"Where is the Grey God?"

"Ah yes, I had almost forgotten him."

The Fallen One lifted the round object sitting in his lap and tossed it at Arra. The thing bounced down the stone steps, making sickening crunching sounds as it did so. When it came to rest at her feet she recognized the face of Ravim, the Grey God. Her rage was immediately replaced with revulsion and she took an involuntary step back. She felt a bone-chilling fear suddenly wash over her.

"He looked almost as shocked as you do," the Fallen One said, a wicked grin splitting his face. "You see, I realized that the only thing keeping our war from really heating up again was not actually the Pact, but the Grey God himself. As I killed another god before him, I figured that it would not be that difficult to accomplish again. I was not wrong in this."

"You will pay."

"How so?" He leaned forward in his seat. "There is nothing that you can do about it, and I don't expect your companions hiding away in Ayyslid to be of much trouble either."

The Fallen One slowly stood and drew his own blade. Arra began to cautiously back away from him, her eyes falling again to the severed head at her feet.

"I have always loved you Arra, even when you no longer held love for me," the Fallen One said. "Be grateful that you won't live long enough to see the Light fall."

Arra spun to escape from the descending figure. She heard a sickening crunch as an explosion of pain wracked her body. The goddess cried out and collapsed to the ground, her knee a ruin. It was Rhenaris, and not the Fallen One, who loomed over her, ready for another strike. Weakly, Arra lifted her sword to block the swing of a second flail. The chained weapon wrapped around her blade just short of her face. She could feel the blood gushing from her crushed knee. The sensation nearly distracted her from the danger she was in.

Arra yanked the flail from Rhenaris' grip just as Vardic plunged his spear through her side. Silver blood ran from the edges of her mouth as she desperately tried to stand, but faltered and fell against the Basin.

As the Fallen One walked past the pool his fingers broke the surface of the silver liquid, sending ripples across it that brought images of the Mortal Plane forth. He approached Arra, who was only just holding onto her own sword while she leaned against the Basin for support. The Fallen One gripped her by her hair and lifted her up so that she could see the surface of the Divine Blood. She couldn't even feel the pain of her hair tearing from her scalp as she looked at the scene that played out beneath the silver liquid. It was a great battle that was being fought on the Mortal Plane, but it seemed that something had caused the fighting to slow.

"I want you to see how badly you have failed," he cooed in her ear. "Our forces caught them again, and my Herald is about to kill your Seraph. I want you to die knowing that you have truly lost."

The Fallen One raised his sword above his head. Somewhere behind her Arra thought that she heard the roar of a tiger. The sword fell toward her neck. She let out a cry of despair, not for her imminent death, but for the final image that she witnessed in the Basin.

# CHAPTER 23

Trent had lost track of how long they had been running.

It felt like it must have been hours, days even. The Accursed followed them in an untiring torrent of death. They would never slow. Never stop. The same could not be said for the humans that tried to escape them. They fell around him, some succumbing to wounds and others to exhaustion. It would be over soon either way.

Everything that had happened since Devin's death was just a blur in Trent's mind. The Paladin was numb to everything that he had seen and done since that moment. He did remember the despair that he had felt upon seeing Devin's body crumple in the beast's hand. And then the rage. After climbing upon Akklor's back it wasn't long before the two were hurtling earthward. He hadn't had any care for self-preservation in that moment, no thoughts of winning the battle or any hopes of victory. He had merely been a vessel of vengeance. The next thing that he remembered was looking up at Ren just before she collapsed. The amount of energy that she had expended to keep him alive must have been staggering, for it had nearly rendered her unconscious. It had taken him several minutes to get her back to her feet, and several more before they had any hope of regaining the fleeing army that they commanded.

She ran beside him, in the center of the retreating men. They had caught up to the army on horseback, catching two of the frightened beasts that were still reeling, riderless, from the attack by Akklor. Whether it had been fear or fatigue Trent was not sure, but the poor creatures had died shortly after he and Ren had joined the retreat. No doubt their bodies had been trampled by the forces of Darkness that followed quickly behind. The only thing that now kept them from being overrun were the few remaining members of the cavalry that guarded the flanks of the retreating force while thinning out the attackers who made it too close.

*She can't last much longer. None of us can. Not like this.*

Ren's face was cold and hard, a determined expression playing across it. Trent could see that behind it, weariness was setting in. She looked haggard and drawn, a far cry from the font of stamina that had led these same troops a few hours before. Whether she had regained the energy to run from the gods or some hidden wellspring of will he wasn't entirely sure, although he had a good guess. Even so, this forced retreat had to have been causing her more pain than she showed. The troops were beginning to slow; an ever-increasing number fell and found themselves at the mercy of the Accursed, ever within reach. The smell of excrement and blood seemed to go before them, the sickly reek of fear. What she hoped to accomplish now was beyond Trent's ability to guess at. It was clear that all was lost.

Under their feet the rocks continued to slide on endlessly, as if tormenting them with the knowledge that they would never again reach the grass of the fields. Exactly which direction they were running he wasn't sure, although he imagined that it was ever toward Illux, a beacon in the distance that was shrouded in dust and death. With the few forces left guarding the city, Trent doubted that they would gain any protection beyond its great walls.

*Even if Castille would open the gates for us. Even if we could last the three days it would take to return. None of us will last the next three hours.*

His mind turned again to Devin, his lifeless body tossed aside by the enraged Akklor, the beast blinded by the large Paladin's final blow. What little victory that it was. It was as if he had lost his brother all over again, the smell of his blood on the snow no different than the sound of Devin snapping in two while he laughed as he always had. It was just as he had dreamed.

The shadow.

The field of death. Just like in the dream, he was unable to save the Dove. He had no wings.

Trent's eyes flicked over to Ren, trying to gauge her progress.

*She never should have saved me. I never wanted her to die for me. I never wanted any of them to die for me.*

In front of them a soldier stumbled and fell, his blade dropping from his loosely clutched fingers. His fellows tried to hoist him up between them, but when he couldn't support himself they let him fall again. Ren stopped and knelt beside the man, spreading her wings wide to force the flow of the retreat to go around them. Trent dropped beside her, looking over her shoulder at the man who would clearly die soon. He was young, the stubble on his face barely longer than the fuzz on a peach. As much as it pained him to do so Trent tried to gently pull Ren away, hoping that she would follow self-preservation rather than duty this one time. She recoiled slightly from his touch and continued to hold the dying man.

"We must stop," she said, her voice hoarse. "We cannot abandon all of these men. Soon there will be none left."

"We cannot stop, my lady," Trent responded. "The Accursed are not far behind."

"Then we fight them. How would you rather die, Trent? Running and afraid, or with a sword in your hand? We cannot escape them."

"We cannot defeat them."

"I would rather see you all die as Devin did than as this man will. We will not fall to cowardice only to be stabbed in the back by our enemy. We must face our death head on. Only then would I feel worthy to join the High God. I lead us to this doom, but I will see that it is a glorious one."

The conviction was finally returning to her voice. Even weakened as she was, she had begun to regain the inner strength that made men follow her. Trent smiled in spite of himself. She was right. Running from the foe was no way to die, and surely they could not hope to live in either case. He pulled free his sword and nodded to her, turning back to face the death that came at them. Ren gently laid the fallen man down and drew forth Nightbreaker. Raising it above her head, she shouted over the din of fleeing soldiers.

"We will run no longer! All those who are not cowards, with me! We die on our feet this day!"

Ren took to the air, flying back toward the front of the retreat. She dipped and swayed at first before her strength slowly returned, struggling to regain the attention of all who saw her. She repeated her words again and again for those who did not hear, an incantation that strengthened the resolve of those in her charge. Within moments the retreat was brought to a grinding halt. The Seraph was aided by members of the cavalry who wished for the glorious death that she promised, riding in wide circles about the fleeing force to slow the rout. It wasn't long before the line was turned about to face the enemy head on. Some still broke away and ran, and more than a few of them fell with an arrow in their backs. Trent could no more blame the cowards who still ran than he could blame the overzealous warriors who spared them the drawn-out death that running promised.

Ren landed at the front of the column, continuing to galvanize those who still followed her. It seemed as if she had regained her glow and all of the energy that she had previously expended. Trent tried to make his way through the sea of men to where she stood, but too many barred his path. Looking from face to face he saw that many still held a deep-seated fear. More than one looked as if they still wanted to flee but feared death from a friendly arrow more than the iron blades of the enemy.

*It won't take much for some of these to break ranks and run again.*

It wasn't long before the battle was resumed. At first it seemed that the Accursed had been given some pause at the sight of their quarry turning to face them head-on. The mindless creatures no doubt lacked the understanding of bravery in the face of destruction. Demons whipped at their backs and drove them forward once the initial shock of the change had worn off. Ren shouted and ran ahead, her makeshift army following closely behind. The two lines collided with more force than Trent would have thought possible coming from the battle-weary warriors that surrounded him.

Attempting to rally those near him, he cried out, "Fear not for your lives, for those are already lost. Instead, take as many of these bastards with you as you can!"

The cry was taken up and down the line as the battle was met, mixed with chants of "For the Seraph! For Illux!" and even Trent's name was called out by those who had seen him take on Akklor by himself. Trent waded ahead as far as he could, ferociously cutting down every fetid warrior that stumbled into his path. As he cut his way forward he drew many others to him, for they either recognized the man or his goal. He was joined at his flanks by two Paladins, both women with braided brown hair who could have been sisters. The two fought side by side, savagely rending their enemies just as he did. What better company to die in?

Demons filed in and out of the front lines, barking orders or killing the stray warrior foolish enough to wander into their path. Those who fell before them were few, for the hulking brutes never truly waded deeper into the thick of battle, choosing instead to remain behind the safety of their underlings. When they did finally cross the lines, it would almost certainly herald the end of those who remained. Even without the direct threat of Demons, Trent knew that they were outnumbered some three to one, and their foes did not tire the way that normal men did. It would not be long before the initial surge of pride and duty wore off and this glorious charge became a bloodbath. He hoped to fall before he saw the ranks break again.

From his current vantage point Trent could just barely see the white hair of the Seraph near the middle of the line, where Ren was no doubt pushing her body to the very limit of her energy reserve. It was a miracle that she was even still standing, a beacon of hope to those who stood firm around her. He could just make out the swath of Accursed that rushed in her direction, only to fall from view, no doubt cut from shoulder to hip by Nightbreaker. Several Paladins had begun to make their way in her direction, hoping for the honor of dying to defend their holy leader. There was no way that Trent could not do the same.

*If the Lady Ren must die, then it will not be before I have given my life for her.*

A red light flashed before his eyes as the air around him was lit ablaze. Pieces of burnt flesh splattered onto his face. One of the Paladins beside him was gone, instantly destroyed by Demon fire. The second cried out in anguish, scanning the battlefield for the creature who had come close enough to kill her companion. Trent saw the armored behemoth some yards away, the red glow of its magic having not yet faded. It was surrounded by a retinue of Accursed that held back from direct combat, instead only engaging those who journeyed too close to their commander.

"There!" Trent shouted at the woman as he pointed toward the Demon. "Together!"

*I am no more than vengeance made flesh.*

Pushing this thought aside, Trent joined the Paladin woman in a rush through the enemy ranks toward their foe. Sword-limbs and rotted heads flew in every direction as they cut a swath to their quarry. Trent's right side had begun to burn from an iron blade that had found its way through a gap in his armor. He gritted his teeth and continued to place one foot in front of the other, never allowing himself to slow. The Demon quickly noticed the advance of the two warriors, which it answered by sending barrage after barrage of red flame in their direction. Trent and his newfound companion alternated providing magic barriers to keep the flames at bay. He knew that he could not keep this up for much longer, and doubted that the woman beside him could either. Nodding to her, he rolled to the side and sprang forward out of the path of the Demon fire. She did the same in the opposite direction, bringing both Paladins to the edge of the Accursed that protected their enemy.

"Coward!" she yelled. "Answer for your crimes!"

The creature hissed and cut down many of its own followers, stepping out of the safety that it had enveloped itself in to answer the challenge of the female warrior. Their blades met in a raucous clang, the fury of the attack ringing out over the sounds of the battle.

Trent finished off the few remaining Accursed that stood between them, attacking the Demon from its flank. It struggled to parry the attacks from both Paladins, which finally forced it to turn so that each warrior attacked its side rather than the front and rear. The red cloak on its shoulders hung in tatters from Trent's advance, like motionless streams of dark red blood that seemed to flow from its neck.

Trent pushed his side for the attack, savagely landing blow after blow against the fiend's black blade, forcing it to defend against him only. This gave the other warrior the opening she required, allowing her the chance to jump upon the Demon's back. She sank her sword deep through its neck into its body with a cry of triumph. The great monster shuddered for a moment before falling to the ground.

Nodding her thanks to Trent, the female Paladin reentered the fighting with renewed vigor, now working her way in the opposite direction that he himself wished to go. The woman seemed to be searching for something, and did not look to need his company any longer.

Trent looked back to where he had last seen Ren. Now a cluster of Paladins had formed around where she must have still been fighting.

He was snapped back to his immediate surroundings by a blinding pain that nearly forced him to collapse. A legless Accursed had pulled itself close enough to dig its blade into his left leg near his foot. He smashed in the creature's skull with his heel and pulled its sword free, releasing a torrent of blood. There was no way that he could go on with such an injury, not without further healing that he didn't have the energy to perform.

It was then that a change came over the forces of Darkness. Within the center of the of the enemy column just near where Ren fought, a clearing had begun to form. After several moments Trent could see a solitary figure clothed in red, walking out toward the location of the Seraph and her Paladins.

*The Herald. So the coward waits until Ren is surely drained of all energy.*

Filled with an undying hate, Trent forced himself forward, wincing with every step. He tore free a strip of cloth from the carcass of the Demon beside him and tightened it on the wound as best he could, only just slowing the bleeding. There was a sudden pause in the combat that allowed him to make better progress. He was only forced to cut down a handful of the Accursed that stood directly in his path, they too being distracted by the sight at the center of the opposing armies. Trent could taste the blood in his mouth from how hard he was forced to bite down on his tongue to continue walking, but he refused to falter. Ahead, the Herald finally reached a point where he stood directly across the makeshift clearing from where Ren and her retinue of Paladins had clustered.

"Face me, Seraph. Die at my feet so that we may end this!" the raspy voice of the Herald called out, the sounds barely drifting to Trent's ear.

Trent continued on his way toward the clearing, no longer swinging his sword but simply shoving through the enemies that blocked his way to Ren. His head was swimming as the pain began to slowly overtake all of his thoughts, save one. The cluster of Paladins with which Ren had surrounded herself moved into the clearing to meet the creature in battle, not wishing to leave their fatigued leader to his mercy. Surely the Seraph would be unhappy with the arrangement, but she was far too weak to fight alone, just as the Herald had wished.

The black figure lifted a clawed hand and began lancing fire at the right side of the group, followed by the left. At first the Paladins kept coming on, their shields holding the torrent of flame back, but it was a short-lived victory. Blue barriers began to fall, followed shortly by the bodies of the warriors who had maintained them. It was then that the Herald took to the air, flying back and forth around the circle in brief flashes of movement. Heads and other limbs were shorn off in the blink of an eye. Even from where he stumbled forward, Trent could hear Ren cry out in anguish. In a matter of moments, all who had stood by her were dead or dying, victims more from the fatigue of the long engagement rather than the awesome power of their foe. None would be able to withstand the Herald in their current states.

"I challenged you alone," it taunted, still circling Ren from the air. It was as if his voice were carried by some foul wind. "Fight me or others will suffer the same fate."

By now Trent had gained a perfect view of the danger that he slowly made his way toward. His progress was halting now, the wound finally taking its toll, and the Accursed finally taking notice of the determined warrior. He would not allow himself to die here and not by her side. Each enemy that he struggled to overcome took more away from him, each blow causing him to fight that much harder to stand. In between his own fighting he could see that Ren had drawn forth Nightbreaker and taken to the sky to answer the challenge of the Herald. Claw met sword in a flash of movement.

*I have to help her. She won't last.*

All around him others struggled to do the same, but he never noticed. He was adrift in a sea of enemies, and the salvation that he swam toward was about to be smashed onto the rocks. Ren cried out as her left wing was torn open. Nightbreaker swung in retaliation, cutting the Herald across the face. She had already begun to fall earthward from her wound when the creature roared in pain. He spiraled down into her, driving her into the ground with an audible crash. The Seraph collapsed into a heap at the Herald's feet, all but defeated. Saving Trent had robbed her of even enough strength to stand. The Herald bent down and grabbed Ren by the throat, lifting her high into the air for all to see. A deathly silence fell over the battlefield as fighters on both sides stopped their attack in order to witness what it was that was about to transpire.

*No! It can't end like this.*

Freed from any further resistance from his enemies, Trent pushed himself to a weak run, unfettered by pain. All around him not a single other soul stirred, all transfixed by the scene unfolding in the center of the clearing. The world turned underneath him as he ran, spinning wildly under his feet while his vision began to blur from the sweat that dripped into his eyes. Still holding the defeated Seraph aloft, the Herald began to speak, his raspy voice echoing across the battlefield. "Your champion is defeated! You have all lost. Fall to your knees, all of you. Or suffer the same."

*I may have no wings. But I have a sword.*

Men and women all across the battlefield complied with the request, falling to their knees and bowing their heads in silence. The resolve of the Light had finally been broken. In some scattered areas they continued to stand and fight, but those who did were quickly cut down.

Trent, still stumbling forward, soon drew the attention of all those gathered near. In the distance he thought he could see the female Paladin whom he had fought alongside earlier still standing. Not all would fall to their knees and forsake the Seraph. He numbly noticed that those who opposed him fell with arrows in their heads. Someone nearby had begun to give him aid.

"Your gods are defeated. Forsake the worship of the Gods of Light. Instead you must now turn your prayers to the Fallen One. He will accept you with open arms as his children. Those who are loyal to him will be rewarded with untold power. Stop those who will not submit!"

This blasphemous new pronouncement was met with rumbles of dissent up and down the ranks of the Light. For a moment Trent had seen himself as the pigeon again, trying to make his way toward the dove, but the Herald's latest decree brought him back from his fever haze to reality. To his horror, he saw many soldiers cast off any symbols of their affiliation to the Light and begin praying aloud to the

Gods of Darkness. With their spirits truly broken, they turned to the only savior that it seemed would materialize. Rage overtook him and he raised his sword above his head, crying a challenge to the traitors and sycophants within earshot.

Suddenly, a hand gripped his leg. But when he looked down it was not an enemy that grabbed him, but a friend. It was Devin who looked up at him with pleading eyes, somehow desperately clinging to life.

Before Trent could react he felt a small bit of healing energy flow into the open wound on his leg. His mind cleared from the fog that had overtaken him and he no longer struggled to stand. But when he looked back down at his old friend he saw that it was another Paladin whom he hadn't recognized, now dead from the energy that he had used to heal his commander.

"It will not be in vain, brother. I promise you," Trent mumbled, more to himself than the corpse at his feet.

He sprinted forward now, knocking over any of those who stood to stop him. One was a Paladin whom he recognized from his own initiation, the great warrior no longer wearing any signs of his place in the order. The other man began to draw steel when Trent beheaded him without pause. The red blood that sprayed his face only added to his rage, causing him to scream so loudly that even the Herald turned to look at him.

"Cowards! How quickly you deny your gods and your Seraph! Those who would not be damned, stand with me and save the woman we have all sworn to serve!"

Many averted their eyes from him, but his cries were met with a stirring response. All across the field kneeling Paladins and soldiers alike began to stand and join Trent's cause, fighting their way toward where Ren was held hostage. Each man that stayed on his knees made Trent's blood boil, but he now ignored them and ran on, joined at his back by countless others.

He finally reached the clearing and began to move directly toward the Herald, who still held the lifeless Ren in his grip. On the fringes of the circle, more and more men advanced, although many of them were stopped short by Accursed and Demons. Trent could hear cries of pain and shouts of attack as fighting once again resumed. He locked eyes with the creature that held the dove in its hands, the squawking of the thing ringing out in his mind. He gripped his sword tighter and sprang through the air, a shout bursting forth from his lungs.

The Herald raised a claw that glowed red with crackling energy. Trent's blade found its mark first, however, and a single horn was ripped from the monster's head. It stumbled slightly as the flame escaped its fingertips and sent the Paladin flying backward into the dust. Dazed, Trent pulled himself to his feet for another advance. He found a shield lying beside him and raised it in front of his face to prevent another direct strike.

Then the sky was torn open.

A blinding flash and thunderous crack split the battlefield nearly in two. Those who did not cover their eyes and ears from the awesomeness of the light and sound were doubled over in agony.

"No!" the voice rang out, filling every ear and mind with an elemental fury.

When vision returned to him, Trent was left in awe by the glorious sight. Hanging above Ren and the Herald was the golden skinned figure of a woman in brilliant armor, slowly descending from Aenna above. Her countenance was one of white hot anger as she surveyed the scene beneath her. Even from where he stood Trent could see that she was gravely injured, dripping silver blood onto the field below from a crushed knee and a torn side. She was the most beautiful and terrifying thing that he had ever seen. The sight of her filled him with reverence, for without a doubt he knew this to be none other than his patron goddess.

*Arra, Goddess of Light.*

Even as she descended, her blood spilled upon the earth, filling small pockets with pools and rivulets of the silvery substance. He could not imagine what had caused such wounds on a figure as powerful as this; yet she seemed more determined in spite of them.

The Herald visibly recoiled from Arra, clutching ever tighter at Ren's throat.

"Release my servant," Arra boomed, her voice rumbling as if spoken by a multitude. She hung just above and in front of the black figure now, her shadow falling across him.

"You cannot walk the Mortal Plane!" he hissed in fear. "You break the Pact!"

"Your master has already done so. I merely return the favor."

The goddess drew forth her greatsword and pointed it directly at the Herald. Black clouds rolled forth over the battlefield, seemingly pouring out of Aenna itself. Lightning struck the blade again and again, covering it in crackling energy. Then in an instant the energy was released directly into the chest of the Herald with a blinding flash. Ren was dropped as the servitor of the Fallen One was sent flying backward into the ranks of his minions. Those who were close to where he fell were turned to dust from the outpouring of energy. Bolts of lightning from the clouds began to strike at the opposing army, causing them to break ranks and flee in all directions. Upon the ground the smoldering body of the Herald remained lifeless.

Arra descended fully to the earth, where she cradled Ren in her arms for several moments. Trent had fallen to his knees in reverence, not wanting to disturb the goddess in her grief. Tears flowed freely down his own cheeks as he looked upon the lifeless face of his beloved. Then Arra was rising again, holding Ren close to her. Once she had regained a fair height above the clearing, the clouds broke. She scanned the field below, now empty of most Demons and Accursed. Those who had turned from the Light threw themselves upon the stone and covered their faces in shame.

Her voice rang out once again. "Those of you who dared to forsake me and my fellows, who dared abandon your Seraph, I curse you and your descendants for all time."

Trent flinched at the inhuman howls that greeted his ears. All around him those same men and women who had forsaken the gods doubled over in agonizing pain. Blood ran from their mouths and eyes as their bodies began to rip forth from their armor, changing into something no longer human, yet not quite animal. Those who had remained loyal to the end backed away from the convulsing figures in horror.

Then the eyes of the goddess fell directly upon Trent.

"And you," she said as his own body began to be wracked with pain, causing him to collapse and grip the earth for support. He was overtaken with fear as he began to feel a tearing sensation from within his back. His ears started to ring and he could hear multiple voices in his head. He dimly noticed that some of the silver blood of Arra was closer to where he knelt than he remembered.

"No," Trent choked out. "I have never wavered in my loyalty. What have I done wrong?"

Images flashed through his mind in rapid succession. Terric falling into the snow. His father lying on the floor of his home, bloodied and broken. Devin being crushed by Akklor. Ren falling to the Herald.

*You failed to save Terric. You failed to save Devin. You even failed to save your Seraph. Ren. The Dove. You deserve this.*

Blackness overtook him and the world before him faded away.

# EPILOGUE

Tess shuddered as she pulled the blade from his throat. The blood that welled from the gash reflected in the light of his eyes that was slowly fading. He was a coward and he deserved to die.

All of them did. But not all of them had.

Something far worse had befallen those who had condemned their souls by forsaking the gods and turning on the Lady. Watching them transform had been horrific, but what happened after made her skin crawl. All about her they ran this way and that in a milling confusion, uttering inhuman growls and gurgles not unlike that of the man at her feet who was drowning in his own blood. They still had the faces of men, but not much else that spoke of what they once were. They reminded her of goats and dogs at the same time, some hybrid of godly wrath.

Returning her knife to its sheath she again brought her bow to bear, landing an arrow deep into the neck of the nearest abomination, sending it squealing away in agony.

Once the thing was gone, the silence was nearly deafening, broken only by the occasional wet gasp from the man beneath her. She studied him for a few moments, running her fingers through her short raven-colored hair. His eyes still pleaded with her, but Tess simply stared back. Once it was clear that most of the other commanders were dead, she had taken it upon herself to lead the survivors to safety. This man hadn't taken kindly to that, insisting that the Seraph was dead, as were the gods, and they would all be better off without them.

Tess hadn't taken kindly to *that.*

She wasn't a Paladin like her sisters before her, but she was a skilled archer and warrior who held a high rank in what little there was of Illux's military. She had enlisted as soon as she had been old enough, which, by now, seemed like a lifetime ago. Most in the army had never expected that they would ever engage in real combat, but Tess had always known better. In her mind, a day like this was always inevitable. What she hadn't expected was to find herself in a leadership role after all of her commanding officers had either disappeared or died. But she was one to adapt.

The dead and dying covered the field like fallen leaves in the autumn. The sight was almost numbing, especially when she remembered that most of the dead were still several miles behind them in the valley where the battle had begun. She had gathered what forces she could, commanding them to search the bodies for wounded who could be saved. None besides the man in front of her had deemed it wise to challenge her leadership. Even the few Paladins that yet lived had fallen into line, themselves the most broken of any who had survived the day's events. The forces of the enemy were mostly routed, but some Accursed still stumbled about like lost children. Even so they posed a threat to the most grievously wounded, and that she could not allow. Tess knew that they would need every hand that could hold a sword in the coming weeks, so it would not do to leave anyone behind. After what she had seen today, the brave warrior worried that without some new weapon they would fall either way.

Another arrow found its mark in one of the abominations and she continued on, leaving the man who had challenged her to stare blankly up at Aenna. He wasn't the first man from Illux that she had killed, nor did she expect him to be the last. Growing up in the villages that were often attacked by bandits made that an unfortunate but unavoidable part of life for a woman such as herself.

Ahead she could see a large man struggling to get free of a pile of corpses. Even though it appeared that he was a Paladin, she could tell that the weight of several fresh bodies would be too much for him. His panting and grunts of exertion would draw more than just Tess if she didn't free him quickly. The man-things that skittered about seemed to like the flesh of the dead and those close to getting there. These scavengers could do more damage even than the handful of Accursed that still walked the field. She chased another of the creatures off with a well-placed arrow and rushed over to the man, helping him struggle free of the pile of bodies. As she rolled them off of him she tried to ignore the faces that stared blankly at her in turn.

"What happened?" he asked, clearly dazed. A sizable cut across his forehead trickled blood into his eyes.

*The world changed.*

"It doesn't matter," she replied, avoiding his gaze. "Those who didn't run are gathering just over that rise. When you get there, if you find Paladins called Ariana or her sister Gwen, tell them Tess is safe."

Before he had a chance to ask any more of her, Tess abruptly turned and continued her solemn walk through the graveyard. His question had forced her to reflect on the events of that day, which she had tried desperately to forget. But she knew that they would forever be burned into her memory. The battle that had begun earlier in the day had raged until just a few hours ago. It had seemed that the forces of Light had had the upper hand until that great beast had come. Tess had been tasked with gathering archers to assault the creature and defend the Seraph shortly after its arrival. It had made little difference. She had watched helplessly as the winged thing ravaged the line and killed good men and women that she had grown up with.

Then it was over.

Something had killed that infernal creature. Some said it was the

Lady Ren, while others claimed it to be the Commander Trent or even the wrath of the gods. Either way it made little difference as the line was still broken and the army routed. She hated the cowardice of it all, but she had run anyway; they all had. The miles that the retreating forces had fled had seemed to drag on for hours before the Seraph had turned them about and promised them a glorious death. Tess was one of the few who welcomed such an end, not like the others who pissed and shivered at her flanks. It was once the battle had finally resumed that everything had changed so quickly. The Herald had finally shown himself and defeated the Lady in a matter of moments, but only after slaughtering a score of Paladins who were attempting to defend her. Most had fallen to their knees by then, defeated in body and spirit. But not all. Tess was proud to recall that she had never wavered in her faith; it wasn't in her nature to do so. Others had stood strong as well, including the Commander Trent, whose very life Tess might have saved by covering his advance on the Lady with a flurry of arrows.

*Little good it did him.*

What happened after that seemed more dream than waking. When the myths and songs were written and sung about this day it was this moment that would seem the most embellished: the sky itself had been torn asunder and a god had descended from the heavens for the first time in over a thousand years. In her wrath she had cast down the cowards and made them into beasts, killed the Herald of the enemy, and routed his army, all in a matter of moments. Before she could even process what was happening, Tess was again looking at an empty sky with no sign of the goddess or the Seraph. What had become of the commander who had assaulted the Herald, she had no clue. In the chaos that followed, she hadn't found either him or her sisters, two brown-haired Paladins who contrasted her dusky hue.

*Where could they be?*

It was doubtful that she would find one without the other, for the two were inseparable. It was Tess who had always seemed the odd one out when they were growing up. She had preferred to remain mortal while they had wished for the greater glory of the Paladin order. It wasn't like Tess to follow in anyone's footsteps, so she had chosen her own path opposite theirs. Even so she still loved them both, and the fear that she wouldn't find them twisted like a knife in her belly.

The sun was slowly beginning to make its way toward the horizon, leaving the battlefield to sink into the shadows created by the rocky outcroppings that rimmed it. Soon darkness would fall and it would be time to give up on those who had not yet been found. There was no telling how long they had before the forces of Darkness regrouped and returned to finish what they had started. Tess had seen the way in which the goddess had broken them and sent them fleeing in every direction. Without a Herald they would be in disarray for a few days at least, but who was to say that another Herald would not be created by nightfall?

Tess suddenly realized that her meandering path had taken her nearly to the middle of the battlefield. It was here that that the goddess had been hovering just some hours before. The waning rays of sunlight glinted off of the pools of silver blood that had formed at the center of it all. She was entranced by the way in which the liquid seemed to shimmer and almost give off an otherworldly glow.

Tess had become so fascinated by the Divine Blood before her that she didn't even notice the corpse-like body that slowly shambled up from behind. She didn't realize anyone else was near her until she heard the iron blade swinging through the air. The lithe warrior twisted at the last moment as the sword of her enemy cut through the flesh and sinew on her arm.

"Shit!" she cried out, stumbling away and dropping her bow.

How could she have been so careless? There was no one left to help her now, and with her right arm hanging limp at her side she wasn't sure that she would be able to fight back. The blood welled out in an unstoppable flow, staining her armor below the elbow a dark scarlet. Suddenly, her attacker wasn't alone and another Accursed stumbled at her from her wounded side. If she didn't act quickly she knew she would die here. Ignoring as much of the pain as she could, Tess drew her long knife from its sheath and jammed it into the cheek of her first attacker, ripping the blade free through the stitched mouth. Turning, she threw the knife into the forehead of the second Accursed, dropping it like a stone. She allowed herself a quick smile. Then she noticed the iron blade sticking out of her stomach.

The first creature hadn't died.

Numbly, Tess touched the edge of the blade with her fingers as it was pulled free from behind. She dropped to her knees and fell face first into the dirt. As she lay there motionless, she could hear the shambling figure slowly stumble away before it finally collapsed.

No one would find her now, and she would die alone. Her sisters were still missing and she would die alone. The others needed a leader but she would die alone. It didn't even hurt any more, she noticed. The numbness had been replaced by burning, but it didn't hurt. She was sure that this meant that the bleeding was almost done already, her life-force nearly emptied into the soil. What other hope did she have besides closing her eyes and willing for it to end quickly?

From behind her she could hear the unfortunate sound of one of the man-things squealing and rooting through the nearby corpses. If she didn't die soon she would suffer through a few more agonizing moments as the thing ate her living. This thought filled her with more fear than she had ever felt in her entire life. She had seen the near-human teeth tear the flesh off of one of her comrades; it would be a pain worse than death. Fear gave her the motivation that she needed to slowly lift her head and gaze at her surroundings. It took more energy than she had first realized; her body was too weak for much else. Just ahead was the silver liquid that had spilled from the veins of the goddess.

Something inside her told her that if she could reach it she would find safety of some sort.

The sounds of the beast grew closer as its human face sniffed along the ground just to the left of her leg. Renewed with a new sense of urgency, Tess gripped the earth with her one good arm and began pulling herself forward as best she could. Each inch she traveled forced her to stop and gather more strength, all the while she could feel it slowly leave her body. Again she reached forward and pulled herself closer and closer to the silver salvation that glimmered just beyond the reach of her fingers. She could smell it now, a smell not unlike the orchard near her home.

Then the creature noticed her movement and its savage teeth bit down on her leg.

Tess screamed and kicked at the thing, frantically digging her fingers at the stone until they bled under the nails. It was no use, her armor had given way under her attacker's bite and its teeth had dug deep into her calf. She could feel that it was attempting to pull her away, as if it knew that she was trying to reach the Divine Blood. Desperately, she glanced back just long enough to see where to plant her final kick. The teeth released their grip and the thing squealed in pain from its crushed eye. This gave Tess just the opening that she needed to pull herself forward and into the pool of silver liquid, submerging her entire face beneath its surface.

The Divine Blood filled her nostrils and mouth, running down her throat in a torrent of tingling sensations. She gasped for air, but simply swallowed more, allowing the feelings it brought to take over all of her senses. It felt as if it were warm and cool at the same time, and it was thicker than normal blood ought to be, yet it flowed freely as if it were no more than water. The energy that filled her body started in her stomach and moved to each appendage. Tears welled out of her eyes and mingled with the pool as she began to feel overwhelmed. It was as if in this moment she felt a connection to every living thing on the Mortal Plane. Fleetingly, she thought she could hear voices in the heavens and beneath the earth. She could feel the wind in the trees miles away and sense the fear of the survivors who had gathered just over the ridge. The mind of the creature that assaulted her was opened, and she could see that other than fear and rage it no longer held any intelligence. The wounds in her body closed and healed as if they had never been formed.

Then she felt power in her blood.

When the euphoric sensation had become too much for her to

handle she pulled her head from the pool of liquid and filled her lungs with air. Without even looking over the rest of her body, Tess could tell that she was somehow more whole than she had been before. The man-thing tried to bite down on her leg again but she kicked it away, this time sending the creature flying backward through the air. It landed hard on the stone, never again to rise. She was filled with a strength unlike any she had ever known.

*Is this how it feels to be a Paladin?*

Standing, Tess surveyed the area around her, looking again for any sign of the enemy. She was alone. Behind her the sun had almost set, but there was still enough light to return here with the wounded. All of them would drink from the silver liquid and be healed before they made for Illux. It was the only way that many of them would survive the night. She looked down at her once injured arm, flexing the muscles as if they were foreign to her. Ahead the creature that had almost devoured her lay in a crumpled heap, some yards from where she stood. One kick had sent the beast tumbling to its death like a rock skipped across a pool of water. If this newfound strength didn't wear off, then she might have stumbled upon the weapon that they would need to stand any chance of winning this war.

*The world has changed.*

# WHAT TO READ NEXT

To find out what happened to Trent and Ren, check out *Cries of the Forsaken!*

For more adventures of our principle cast prior to the events of this book, read *The Bard's Demons, A Bandit's Balance, The Sons of Lighthammer*, and *White Wings from Grey Ash*.

# ABOUT THE AUTHOR

Kris Jerome was born in the middle of a snowstorm in Pendleton, Oregon, several decades ago. Since then he moved the great distance across the state to study at Willamette University. He obtained a BFA in Digital Communication Arts in June of 2016 from Oregon State University. Kris enjoys reading books and comics while sipping wine and craft beer. He currently lives in Albany, Oregon with his wife, seven children and two cats.

darktidingspress.com
darktidingspress@gmail.com

www.ingramcontent.com/pod-product-compliance
Lightning Source LLC
Chambersburg PA
CBHW030537310726
48979CB00010B/1945/J
* 9 7 8 1 9 5 1 1 3 8 1 2 7 *